HORROR AT HALLOWEEN

Also available from Pumpkin Books

Peter Atkins
WISHMASTER AND OTHER STORIES

Ramsey Campbell
GHOSTS AND GRISLY THINGS

David Case
BROTHERLY LOVE AND OTHER TALES OF FAITH AND KNOWLEDGE

Hugh B. Cave
ISLE OF THE WHISPERERS

Dennis Etchison
DOUBLE EDGE

Stephen Jones
DARK OF THE NIGHT
NEW TALES OF HORROR AND THE SUPERNATURAL

WHITE OF THE MOON
NEW TALES OF MADNESS AND DREAD

Nancy Kilpatrick
CHILD OF THE NIGHT
POWER OF THE BLOOD VOL I

NEAR DEATH
POWER OF THE BLOOD VOL II

REBORN
POWER OF THE BLOOD VOL III

Jay Russell
WALTZES AND WHISPERS

Sylvia Starshine
DRACULA: or THE UN-DEAD
A PLAY IN PROLOGUE AND FIVE ACTS

HORROR AT HALLOWEEN

Written by
STEPHEN BOWKETT * DIANE DUANE
CRAIG SHAW GARDNER
JOHN GORDON * CHARLES GRANT

Edited by
Jo Fletcher

Created by
Stephen Jones

PUMPKIN BOOKS
NOTTINGHAM

Published in Great Britain by Pumpkin Books

An imprint of MeG Publishing Limited
PO Box 297, Nottingham NG2 4GW, ENGLAND.
Also at http://www.netcentral.co.uk/pumpkin/

First edition, October, 1999.

'Horror at Halloween' copyright © 1999 by Stephen Jones.
This selection copyright © 1999 by Stephen Jones and Jo Fletcher.
Dustjacket artwork © 1999 by Terry Oakes.

The moral right of the editors and authors to be identified as the authors of this work has been asserted by them in accordance with the Copyright Designs and Patents Act 1988.

All characters in this book are fictitious and any resemblance to real persons, living or dead, is purely coincidental.

All rights reserved. No part of this publication may be reproduced or transmitted in any form or by any means, electronic or mechanical including photocopying, recording or any information storage or retrieval system, without the prior permission in writing from the publisher, nor be otherwise circulated in any form of binding or cover other than that in which it is published and without a similar condition including this condition imposed on the subsequent purchaser.

ISBN 1 901914 19 4

A CIP catalogue record for this book is available from the British Library.

Printed in Great Britain by Creative Print & Design Group.

Contents

PROLOGUE
1

Part 1
SAM
9

Part 2
ELEANOR
87

Part 3
TINA
179

Part 4
CHUCK
275

Part 5
CODY
349

EPILOGUE
401

Acknowledgements

Special thanks to Charlie Grant for allowing this book to be set in the town he created.

'Sam' copyright © 1999 by John Gordon.
'Eleanor' copyright © 1999 by Stephen Bowkett.
'Tina' copyright © 1999 by Diane Duane.
'Chuck' copyright © 1999 by Craig Shaw Gardner.
'Cody' copyright © 1999 by Charles Grant.

About the Contributors

STEPHEN BOWKETT was born and brought up in the mining valleys of South Wales. He began writing at the age of thirteen, and had his first book published in 1985. Since then he has become a full-time writer and qualified hypnotherapist. His early published work consisted of fantasy for teenagers. He has since diversified into teen and adult horror (the latter under the pseudonym 'Ben Leech'), teen romance, mainstream fiction for pre-teens, fiction for younger readers, non-fiction, and poetry for all ages. The author still enjoys visiting schools and libraries to tell stories, but points out that "Although some of them are funny . . . others are very, *very* scary . . . "

DIANE DUANE was born in Manhattan (a direct descendant of the first mayor of New York City after the Revolutionary War) and she now lives in Ireland with her husband, science fiction and fantasy writer Peter Morwood. She has written thirty or so novels, numerous short stories, plus scripts for TV series (such as *Star Trek: The Next Generation*, *Gargoyles*, and *Batman: The Animated Series*), computer games, comic books and audio works. She is most widely known for her series of young adult books featuring the teenage wizards Nita Callahan and Kit Rodriguez, starting with *So You Want to Be a Wizard* and continuing through *Deep Wizardry*, *High Wizardry*, *A Wizard Abroad*, and the recent *The Wizard's Dilemma*.

CRAIG SHAW GARDNER was born in Rochester, New York, a place where it snows far too often. He has written more than two dozen novels, as well as several best-selling film and television novelisations, including *Batman*, *Back to the Future Parts II* and *III*, the Hallmark Entertainment miniseries *Leprechauns* and the *Buffy the Vampire Slayer* series. He is a past president of the Horror Writers Association and has seen his short stories appear in numerous anthologies with names like *Shadows*, *Ghosts*, *Midnight* and *Doom City*. Under another name, which might be Peter

Garrison, he has written an entire fantasy trilogy based on the high concept of "*Pulp Fiction* meets *The Lord of the Rings*".

JOHN GORDON is a Geordie born in Jarrow-on-Tyne who moved to the fen country of East Anglia with his family at the age of twelve. He served in the Royal Navy during World War II and afterwards worked as a journalist on various local newspapers. He has written a number of novels of the supernatural, including *Gilray's Ghost*, *The Flesh Eater* and *Skinners*. His children's story *The Midwinter Watch* was named Children's Book of the Week in *The Guardian* newspaper, and his collection *The Burning Baby and Other Ghosts* was recently reissued in Britain. About the latter, Ramsey Campbell wrote: "All the stories include hauntingly memorable apparitions . . . "

CHARLES GRANT has lived most his life in north-western New Jersey. A prolific editor, short story writer and novelist, he has won the Nebula Award, the World Fantasy Award and the British Fantasy Award. He first introduced readers to the old New England town of Oxrun Station, where strange events occur, in the novel *The Hour of the Oxrun Dead* (1977). Since then he has published such titles as *The Sound of Midnight*, *The Bloodwind*, *The Soft Whisper of the Dead*, *For Fear of the Night*, *In a Dark Dream*, *Something Stirs* and the first two *X Files* novels, *Goblin* and *Whirlwind*. His latest books are *Riders in the Sky*, the fourth in the Millennium Quartet, and *Winter Knight*, the third book in the Black Oak series.

JO FLETCHER is a writer, critic, journalist and editor for a major London publishing house. Winner of the International Society of Poets Editor's Award and the British Fantasy Society's first Karl Edward Wagner Special Award, her work has appeared in *The Mammoth Book of Werewolves*, *The Mammoth Book of Frankenstein*, *The Mammoth Book of Dracula*, *Now We Are Sick*, *Voices on the Wind*, *The Tiger Garden: A Book of Writers' Dreams*, *Dark of the Night* and *White of the Moon*. A collection of her poetry, *Shadows of Light and Dark*, was published in 1998, and she has co-edited *Gaslight & Ghosts* and *Secret City: Strange Tales of London*, both with Stephen Jones.

STEPHEN JONES is the winner of two World Fantasy Awards, three Horror Writers Association Bram Stoker Awards and two International Horror Guild Awards, as well as being a twelve-time recipient of the British Fantasy Award and a Hugo Award nominee. One of Britain's most acclaimed anthologists of horror and dark fantasy, he has edited and written more than fifty books. He lives in London, England.

PROLOGUE

Prologue

SNOW HAS A WAY OF CALMING THINGS DOWN. Once it covers the ground, everything gets soft and quiet. The kind of quiet you can almost hear. The kind of quiet that tells you what has happened overnight, even before you look out of the window.

And when you do finally get up and look outside and see all that unbroken white on the ground, and the snow still falling without any wind, it kind of makes everything okay for a while, you know what I mean?

Everything is beautiful; everything's at peace.

You almost hate to go outside and spoil it.

That's the way it used to be for me.

That's the way it always used to be, before I moved to Oxrun Station.

Now, watching the season's first real storm, watching a bluejay try to hop through the snow to fallen bird seed beneath the feeder, all I can do is remember Halloween.

Weird, right?

Well, no, not really . . .

See, the Station is different. I can't really explain it. And, if nothing else, you have to understand that things happen here. No-one knows why, they just do.

And when they do, nothing . . . nothing . . . is ever the same again.

You wouldn't know that to look at it, though. I mean, it's real small, and it has lots of money and it's tucked away in a corner of Connecticut that hardly anyone ever visits unless they're on their way to somewhere else. It has a big park and a college and a train station; there's a cinema and lots of places to eat, a graveyard and a few churches. All the blocks are pretty long and the houses pretty big and old — for America, that is. The cops are okay, for cops, and even the teachers aren't all that bad, for teachers.

I mean, if you came here, you'd think everyone is just like everyone else, everyplace else.

Well, they are.

Except . . . things happen to them.

Weird things.

The kind of things you don't even want to dream about in your nightmares.

Like what happened on Halloween.

The snow keeps falling and there's a breeze now and then, and the flakes twist and dance and kind of form pictures.

I don't want to look, but I can't help it.

Over there by the big maple tree I can see Eleanor Trent from New York; on the sidewalk I think I can see Sam Jones from Norwich, all the way over in England; and across the street, getting out of his father's car, the snow lets me see Chuck Antrim, born and bred right here in the Station. Cody Banning is right beside him. Tina Broadbent, smart as her dad, is whispering something to her best friend Cerise.

It wouldn't be all that bad, seeing them again, but they're all gone now.

It's not exactly that they all . . . lost.

It's more like they had to get away — those that were left.

And I know I said that strange things just happen in Oxrun Station, but this Halloween was different. Maybe it really was the rare conjunction of Mars and Saturn with Venus, lowering the barriers between our world and another, shadowy realm . . . or maybe it was just that the full moon always makes the weirdnesses come out in this place. Trick or treat is crazy enough, I guess, with ghosts and goblins and witches and warlocks and all manner of nasties roaming the streets — and it's true that you can never tell what's really going on underneath a mask . . . it's just that in Oxrun Station, the masks aren't always made of rubber . . .

And now the guys want to tell me what happened to them to change their lives so totally . . .

Some are telling their own stories, others are showing me just what happened to them when the moon was full in the sky, Saturn gleamed yellow and Venus shone down so brightly, making the shadows even more dense and threatening . . .

Prologue

Whether I want to or not, they're going to tell me.

You see, they want me to know what really goes on in Oxrun Station.

I have no choice now. The snow is telling me why . . .

Prologue

SAM

1

TWO YEARS HAVE GONE BY SINCE I LEFT OXRUN Station. It is autumn again, the leaves have begun to fall, and I keep thinking of a girl who lives in Mildenhall Woods in the hills above the town. I long to see her again.

Something strange happened to me on the evening we arrived in Oxrun. It was a welcome — and a warning, although I didn't recognise it at the time.

We came to Oxrun because my father's work took him there — and my mother loves to travel. He is a researcher in plant biology at the John Hammond Institute in England, and when the chance came for him to take up an appointment to carry out a project linked up with Hawksted College in Connecticut my mother jumped at it. Dad is much more cautious than my mother, but he is the true 'plantsman' that he calls himself, and investigating the medicinal properties of the bark of a fairly rare woodland shrub is what lured him to the United States and to the forests of Oxrun Station.

There is mystery in the air at Oxrun. Not everyone thinks so — perhaps you lose the sense of it as you become familiar with the place — but as we stepped off the little plane that brought us to Harley Airport, just the other side of the mountains, I already sensed that I was entering a hidden world. The air was heavy with the scent of the pine and spruce forest and as I breathed it in I felt that I was in a land cut off from everything I knew.

It was dusk, there were no more flights that summer night, and the silence that seeped down from the darkening hillsides seemed to smother the putter of the engine of the private plane as it found its parking place for the night.

London was twenty-four hours behind us, and the noise of aircraft, which had been our constant companion, suddenly ceased. The luggage trolley had gone on ahead of us and had disappeared among the airport buildings, leaving a straggle of passengers to cross the tarmac on foot. The noise of our footsteps was lost in the huge silence around us, and it was then that I heard the whispering for the first time. I stood still.

"What is it, Sam?" My mother turned to look back.

I shook my head, trying to clear my hearing. "My eardrums," I said. "The cabin pressure's got through to me." Which was hardly surprising considering all the plane-hopping we'd had to do to get here.

"A good night's rest is what you need," she said, and my father, loaded down with hand luggage, grunted.

But the whispering, an illusion or not, was in my ears again. There were no words, but somewhere, just out of reach of my hearing, words were being formed only to die like the lisp of wavelets on a beach. Even stranger than the sounds themselves was that I sensed they came from a particular direction. I found myself turning to face the source, expecting to see ground crew talking quietly among themselves as they came out to service the aircraft. It was true that the intensity of the whispering increased as I turned, but the tarmac was unpeopled.

I paused, and the formless whispering steadied. It was as though I had tuned in to a radio beacon and had found the direction of its source, so I listened carefully as my eyes scoured the shadows of the airport buildings. Something in its tone encouraged me to lift my eyes beyond the roofs and radio aerials. On the nearest hills the shapes of the trees were already dissolving in the twilight, and further away the slopes themselves were blurred, but the whisper, as if it came from the heart of the dark forests, increased in intensity until, obeying it, I shifted my gaze to where one hill, above the rest, lifted itself on the distant horizon.

It was then, with a thin shriek, that my ears cleared themselves. A huge silence swept over me as if the night, satisfied that I had arrived as expected, had fallen asleep.

"Stop daydreaming, Sam!" It was my mother's voice. "You're keeping everyone waiting."

Mr. Galbraith, who was to be a colleague of my father, was there with his camper — and his daughter — to welcome us and take us on the last lap of our journey. Oxrun Station, he said, was just over the horizon, which was a strange way to put it but was very much in tune with my state of mind. Oxrun was a place out of this world, but it wanted me. And Penny Galbraith was very pretty.

2

That night, as he drove us to our new home, Mr. Galbraith told us a lot about 'the real friendly folk' who would soon absorb us in 'community activities', but it was his daughter, sitting next to me and saying hardly a word, who told me most. Just to look at her made me realise I would enjoy Oxrun.

Mr. Galbraith, who taught at Hawksted College and would be working with my father, was a tall, lanky man with a slow way of speaking that seemed to exasperate his daughter but which I'm sure he exaggerated in order to amuse us, me in particular.

"Getting dark," he said, "and we're going to climb." The road snaked steeply upwards through the forest. "Penny, give these good people some candy to suck to stop their ears popping."

"Father," she said, "stop being so childish."

"My ears have been popping ever since we got off the plane," I said.

He glanced back at us over the wire frames of his glasses, and even in the dimness inside the car I could see the amusement in the faded blue of his eyes. "You'll have to excuse her, Sam," he said, "but she's a little excited to discover you're in her grade at school and she'll want to show you off to her friends," he chuckled, "as a novelty."

"Father!" I've never really believed that girls look beautiful when they're angry, and it is true that the sudden redness in Penny's cheeks did nothing for her looks, but when she caught me looking at her and turned away as if to hide herself she added to the mystery of this unknown world that was already beginning to absorb me.

Mr. Galbraith drove with one elbow resting on the sill of the open window. He asked us if the rush of air troubled us, but we all said no, not at all.

"It's such a hot night," said my mother, "and the scent of all these trees is lovely."

He was pleased, and tried to bring his daughter into the conversation. "We hardly notice it, do we, Penny?"

Beside me in the back seat she shrugged and gazed indifferently at the columns of black trees that pressed so close to the road that the branches seemed to be reaching out to touch us. We rounded a bend that made our headlights swing suddenly beyond the road edge and their beams were lost in nothingness. For an instant I felt giddy, as if we had suddenly become airborne, and all of us, except Penny and her father, gasped.

Mr. Galbraith heard us. "Night flying," he said, "it's one of our pleasures hereabouts."

"Pay no attention to my father," said Penny, speaking directly to me, "he's an embarrassment." She raised her voice. "Daddy, will you stop being so scary!"

Now it was my own father's turn to speak. "Don't worry about us, Penny," he said, "we just find it all so stimulating."

That's one of my father's words, 'stimulating'. The grotty bits of bark he peels off trees and puts into test tubes are 'stimulating', and I feared a little lecture coming on. 'Instructive' is another word he goes for, and when he went on to say that a stimulating experience was also instructive, I had to interrupt.

"I like it here," I said quickly. "It's not the same as Norwich."

"Where's that?" said Penny, and her father answered.

"You'd likely call it Nor-witch," he said, and repeated it. Fathers were being a pain.

"Oh," she said, not at all impressed. "Is that near London?"

London, I was soon to discover, was the only place in Britain that any of Penny's friends seemed to know about. "No," I said, "it's nowhere near London. It's at least a hundred miles away."

"Oh," she said again, and I could tell that a hundred miles didn't mean much in a country where cities were separated by thousands. "Is it old?" she asked.

"Oh, yes," I said. I'd never before been asked if a *place* was old. "It's very old."

"I'd love to live somewhere old," she said. She raised her voice, "And Daddy, you can be quiet. I'm not going to ask him about castles and dungeons and stuff. I'm not a kid any more." She turned back to me. "He thinks I still believe in fairy tales."

"Well," I said, not quite sure what effect it would have, "there is a castle. On a hill. Right in the middle of town."

"Oh."

"And it does have dungeons."

She drew in her breath. "There you are, you see," she said. "My father is probably the most ignorant man on this planet."

Mr. Galbraith laughed, and he and my parents in the front began talking among themselves.

"There's also a place inside the castle where they used to hang people," I said, "and it's probably haunted."

She was very matter of fact. "Quite likely," she said. "I don't like to go any place where people have died."

Then I made myself wince as I asked, "Do you have ghosts here?"

"Oh, yes," but she no longer appeared interested.

I thought I must have offended her. "I'm sorry," I said.

"Sorry?" She was mystified.

"It's stupid of me to be talking about ghosts when I've just arrived."

"Do you always apologise about everything?" she asked. A hand flew to her mouth. "Have I embarrassed you, Sam? I'm so *sorry!*"

We were both laughing as the car, having crossed the pass, began to slide downhill into Oxrun.

3

That night I slept well, but I dreamt. The house we were to occupy for the next year and a half was on Thorn Road, and was larger than anything I was used to in England, but not as large as the house in my dream. The rooms in that house were enormous and were connected by corridors and staircases that were endless, and they were magnificent but empty. And I was lost, and no matter how loudly I cried out there was no-one to hear me. And when I woke up in the night, in a strange room, the house on Thorn seemed too big, and the whole of Oxrun outside was too mysterious, and faintly menacing.

But in the morning the sun shone and I thought I saw a bluejay in the garden. A bluejay was something new and it made a change from starlings. And the refrigerator in the kitchen was twice the size of the one we had at home. Bluejays and refrigerators — just two things among many that came to me that day so vividly that they appeared to be deliberate signs showing me into a world that, like an enchanted forest, would be full of surprises.

And the streets were very wide and the kerbs higher than any I had known. Penny Galbraith laughed to see me hesitate before crossing the road. "Sorry," I said, "I can't get used to the traffic coming at me from the wrong direction."

"There you go again," she said, and when I looked puzzled, she added, "Apologising — you don't have to be sorry about everything, do you?"

"Sorry," I said, and she dragged me across the road to the Herbert Bass Museum. We were on Chancellor Avenue and she was showing me the town. "I don't know what you think of museums and stuff," she said.

"Now it's you who's apologising. Museums are just what I need." And I did. There was so much around me that had to be digested that I welcomed the chance to breathe the air in some quiet place.

And the museum was quiet. Apart from a fat lady who sat at a desk in the hall and was busy on the phone or answering letters, there was just one other person, a girl with long, pale blonde hair and quite startling green eyes, who was peering intently at a display of ancient folk customs and traditions. She tucked her left hand into her pocket as we passed her.

"Who's she?" I whispered, and got a sharp jab in the ribs from Penny.

"That's stuck-up Eleanor Trent. She's kind of new in Oxrun Station. She's definitely not your type — so keep your mind on why we're here."

Penny kept her voice lowered as we walked through the rooms. "This place is weird," she said. "My parents recall when it was still a house and people actually lived here."

"Mr. Herbert Bass," I said, "and his wife Ida." The lady at the desk had given me a leaflet.

Penny giggled. "Well, Mr. Bass was a little before Mom's time," she said. "He built the place way back."

The leaflet said 1898, which was about the time our own house in Norwich had been built, and that wasn't reckoned to be all that old, but it was nevertheless strange to be walking through rooms and opening doors and hearing the floorboards creak where once the footsteps of Herbert and Ida or one of their four daughters had made the same soft sounds that we were making now.

"I can just hear their dresses swishing as they went up these stairs," said Penny, and in a room at the top there were some of the very dresses the girls had worn, preserved in glass cases. "Elegant," said Penny, and a bluejay outside the window gave a harsh cough that made us both jump.

The windows were large and filled the room with sunshine, but that solitary sound from outside reminded me that we were upstairs in an almost empty house and brought my dream to mind with all the hollow loneliness of the empty mansion I had been lost in while I slept. I was not sorry to leave the room and come out on to the landing where we were once more in sight of the curator in the hall.

The landing circled the stair well, and Penny had gone ahead to a room at the back of the house.

"Sam," she said, "this will interest you more than a bunch of old dresses."

She was right. The room was set out to show the earliest years of Oxrun, which happened to coincide with the early generations of the Bass family, so there was a great deal about the interests of Herbert Bass himself. He was a businessman involved in hotels, stores and homesteading, and even telephone lines — but he had made his fortune in logging, and it was the forests surrounding Oxrun Station that dominated the room. It was then I realised why, ever since I'd entered it, that the house had seemed to remind me of something that just eluded me, as haunting as the dream but not quite the same. And then, as we trod the floorboards, it came back to me.

"It's the way the house is built!" I exclaimed suddenly, and saw instantly that I had puzzled her. "What I mean," I said, "is that it's built of wood."

She had startling light blue eyes. "Uh-huh," she said, and kept those eyes fixed on me until I explained myself.

"It's the way it smells," I said. "It's the scent of all the wood and wax."

"Don't you like it?"

"Yes I do, very much. But it's just the same as when you step off the plane at Harley — all those trees fill the air with a . . . I don't know, a woody kind of smell that goes with the whispering."

I had said too much.

"Whispering?" She was puzzled again, and I couldn't blame her. So I told her about the aeroplane noise that had lingered in my ears.

"Well, sure," she said, trying to understand. "I guess we've all had that, getting off an air-o-plane." She was laughing at my accent again. "And don't you dare apologise about it, Sam, or I won't buy you a coffee." She puckered her brow. "You do drink coffee?"

"Sure," I said, putting as much of her drawl into the word as I could.

"Help!" she cried. "That sounds awful! Just speak the way you do, Sam, or I won't think you're cute any more."

Cute was not quite what I wanted to be, but it was what she certainly was. And at least I had changed the subject.

4

Last night's dream had faded, but strolling with Penny Galbraith through the streets of Oxrun Station was a kind of waking dream. Facts that had lain, half-forgotten, in the base of my mind, kept floating to the surface so that I recognised a fire plug when I saw it, although there are no such things in England, and I was familiar with huge flat-fronted trucks as if I'd known them all my life, storm drains, and traffic lights on long stalks bending over roads like praying mantis. All from films I had seen. But when we paused before crossing to The Luncheonette on the corner of High and Centre, a much more vivid picture leapt to my mind.

"Nighthawks," I said.

Penny's blue stare was on me again, waiting for an explanation. I nodded towards The Luncheonette. Its long window on Centre was continued around the corner so that the whole length of the counter was in view. "It's that painting," I said. I even remembered the artist's name. "The one by Edward Hopper — you know, with three people sitting on stools at the counter and a waiter at the bar stooping to get them coffee."

There was no waiter visible in The Luncheonette, but it did look exactly like that late-night picture of a lonely lunch counter in a deserted street, and there were three people hunched on bar stools. Whether Penny knew the picture I never found out because at that moment she recognised one of the customers and waved to him.

It was, after all, only a small coincidence, and I was about to follow her across the road when a waitress came from the kitchen and moved along behind the bar. I smiled at the little surge of disappointment I felt, for the waitress should have been a man with a white hat to match Edward Hopper's picture, not a dark-haired girl. She bent forward to take care of something behind the counter, and as she did so the little white cap pinned to her hair showed for the first time, and for one long second her solemn profile was exactly where it should be . . . and the whole night-time picture, in which nothing moves, was frozen there in the middle of Oxrun on the corner of High and Centre in broad daylight.

"Sam, I want you to meet Jeff Dacre."

I had walked into Edward Hopper's picture with Penny, but it was no longer 'Nighthawks', and Jeff Dacre was not a lonely man wearing a fedora. He was tall and blond, and he wore a baseball cap.

We sat in a booth. "I was in England once," he said.

"London — you know it?"

"Doesn't just everybody ask you that?" said Penny to me, and then she turned to him. "He lives in Nor-witch and he doesn't know anything about London because it's too far away." She laughed at me. She had very even white teeth. "And he says sorry all the time, which is very sweet — not like you, Jeffrey Dacre, you hulk."

He grinned. He never took offence — not, at least, at anything a girl said to him. "I apologise," he said. He stuck out a hand across the table even though we had shaken hands just a moment before, and I shook it. "It was just the same for me in your country, Sam, when they asked me where I came from and I'd say Oxrun Station and they'd say where's that — is it a part of New York?" He sat back. "I guess we all think that where we live is the centre of the world. Isn't that so, Penny?"

"Oxrun Station may be the centre of your world, Jeff Dacre, but it certainly isn't mine."

His face fell a little at that, and for some reason I shared his disappointment. Before I'd thought about it I was backing him up.

"Well," I said, "I think Oxrun Station might just possibly be the true centre of the earth." And that sounded so phoney that I blushed. "Sorry," I said, and saw Penny grin, "but I've had a strange feeling ever since I arrived that there's more going on here than you'd believe."

That made him laugh and slap the table. "You can say that again," he said. "What's Penny been telling you?"

"Isn't that truly typical!" Penny turned her eyes to the ceiling. "Everything's got to have a double meaning for him."

He was about to respond when the waitress came from behind the counter to take our order. She was a girl of about our own age, maybe a year or two older, and they both knew her. "Hi, Glyn," said Jeff and introduced her to me. She nodded but remained silent. "Glyn's folks come from England," he said, but this seemed to embarrass her.

"Way back," she said, as if apologising. She paused, biting her lip. "And they didn't come from England. They were from Wales." Her eyes flickered towards me as though she had said too much and needed help.

"There's a big difference," I said. Wales was like Norwich, neither Penny nor Jeff had much idea about either, and for the first time I realised that I was as much a mystery to them as they were to me. But the girl knew about Wales. I had opened my mouth to say more when she became the waitress once again. "Coffee," she said abruptly, and hurried away.

"That Glyn." Jeff shook his head. "She never did say much to anyone."

Penny had looked sourly at the girl as she retreated. "She's so uncouth," she said, which told me that further questions from me would be unwelcome.

Jeff, intent on making me feel at home in his town, asked if I went fishing, and when I said yes but my tackle was far away, he was all for lending me some right now and taking me to a particular stream he knew in the woods.

"Can't you see Sam's jet-lagged?" Penny protested. "Give him a chance."

He held up both hands in surrender. "Me," he said. "I'm the dumb ox of Oxrun. Sorry, Sam."

"That's my line," I said.

He laughed. "But really, Sam, you'll love it up there in the hills, won't he, Penny?"

"It all depends where you take him."

This amused him. "Do you know what this girl's worried about, Sam? She thinks those woods are spooked."

Penny was indignant. "I don't *think* so — I *know* so!"

He was having a good time teasing her, and neither of them noticed the waitress returning with our coffee.

"Penny thinks there's a great old ghost up there amongst the trees just aching to get his slimy old hands on any living person and snatch them away to hell and damnation."

"Well, I've heard of it," she said, "and so has everyone."

Jeff had been waving his arms about so that the waitress had had to wait before she could set down her tray. He noticed her. "Glyn lives out of town," he said.

"What of it?" Her voice was as cool as the expression in her dark eyes.

"Hold on!" Once again he held up both hands. "I didn't mean any offence, Glyn."

"Okay." There was a suggestion of a blush in her cheeks. "I guess I'm a little tired this morning."

"Look, all I meant was that you live a little way out among the woods and you don't find anything to be scared of . . . " His voice died away and he looked awkward as she poured our coffee and left. "Wow!" He pretended to mop his brow. "That was a close one." He saw I did not understand, and he lowered his voice. "I shouldn't have spoken about that old ghost in front of her — they say it was a member of her family."

Penny was unimpressed. "But so far back it hardly matters, she said. "That Glyn's so touchy it's ridiculous."

"Well," said Jeff, "she's certainly got nerve, I'll say that for her." He was big and good-natured and he smiled as he said to me, "Now Penny, she wouldn't dare live up there in those woods. She'd be up among the top branches like a squirrel if a little old mouse squeaked."

"Pay no attention to him, Sam," said Penny.

There was mischief in Jeff's face. "Okay, Penny," he said, "if you're so big and bold, just tell us the name of that little old ghost."

She lifted her nose and sniffed. "Don't be so silly."

He spoke to me. "This ghost was a lumberjack, up there in Mildenhall Woods — where Glyn lives. And he was reckoned to have done away with several people — with his axe."

"You don't know that!" Penny was suddenly vehement. "No-one's ever said anything about an axe. You're trying to make it worse than it is."

"See what I mean? She daren't even think of it."

"That's just nonsense!"

Jeff continued to smile. "Well then, Penny, you go ahead and tell Sam what he was called."

"He already knows."

Jeff laughed. "How can he? He's only just arrived in Oxrun."

"Because there's a photograph of him in the museum with his name underneath it — that's why." She spoke in a rush and added, "That's true, isn't it, Sam?"

I nodded, because I knew she wanted me to agree, but I had to admit I could recall no name.

"That's okay," said Jeff. "Penny will remind you."

"I will do no such thing."

"Just what I said, she's a squirrel." He sat back, well pleased with himself. "You noticed that, Sam — she won't say his name. And she won't say it because she's afraid that if she does say it, that old spook lumberjack will answer to his name and come looking for her. He likes girls." He tilted his head. "Now me," he said, "*I* can say it."

"Don't you dare." Penny glowered at him.

"Well, as he used an axe, you could always call him Hugh . . ."

"Stop it!"

"I was only going to say that he isn't human, but he did hew wood so you *could* call him the Hew Man."

I was facing them across the table. Behind their backs, unseen by either of them, the waitress had come out from behind the counter and was approaching our booth. Jeff had at last coaxed a smile from Penny, and I pushed out my cup for the waitress to refill it. The crisis was over and I was watching the black whirlpool of coffee as she poured.

Jeff and Penny had their foreheads close together and were not aware of me or anyone else as he said, "That's all I was trying to tell you, Penny. I was never going to say his real name, because you're so frightened of it. I was never going to say it out loud — not Hugh Morgan, I was never going to say *Hugh Morgan*."

He chuckled and I was aware that Penny was angry with him but I did not hear her words. The frothing of the coffee seemed to drown them out. I heard the hiss of the bubbles and it intensified until the noise filled my head. I started back just as the coffee spilled over the edge of the cup and Jeff called out to warn the waitress.

I looked up. She was gazing down at me. She was startled and, as our eyes met, the noise in my ears rose in a crescendo, thundering in my head like a waterfall and pressing in on me until the pain of it blurred my vision.

I saw Jeff prise the coffee pot from her fingers, and I saw her turn and move away. And then Penny and Jeff were mopping spilled coffee with paper napkins, and the clamour in my head diminished and ceased.

We sat for a while. Neither of the others could make out what had happened, and I said nothing. I think I would have let them know that yesterday's whispering had increased suddenly and violently . . . I would have told them all about it if it hadn't been for the expression on the girl's face as she had looked down on me. She knew what was happening, and she was afraid.

Jeff went to the counter to ask after her. "She's sick," he said, "and they've sent her home."

5

It was vacation time and everyone of my age seemed to leave Oxrun. Jeff's family always visited relatives in the South, and Penny and her parents went to Europe, so I was left pretty much on my own. It didn't bother me because I still had a lot of exploring to do.

The whispering did not come again, and I certainly did not mention it to anyone. It had all been caused by the fatigue of travel and I felt foolish at having overreacted. Even the incident in The Luncheonette became insignificant, and as I had no wish to go back there I didn't see the girl — I'd even forgotten her name — who had been so unwell she had spilt a pot of coffee. But I did discover something about Penny. She'd lied to me.

One sunny morning — and even to wake up and know that the day ahead was almost certain to have unbroken sunshine was new to someone born on an island that collected Atlantic rains — I was strolling out along Chancellor Avenue with the vague idea of getting to the end of the houses and seeing what lay beyond the outskirts of town when I realised I was passing the Herbert Bass Museum.

By now I was recognising the styles of some of the buildings in Oxrun and it was obvious that Herbert Bass must have been a man of wealth when he built his residence a hundred years ago. It was a Queen Anne style house with steps up to a verandah (which I was learning to call a porch) and a spread of lawn and shrubs that set it well back from the road. It gathered an imposing silence around it, and I felt like an interloper as I climbed to the sunbaked porch and pushed open the door.

Nothing had changed since I'd visited it with Penny; not that I expected anything to be different, but it was so precisely what it had been before that I felt that, like a doll's house, nothing had so much as stirred until I'd opened the door a second time. The same green light filtered through the windows, the upper floors held the same secret silence, and the same fat woman sat at her desk in the foyer with the telephone to her ear. Only the pale blonde, Eleanor Trent, was missing.

I was about the pass the curator and climb the stairs when her conversation ended and she put down the phone. "I've seen you before," she said. The plumpness of her cheeks narrowed her eyes.

I admitted that this was my second visit.

"You English?" She may have been friendly, but her smile pushed her glasses further up her face and intensified the fierce glitter of her eyes. "What do they call you?"

I told her.

"Sam Jones," she repeated, "then I guess you're of Welsh extraction — am I right, Sam Jones?"

"Almost," I said. "It's my mother who is Welsh, not my father, in spite of his name."

"Welsh," she said. "Are you surprised I guessed that — you wouldn't have expected a person in Oxrun to recognise a Welsh name, would you?" I shook my head. "It's because there're loads of folks hereabouts who have Welsh blood in their veins — me, too." She laughed, and there was so much of her that it was like watching a minor earthquake. "And a mighty weird lot we are. What about you, Sam Jones?"

"I'm a rum 'un," I said.

"What's that? A rum 'un?"

"That's what we call someone peculiar in Norwich."

"Is that near London?"

"Almost part of it," I said.

"Rum 'un." She liked it. "So what do rum 'uns do? No, don't tell me — I know what they do. Yes, indeed I do. They're neither here nor there, out of their minds, gone to lunch — am I right? If a Norwich rum 'un is like an Oxrun rum 'un they believe in all manner of kooky things — what say you, Sam Jones? Things like . . . "

She left a gap for me to fill. "Kooky spooky," I said, entering into the spirit of it, "like ghosts, you mean?"

"On the button, Sam Jones." She slapped the desk and cocked her head. "And no doubt — you being Welsh and all — you felt something strange in the atmosphere just as soon as you set foot in this peculiar little town."

"Even before," I said.

"How's that?" she asked, but I didn't tell her. Instead I said, "I came here today because of the ghost of Mildenhall Woods."

"You did? And why is that?"

I hadn't even thought about it until the idea popped out of my mouth, but suddenly I remembered something Penny had told me. "You've got a photograph of him — before he was dead, I mean."

"That's news to me."

I told her about the big picture of the lumberjack upstairs in the logging display.

"In the lumber room, you mean — isn't that what you British call the junk room?" I nodded, and she was laughing again. "Well there may be a lot of old rubbish in there but Hugh Morgan ain't among it. This is a serious institution, sir, and we hold no truck with ghosts and such stuff. The very idea!"

"Oh, but I was told . . . " I broke off as the fat lady shook her head.

"Sam Jones," she said solemnly, "that pretty young lady who brought you here has been having you on. It was the young lady who told you, wasn't it?"

I nodded, and she was pleased she'd got it right. "There you are, you see. I knew it all along. It's the Welsh in me — it's not only the Irish who've got the second sight. But you'd better go up and see that I'm not kidding."

I obeyed her, and she was right. Among the exhibits there were many old photographs of sawmills and tree felling, but none of any individual lumberjack, let alone an enlarged portrait of one, as Penny had insisted.

"Young man!" I went out on to the landing and saw the curator at the foot of the stairs. She knew I had found nothing. "Are you very disappointed with that pretty young thing?"

"Well," I replied, "she told me the picture had his name printed underneath. I don't think she wanted to say it out loud."

Her guffaw made the staircase tremble. "So you kids still believe that one, do you — that old Hugh Morgan will come for you if you call him?"

"Not me," I said. "I'm a stranger here."

"But you're Welsh, Sam Jones, and so was he. You'd better watch your step." Still shaking with amusement she went back to her desk, and I, now that I was up here, took a more leisurely tour than I'd had with Penny.

There was one room that we had not bothered with, and I entered it more with a sense of duty than any real interest. I had heard of the Ox River Project but had shunted it to the side of my mind where I'd heaped up all those important but dull facts that one day, given a push from someone like a teacher, you might have to rummage among to pass an exam. But here was a room where the Project was spread out all around me and I recognised that I had better take some account of it just in case I was cross-questioned about it by the fat lady downstairs.

My ignorance was so great that I was surprised to discover that the Project was the building of the Ox River Dam, of which I had heard because several of our neighbours had offered to take us there, but sightseeing trips had not yet taken us that far into the mountains. Now, in a lonely room that few people seemed to visit, I found something to fascinate me.

I have always liked models, and I had no sooner walked through the door than I found one of such mechanical complexity that it engrossed me completely. The dam had needed a lot of a particular kind of rock in its construction, such a vast amount that it could not be cut from the mountain sides nearby but had to be quarried down in the valley near Oxrun Station. I knew there was a quarry, but what I did not know was just how that rock got to the dam six miles away. And here, in a glass case that ran the entire length of one wall, was a model that showed me.

The engineers had lifted the rock by conveyor belt, millions of tons of it on a moving belt that ran for six miles up hills, through forests and across gullies to the site of the dam high up in the mountains. The model showed it all. It was behind glass but the tiny sponge-rubber trees were realistic enough to look as if the wind blew through them, and the quarry had rocks the size of thumbnails that nevertheless seemed weighty enough to crash down in a landslide. And the machinery worked. When I pressed a button the endless belt of the conveyor, grey and clogged with rock dust, ground its ponderous way up the hillside until it spilled its boulders into the head of the Ox River Valley to choke the river.

The thrum of the electric motor broke the silence of the room, and I was up there in the hills listening to the heave and strain of the belt as it shifted itself through the treetops, groaning with the load it shouldered while the rumble and squeal of the great pulleys shed dust like sweat. I could hear it all, rending the silence of the forest, but, as I listened, another sound broke in. It seemed to be words, some faint commentary on what I was looking at, and I strove to hear it. I succeeded too well, for suddenly my head was filled with such a screaming that it pounded my brain, and dizziness made me snatch at the exhibition case to hold myself upright.

I know I fell to the floor, although I do not remember it, but I do recall the terror that swept over me as I recognised the sound for what it was. The whispering had returned, now with an intensity that overwhelmed my brain.

Then, through it all, I heard footsteps, and a voice. "Young man?" I found that I was crouching, and I turned to look over my shoulder. "Are you quite well?"

The curator was looking at me from the doorway, and I realised that the noise in my head had ceased.

"You okay?"

"Yes," I said. "I'm fine. I just . . . " and then I saw that something had fallen from my shirt pocket, " . . . I was just picking up my pen." I got to my feet but had to hold the edge of the exhibition case.

"You are very pale, Sam Jones. Will you kindly give me your telephone number?"

I wasn't even puzzled that she should ask, and I dumbly watched her write it down. "Can you make it down to the hall?"

Of course I could.

"Very well, then. Take care. I'm going to call your parents."

"Why? What have I done?"

This made her laugh. "Ease up, Sam Jones, don't try to act tough. Right now I'm looking at a young fellow who isn't feeling all that well and I'm going to put him in good hands."

It was ridiculous. "There's nothing wrong with me," I protested.

"You didn't drop that pen," she said. "It came out of your pocket when you fell. I heard you."

There was no stopping her. She had me sit in the hall while she telephoned. I felt foolish, a weakling, and she saw it. She put her hand over the mouthpiece. "Don't you fret about this, Sam Jones. I'm not going to let on to any of your friends about it — everyone has a fainting fit once in a while."

But not me, I wanted to say. No, no, no. And then, no matter how I fought it, I went pale once more, because that was the word that the voice was repeating when it reached such a scream of terror that it blotted everything else from my mind. No! No! No!

6

I know everyone is supposed to enjoy being fussed over, but I'm fairly healthy and one thing I did not want was to be an invalid. So when my parents arrived at the museum in such a lather of anxiety about me, I was pretty brusque with them and made a point of leaping down the porch steps to prove how fit I was.

But I have to admit that I was secretly relieved that the doctor — or doctors, because I was sent to the hospital for tests — decided there was nothing wrong with my heart or lungs or anything else. I had suffered 'a stress-related syndrome' due to the experience of moving house, and they said it was unlikely to affect me further. I had told them about the buzzing sound in my head, but not that it had resolved itself into words — and I got round to accepting that it was all due to an overwrought imagination.

So I was fit and well, and in the days that followed I ceased to be a stranger in Oxrun and became much like anyone else — except for my accent, which I was determined not to lose. Penny Galbraith had said she liked it, and it is putting it far too mildly to say I liked her, although I disguised the way I felt because I had guessed from the very first that she and Jeff Dacre had something going together.

I can't pretend that I did not envy him, but after a while I discovered, confusingly, that it was possible to be both jealous and friendly with someone at the same time. It was made easier when, with Penny still away on her travels in Europe, Jeff came home and he and I were often in each other's company.

We went fishing. At home in Norfolk I would go float fishing for pike or ledgering on the river bottom for bream, but he angled for trout and he had a book of flies which, when he opened it, almost took my breath away. They were like tiny jewels and so delicate I could hardly credit they could be secured to a line, but he did it and, watching his fingers work so dexterously, I became fired with the urge to do the same. He instructed me in fly tying, but I never could match him so I was forced to be modest about my efforts, or even secretive.

He had a favourite trout stream in the foothills above Oxrun, and one particular stretch where a deep pool lay in a hollow the stream had carved in the rock.

"Not many people know about this," he said, and I told him I wasn't surprised. We had driven some miles out of town and had turned off into a dirt track that had petered out when the ground got too steep. Then it had taken us more than an hour to clamber up a slope through rocks and trees to where the pool lay on a broad ledge. It was a natural amphitheatre where the trees, rank on rank of them, looked down on us as if they were a silent audience.

He slid the creel from his shoulder and pointed to where, in the vee between two mountains, something white shone in the sun. "The nearest sign of human habitation," he said.

"What is it?" It looked like the wall of a castle, but I knew it couldn't be that.

"Ox River Dam," he said. "Listen."

We stood still. We were high above the valley floor but nowhere near the summit of the hill, and the pool lay at our feet. The stream that fed it was cushioned to silence among the trees, and nowhere, either near at hand or far away in the blue haze of the mountains, did a single branch stir. It was as though the world listened to the silence of the universe.

"Awesome," he said, but I could hear nothing.

From the lip of the pool the stream split into runlets that were so deeply embedded in moss they seemed to be designed to flow in silence. "There isn't a sound," I said.

"Sometimes," he said, "you can hear it quite plain."

"Hear what?"

"The dam."

I waited for him to explain, but he said nothing. I was hot, but a chill touched my backbone. "I didn't know a dam could make any noise," I said. "It's solid concrete."

"The people who built it could hear it." He was gazing towards the white wall far away. "They said it was all the stonework settling. That's what they said then. They sometimes say other things now."

"You mean it still makes a noise?"

"Nights," he said. "You sometimes hear a kind of groaning from a long ways off. And some say it's not the dam itself, but something else." He pointed, not directly at the dam itself, but towards the nearer slopes above us. "They say it's that great old conveyor belt still turning." He tilted his head towards me and put an old man's tremble in his voice. "Which is kinda strange, as it ain't there no more."

I kept a straight face, playing along with him. "Another ghost," I said. "Does it have anything to do with the . . . " I let my voice trail away.

"With the . . . ?" He was grinning, tempting me to say it. "With the Nameless One," I said.

"Oh, him." His eyes were bright with mischief. "You mean the . . . one who frightens the girls." He paused and his mouth was open. I knew he was about to pronounce the forbidden name of the dead lumberjack, and I did not wish to hear it. I had been ill, no matter what I pretended, and at that moment, alone in the hills, I simply did not want to increase the tension that this discussion, playful though it was, was already causing the muscles of my jaw to stiffen.

I opened the lid of my tackle box. "I've got a new fly," I said. "It's a world beater — just take a gander at this." I held it out on the palm of my hand.

He took his time. "It ain't pretty," he said. It was brown and fluffy. "And it ain't small." He made it sound as big as a walnut.

I turned it over, trying to squeeze the fibres together. "Its size is the point," I said. "The fish have got to be able to see it."

"They'll see it, all right." He weighed it in his hand. "What's it made of?"

I didn't tell him I'd taken a tuft out of a carpet and then embellished it. "Only the finest materials," I said.

"Hmm." He took time to examine it before he complimented me. "About the size of an orange, and hefts like a rock — if it don't choke the life out of 'em it'll bomb 'em to death."

On my first cast it caught on a high branch and the line broke. "Now we shall never know," he said, and I had to admit as we sat in the shade and ate our sandwiches that the ball of fluff above our heads was one of life's great mysteries, "like Bermuda shorts and aftershave," I added.

"Hell now, Sam, you know I wouldn't ever use aftershave."

"And I swear you'll never see me in Bermudas."

"That's because you're British, old buddy."

"Too long for shorts and too short for strides — they're still a mystery. Just like your ghostly lumberjack." I had brought the subject back deliberately. I wanted him to know that I wasn't as timid as I might have appeared.

Jeff looked sideways at me. "He seems to be on your mind, that old feller."

"Feller is good."

We laughed.

"Does he trouble you?"

"Of course not. I'm just interested, that's all."

"Like in The Luncheonette that day?" I did not answer, but he persisted. "Remember? — that time you didn't feel well. We were talking about it then."

I thought I had disguised it, but Jeff had noticed. "I don't see what that's got to do with it," I said.

"Me neither."

The sun shone and the pond mirrored the blue sky, the scatter of clouds and the bright green of the hilltops. There was an enormous peacefulness around us, but now, like a little breeze that can bring goose bumps to your skin on the hottest day, a thin thread twitched in my mind and would not ease off. A girl talking about a ghost, the buzz of a working model in a museum, and now a tale of a groaning dam was making me feverish. I glanced at the white wall in the hills far away and my galloping mind saw a crack split it from top to bottom and a thundering torrent went lashing down the valley.

I hauled back. "What is all this about the lumberjack?" I said. The dam was where it was, no water thundered, and no whispered words came to me through the trees. I threw a pebble into the pool. "Nobody has ever told me exactly what he's supposed to have done, this woodman."

"I guess it's because you never asked." He was being tactful.

"All I know is that he killed his wife."

"She was never found. Maybe even that isn't true."

"Even that?" I repeated. "You mean there's more?"

"Well . . ." Now it was his turn to throw a stone into the pool and I could see he was embarrassed. "He had a daughter."

"And she disappeared, too?"

"No. She stayed." He was too decent to say any more, so I said it for him.

"They lived together."

"Hell, Sam, it was a long time ago. It's about time folk stopped talking about it." Indignation had reddened his face, but I could not understand why he was so troubled.

"Surely that doesn't matter any more," I said. "There's no-one left to be hurt by it." He did not answer. "Am I right?"

He sat with his hands resting on his knees, and his head drooped as he spoke into his lap. "You weren't the only one who felt sick to the stomach that day in The Luncheonette," he said.

My own feelings at that time had blurred my memory and I had to think. It couldn't have been Penny, and it wasn't Jeff. "There was only the waitress," I began, and then I recalled seeing Jeff go to the counter and come back to say that something had upset her. "Is she the one you mean?" I asked. I could not remember her name. He nodded. "But why does it matter to her?"

"Family," he said. "It's her family — and she still lives in the middle of those goddam woods." He stood up. "Can you think what it's like for her, with a man like that as your . . ."

He broke off, and I wanted to ask more, but the whole business of the messy past embarrassed him and he'd had enough of speculation. The sky had clouded over and he thought we should call it a day.

Just before we left he picked up a large stone and pitched it high in the air. "To hell with you, Hugh Morgan, you lousy old ratfink!"

The stone came down vertically and hit the water with the deep plunk of a deadened guitar string. I even heard it click against other stones at the bottom and there were no reverberations, so the soft thud we heard immediately afterwards could have had no connection with it. Nevertheless we lifted our heads. Somewhere in the forest a rotten limb had fallen into the moss.

We grinned at each other, mocking the moment's alarm we had each felt. We had already collected our gear and it was time to go. I was hoisting the strap of my creel to my shoulder when the thud was repeated, and with it came a soft sound that could have been something pushing its way through the undergrowth — or, more likely, the rotten branch completing its fall to the forest floor.

Neither of us wished to be the first to move, but when a jay sent up a screech that was like a woman's scream, we both went charging down the hillside, in broad daylight but as if something from the blackest night was at our heels.

7

Next day neither Jeff nor I attached any importance to what had happened at the rock pool. We had built up the atmosphere quite deliberately, and had enjoyed giving ourselves a scare. It was easy to explain, and so was everything else that had happened to me. Taken one by one they were nothing. It was when they were added together that a picture formed in my mind in which, whether I liked it or not, I was finding a place. Why me — a stranger from far away?

And then there was Penny. She had been away all summer, and altogether I had known her for only a few days, but she was always in my thoughts, so much so that I could feel uncomfortable about it when I was with Jeff. I was in danger of being disloyal to the best friend I had in Oxrun, so I was glad that the picture I had of her in my mind faded so fast that, whenever I tried to recall her, I was more and more uncertain of what it was about her looks that attracted me so strongly. I told myself this must mean my feelings towards her were weakening, and I was glad, because then I would have nothing to hide from Jeff.

Then, one day, she sent me a snapshot of herself from London. I know that no camera is ever capable of seeing what you see yourself, so the Penny I saw smiling on the Thames Embankment with the Houses of Parliament behind her was not at all like Penny herself. That was what I told myself, but I fell in love with the photograph. I did not show it to Jeff, and it was because I felt I had to avoid him for a time that I wandered into town alone.

The day was overcast and the clouds were low enough to lie as mist among the trees on the higher slopes beyond the roof tops, and lights had come on in the windows of shops and offices. A row of small table lamps glowed in The Luncheonette, which should have made it even more like 'Nighthawks' than before, but now it was an unfinished picture without a single figure slouched at the long counter. It was typical of the way my mind was working that I chose to sit at just the spot the man wearing the fedora occupied in the picture, but even that did not gel and I merely felt awkward as the waitress came out of the kitchen and walked along to be opposite me.

It was the girl of a few weeks ago and we recognised each other, but her name had completely escaped me by now. Nor, from the way she greeted me, could she recall mine. I ordered coffee, and she turned away to make it at the espresso machine.

All I knew about her, and all I needed to know, was that she was not as good-looking as Penny. Everything about her was subdued. She had a thinner, smaller mouth than Penny, and her cheeks were pallid, less rounded, and her eyes did not gaze into yours with the bright inquisitiveness that always made me feel as if Penny was paying me the compliment of being interested. The dark girl kept her thoughts hidden behind lowered eyelids.

She put the coffee on the counter in front of me. "Is there anything else, sir?"

"There's no need to call me that."

"I beg your pardon, sir?" She was very soft spoken.

"Sir," I said. "I'm not sir to anyone." I was embarrassed, and I said more, trying to explain myself and making it worse.

"It's just that I'm not used to it . . . I mean I don't seem to deserve it from someone my own age." But she was older than me. She stood motionless, not looking at me, and saying nothing. It was a reproof, and I dried up.

Then she spoke. "You're British, aren't you?" Her eyes glanced quickly at me and were hidden again.

I said I was. And then, in order to redeem myself, I snatched at anything to keep the conversation going. "You live in Mildenhall Woods, don't you?" Again that look, quickly shrouded but not fast enough to hide the fact that she resented the question. I spoke quickly. "It's just that there's a place near where I live in England called Mildenhall and there's a forest there, too. Have you heard of it?" She shook her head.

I had failed again. "I just wondered if there was some connection, that's all," I said lamely and looked away.

She gave a bitter little laugh. "That's not what you meant." She must have seen the surprise on my face, but that did not prevent her accusing me. "You want me to tell you what it's like living out there when everyone tells stories about the place. That's what you want — you want to know what the hell it was that happened all those years ago, and what the hell I'm doing still living in the same place."

There was anger in her words but she had not raised her voice, and now she was gazing directly at me. She defied what people said and she rejected me, but she was hurt, and her eyes betrayed her. Their darkness was intensified and enlarged by the beginning of tears she refused to let fall.

I was about to drink my coffee when anger suddenly swelled up inside me. She was accusing me of other people's stupidity. "I don't give a damn about Mildenhall Woods," I said. "Let 'em say what they like — what's it to me?" I lifted my cup and drank. Let her cry, if she feels she must. What's she to me?

I put my cup down. Like two fighters we gazed steadily at each other. I was right, and she knew it. I faced her down. Her lips parted slightly and she drew in her breath in a series of little gasps, and lowered her eyelids. I had won, but those shuddering little gasps gained the better of me. She had not intended it, but she had defeated me.

"People scare too easily," I said.

She could not bear to bring her eyes back to me, but she nodded. I don't think she could speak.

"They get scared even in daylight." I was speaking only to help her out. "I was darn near frightened out of my wits just the other day near here."

"Where?" She managed just the one word.

"In the hills," I said. "Up towards the dam." Her mouth became small and round, almost as if she was about to whistle, and her eyes were on me again. "I was up near where the old conveyor belt used to run — you know, the one that's supposed to squeal in the night?" I was smiling, making fun of all the stories, when she spoke quite seriously.

"You heard it?" She was so absurdly solemn that I lost patience with her again.

"No," I said, "I didn't hear it. I heard something much worse. I heard footsteps through the trees and I heard a woman scream." It was brutally satisfying to see the effect this had. Her face which, with its pursed lips and wide, dark eyes, had become innocent and attractive, crumbled. She was afraid. My words had frightened her, and in my disgust I let go. "I guess it was that old idiot who's supposed to wander about up there!" I cried. "Hugh Morgan!"

I felt cold and I thought the outer door had opened. I tried to turn to see who had entered, but my head would not move. It would not move because, directly in front of me, someone was whimpering. It was the most pitiful sound I had ever heard, pleading for help, and I could not turn away. But it was not the girl. Her small mouth was still open but no sound came from her. No sound at all. And she, too, heard it. Her eyes told me so, and in the moment that we recognised it, the whimper, as if it had been waiting to be heard by both of us, rose to a shriek.

It came with all the terror that had forced me to the floor of the museum. It pierced my head and I was half blinded by it. Panic made my muscles freeze, yet one thing was necessary above all else. To be alone was unbearable. We had to touch.

I remember seeing my hand move crabwise across the counter. I saw my arm brush against the coffee cup and I watched it spill. I felt the liquid burn my arm but I ignored it. Her hand, smaller than mine and paler, was reaching for me. I knew I ought to cover it and protect it, but my true feeling was selfish. Only by reaching her could I save myself. Our fingers touched, and what went through us next was purely mechanical, out of our control. A shock jolted through us and a door slammed shut on the din. It ceased. Ordinary sounds came back. The espresso machine hissed, and I drew in my breath as I felt the pain in my arm.

She poured ice water on to a napkin and laid it on my burning skin, and as I thanked her I remembered her name.

8

Penny returned. The photograph she had sent me was wildly wrong; she was prettier than ever. We were neighbours and we were often together.

I did not go back to The Luncheonette. It was partly cowardice, but mainly embarrassment at what had happened there. The waitress — I could not bring myself to think of her as Glyn — must have been caught up in the hysteria that had been plaguing me, and all I wanted to do was put it behind me once and for all.

And besides, as she had pressed the ice water to my arm until the pain eased, she had seemed to regard me as some sort of accomplice. I had no idea what might have been in her mind, but I did know that the last thing I wanted was to be involved. So I was content with the Mariner Cove which was the place that Jeff, and Penny, preferred. The Luncheonette was only a couple of blocks away but somehow I never seemed to be anywhere near it. My mind was filled with Penny.

The days shortened and the weather got colder, but the trees on the hillsides glowed with such reds and yellows that when the sun, dipping towards the horizon, caught the slopes at an angle the trees flared like a forest fire. I said so to Penny when we sat on the steps of our porch and saw the blaze of colour blocking off the end of the street.

She said, "I know it's lovely, but it's getting very cold."

"Just like England," I said.

"You're knocking it. Why do you do that?"

I shrugged. "School tomorrow," I said.

"What's that got to do with anything? I was telling you how much I liked England." She paused, then added, "And English people."

If she had not paused I would not have turned towards her and would have missed the wistful expression in the blue eyes that were resting on me.

"I do," she said. "I like English people." She kept her eyes on me, and colour came into her cheeks.

I said, "I'm half Welsh."

"Oh!" She banged her hand on the wooden step. "You're half stupid, too!"

It was then that I leant towards her. The top of her nose was cold against my cheek but her lips, when my own lips touched them, were warm and very soft.

We were still kissing when my father's car drifted into sight. She sprang back and was two steps down from me when he pulled up and she raised a hand to greet him. Mr. Galbraith was sitting beside my Dad. "Don't," she said over her shoulder. "Whatever you do, don't say anything."

I was hardly likely to, but I did not believe she was thinking of our parents. She was thinking of Jeff, and so was I.

We helped my father and Mr. Galbraith unload the trunk. They had been into the hills, exploring the woods to help my father's research into shrubs, and had rooted up some specimens which we carried to the miniature forest of plants that filled our backyard. We had only just finished when my mother drove up with Mrs. Galbraith and came indoors with an armful of books from the library, and soon Penny and I were handing round mugs of tea and Welsh scones my mother had made. I would have gone out to sit on the stoop again, but Penny made sure we had too much to do. So I had to listen to my father telling my mother about the quarry they had explored in the hills.

"You've no idea of the size of it, Mai." Her name is Mary but he likes to give it the Welsh pronunciation.

"No idea, haven't I?" She and Penny's mother exchanged glances. "That's just where you're mistaken. They had to dig out ten million tons of stone, which makes it a pretty big hole in the ground."

He raised his eyebrows at this, and Joe Galbraith laughed and said, "You've been upstaged, old sport. While we've been digging up the forests, they've been digging into local history."

My mother wasn't one to let it rest there. She told him about the Oxrun conveyor belt. "It went over hills and highways and railways," she said, "and it ran day and night for I don't know how many years."

"Five," said my father, who had also done some homework.

"Well, maybe," she admitted, and then she put on that prim little smile that always means she knows something that's going to shoot you down in flames. "And what about the men?" she said. "The men who worked in the quarry — what about them?"

"I don't know, Mai. What about them?"

"They were miners." The Welsh lilt had come back to her voice. "That's what a lot of them were — miners. There now, what do you think of that!"

My father was mystified and looked to Joe Galbraith for an explanation but he was equally puzzled.

Mrs. Galbraith put a hand on my mother's arm. "We've got them beat, Mary," she said. "Just tell them what you unearthed in the library this afternoon."

Keeping my father pinned down, my mother said, "Well, there was a labour shortage here in Oxrun, see — and there weren't enough quarrymen so they set about looking for miners, and the news got around . . . " she paused, and her eyes were shining, " . . . even as far as Wales, would you believe!"

Mrs. Galbraith broke in to explain to her husband. "Mary's been telling me what it was like in the coalmining valleys where she used to live, and how poor some of the people were, so it wasn't surprising that they should look to this country if they got the chance."

"And they came — some of them, a few — but listen, Dai." My father's name is David but she sometimes shortened it, Welsh fashion. "I'm sure someone came from my own valley — my own village, even!"

"That's very interesting," he said, but it was obvious he thought the excitement was out of proportion.

"You stuffy old so-and-so," she said, and turned to Penny's mother. "Now then, Dorothy, didn't I tell you he'd be a wet blanket — just like an Englishman?"

This was an old tease, and my father smiled. "Better to keep your feet on the ground like a sensible scientist than fly around like a wild Welsh witch."

"Witch, is it? I'll give you witch!"

It was always a battle between the Welsh and the English in our house, and they loved it, but I began to wonder if it was just as amusing to the Galbraiths, so I said to Penny, "With a background like mine, you can't blame me for being a nut case." It was a mistake because then I was in the middle of all their kidding, and I had to try again. "Mum," I said, "was the miner from your village called Morgan?"

"Which Morgan?" she said. "There are a lot of Morgans about."

It had crossed my mind that the lumberjack that Penny was so afraid to name could have started out as a miner, and I was about to say so when I glimpsed Penny's face. She was biting her lip, and there was real anxiety in her eyes. "Oh, I don't know," I said to my mother, "it's just that I've heard you talk about people."

"But not Morgans. There wasn't a single Morgan in my village, can you believe? No, I wasn't exactly thinking of a miner who could have come here, I was thinking of a girl. I used to hear my mother talk about a girl who years and years ago married someone and went to live abroad." She threw up her hands. "But Morgan . . . Morgan . . . No, I don't think so."

As she repeated the name I was listening to the silence beyond the house and after a moment I realised uncomfortably, that I had been hoping to pick up the whispering once more, and even hear it rise to a shriek to din in my ears. There was nothing. I had been terrified when it struck, but now I felt I had lost touch with something that lay all around us, just below the surface of the ordinary world, and which almost nobody else had been able to detect. I went outside, but there was not even a breeze to stir the yellow leaves that littered the porch. All was silent.

9

There is no excuse for the way Penny and I behaved towards Jeff. We were deceitful. Even if it were true, as she insisted, that she and Jeff had no claim on each other, there was no doubt in my mind that he thought of Penny as his girlfriend.

It had always seemed to be something understood between them and he, in his gentle, good-natured manner, was in awe of her and never made demands.

We could have said we kept our feelings hidden in order to spare him, but that was not true. We enjoyed the secrecy.

Penny and I had a kind of sign language, or at least we understood each other's nods and gestures, so that even if she was explaining something very simple to me — and school was a minefield she enjoyed leading me through — there was more to it than Jeff could guess. Not that he was left out in the cold completely; I mean he taught me baseball and I told him about cricket.

"You hit the ball with a paddle, isn't that so?" he asked me.

"We call it a bat, same as you."

"And the pitcher *runs* up to the mound before he pitches?"

I put him right. "The bowler runs up to the stumps before he bowls."

"Okay — but the catcher is behind the batter just the same."

"The wicketkeeper is behind the batsman."

"Right," he said. But what really got to him was that the cricket ball hits the ground before the batsman strikes it, and when I said that some games lasted for five full days he said, "Uh-huh," and bought me a root beer, which I hated.

I think that maybe, about this time, he'd begun to suspect that Penny was not playing fair with him, but he never said anything to either of us. I do know that I was feeling increasingly guilty but it still did not prevent me, every evening, leaving home to wander, as if by accident, along the narrow trail into the deep woods at the end of the road where Penny was waiting.

We were together when an owl sent its mournful feathery cry through the trees and made us both start. We were at the mouth of a fire break and Penny gazed into the long avenue cut through the forest and shuddered. "I wouldn't live where she does if you paid me a million dollars," she said.

"You don't need to worry about her," I said. "She doesn't care."

Penny looked at me from the corner of her eye. "How do you know? I haven't told you who I'm talking about."

It was no great feat of deduction to have guessed she meant the waitress at The Luncheonette, but it was true that neither of us had spoken of her for weeks, so I made the most of my lucky guess. "It's my sixth sense," I said. "I'm afraid I carry the burden of knowing far too much."

"You phoney!" She batted at me with one of her gloves, but I held her close.

"It's because I'm Welsh," I said. "Our minds move through the twilight world and we speak of things that mundane mortals can never know." I was kissing her as I said it and she was pretending to try to escape.

"You arrogant, big-headed . . . " and then our lips were joined and we were silent. The owl hooted, further away now, less menacing, and Penny drew her head back a fraction.

"It still scares me," she said. "Just the thought of being in that house in Mildenhall Woods right now makes me feel awful."

I had my arms round her and I was the hero. "Let's go take a look," I said, and started to walk away along the fire break.

"Come back!" she cried, but I had committed myself, and after a few moments I heard her footsteps behind me.

"You can't do it," she said.

"Why not?" I knew we were heading vaguely in the direction of Mildenhall Woods but I was already not quite so enthusiastic and I hoped she would tell me that the fire break would never get us there. But that was not her reason for wanting to turn back.

"It's too spooky," she said. "And it's through the woods all the way."

"Then we'd better hurry." It was the only way to keep my self-respect. "It's getting dark."

The fallen leaves rustled under our feet, but the woods had become silent and dead. If any creatures were stirring, their movements were muffled.

We came to a place where two trails crossed and stood in the centre looking up at the stars. Venus seemed to be brighter than ever. "It's beautiful," she said, "but it's time to go back."

I ignored that. "Which way?" I said, and when she pointed ahead we entered a new part of the forest. The trail climbed and the trees became denser. Darkness walled us in, folding in behind us as we went deeper.

"I don't know how we'll be sure when we get there," she said.

I was glad to have an excuse to stop. Our breath, just visible in front of our faces, misted the air. We must have circled the edge of town and we could have turned back without disgrace. I had opened my mouth to say so when something caught my eye.

We had reached a shoulder of the hillside and the land fell away steeply to our left. Below us, a speck of light hung in the trees. We moved closer together until our breath mingled. We listened. The night was silent, and the light did not move.

"What is it?" The words had hardly escaped my lips when she answered.

"It's a house," she said. "We're there."

Piecing the shadows together I saw a roof top, and then, by moving my head, I saw that the light came from a window. Quite suddenly the night became less frightening. If someone could spend every night out here in the forest, then so could I.

"Come on," I said. "We'll call on her."

"No." Penny held back. "We'd scare her out of her life coming out of the forest like this."

"She won't be scared by us. She lives in a haunted house, don't forget."

"She does not." Through the mist of her breath I could see that Penny was shaking her head.

"But you told me she lived in the house where . . . " She need not have grabbed my arm to make me stop. I was not going to speak his name.

"No. No. He didn't live in that house — he had a cabin up the hill behind it. Nobody ever goes there — not even Glyn." I took a step away from her. "And I forbid you to go there, Sam Jones. Stay right here!"

I had, in fact, hoped I was moving away from the invisible cabin, but now a strange perversity made me disobey her. "Just one quick look," I said, "to prove we dare."

We went downhill, circling the house as we did so, and I held her hand as we slithered knee deep in leaves. The ground levelled and we came to a clearing. The air was heavy with the scent of earth and fungus.

"This is it," she breathed. "We don't have to go any closer." The stars threw down enough light for me to see that the clearing was empty. "I can see no cabin," I said softly.

"Of course you can't. It fell down years ago. It's all rotted away."

"Is nothing left at all?"

"I shouldn't think so. He . . . " she hesitated, " . . . he disappeared so long ago, and nobody lived there."

She was tugging at me to turn away and climb back to the track when I thought I saw a more solid shape among the tangle of undergrowth at the centre of the clearing. I had to see what it was.

"It's just a fallen tree," she complained, but she came with me.

She was mistaken. "It's a wall," I said, "what's left of one."

"I hate this. I just hate this. We are standing right on the spot where he used to walk."

But I was looking further than the rotten, collapsing wall. Beyond it I saw what seemed to be a doorway, and I realised I was looking across a room. The door had gone, but the two uprights of its frame remained. And something else. I could not make it out. Perhaps the remains of a stove still stood in the room beyond. I squeezed my eyes shut and opened them wide. And then I saw it for what it was. In the centre of the empty door frame, motionless, a figure stood watching us.

10

Next day I went to The Luncheonette, but I chose the wrong time and there were too many people for me to see the waitress alone. The best I could do was to sit in one of the booths she served and hope to talk to her without being overheard.

But then she caught sight of me and I could see she was nervous. For a long time she avoided me, but eventually she had to stand at my table.

"What can I get you, sir?"

"Can you sit down?"

"I'm afraid not, sir." She raised her voice. "What can I get you?"

There was a hum of conversation and no-one was paying us any attention. "I want to apologise," I said, "for last night."

"There's no need." She remained as upright as when she had stood in the cabin's doorway, watching Penny and me. "Would you like coffee?"

"I want to explain."

It was then she became uncertain. She had hardly looked at me but now her dark eyes were on mine and she had seen that I was determined. She bent forward, notebook in hand, as though she was taking my order, just in case May Levowitz, who ran the place, was watching us. "I finish at five," she said. "Be on the corner of Centre and Williamston Pike." And she turned to fetch the coffee I had not ordered.

When, in the night, I had seen the dark figure, the shock of fear that went through me had made my hand grip Penny's fingers with such a spasm that she had cried out. And she had not stopped shrieking even when the girl switched on her flashlight and we had seen her, but by then Penny's cries had turned to abuse. The girl herself had said hardly a word, and we had left her standing alone in the blackness of the forest.

Now I gazed obliquely across the street towards The Luncheonette a block away. It was getting dark and a bitter wind pressed my jeans against my legs and made me stamp to keep warm. I missed seeing her leave, and when her voice came from behind me I realised she must have circled the block. I asked why she was so cautious.

"Your girlfriend might have seen me talking to you," she said. "She doesn't like me."

She pulled her coat tighter around her and I saw she had put it on over the short dress of her waitress uniform. She was cold. She pressed her knees together as she bent into the wind and she hugged herself, in the way girls do.

"Let's get out of this," I said. I had no idea where to go, but she pointed along the Pike and the wind at our backs helped to hurry us along and around a corner. There was a windswept parking lot. "I'm over there." We walked to an old Buick that stood alone in a far corner. We got in and she started the engine.

"Where are we going?" I asked.

"Nowhere. I want to get warm." The blower was still cold on our feet when she turned to face me. "Why?" she said.

"We must have frightened you last night. I wanted to apologise."

I saw her in the dim light from the dashboard with her coat collar pulled up to her cheeks and I realised, with a sudden small shock, that I had very little idea of what she really looked like. "Why are you lying to me?" she said.

I was confused. She was suddenly no longer an aloof waitress, older than myself. She was a girl whose large dark eyes sought the answer to an impossible question. I began to mumble something meaningless, but she cut me short.

"I'm not talking about last night," she said. "There's something else." I saw the tip of her tongue touch her lips and she gave a shallow little gasp before she said, "That last time you saw me — what made you spill the coffee and burn your arm? You went away and you didn't come back."

"I'm sorry — I should have thanked you for what you did." I was putting up a smokescreen, and she was impatient with me.

"Sam." I did not even realise she knew my name. "Listen to me." Again the short intake of breath. "It wasn't the first time it had happened, was it?"

I shook my head. I noted that her face was smaller than Penny's, and she was older than Penny but she seemed younger. Comparisons seemed more important than what I was saying. "I hear something in my head," I told her. "It begins as a whisper but then it gets worse until I feel my brain is splitting and I'm falling apart." I tried to smile. "Then I burn my arm and you put ice water on it."

She sat silent, not looking at me. Then she said my name softly. "Sam."

"Yes."

"We both know that I heard it, too."

I murmured that I guessed so.

"And always at the same time," she said. "When somebody mentions something."

"Yes." We both knew what we were talking about, and we knew where the danger lay.

"Will you understand me, Sam, if I tell you that I have a connection to that terrible thing that happened all those years ago?" She waited until she heard my murmur, then she went on, "My grandmother knew the man that everyone talks about. She knew him when she was a young girl. She was living in that cabin, Sam, when her mother disappeared and everyone said he had murdered her."

I had to know for certain. "So your grandmother was the one who carried on living there even after her mother vanished?" I saw her nod. "What happened to her?" I asked.

"She's very old."

I was still absorbing the fact that someone from that time was still living when the girl said, "She never talks about it." But suddenly she turned towards me. "And nothing happened until you came here! Why does it happen to us?" It was the first time she had raised her voice. "What do you know? — you've got to tell me!"

I took my time before I answered. "I'm partly Welsh — and so are you, Glyn." I don't think she noticed that I had used her name. "My mother even thought someone from her own village might have come here." She looked at me expectantly, but I had to disappoint her. "No," I said, "there was no-one called . . ."

I broke off, unsure whether to mention the name, and she understood.

"Last time," she said, and her voice was uncertain, "when you spilled the coffee, do you remember what we did?"

I nodded. We had held hands and the noise had died. Now she put her hand in mine.

"Say it now," she said.

"There was no-one from my mother's village called Hugh Morgan," I said.

Her fingers were cold. Her grip on my hand tightened.

"Hugh Morgan," I said distinctly. "Hugh Morgan."

No sound but the grumble of the car engine and the purr of the fan reached us. She smiled, but doubts were still filling my mind. Hugh Morgan had never had any connection with my mother's village. He was nothing to do with me. But he had everything to do with Glyn.

"I'm sorry," I said. I felt I had deserted her.

She was mystified. "Sorry? What for?"

"I thought I could help — but all I've done is blunder in and stir up old trouble because I imagined I heard strange noises. Trouble for you, Glyn."

"I heard something, too. No-one else did."

A car swung out of the car park and its light brushed our faces. We were spotlighted; two people gazing at each other at the moment they recognised they were locked together in the same predicament. I even had her hand in mine. Then we were in darkness again, and she was freeing her fingers.

"I must go," she said.

"Not yet." I needed to stay with her, find out more. I looked out through the windscreen. "Where are we?"

"Library parking lot," she said, and I seized on it.

"That's it," I said, "we've got some research to do." Before she could protest, I had opened the door and we stepped out into the biting wind.

11

It was warm in the library. We shook the rain from our coats as we went to the main desk where Glyn asked where we could find something about the history of Oxrun.

"We have an extensive holding of material relating to Oxrun Station," said the librarian, and he indicated a section at the far end of the long room. "Can you tell me what specifically engages your attention?"

That was the one thing neither of us wanted to reveal, and she replied, "Just anything to do with the early days."

She thanked him and we walked down the room feeling he was following us with his eyes.

We passed an odd-looking girl dressed like a Goth; I'd seen her at school, but only to know her by her nickname: CF, which Chuck Antrim had told me stood for Colossal Flake.

We were relieved to find that Local History was in a deep alcove where we were out of sight of the desk.

We searched the shelves. There were many books about the history of the State but comparatively few about Oxrun Station itself. In recent times Charles Grant had been extremely industrious in collecting material about contemporary Oxrun, but there was no-one to match him for earlier times, and the further back we went the sparser the material became. There was very little about ordinary folk.

But then we came across a local historian, a former librarian, who had spent his retirement seeking out oldsters to get them to speak about what life was like when the logging industry was the only thing that mattered in Oxrun. In no time we had his pamphlets spread out on a desk.

They were an odd collection: 'Old Oxrun', 'When Times Were Hard', 'Woodland Tales', and 'The Jailhouse Gazette'.

"This is it," I said, but I was disappointed. Old lumberjacks and their wives and children gazed out from faded photographs, and we scanned the tales they told, but nowhere was there mention of anyone called Morgan, not even in jail. The pamphlets were thin and it did not take long.

"What next?" I asked. My head was still bent over the pages, and when she did not reply I looked up. She was sitting back as though she wanted to take no further part. Her coat was open and showed the pink and white of her waitress uniform. It did not suit her. Penny would have made something of it, but the dark girl wore it as if clothes were unimportant to her.

"Glyn?"

She did not immediately raise her eyes, and her face was secretive again. I noticed for the first time that she had a slender, elegant neck and small ears. There was a delicacy about her that even she seemed to ignore.

"Glyn?" I repeated, and her eyelids lifted. "What's the matter?"

"You don't know anything about me," she said.

"I don't want to." That was clumsy and I reddened.

"You don't know what you're getting into," she said.

I was about to reply when footfalls approached our alcove, and a voice asked, "Did you find what you were looking for?"

The librarian was a tall, grey-haired man and he smiled, eager to put his books to work for us.

"We've just been looking through these booklets," I said, wondering how to bring the subject around to Hugh Morgan without distressing Glyn, when he played into my hands.

"You're British!" he exclaimed, and he held up a finger to indicate he had more to say. "And I know exactly what you are seeking — information on British folk who found their way to Oxrun in earlier times. Am I right?"

"Yes," I agreed. "Some were in logging, weren't they?"

"Perhaps, but it is difficult to check because the early records of the logging industry are unreliable." His eyes, however, twinkled with a piece of special knowledge that was going to surprise me. "Were you aware there was an influx of miners when we were digging the quarry for the great river dam project?"

I did not wish to disappoint him, so I asked, "Did any of them happen to come from Wales?"

"Indeed they did."

"Because my mother is Welsh," I told him, "and she wondered if a relative of hers had emigrated to America. He was a miner, by the name of Morgan."

"We can very soon ascertain if your mother's conjecture is correct." His enthusiasm was aroused and he squeezed past us to a very dull-looking range of books under a heading that had not drawn my eye — Statistics. He ran a finger along the row, humming happily to himself.

"Here we are . . . " He took down a thick volume and opened it on the table. "We have only recently had these reports rebound and I happen to recall . . . let me see — ah! here we are . . . a complete list of employees working on the Ox River Project for the year of our Lord 1901." He began reading down the list. "Jones . . . Jones . . . Jones . . . My word, a sizable contingent of your mother's countrymen, it seems." He lifted his head. "But it's Morgan you want, isn't it?"

I nodded, and as he lowered his head over the page I leant over the table as if to give a book to Glyn, but really to touch her hand as I spoke. "Hugh," I said. "Hugh Morgan."

She was pale, but I could tell she heard nothing except the name. Nor had I; nothing had echoed in our heads. Then the librarian said, "There is a Morgan, but I'm afraid it's not Hugh. Pity — this one is David." He was about to raise his head when he said, "However, there's a footnote." He put his finger on it and read aloud: "David Morgan was one of eight workers who lost their lives during the five years of the project. See Appendix Y."

It was the wrong man, but there was no stopping the librarian. I had never seen a man so happy in his work. He spun around and counted his way along the shelf until he came to the book he sought. "Ah — a very slim volume. I fear industrial accidents did not merit long reports in those brutal times."

His eyes twinkled at us and he bent to his task. "Only a single Jones, I see — a quarryman killed by a fall of rock. O'Shay — died when he plunged from the wall of the dam. And, here we are, Morgan."

He fell silent, reading to himself for a full minute. In spite of the fact that we already knew it was entirely the wrong man, we waited impatiently to find out what absorbed him so deeply. At length, he apologised for keeping us waiting.

"Excuse me, but this is an oddly interesting little tale." He began to read aloud: "Morgan, David, was a married man, a miner, an immigrant to the United States from Wales, recruited to work on the project. Some mystery surrounds his death. Although there can be little doubt that he lost his life as the result of a tragic accident, his body was never recovered.

"Morgan was at work in the quarry on the evening of 31st October, 1901, loading rock into the hoppers that fed the conveyor belt when he disappeared, unnoticed by other labourers on his shift. A search was instituted but was abandoned at nightfall. Three days later, however, a boot was discovered on the quarry floor beneath the hoppers and, upon investigation, it was found to contain the foot of David Morgan, severed just above the ankle."

The librarian grimaced at us. "Gruesome," he said, and then bent to his reading again: "At the inquiry it was presumed that, while working alone and out of sight of other members of his work-gang, Morgan had slipped and fallen into the hopper. The inquiry concluded that he had been dismembered by the machinery and the churning action of the rocks, and that his trunk and limbs, with the sole exception of his right foot, had been transported on the conveyor belt to the site of the dam where it had been submerged in the aggregate and cement that was in process of being piped into the core of the dam.

"Work ceased immediately on the discovery of the severed foot but, despite probes into the several thousand tons of concrete poured since Morgan's disappearance, no more of his remains were recovered.

"Several witnesses deposed that they had heard cries or shrieks at the time of Morgan's disappearance, but had paid little attention because both the machinery and the conveyor belt itself frequently emitted loud sounds which could easily be construed as screams from the quarry or the hillside.

"Morgan's widow soon after left the quarrymen's settlement where she and her husband had lived."

The librarian ceased reading. "I am much obliged to you both for pointing me in the direction of this incident," he said, gazing benignly at each of us in turn. "I was quite unaware of it. A fascinating footnote to the history of the times."

He glanced down, idly turning the page. "Hullo, hullo," he said, "it goes on — but only for a sentence or so: 'The unfortunate young wife, who was expecting a child at the time of the accident, was in receipt of a pension from the company, but she is believed to have been cared for by a relative.'"

The librarian closed the book. "Interesting," he said, "but hardly of use to you, I am afraid."

12

"You weren't there," said Penny.

"Well, I'm here now." We were in the lounge of the Mariner Cover which, at weekends, was a regular place for a lot of people we knew. Penny had been looking around, paying me little attention as I tried to apologise for not keeping our date the night before.

"I waited for half an hour," she said, "and I *froze*."

"I rang," I said.

"I am well aware of that."

"You weren't there."

"I know I wasn't."

"Where were you?" I asked politely.

"Where were *you*!" She had a hand on the table between us and her fingers were tapping. It did not seem a good time to tell her about Glyn. I played for time.

"Are you mad at me?" I asked innocently.

A fingernail scraped the table top and her eyes flashed. "You haven't even said where you were!"

"I called in at the library and a guy there kept me talking." She raised her eyebrows. "The librarian," I explained. "He kept me talking late and I didn't realise . . . "

"The librarian?"

"He was very interesting." I kept on speaking but I knew I was lost. "He told me a lot of stuff about the early days in Oxrun."

Her eyes were searching the room, and she spoke absently as if it were a matter of no consequence. "Someone saw you with a girl." She smiled at some person behind me, but her smile vanished as she turned back to me. "Jeff Dacre saw you with that waitress." He must have just come in, for she broke off to greet him as he approached. "Jeff," she said, "what is the name of that girl who serves table at The Luncheonette? I've quite forgotten."

Penny had suddenly gained twenty years. Her voice went with a hat and gloves. She was chairperson at a PTA meeting, and I was getting the treatment. But at least Jeff knew the girl's name.

"Glyn," he said. "Glynis." He looked at me and shrugged. "Couldn't Sam tell you?"

"It's such a little thing," she said, "it has slipped his memory."

"Not a very memorable girl, huh?" He was laughing as he sat down next to Penny. "I always thought she was kinda pretty — if you looked real close. What d'you say, Sam?" He was quite unaware of what was going on.

"I hadn't paid her much attention," I said, and Penny abruptly seemed to change the subject.

"They are strange," she said to Jeff, "don't you think so?" He was mystified, but she drilled on, "I don't know about their looks, but they are all very strange, the women who live in that house."

"Hold on, Penny." He had wrinkled his brow and was smiling across at me and he repeated her words: *All those women in that house?* . . . You make it sound as if something wasn't quite right up there in Mildenhall Woods."

"You can't get away from it." The hardness had not left Penny's face. "Look at how they keep to themselves so much — her and her grandmother living alone like that."

"Well the poor kid's father upped and left them years ago," said Jeff, "and then her Mom died."

"Something is *always* happening to them," said Penny as if they were responsible for all their own misfortunes.

Jeff was compassionate. "Well she can't get around much. Her grandmother's pretty old, Penny — way over ninety, they reckon, and that poor kid looks after her."

"Kid!" Penny was scornful. "She quit school two years ago — she's older than you." She turned and spoke to me with particular emphasis. "And you!"

Jeff laughed again. "Don't blame poor Sam for that — he can't help being a little bitty kid, can you, Sam?"

I had to speak up for Glyn. "She has a tough time," I said, "what with an old lady to look after and . . . " I hesitated, on the verge of mentioning the haunted ruins, then ended lamely " . . . and everything."

Penny raised the tip of her very pretty nose to give a ladylike snort of disbelief. "They say strange things about Granny Morgan, too. Did you know she was only fifteen years old when her mother was killed and she was left alone in that cabin with the man who committed the murder?"

"He was her father," I said, as if that was an excuse.

"Oh no," said Penny. "He was her uncle — or so they say. He'd already murdered his brother, and then he went on to murder his brother's wife!"

"Hold on," said Jeff. "None of this was ever proved. No-one ever found a body."

Penny was not impressed. "Well, can you tell me why Granny Morgan has kept out of people's way all these years? It is because there are so many awful things in her family they don't bear thinking of."

"People say far too much," said Jeff. "So he murdered his brother and shacked up with his brother's wife — and then he murdered her? It's just too much, Penny. No-one ever proved that this mysterious brother ever existed. It's just a lot of old wives' tales, if you ask me."

"Nobody is asking you anything, Jeff Dacre. Granny Morgan stayed with her uncle in that ghastly cabin, and then *he* disappeared . . . and she *still* didn't leave!"

"Hold it, Penny." It pained Jeff to hear her talk like this. "There's nothing wrong with living alone. She got married after a while, and that's a fact."

Penny gave a short, harsh laugh. "And then the cabin burned down!"

"Give her a break, Penny. Her husband built her a new house, didn't he?"

"Maybe he did, but can you wonder at this girl you both seem so keen on being the way she is — so secret and deceitful — with her background!"

"None of this is Glyn's fault — you can't make her pay for things that happened way, way before she was born."

I had ceased to listen. Hugh Morgan, the man in the cabin, had had a brother. My mind was racing, and I hardly noticed that Penny had fallen silent at last. She had made her point, and her reason for gloating over all these old stories about Glyn's family was hidden from Jeff. It was me she was getting at, and she had done it without revealing anything about how we had behaved behind his back. Jeff was the only innocent one.

"Well," he said, "I'd come along here with an idea of something we should do, but it hardly seems right in view of everything that's just been said."

Penny, studiously not looking at me, was silent. I had to say something so I asked him what he'd had in mind.

"I was thinking," he said slowly, "that as it's only a couple of nights to Halloween we could do something a bit different to ordinary trick or treat. Try a spot of ghost hunting maybe. Hold a little party in the woods." He looked cautiously from Penny to me, trying to gauge our reaction, and when we did not respond he went on, "Mildenhall Woods. I was thinking of the old ruined cabin." He held up a hand as if to stop our protests. "But I must admit we can't go charging up to her place and revive old memories for those folk."

"No!" The idea horrified me after what I had just heard. "We can't go trespassing up there."

"Trespassing!" Penny was indignant. "How can you call that trespassing? Those woods are public property and we have every right to go there if we wish!"

I was about to say something more but she had made up her mind to obliterate me.

"Whatever *you* decide to do," her eyes were on Jeff, but her words were meant for me, "whatever you do, *I* am determined to go to Mildenhall Woods Halloween night!"

It was a crusade. Nothing I said was going to stop her. I was already part of her past, a has-been.

13

I kept clear of Penny for the rest of the day, and late in the afternoon I was in a bookstore on Centre where I could browse and at the same time keep an eye on The Luncheonette across the way. Glyn and I had talked for a long time after leaving the library the night before, but as we had approached closer to the secrets of her family I had come to see there was much that was mysterious even to Glyn herself.

She had become more and more silent as we talked, until in the end she said hardly a word and I felt I was prying into affairs that were none of my business. Now, after hearing what Penny had revealed, I had to see Glyn, whether she wanted to talk to me again or not.

I saw customers come and go in The Luncheonette and realised how little you can read from gestures seen at a distance. If a man raised a hand it was only to tug at the lobe of his ear as he talked, or a woman would shake out her hair over her collar, and even when someone stood up or sat down it revealed as little of his mood as a caterpillar looping along a leaf.

With Glyn it was different. I could tell by no more than the tilt of her head or the way she wrote an order on her notepad exactly the expression there would be in the shrouded darkness of her eyes or the slight downward tug at the corners of her mouth.

There was something appropriate to the way I was feeling in the title of the book I was holding, so when she disappeared into the back of The Luncheonette for what I guessed was the last time in her day's work, I bought it and went out to meet her.

I had not moved quickly enough. By the time I was on the sidewalk, she had put the diner behind her and was the best part of a block away along Centre and heading for the Pike. I ran, but she had turned on to the Pike before I reached the corner, and when I got there she was nowhere to be seen. Raindrops carried on the bitter wind pecked at my face and I ran almost blindly. I came to the library. There was a double set of glass doors, and the inner pair were still slowly closing. There was no-one in sight, but this was where she must have gone. I went in. The long room was nearly deserted except for the Goth girl, bent over an old newspaper file; the alcove where we had sat the day before was empty.

I was casting around when a voice behind me said, "If you are seeking the dark young lady you were with yesterday you had best make haste." The librarian had come from behind his desk. "That is," he added, "unless it was more information you sought from me — although your expression appears to suggest more important matters." He was smiling.

"Yes." I was panting. "I do want to see her."

"Then follow me." He hastened away down a corridor with me half trotting at his heels like the White Rabbit in a panic. He came to a door. What other secrets did she have? "You will find her in the far corner, I imagine." He flung the door open and the wind came gusting in. "There she is," and he pointed across the parking lot.

There were no secrets, after all. I laughed. "Thanks — I thought she'd got away."

"Oh no," he said. "From what I've seen, I don't think she wants to avoid you." I looked at him, but he was already closing the door. "She'll wait," he said, and I heard him laugh softly to himself.

He was mistaken about one thing. Her car was already moving. I ran towards the exit and raised my arms. She must have seen me, but I thought she was going to ignore me. She drove on before she seemed to change her mind, and the car slowed and her window wound down.

"I thought for a minute that you weren't going to stop," I said.

"I wasn't."

"Why not?" I think the wind blustering around us disguised that I was hurt.

"You don't need to know me," she said.

"I do!" But already her window was going up. I lifted my hand and caught a glimpse of the book I held. I called out, "I've bought you a present!" The window closed and I stood back to let her go, but the car turned into a slot and stopped.

I got in. "I was in a bookstore," I said.

"Which store was that?"

I told her.

"I could have looked across and seen you." She spoke towards the windscreen where the rain rattled.

"I know. That's why I thought of you. I bought you this."

She took the paper bag but did not attempt to look inside. "It's too dark," she said. "What is it?"

"Fritz Leiber," I said. "It's called *Our Lady of Darkness*."

She bent her head over the package. "Have you read it?"

"No. I just liked the title."

Her head turned my way and the most unlikely sound came from between her lips. At first I thought she was sobbing, but then I realised it was the opposite. She was chuckling.

"Do you know what this book's about, Sam?"

"No."

"A man looks from a hilltop in San Francisco towards the high rise where he lives and sees someone beckoning to him from his own apartment."

"Oh," I said.

"A figure beckoned to him, Sam, but he knew his apartment was empty."

"So you've read it."

"Yes, Sam."

I was silent. Had she told me what the book was about because she knew that I was beckoning towards an empty apartment? Or was she telling me that I would not like what I might find there?

"You didn't really buy it for me, did you?" she said.

"No. But I'd like you to have it."

She did not answer and we sat and watched the rain make crooked fingers on the glass.

"Sam," she said, "leave me alone. You don't know what you are getting into."

"I know something you didn't tell me yesterday," I said. She gazed straight ahead and waited for me to speak. "There were two brothers. One of them lived alone in Mildenhall Woods, and one of them was married and worked in the quarry." I paused, but she did not interrupt. "And there was a rumour that the unmarried one did away with his brother, and then he murdered his brother's wife. You knew all that."

"I only knew what people said." It was my turn to wait, and after a while she faced me. "My grandmother told me nothing. She never speaks of it. She is afraid to."

"But you and I know who the married brother was," I said.

"And what became of him. And where he is now."

"Yes."

We sat together, and there seemed to be no need to speak. David Morgan, killed by his brother and torn to pieces on the conveyor belt, lay entombed in the dam. "Is she there, too?" I asked. "Is his wife with him?"

Glyn did not reply, and I had no right to go any further. It was not my affair.

She sat with the book I had given her on her lap. Her head had drooped forward as though she was studying it, and I could not get the picture out of my mind of a spectre beckoning from a great distance. "Ox River Dam," I said. The white wall in the distant vee of the hills had seemed to beckon to me at the rock pool. "It's a long way off, but you can see it from down in the valley."

"And hear it," she murmured. "We both hear it — you and me."

What I did next was inappropriate. I leant forward and kissed her. Her lips were warm and dry against mine, and she did not respond. But neither did she draw away. I sat back in my seat.

"I am afraid," she said.

"I know."

"I hear things and I am afraid I may be mad."

"I am mad too."

Then it was she who kissed me. She was trembling but fierce, and I tasted the tears on her cheek.

14

It was bright and it was cold and I was lacing my boots.

"Not fishing again?" said my mother.

"Yes," I lied.

"Where you went last time? With Jeff?"

"Yes."

"You must be mad, the pair of you."

"Yes." And this time it was true. Glyn and I were mad indeed, and I didn't care.

She had driven me home the night before and dropped me a block away so we should not be seen together. This was shyness on her part, not on mine, and partly because she was afraid of Penny. There was also the embarrassment for her that she was two years older than me and had a job, while I was still at school. For me this only added to her allure, but she insisted that if we met on her day off it had to be in the library car park.

She saw my fishing gear and was startled by it, as though I had badly mistaken the purpose of our meeting. I began to stow it in the trunk. "Camouflage," I said, and for the first time I heard her really laugh.

I am not going to say her laughter was like the bubbling of a mountain stream — I thought it, but I'm not going to say it — no, it was a little girl's chuckle, amused and surprised and without any trace that she was aware of how attractive it was. And I laughed, too, because she delighted me.

The old Buick wallowed as we turned on to the Pike.

"It's a lovely day," I said, and caught her taking a sideways look at me. Something amused her. "What are you smiling at?" I asked.

"Nothing." Then she gazed straight ahead and told me. "It's because every time we meet you say it's a lovely day."

"Crikey." I hung my head. "It's because I'm British — we always talk about the weather."

"Don't change, Sam," she said.

"And," I said, "every time I meet you it *is* a lovely day." That was so corny it made us both laugh.

The quarry was only a few miles out of town, and when the car had heaved itself a short distance up a rough track she pulled into the side and we got out. The far peaks and the nearer hilltops were cut out clear and sharp against the blue where a few white clouds lay high and motionless, looking down on where the quarry had bitten a huge mouthful out of the hill. The wound was still raw in spite of the vegetation which grew in the crevices of the split rock.

"The settlement where the quarrymen lived was over there." She pointed. "Do you want to go look?"

I shook my head. We had both turned to get what we needed from the trunk of the car before we realised that we had each known with absolute certainty that, whatever it was we were seeking, it did not lie in the bottom of the valley. "There's no point in hanging about down here," I said.

I had a small haversack and she put her flask in alongside mine. We did not touch, as if contact would diffuse some tension that lay between us and would guide us as surely as a compass.

"There it is." She pointed to the upper lip of the quarry. "Do you see it?" Something that looked like a pylon rose above the scrub. "They took all the machinery away when they finished digging. That's about all that's left."

It marked the place where we had to start, and reaching it meant a stiff climb through the stunted growth at the quarry's edge.

"There are rock falls," she said, "so take care." She wore jeans and a windcheater and her hair was tied back in a ponytail.

"You've been here before," I said. She was dressed for hill walking.

"Not here. I've never wanted to." I raised my eyebrows and she looked away. "You know how I felt, Sam. I was afraid."

"For all these years?"

She did not answer, and when we got to the top neither of us said a word as we stood at the foot of what, from below, had appeared to be a pylon. It was a latticework of heavy iron with its feet set in a platform of concrete. It was one of the supports on which the conveyor belt had run. They had been too massive to be worth dismantling when the quarry was abandoned, and even the great pulley wheels that had borne the conveyor belt were still held aloft where they had groaned and squealed under the weight of rock nearly a century ago.

She pointed again. Far away, the dam showed as a white wedge between the hills and the track of the conveyor was marked by the iron towers that climbed away from where we stood. They disappeared at the crest of a rise but rose again on the slope beyond, marching across the landscape in a way that seemed strangely familiar to me. It did not strike me what it was until, coming closer to the concrete platform, I looked up through the iron lattice and saw the wheels against the sky.

"Pitheads," I said. "They look exactly like pitheads." Everything was fitting into place. The hills around us could easily have been a Welsh landscape, and the iron towers looked very like the pithead winding gear that lifted tubs of coal from the mines in Wales. But Glyn was puzzled, and more so when I added, "It must have made it all seem like home to her."

"Who?"

"His wife," I said. "David Morgan's wife."

Neither of us had so far spoken a word about what had brought us here. It had simply been necessary to follow whatever faint trace remained of the terrible acts of so long ago. It was Glyn's tragedy, it belonged to her, but now I was taking part in it myself.

"I'm sure she was from my mother's village," I said. I had no proof, but I knew it. "She was a relative of my mother's — a distant, distant cousin." I fell silent. I had become part of the past, Glyn's past as well as my own.

"The sounds," said Glyn softly. "Why doesn't your mother hear them? Why is it only you?"

I touched her hand. "It's you," I said. "It's between you and me."

She turned abruptly and I followed. There was still an avenue through the trees where once the conveyor had run but the scrub had encroached and it was hard going. When we came to the crest of one rise there was always another slope to climb, and gradually they became steeper. But by midday we were high above Oxrun, and the difficult part of our journey was over. Only a short span of towers lay between us and the huge wall of the dam that blocked off the valley.

We rested on one of the concrete platforms with our backs against the ironwork and I took our food from the haversack.

"I keep listening," she said, "but I hear nothing."

The silence had become so intense that even the faint sound I made brushing crumbs from my jeans seemed loud, and when I spoke I kept my voice low.

"Perhaps," I said, "sounds build up among the hills very gradually and the crags store up the echoes until they overflow, and then people down below think they hear the conveyor grinding away." It was too fanciful, and I shrugged and laughed and said, "So it's not ghosts they hear, nothing to do with David Morgan or his wife."

I did not, in fact, finish the sentence. The last word was on my lips but was never spoken, for at that moment Glyn's arm suddenly jerked and her flask flew from her hand. I saw the droplets of coffee make an arc against the sky and I watched the flask spinning as it fell, and then I saw Glyn's startled face.

"What happened?" I asked.

"I don't know. It was just as if . . . " She turned to look at the ironwork she rested against. "It felt like an electric shock."

She jumped down from the platform and went to rescue her flask. It had come to rest in one of the spillages of broken rock that still littered the hillside along the track of the conveyor. I saw the loose rock made it difficult for her, so I went down to help.

The slope fell sharply beneath us, and as I reached for her hand we overbalanced and dislodged a rock that went bounding away down the slope. Then, as we scrambled to stand upright, our feet began a minor landslip and we went slithering down the slope on a tongue of dust and fragments before the bushes brought us to a standstill.

She was crouching below me, and I heard sobbing.

"Are you hurt?" I scrambled down alongside her, but her face was calm and the sobbing had not come from her. I heard it again, but then a few last rocks went bounding away through the bushes and I realised the sound came from them as they brushed the undergrowth. I was about to say so when I saw that her attention had been caught by something else.

She was examining some object that lay within inches of her hand. She picked it up. It was a small pencil of pale stone, and she let it lie on her palm.

I asked her what she had found, and she held her open hand towards me. She turned the object with a finger of her other hand so that I could see what it was.

The pale grey pencil was not a rock. It was a bone, dried and calcified. A finger bone, and circling it loosely, but prevented by the knuckles from falling off, was a thin gold ring.

15

Night had fallen, and there was little traffic on the mountain road as we drove back towards Oxrun. We said nothing until we turned into the track through Mildenhall Woods. Then I said, "Do you want me with you?"

"None of this would have happened without you."

I saw her in the light reflected from the trees as she concentrated on the narrow track, and she was as far from me as she had ever been. Her silence had begun as we walked down from the mountain, and now, as I climbed the steps to the porch of her house, the silence of the forest closed around us.

A dim light showed through the curtains of a downstairs room, and even when Glyn opened the door and stepped inside it was not much brighter.

I was familiar by now with the greater space in American houses than I was used to in England, but as I followed her inside, our footsteps echoed as if the house was empty. The light came from one corner and we were so much at its outer fringe that we must have been little more than shadows to the woman who sat there. Granny Morgan had been reading, but the book now lay in her lap and she had turned her face so that only half of it caught the light.

"Granny," said Glyn, "I've brought someone home with me."

"So I see." The downturn of the thin mouth was emphasised by the shadows which also deepened the darkness around the invisible eyes. She saw me clearly enough, and her voice was sharp. "Who is he?"

"He's from England."

But her grandmother was uninterested. "You're late. Where have you been?"

Glyn went ahead of me across the room. "I told you, Granny. We went out towards the dam."

The thin white hair caught the light and made a haze over the head which was suddenly turned towards me. "She took you there, did she?" And without waiting for an answer she shot another question at me. "What has she been telling you?"

I protected Glyn. "Nothing I didn't know already."

"Ha!" She was amused. "Well that won't do you much good! Nobody knows anything down there." Her hand stabbed in what may have been the direction of Oxrun. "They reckon they know it all, but they don't know spit. There's only one human soul in the whole of creation who knows what went on up here all those years gone by, and she ain't saying. Not now. Not ever."

Glyn had shown me to a seat. It was outside the immediate ring of light that the old lady's reading lamp threw around her, so that when Glyn went forward it was as if she and her grandmother were on a stage and I was the audience. I could see that Glyn was nervous.

"Granny." She stood alongside her grandmother's chair awaiting permission to continue. The old lady glanced up at her, and as she tilted her head the light fell full on her face so that I saw the change that had come over it. The harsh lines had softened, and the hand that had stabbed the air a moment before now trembled with age and helplessness as she put it out for her granddaughter to hold. "Don't let them frighten you with all them old tales," she told Glyn. "It's all over and done with long years gone by."

"Granny," said Glyn. "He's Welsh."

"That don't mean a thing."

"His mother comes from the same village your mother came from."

The old lady ignored her. She was busy with her footstool, bending to push it towards her granddaughter. "Sit yourself down," she said. "I get a crick in my neck looking up at you like this."

"I've been up to the conveyor," said Glyn. "All the way — right to the top." They sat with their heads close together and they were murmuring so softly I could barely hear them. I no longer existed and Glyn spoke as if she had been on the hillside alone. "I was near the top when I heard something . . . someone was sobbing, Granny."

The old head nodded. "I know, I know."

"I slipped and fell among the rocks." Glyn's hand went to the pocket of her shirt. "I found something, Granny."

"Did you, darlin'?" It was said as though Granny Morgan was taking an interest in some trinket brought to her by a little girl. Glyn opened her hand.

"I can't see it, my lovely." The old lady shifted her head. "Put it into the light."

Glyn raised her hand closer to the lamp. I saw the glint of the ring before I caught sight of the greyish white of the bone, and I raised my eyes to the narrow features gazing down on it.

Her grandmother asked no questions. Her face, sunken and narrow, was poised over the bone like an eagle with prey in its talons, and she took her time to examine the bone and then examine the ring, and still she did not touch them. When she raised her head she was more like an eagle than ever. There was rage in her eyes, and her voice was thin and raw.

"I never found her," she said. "I was on the hills day after day. I called out and cried for my mother. But I never found her."

"You've found her now," said Glyn.

The long fingers went out and, at last, rested on Glyn's upturned palm covering the ring. "Yes, I've found her now." And the old, stem face crumpled suddenly and her narrow shoulders shook with dangerous sobs.

I don't think either of them saw me leave the room. I went out and sat on the steps of the porch and watched the progress of the stars through the trees until, deep into the night, Glyn came out to me.

16

Trade was slack in The Luncheonette, so Glyn and I knew we would not be disturbed as we sat in the corner booth which staff were allowed to use when there was a chance for them to take a break. We had talked for a long time on the porch the night before and it had been the early hours before she had driven me home. We had not even noticed the sudden storm that had knocked out the power in the town centre for a few hours.

I asked her if she had slept.

"Not much." She took off the waitress cap with the ribbons that was always far too cute for her.

"You look tired." She nodded. She had dark rings under her eyes, but was never going to make excuses for her looks. She was a girl on the edge of sleep. "But you look fine," I said.

She gave me her slow, reluctant smile, and shook her head.

In the night, as we sat shivering together on the porch steps, she had told me secrets unlocked by the ring. Her grandmother was the only person alive who had known Hugh Morgan, and even now, in daylight, I felt the chill strike through me once more as Glyn said, "She's afraid of him still."

Her grandmother had always known that he had murdered her father. There was never proof, but her mother had told her of savage quarrels between the two brothers, and of how Hugh Morgan, when he was drunk, let fall hints of what he had done, and yet she had always been too terrified to leave the cabin where they lived. She had a baby to care for, and nowhere else to go.

"That's how my Granny was raised," said Glyn. She was tracing her fingertip through a spot of spilled coffee on the table. "Frightened out of her skin from the moment she was born."

"And then her mother disappeared," I said.

"When she was still only a child. And she searched the hills and woods for miles around and never found her."

"Until last night." I paused, wondering whether to ask the question, but then I said quietly, "Does she know where they are now?"

Glyn drew in her breath and nodded. "They are together. She knows that." Their broken bodies were entombed in millions of tons of rock.

But there was still one question that had not been asked. The man everyone had feared, Hugh Morgan, had himself vanished soon afterwards, leaving a girl of fifteen alone in the cabin in the woods. "What happened to him?" I asked.

"Does anyone know?"

Glyn's lips opened and she was about to answer when I heard the door of The Luncheonette open. It was at my back so I did not know who had entered until I heard the voice.

"Well, look who's here." I turned to see Penny pull off the hat she'd been wearing and shake out her long blonde hair. "No, don't get up."

I was still sitting. It was Glyn who had got to her feet.

"It's *so* cold and wet outside." Penny was unzipping her padded anorak as she spoke to Glyn. "I'm so sorry to interrupt you just when you are taking a rest from your chores."

Jeff was behind her. "We can wait," he said. "There's no hurry. Sit down, Glyn."

"Don't be silly, Jeff." Penny's cheeks and eyes were bright with the cold. "She's a working girl and she has things to do." She smiled at me and then at Glyn. "Besides, we shall be seeing you later on, won't we?"

Glyn was on the point of moving away. "I don't know," she said.

"But of course we will. Hasn't he told you?"

I was as mystified as Glyn herself.

"Don't look so blank, Sam." Penny was pretty even when she laughed too loudly. "You can't have forgotten it's Halloween and we're going to meet at the old log cabin tonight."

"But you can't do that," I protested. "Not now."

"Why not now? Don't be such a wimp, Sam, I'm sure Glyn won't mind." She did have beautifully even white teeth when she smiled. "We are just going to try to raise the spirit of you know who . . . he who shall not be named. Not by me, at least, because I'm such a scaredy cat. Oh dear . . . "

She broke off and a look of fake astonishment crossed her face as Glyn turned her back and walked away. "Do you think I have offended her in some particular?"

17

Trick or treat brought kids to the door. My mother was charmed, my father was tolerant, and I regretted I was too old for white sheets and skeleton masks. At home I had bobbed for apples in tubs of water and made turnip lanterns — my mother was mad keen on Halloween traditions — but there had been nothing as elaborate as this.

I left home early in the evening. I had to get to the cabin before Penny, and I had to walk. The coldness was fierce but there was something in the air, a stir of excitement as kids scampered across lawns to haunt neighbours' houses, that caught up with me and I was still exhilarated as I put the outskirts of Oxrun behind me and took the road that rose slowly into the forests. Cars swept by from time to time, pushing their own corridors of light into the darkness, and I watched them flicker for a moment in the distance before the night closed in on them and cut them off. The town lights were out of sight long before I turned into the track through Mildenhall Woods.

The silence that had deadened the sound of cars on the mountain road closed in on me so completely that even the soft footfalls of my walking boots seemed furtive in that vast nothingness, and when I climbed the porch steps in order to rap at Glyn's door the sound startled me enough to make me wince.

"It's me," I called as I heard footsteps inside. "It's Sam." The door opened on the dim light within. I wondered if she would have opened to any other caller, and the trembling touch of her hand told me that she would have kept the door shut.

"I came early," I said, "to keep away from them."

"They are still going to do it?"

I nodded. Nothing I had said, nor Jeff's doubts, had weakened Penny's determination. "We'll sit with your grandmother till they've gone," I said.

Spontaneous acts were so rare with her that I very nearly drew back when she leant forward. But she kissed me, and I held her close so that what began as a touch of her lips to show her gratitude became breathless as we clung together.

We were still standing there and the door was ajar when we heard sounds of movement within the house. Glyn eased herself away from me. "It's my grandmother," she said, "she's restless tonight."

"That sounds as if she's been ill." The old lady had been sharp and bright only a day or so before.

"Something's on her mind. Finding that ring upset her." Inside, everything was exactly as before. Her grandmother sat where I had last seen her, and she was gazing towards us in the same way except that she was making strange little jerking movements with her head as if she could not quite bring us into focus.

"Glynis," she said, "who's that with you?"

Glyn told her. "He said he'd sit with us, Granny."

"Why? What for?" Nervous questions spilled from her, and her eyes were restless, peering everywhere but not seeming to see anything. Her eyesight was not as good as I had taken it to be when I saw her reading. "What do we want with a young feller? He's got nothing to do with us."

"It's Sam. You remember Sam — that Welsh boy." Glyn glanced swiftly at me so that I would not deny it. Perhaps Welshness was my passport. "He's going to sit with us because some people are coming up to the old cabin tonight. He doesn't want us to be afraid of noises in the woods."

"What does he intend to do about it?" Her voice was sharp. "We've heard noises before — you and me. What's he got to do with it?"

Glyn sat on the stool at her grandmother's side, and once again I watched from outside the ring of light from the reading lamp. It seemed appropriate that I should be separate, especially when Granny Morgan leant forward to whisper something that was meant for Glyn alone. "Get rid of him, girl. Get rid of him."

"But why, Granny? — he only wants to help."

"I don't trust him!"

Their voices diminished so that I could hardly hear the words, and it was then I heard the first sound from outside. It was slight, as though something small and light was running swiftly through fallen leaves, but I had no sooner focused on it than it was gone and the talkers had noticed nothing.

"Glynis, Glynis child!" The old voice was suddenly clear. "For all these years we have never needed anyone. Send him away!"

Glyn paused. She knew I was listening and, when she spoke, she meant me to hear. "Granny, listen to me. Sam was with me when we climbed all the way up to the conveyor." She was tugging at the old lady's hand, keeping her attention. "He was with me — he knows everything."

Her grandmother seemed suddenly to shrink. Her shoulders were pressed into the back of her chair, and her head drooped. She wanted to hear no more, but Glyn held tightly to her hand and forced her to listen. "He knows your mother died up there. And he knows how your father died, too. He knows it all, Granny — he knows who murdered them."

We were hushed. Silence had fallen in the forest outside, and everything within the house was still. I saw the frail fingers free themselves from her granddaughter's grasp.

"Does he know what I did, Glynis?" There was a huge weariness in the old lady's voice, and she did not wait for an answer. "No, he doesn't know. I have never told a living soul — not even you." She paused as if considering whether to tell us, but I believe she had made up her mind. It was time to unburden herself of what she had kept hidden for so long. Her voice was quiet but it was steady.

"When I knew my mother had gone and I would never see her again, I killed him."

Glyn stirred as if she wanted to put an arm round her grandmother's shoulders, but I saw the knuckles of the old hands whiten as she held her still. "Listen, child. I came down from the hills where I'd searched for my mother and he was drunk and said I never would find her. So I took his axe when he fell asleep in his chair and I killed him." She did not raise her voice. "I killed him, and no-one ever asked what had become of him. So I buried him . . . and no-one ever came."

She gazed in front of her, seeing nothing, but she suddenly gave a great shuddering breath and cried out, "I killed Hugh Morgan! I buried him in the night . . . and his eyes did not close!"

The thin scream that reached us from outside may have been an owl, but was more human. The old lady snatched at her granddaughter. "Glynis!" she wailed. "They are coming for me! They are coming to take me away!"

I was on my feet. There was movement outside, and laughter, and I was running for the door, filled with fury and shouting, "I'll get rid of them!"

18

I thrashed my way through the bushes. Anger made me sure-footed and somewhere, invisible to me, the moon shed enough light through the branches to show me the ruined cabin when I was still climbing the slope beneath it.

I shouted as I ran, anything to ruin the Halloween party, and I succeeded more easily than I expected. Even as I climbed I heard them running, and by the time I reached the stumps of the cabin the ghost hunters were far away down the hill. I heard a boy swear and a girl laugh. It must have been Penny. It was a triumph of a sort, but as I stood panting at the edge of the clearing I did not believe that they had run because of me; they must, in the end, have thought of the two terrified women in the house below.

I was slightly surprised that Jeff had gone with the rest. It would have been like him to stay behind to make sure no harm had been done, but perhaps he had to be with Penny. And I had not behaved very well myself; none of this would have happened if I had not interfered in what was none of my affair. And then from the corner of my eye I saw something that made me smile.

"I knew it," I said aloud. Jeff had not left with the others. I saw him across the space. "So who's looking after Penny?"

I could hear her laughter in the distance.

He stood on the other side of the clearing among what little remained of the cabin. And I laughed again, for he was framed in the broken doorway where Glyn had stood and terrified Penny and me. It was not going to happen a second time.

"Okay, Jeff," I said. "You've proved your point."

Penny's voice had faded and gone, but Jeff had still said nothing. I was about to speak again when I heard something pushing towards me through the undergrowth at my back. A hideous ripple went through my skin as if a hand had grabbed at my neck, and I spun around. Then I saw Glyn. She had followed me.

The warmth of relief was still washing away the last tingle of fear when, in the grey light of the hidden moon, I saw the expression on her face. Her eyes and mouth were open and terror hollowed cavities in her face. She gazed at something beyond me. Once more I turned, and then I saw it, too.

The figure in the doorway was not Jeff. It had moved. The arm that had rested against the doorpost was now by its side, but that slight movement had shown a tatter of shirt sleeve and stirred the air. A waft of ancient rot found our nostrils and coiled around us as if to drag us into a grave.

I stumbled and fell. Glyn reached for me. I even shrank from her as her cold fingers clawed at my hand, but then I was upright and we were running.

The forest seemed to lean towards us as we clattered up the porch steps and burst into the house.

We leant against a table, staring at each other, our chests heaving as we fought for breath. And outside the house we heard movement. Nothing was still. In the windless night we heard the trees sighing as if, by shaking their branches, they would shed the heavy dread that thickened the air. And when that sound was stilled, a new sound took its place. Something was circling the house.

There was no definite footstep, but we sensed movement on the porch. It was a whisper such as cloth makes dragged across a floor, and it paused at every window, and at every door it waited, and our concentration was so intense on what was happening outside that the sound of a voice from the next room jolted us against the table.

"Glynis!" Her grandmother was on her feet, steadying herself against the back of her chair. She called again, but as Glyn moved closer she raised an arm and stabbed a finger towards her, jabbing again and again in a gesture to make her stand where she was. I understood, and held Glyn back.

"The ring." The old voice was feeble as she gasped for air. "He knows I have found her. He seeks his revenge — and the ring has brought him out." She was on the point of collapsing but she flapped a hand to keep Glyn at bay. "My mother's not at rest. Nothing is at rest. She must have the ring."

"Give it to me." Glyn put out a hand. "Give me the ring."

"No! Nothing is at rest until my mother gets the ring. I've got to give it to her."

Glyn, pleading with her, edged forward. "Why not me? I can take it to her."

"Child! Will you leave me!" The eagle's glare made the old face fierce. "He will destroy you. I am near the end of my days — leave it to me!"

But she was too late and too weak to prevent Glyn taking the last step. Her grandmother had the ring and the bone in her clenched fist and Glyn's hand closed over it. "Please," she pleaded, "one of us can take it."

Too frail and breathless to speak, her grandmother shook her head. When her voice came it was almost too weak to hear.

"You and me are of my mother's blood and we hold the ring . . . it draws him to us, and he comes to destroy us."

She was at the end of her strength. I saw her fingers relax and I saw the ring and the bone pass into Glyn's hand. There was a sudden slithering rush outside, and something shapeless pressed against a window pane. The old lady had sagged against Glyn. I stepped forward and reached out. Glyn, expecting me to help her, drew in her breath sharply when I ignored her and instead clutched at her hand to prise her fingers open.

I backed away. "I'll take the ring," I said.

I tightened my grip on the bone, and listened. There was a breathless hush outside. I crossed the room and stood beside the door. With my free hand I turned the handle, but kept the door closed as I turned to Glyn.

"Your car's out there," I said. I would soon discover if I could drive it. "Give me the keys."

19

Glyn came and stood alongside me. We were the same height and, as we stood face to face, we were suddenly a pair of warriors.

"I drive," she said.

I clenched my fist over the bone and the ring. We glanced at each other once, and I flung open the door.

She went ahead of me and leapt down the porch steps. I slammed the door behind me and hit the dirt a pace behind her. The starter was churning as I slid into the seat beside her and, with a screech of wheelspin and a shower of stones, she spun the car and we were rocketing and bouncing down the track.

No lights. She had forgotten them in our haste. "Damn!" she said, and reached to switch them on — but never made it for at that moment some night walker stepped from the trees ahead of us. He was just visible. Her foot jammed the brake. The tyres bit the ruts, but we could not avoid him.

"Oh God!" Her head had jerked forward as we came to a standstill, but now her eyes lifted and she looked above the dash.

"What have I done!"

I had cracked my head but I had never taken my eyes from the figure. "You didn't hit him," I said. "He's okay." Only a pace in front of the hood the walker still stood.

Glyn was about to fling open her door but I reached across and held it shut.

"What are you doing!"

Even as her cry rang out I had switched on the lights. What we saw made her moan. The engine had died.

"Don't look!" I covered her eyes with my hand.

I had seen him before. I had smelled the rot of the rags that clung to him. What I had not see was his face. The old lady was right. His eyes were open. And so was his face. Open in places where it should not have been.

"Start up." I remember that my voice was quiet. We had to move carefully.

She fumbled, but the engine coughed and caught with a roar as her foot stabbed the throttle. I saw from the corner of my eye that she was raising her head. "Don't look!" I yelled. "Drive!"

She turned to me, her eyes wide, unbelieving.

"Drive! Drive him down!" I hammered at her knee with my fist, her leg jerked and the car, out of control, hurled itself forward. The windscreen blanked out, branches thrashed against our sides, we bumped and bucketed and then we were roaring and slithering sideways on to the highway and she was fighting to straighten up as the headlight beams pierced the darkness of the road.

For long seconds we screamed like a dragster along the empty highway, putting Mildenhall Woods behind us.

"The washers," I said. "Put the windscreen washers on." The screen was streaked and the car stank like a collapsed coffin.

I had no need to explain; we both knew what had happened. "Is that the end of him?" I asked.

"I don't know. We must hurry." She drove fast, and for a long time neither of us spoke. Oxrun was behind us and we had climbed high enough to see the lights marking the grid of the streets, but then they were gone and I realised that I was climbing out of the valley just as, a few months earlier, I had come down through the hills into the town for the first time. And each time sitting alongside a girl.

"I heard the whispering," I said, "when I first came to Oxrun."

"Can't you hear it now?"

"No." There was nothing but the rush of air past the car.

"Then listen." She wound down her window. The wide night yawned, but no voice reached me.

She put out a hand and touched my fingers. "Now do you hear?"

It was as though I had been outside a closed door and she had opened it for me. I heard a sighing, scampering, whimpering noise as though some panic-stricken night creature was keeping pace with us.

"She's worried for us," said Glyn. We had put the horror behind us, and her attention was on what lay hidden in the dam.

Above us, where the full moon had climbed the sky, I saw the last jagged teeth of the conveyor pylons jutting above the trees. On our other side the valley was already walled off by the dam, and our road had levelled.

She slowed and turned into the wide car park at the head of the dam and we were crossing the deserted space when the engine died. She turned the starter but nothing happened. We got out. The car's doors hung open like elephant's ears and we left them. We were alone, with emptiness all around.

In the moon's shadow, the black hillside frowned down on us, still scarred by the final rock spill at the conveyor's end. Nothing moved except ourselves.

"Give me the ring." She held out her hand, but I delayed.

"We've got to get on to the dam," I said.

We crossed black tyre marks left by cars and came to the empty pay booth. A tiny green light showed that some equipment lay with one eye open, but all was quiet. From here the road swung away from the slope towards the enormous drop of the dam's curved wall and the soundless foam of an outfall far below. I held out the ring and the bone, and she reached for them.

Our fingers had not met when, from high overhead, a squeal pierced the night. We shrank together as it came again, the screech of tortured wheels and the groan of the belt. Our mouths were open as if we were facing a gale as we looked up. The steep slope loomed above us, but no wind stirred the trees and there was no conveyor to tear at the air, and the sound fell away.

I breathed deeply, and my head drooped forward. We had passed the final test. I glanced at her. The screeching had died but she was still listening. She must have heard the first trickle of stone on the hillside. I was not aware of it until I heard a heavy beat on the wooded slope. It thudded unevenly, and then there was a slither before a rattle of stones spilled into the brushwood at the roadside and a boulder, dislodged from high up, bounded over them and came to rest in the road ahead of us.

We were running for the dam when the boulder, with the last of its momentum, rolled once more, and subsided. But it was not a rock. It was a heap of tattered garments, and we saw them uncoil. And more than garments. The dome of a head pushed up from the mass, shoulders heaved and rose, and what had seemed to be dangling shreds stiffened to fingers. Hugh Morgan blocked our way to the dam.

"The ring!" She was fierce. "Give me the ring!"

It glinted in my palm, pierced by the bone. She must take the ring. I needed a weapon. I tugged to get the ring free. It jammed on the knuckle. I held the bone in both hands and brought my thumbs to bear on its slenderest part. It snapped and I put the ring in Glyn's cold palm. Then I jammed the broken bone between my fingers like a jagged fork, a deer's antlers, a goat's head, and I charged.

I saw the pitted hollows and the disintegrating flesh and I struck at it. My jagged hand sliced nothing but air and then, as if in friendliness, a soft and rotting arm was laid around my shoulders. It pulled me closer and leaned a head towards me that grinned because it had no lips and breathed a waft of putrid corpse gas over me.

Glyn, running, glanced back. I saw her horrified face look over her shoulder as I went down, and then her arm went back and she hurled the ring. I saw the tiniest spark of light leave her hand and curve towards the hidden water of the lake. I did not see it fall. All I knew was that the clammy grasp slid from me as Hugh Morgan left me behind and reached for her.

She clutched the railing but the tatters engulfed her. I heard her desperate moan as she sank to the ground, and with the last of my strength I threw the broken bone and began to crawl towards her.

I heard the fragments of bone break the surface of the lake. They sank alongside the great wall that was also a tomb, and at that moment the shreds that engulfed Glyn slid from her. With a thin, tortured squeal they twisted like smoke in a tighter and tighter spiral until they collapsed inwards into a ball of rags that hurled itself away from her. It flew out over the towering curved wall of the dam into empty space. I saw it fall, and as it went down the tormented squeal faded until it was lost in the foam of the outfall far below and the rags were washed away into silence.

I stooped over Glyn. She did not seem to be breathing, but when I lifted her her breath fluttered against my cheek. I carried her back to the car. She was not heavy, and I did not need to look back for fear we were being followed. It was over. The car started, and I drove down from the mountains on deserted roads.

She woke when we turned into the forest track to her house. Granny Morgan was asleep in her chair and we did not wake her. For her, the past was over and, far away in the hills where they would never be disturbed, her parents were at rest.

We left her and sat together on the porch until the first light showed the tips of the bare branches and we could see each other.

My family left Oxrun soon afterwards, but my father kept in touch with the college in the hope that I would eventually study there.

Two years have gone by. It is autumn again and the leaves have begun to fall. Glyn's grandmother died a year ago, and now Glyn lives alone in Mildenhall Woods. It is time for me to return.

ELEANOR

1

ELEANOR TRENT WATCHED THE SKY DARKEN through the dusty window of Oxrun Station Public Library. Across the way, beyond Williamston Pike and Park Street, the woods that fringed the town were already deep in shadow although — perversely, Eleanor thought — late sunlight was shining in through the library's far window, so that a bright fiery pattern was cast on the high bookshelves lining the cast wall.

Eleanor checked her watch. It was already past four o'clock and time she set off for Hawksted. She admitted to herself that she was not particularly looking forward to her meeting with Robert Gill, for all kinds of reasons. He was, for a start, Rob Gill's father. Eleanor had grown fond of Rob over the past couple of months: he had become important to her and so, it seemed, had she to him. But she had hoped that the relationship would not grow too serious, though when Rob suggested the meeting with Rob Gill senior, she feared it might have done so.

Then there was Eleanor's mid-term project for the folklore module of her American Studies course: *Halloween, An American Holiday*. It sounded grand, and Eleanor felt sure that Miss Lance, her history tutor, would credit her fairly. But there was some considerable difference between earning the praise of a high school ma'am five years off retirement, and impressing the author of *The Origins, Rites and Ceremonies of Halloween in the Northeastern States of America*; a definitive text that Eleanor had drawn from heavily in the writing of her own work. She just knew that Doctor Gill would pick up on every phrase she had lifted, every fact she had got wrong, every opinion that was unfounded, and embarrass her dreadfully in front of his son. She just knew it . . .

"No, you don't know it. Stop being such a scaredy cat and go on over to Hawksted!"

She had been talking to her reflection in the window, cast clearly by the library's fluorescent lights, which Miss Ross, the senior librarian, had switched on a few minutes ago. The same Miss Ross now *shushed* Eleanor sternly from behind the issuing desk. Eleanor stuck her tongue out and smiled at her reflected face. She would never dare show such disrespect openly. And besides, more seriously, Kay Ross would ban her from using the library for months!

Eleanor's thoughts tilted back to Rob junior. He'd offered to drive her over to Hawksted College, and bring her back home too and, maybe, they could stop off for a pizza on the way . . . But Eleanor said she'd prefer to cycle across by herself. Trying to make small talk while she sweated over what Doctor Gill might say would be impossible. The ordeal was going to be bad enough anyway, without feigning ease and cheerfulness for Rob's benefit.

But with Rob in mind, Eleanor checked that her hair was tied back neatly in the ponytail he said he liked, and which she found sensible for a bike ride. It was long hair, pale blonde, and, in Eleanor's estimation, her best feature. It outweighed the disadvantage of a thinnish face, eyes of a startling green that betrayed far too many of Eleanor's innermost emotions, and a mouth that she thought was just a little too wide, though plenty of people said that her smile was 'sunny'. Eleanor hoped that associations of 'cute' would gradually be replaced by associations of 'sensual'. She was no longer a little girl and no longer wanted to be one . . . though the pale window-mirrored face was still innocent and still slept serenely each night on the soft pillow of ignorance. Most of all, she hoped that what beauty she possessed made up for her twisted left hand. She'd been born with it, and while it meant or mattered little to her now, she knew that it tainted some people's impressions of her for the worse.

Eleanor packed up her folders and books and tucked them away into the canvas shoulder bag she'd bought cheap at the surplus store. She said good evening to Miss Ross and offered her sunniest of smiles. Miss Ross's reply was a rather thin stretching of the lips and a lingering stare that Eleanor felt was perhaps tinged with envy . . . I'm young, Eleanor thought, I'm happy; I have all that I want or need. Life has not been bad to me . . .

Juggling those advantages in her head like polished pennies, Eleanor hurried down the library steps, unchained her bicycle from its rack and set off to the east, into the gathering gloom, flicking on her lights as the last street lamps on Chancellor Avenue gave way to trees.

2

Hawksted College lay three miles east of Oxrun. Its appearance matched the prestigious nature of its reputation. You had to earn your place there, as Eleanor hoped one day to do. Kids that didn't make the grade went to college at Harley, though that option soaked like a stain into one's academic record and made a career in medicine, law or research a little less likely. Eleanor was still far enough away from the hurdle of Hawksted's entrance exam to regard it with confidence and optimism. Even so, Harley wouldn't be so bad, she thought, as the wind lifted in the trees around her and made the woods roar softly. At least Harley would be better than dropping out early to stack supermarket shelves, or wait tables like the strange dark girl Glynis from Mildenhall Woods. Eleanor gripped the bike's handlebars more tightly thinking of that ultimate humiliation: serving cokes and pizzas to the likes of John Montague or Jeff Dacre or Benjamin Leech, three of several boys she'd dated briefly during the year she'd lived in Oxrun. The vision actually made her sweat, and her suddenly increased determination to reach Hawksted educationally made her push down harder on the pedals in order to get there more quickly.

Minutes later she swished off the road and into the long sweeping driveway to the College, standing on the pedals to manage the upward slope towards the main entrance in the south-facing facade. Eleanor had been on the campus several times and never failed to be impressed by the imposing Gothic-style buildings and the air of ancient academe that they evoked. The quadrangle that formed the old nucleus of Hawksted, a place of towers and turrets and high leaded windows, looked more Old England than New. Eleanor wondered if the place had been transported from Britain brick by brick — then chuckled and dismissed the notion as fanciful.

She leaned her bicycle against one of the glass-globed lampposts in the quad, picked up the lock chain and then dropped it back into the pannier. No-one was likely to steal the bike in a place like this, were they? She hefted her folder under her arm, swept a final glance across the rather dark and solid architecture all around her, and went in the side door to find Robert Gill's study.

Eleanor's smile, she was surprised herself to discover, was both sunny and unforced. Doctor Robert Gill was delightful; friendly, chatty, not at all superior or stuffy. He treated Eleanor from the start like a favourite niece — though she found it impossible to treat him like a favourite uncle, exactly. He was far too handsome for that, despite his corduroy trousers and the fact that he wore them with a tweed jacket leather-patched at the elbow and hem. He had hair that was much darker than his son's, and had combed it back severely with some hair cream, so that it shone glossily. His dark moustache made him look older than he was; his twinkling eyes made him look younger. Eleanor enjoyed this paradox and the way his easy manner threw her a little off balance.

"*Halloween, An American Holiday.* Hmm . . . It sounds very grand." He smiled, and so did Eleanor. "Are you pleased?"

"Yes, sir, I'm happy with it, I—"

Gill held up his hand. "No, no. Not 'sir', please. That embarrasses me. Makes me sound like some kind of expert."

Eleanor's laughter bubbled out. "But you *are* an expert! You know more about Halloween than — anyone!"

Gill smiled again, so that attractive crowsfeet crinkled at the corners of his eyes. "I think not."

He stood up and walked over to a small chalkboard framed on the wall between bookcases. He began drawing circles.

"There is an old story, and a very wise one, that goes like this . . . When the white man came to America, he was very keen to impress the native Indians, whom he thought simple and primitive. Arrogantly, the white man showed the chief of a local tribe his guns and his pocketwatch. Then he drew a circle in the dust with a stick. 'This is what the red man knows', he said. He drew a larger circle around the first. 'And this is what the white man knows — so you should beware.'

"The Indian chief nodded slowly. He took the stick off the white man and, around both circles, drew a much, much larger one. 'And this,' said the chief, 'is what neither of us knows. So we should *all* beware . . . '"

Gill took a thin pointer from the chalk ledge. "This circle is your project, Eleanor. This circle is my book . . . "

"And the outer circle?" Eleanor asked, as Gill's smile dropped away and his eyes turned very dark and serious.

"This is what neither of us knows about Halloween. So we should all beware."

Eleanor giggled and felt stupid for it. The study's cosy atmosphere seemed changed, and she looked around to see if a door had blown ajar.

The evening's first specks of rain flickered on the window, rattling the old loose latch. Robert Gill left the chalkboard and walked across to draw the drapes. He paused, looking out, then turned to beckon Eleanor over.

She stood up from the leather armchair where she'd been sitting and gazed through the small panes of the leaded window that made a glimmering tangram of the night. She'd imagined the sun had set long ago, but a final deep red gleam caught her attention, like a closing eye bleeding among the trees. The wind was strengthening and pulling leaves loose by the thousand. Swarms of them tumbled through the dimly lit quadrangle and past Eleanor's bicycle which, she thought, looked so lonely down there by itself. Above, the clouds were churning like dirty oil.

"Doctor Gill, what should we all beware *of*?" she asked quietly.

"Well, Eleanor, maybe we'll know that when we find it. Or when it finds us," he added. Which prompted her to wonder:

"Where's Robert? I thought he'd be here."

Gill drew the drapes and walked back to his seat. Eleanor did likewise. He flipped open the folder, then fumbled in his jacket breast pocket for some gold-framed glasses. They made him resemble the stern academic that Eleanor had feared.

"Oh, he said he'd be along. I think he's down in the library ... We have a very good library at Hawksted," Gill commented. "Several old local families have bequeathed collections to us ... One reason why I came to teach here, actually ... "

He became preoccupied. "Hmm. 'Long before the coming of Christianity, Hallowtide was a holy season when the barriers between this world and the next grew weak. This allowed the dead to return from the grave, and gods and strangers from the darkness of the Underworld walked abroad! It was also a time of new beginnings, when divination was practised to see what the coming year would bring ... Ceremonies were performed, young men and women foretold their future loves, games were played and ritual fires were kindled upon the hilltops. This cleansed and purified the people and the land, and helped to defeat the powers of evil which were then at their strongest ... ' This is very well written, Eleanor," Gill said with a smile and a gleam in his eyes. They were brown eyes, as rich and bright as the polished mahogany of his desk.

Eleanor blushed, recognising one of the passages she'd taken from Gill's own book. But if he'd noticed, he was far too polite to mention it.

"I wonder," he said, "how long before the coming of Christianity you think this festival was celebrated?"

"Um ... " Eleanor struggled to remember her studying, disconcerting herself as her blush deepened.

"I'll tell you. It has gone on for as long as man has walked on this Earth. And even then, even when humanity was young, the powers that visited at this time of the year were ancient ... so incredibly old, it's beyond imagining. But we've turned it into a moneyspinner, haven't we? An excuse for kids to beg candy and put grease on door handles and balloons on cats' tails ... It's become another party, another joke. But wipe away the make-up, tear off the mask, and at the bottom of it all you've got something astonishing: something wonderful and terrifying and awesome."

Gill jabbed a finger at the blackboard. "At Halloween the circles are not separate things. The barriers are down. We share the world with strangers . . . "

Had this been a summer's evening full of sunlight and people and the scents of flowers, Eleanor would not have shivered. But Hallowtide itself was just a few days distant, and the rain was lashing like flung beads at the windows now, and the temperature in the room was way down. She felt all of her confidence ebb to nothing, and the first fear creep in to take its place.

"I think," she said uneasily, "I think I'd better be going now."

The soft focus of Gill's eyes sharpened. He realised he'd been far away, and apologised. "It's all too easy these days for me to leap on my hobbyhorse and go galloping off. I'm sorry. At first glance I think your project is a good one, striking a fine and healthy balance between solid information and entertainment. Your research is sound—" He grinned wickedly. "And the sources you've quoted are reliable. I'd award a beta-plus, and a free ride home."

Eleanor started to protest. "No," Gill said, "I insist. You can't cycle back in this weather. We'll find Rob and I'll take you both over to town . . . Oh, I use a room here to sleep when I'm especially busy, as I am right now. But Rob copes very well by himself, though I'm sure he plays his hi-fi far too loudly . . . "

The drive to Oxrun took ten minutes. Eleanor sat by herself in the rear seat. Robert Gill senior chatted with his son about the work he'd done in Hawksted's library rooms. Rob junior turned to glance at Eleanor from time to time and ask if she was okay. She nodded, wrapped in the visions conjured by Robert Gill's words, and the passion with which he'd spoken them. As far as Eleanor had been concerned, Halloween was nothing more than an excuse for trick-or-treat nonsense, a reason to party and let your hair down . . . but now she was not so sure.

She saw the bright lights of The Luncheonette as they cruised by on Centre Street, and smiled to think that she'd enjoy nothing more now than to sit with Rob over a drink and a meal, and ask him a few of the hundred questions that had occurred to her during the evening. Like his son, Robert Gill was good-looking, intelligent and charming. But he was an enigma: there was something about him that was as dark and chilling as the season itself. Eleanor found herself curious to know more, though perhaps not too much more, about him. Maybe tomorrow, she thought, feeling heavy with sleep. Everything tomorrow . . .

Gill dropped Rob off at the family home on the corner of Devon Street and High, before driving south to Thorn Street where Eleanor lived. She saw her mother waiting anxiously by the window.

"Mothers worry," Eleanor said.

"And fathers too . . . Good night Eleanor. I've enjoyed meeting you. Come over again, won't you? I'll show you the college library, if you like."

"Thank you. I'd enjoy that. And I'll let you know what Miss Lance gives me for my project, when it's finished."

"Anything less than beta-plus, and she'll have me to answer to. Now get yourself indoors. It's a wild night."

"Yes. Goodnight."

Eleanor stepped from the car and ran up the concrete drive to shelter under the porch. She watched Gill drive away through grey veils of rain, the tyres sweeping skirts of leaves up behind them that had blown over from the woods across the way. Maybe a hundred yards down the road, brake lights flared and the car stopped briefly. Eleanor could barely see, but it seemed that a gust of wind and raindrops swirled around the car . . . And did the passenger door open just before Gill drove off? Or was it just an illusion in the gloom?

Eleanor was still trying to decide when the front door opened and her mother said, "Come inside girl, you'll catch your death!" in a tone of both anger and relief.

The rain had stopped, but the wind was still high and the deep woods were filled with the rush and boom of it. Everywhere there was movement, uncontrolled and inexorable.

Eleanor felt herself tumbling along, tossed lightly up high to the leaf canopy, then plunged back down to ground level. It was all a blur, but it seemed that hundreds of others were being similarly spun and spiralled through the woods to the lonely nowheres outside the town.

Leaves streamed by, and each leaf had a face. Some were wide-eyed with wonder, others looked frightened; a few were screaming in absolute terror.

Suddenly Eleanor realised. They were all leaves. All the people of Oxrun were no more than that, plucked loose by the wild autumn gales and driven on and on through the endless night towards . . .

Towards where, she wondered. And no sooner had the thought occurred to her than she saw faint and fitful flames through the trees up ahead.

The wind lifted and she was snatched up high, beyond the tallest branches, into a sky blown clear of clouds where the stars glittered fiercely.

Now she could see the sacrificial fire: the fire of purification and new beginnings. She felt its heat from here, this far off. But as the gusts blew her closer and closer, so she began to curl and wither in an agony of scalding. There was no escape from it. There was no release. No hope.

Eleanor started screaming too.

3

Eleanor reached for the milk jug. Her hand clipped the top of her glass and toppled it, spilling orange juice across the blue gingham cloth. She fumbled to retrieve it and succeeded only in spinning the tumbler into the condiment set in the middle of the table.

The dream was still with her, clinging like cellophane to the back of her eyes: *all those leaves*, all those souls consigned in horror and confusion to the flames. It made her shudder. It made her angry too, with a flash of passion that coloured her cheeks and set her eyes glinting.

"God damn it!"

"Eleanor! That's enough from you!" Mrs. Trent had mistaken the remark. She looked strained herself, and annoyed too as Eleanor glanced up, still dream-dizzy and tired.

"Um . . . I'm sorry, Mum. Still, no use crying over spilt . . ."

"Orange juice," Mrs. Trent finished for her, and they both laughed, knowing that breakfast-time temper sets the tone for the day. But besides that, and beyond it, each of them shared a little of what the other was feeling. It was a mother-and-daughter closeness that they both appreciated. It had seen them through plenty of hard times together.

Eleanor's brother, five years younger, brasher, less sensitive to meanings under the surface, made a tutting sound and a big show of dabbing at the juice with his napkin.

"Okay, I'll do it. Don't bother to help, Nell. You just enjoy the joke . . ."

Eleanor's pet hate was being called 'Nell'. Everyone she knew at all well was aware of it. The raw anger came up again, like a heartburn. But Eleanor kept her smile intact and convincing. Shouting at David wouldn't help anyone, besides which, she'd only be shouting again at the dream. That awful, hopeless dream.

"Thanks, brother. I appreciate your kindness."

"Are you all right?" Mrs. Trent asked gently, noting her daughter's paleness and the contrasting shadows around her eyes. Eleanor shrugged, an encompassing gesture.

"Time of the month, Mum. And the pressure's on at school at the moment."

"Yeah, that Rob Gill kid wants to take her out *every* night!" David leaned back grinning and dumped his sodden napkin in his cereal bowl. Eleanor's face made a small expression of pain.

"It's not like that at all—"

"I hope he's not getting too serious with—"

"I *said*, Mum, it's not like that. We're dating occasionally. Rob has his studies too. He's not likely to ruin his chances because of me!"

Both Eleanor and her mother knew how serious and studious Rob always was. Almost two years older than Eleanor, he was working hard — and needed to — to keep his place at Hawksted.

If she was completely truthful with herself, Rob's attitude did cause Eleanor some irritation. She loved, when it happened, unconditionally, and probably too deeply for her own good. Whereas Rob apportioned his time and always kept some distance between Eleanor and his innermost dreams. She guessed that when the time came for him to graduate from the High, he'd end it between them and pick up with some pretty co-ed at the college. They would both get good jobs and a fine house, maybe in Providence or perhaps Boston (unless he worked in New York, in which case they'd have a classy apartment there): she'd take a career break to raise a family — two kids, one of each, both blonde and rather quiet — and for their twilight years they'd invest in a ranch somewhere out west. He'd write a textbook, she'd devote her time to charity functions . . .

Eleanor found herself smiling at the vividness and absurdity of this mental map of Rob's life. Of course it was bound to be totally different! But even so, it was not likely to feature her beyond the next six months. Her smile went away.

"I'm off to school now," she said curtly, to break her own reverie. "Sorry about the mess, Mum."

"Eleanor, really, it's all right . . . "

"I'll walk with you," David said, and avoided looking too disappointed when Eleanor said that was fine.

There was nothing left of last night's storm except a tangy freshness in the air and some roadside puddles reflecting the pure perfect blue of a cloudless sky.

Eleanor and David waved to their mother as they turned out of the drive, and then turned right off Thorn, past the Welsh boy, Sam Jones's house, for the long, easy walk down Northland Avenue to the school.

David inhaled deeply and "Aahhh'd" with pleasure. New York had been nothing like this. The air there was dead and metallic, a rich dark weave of traffic exhaust and cosmopolitan cooking smells out on the streets. But here at Oxrun the atmosphere smelled and *felt* alive. The town was surrounded by woods and forests and some farmland. Its mood changed with the weather — and that was a constantly moving thing, hour by hour — and not merely a seasonal swing from hot to cold and back again. So Eleanor knew exactly what David meant, and agreed with him . . . though there was a strangeness here, too. It was as if the air was charged with static.

"Was there lightning last night?" Eleanor wondered aloud. She thought back, but could remember only how Rob Gill senior had impressed her, and how her dark and unexpected nightmare had impressed her far more, yet in a totally different way.

"I think once or twice," David said. These days he walked with the studied, heel-scuffing slouch of the adolescent, enhancing his street cred with a baggy blue sweatshirt hanging down over equally shapeless brushed denims, and a New York Jets baseball cap worn back to front. Eleanor glanced at him as he replied and tried to hide her amusement.

He went on without prompting, "I dunno. It was weird, Ne— I mean, Eleanor. I saw lightning, but I was asleep. And then, when I woke up and went to the window to check it out, it felt like I was dreaming." He shook his head. "I mean, really strange . . . "

She wanted to question him further, because deep down she saw some significance in his troubled slumber. But they had crossed Chancellor Avenue and now were waiting to cross Steuben, and there were more kids about, and David was starting to get embarrassed to be seen with his big sister.

He looked at her sheepishly. "I'll, um, see you later."

"Yeah." Eleanor leaned over to kiss his cheek, and with a squeal of utter panic, David sidestepped and ducked away through the scatter of pedestrians.

Eleanor crossed over to Oxrun Station High School, went straight inside to her locker, sorted her day's books and papers, then walked through to the toilet block closest to her tutor room.

Tina Broadbent and her friend Cerise Fallon were just leaving; Sarah Jane Smith was still there, prettying herself up and not, Eleanor judged objectively, making a very good job of it.

Eleanor and Sarah Jane — though she insisted on SJ — had never been friends. From the outset there was friction between them, which in the beginning had been unfocused, but quickly sharpened up to a rivalry for grades and boyfriends. SJ was marginally ahead on the science side, but in arts, English Lit and History, Eleanor had no worries at all, scoring high betas or alphas to SJ's barely scraped beta-minuses.

"Nice morning, SJ," Eleanor said breezily. She could afford good cheer, because Sarah Jane had set her sights on Rob at the summer dance and failed to hook him, for the simple reason that Eleanor had caught his eye instead. SJ had barely spoken to Eleanor since, but at least now treated her with a certain cold respect.

When Sarah Jane failed to answer, Eleanor flicked a glance at her with a choice of slick one-liners ready on her lips . . . But she kept all of them back at the sight of SJ's reflection in the mirror over the sink.

"Sarah Jane, are you all right?"

She looked — Eleanor struggled for the word — she looked lost, abandoned . . . but more than that: SJ looked frightened and badly shaken. Her hand was quivering as she attempted, unsuccessfully, to apply some eyeliner. Failing to steady herself, she dropped the tiny brush and snatched up a comb that she dragged through her long dark hair, worn loosely today: Eleanor thought it looked a mess.

"SJ," she said more quietly, stepping closer, "has someone hurt you?" The idea clicked into place as Eleanor spoke the words: her gut instinct was telling her that, somehow, Sarah Jane had been abused.

SJ stared Eleanor straight in the eye, and all the slow burning hatreds and jealousies were there, in that one fierce expression.

"Oh no, not *hurt* me." SJ's smile was ghastly, her mouth shockingly red in contrast to the paleness of her skin. "At last — Nell — there's someone who hasn't hurt me."

"I don't understand . . ."

"No," SJ shook her head and laughed, sharp as glass. "You wouldn't. You never could."

"Maybe you should speak to Mrs. Wallace," Eleanor suggested. Mrs. Wallace dealt with girls' social and personal problems in the school.

SJ's odd laughter cut off like a shutter coming down. She sneered, her lips actually curling away from her gums, and jabbed her index finger in the air a few inches from Eleanor's face.

"It's none of her business — the interfering old bitch! And it's none of yours, Nellie my Nell. It's nobody's business! So just stay out of my life. Got that?"

"Yeah . . . " Eleanor was too taken aback to be angry at the insults or rebuke. She nodded, stunned, as SJ grinned and spat on the tiled floor between Eleanor's feet. Then she turned and sashayed away as the bell rang for first registration.

Breaktime brought the chance to talk it all through with Natalie Dayne, Eleanor's best friend at the High, though they did not share many classes. Like Eleanor, Natalie had moved into town about a year ago. But they were kindred spirits above and beyond that; both right-brain thinkers, as Mrs. Dayne had once described them. The family lived in a large house at the top end of Devon Street, close to the Memorial Park. Natalie called it 'The Barn', because it was big and it was still very largely in a state of disrepair, apart from the few rooms that Mr. Dayne had renovated. He worked for an insurance company and travelled away a lot, so restoring the house had been a slow process. Natalie had recently confessed that she, her mother and kid sister Susie had reached the stage where living in the country was not the dream they'd expected it to be. It was certainly causing tension in the household, and Natalie had seen her grades drop since the summer semester with the worry of it all.

Now she shook her head and stirred her coffee idly. The fine weather meant that most kids had gone outside, so the refectory was almost deserted.

"I can't say I feel sorry for her. SJ has tried to put you down whenever she's had the chance, Eleanor. Quite frankly it's about time she knew what it felt like to be on the receiving end!"

"But the receiving end of what?" Eleanor wondered. "You didn't see her, Nat. I mean, she looked awful—"

"Like someone had *beaten* her?" Natalie's steady expression was challenging.

Eleanor thought about it again. Nodded.

"Like someone had beaten her. But there were no bruises . . . Maybe . . . maybe the word I want is 'defeated'. She looked beaten in that sense."

"Now you've lost me. SJ is never beaten, not by anyone. She'll find a way to get even sooner or later. I'm surprised you've survived intact so far, dating Rob as you do."

Eleanor smiled wryly at the truth of it, and at her friend's unshakeable cynicism. But the change in SJ still troubled her. She gazed past Natalie and out through the refectory window at the sky, the blue fleeced patchily with bright cloud. Her thoughts seemed to be drifting in the same way, all blowing steadily towards an unwelcome conclusion.

"Oh, anyway . . . " Natalie drank some coffee and waved a hand dismissively. "It's too nice a day to worry about Sarah Jane Bitch, I mean, Smith . . . are you going to the party?"

Eleanor's eyebrows lifted. "Party? What party?"

"You don't know?" Natalie brightened at the chance to explain. "Well, apparently, each year at Halloween a grand celebration is arranged up at the Craine house: you know, the big place set back off the road out past Beacon Hill?"

Eleanor nodded mid-sip and shrugged in reply.

"The Craines were one of the founding families of Oxrun Station, oh, nearly three hundred years ago. All the others have gone;

moved away, died out . . . In fact, old Abraham Craine is the last of his line. You see him sometimes when he comes into town—"

"Black Daimler half a block long, mirrored windows?" Eleanor supplied. "That's him?"

"Yeah. Mum reckons he shows his face occasionally to let folks know who's still the boss around the place. And I heard somewhere that townsfolk paid a tithe to the Craine estate right up until the nineteen-thirties."

Eleanor spluttered her final mouthful. "What! But that's mediaeval."

"Maybe it is, but you'll still find locals who'll tell you that Oxrun will only prosper as long as the Craine family prospers. The citizens paid Craine in money, or with produce, and Craine ensured the safety of their souls. Crazy, eh?"

"Absurd," Eleanor added. And more softly, "And evil. It's the way the landed classes have always kept the peasants under their thumb."

"No doubt." Natalie dipped a tongue-moistened finger into the sugar bowl and sucked it. "But you should check it out . . . Hey, I've thought of something. You can use this in your project, Eleanor. The celebration that Abraham Craine holds on his land is called a 'play party'. It's like an early Thanksgiving for a fine harvest, and to pray for a prosperous new year. It goes right back to pagan times. Maybe that's why it's tied in with Halloween."

"I'll, uh, yes, I will check it out. Thanks, Nat."

Eleanor glanced at her watch. "And we'll get together again soon and really swap gossip!"

Natalie chuckled as Eleanor stood and picked up her slim sheaf of schoolbooks.

"Yeah, let's jaw one evening. We could take in a movie and then go to eat — The Luncheonette maybe. Or how about some takeaway?"

"We'll do it." Eleanor smiled ambiguously, and Natalie read it right.

"And stop worrying about SJ. She deserves whatever she gets!"

"Sure. See you soon, Nat."

Eleanor hit the corridor ahead of the rush, thinking all the way along to Maths that surely no-one deserved whatever had been done to Sarah Jane Smith . . .

4

Rob called late afternoon and suggested a walk and a talk and a meal out — or a home-cooked meal at his place if she preferred that.

"A stroll and a pizza sound fine," Eleanor agreed, waving David away from her. He was alternately making grotesque faces and miming a passionate embrace. Eleanor found herself swinging between mirth and irritation. "I'll take a raincheck on the home-cooked . . ."

"You doubt me?" Rob said, mock hurt heavy in his voice. "I can throw together the best tagliatelle in town!"

David mimed being violently sick, then he clutched his throat and staggered about. Eleanor grinned and shook her fist at him.

"Tagliatelle another time, Rob. Let's take advantage of the fine weather and enjoy a walk."

"Okay. It's getting dark early these days. I'll pick you up in, say, an hour?"

There were assignments to finish, and tidying up to do on the Halloween project, and Eleanor's share of the household chores was piling up. More than that, she still felt oddly disturbed at the state of SJ that morning. Natalie had reported with some relish that SJ had gone home before lunch and missed the weekly science quiz . . .

"In an hour, then," Eleanor agreed. "It gives me time to put my face on."

Rob laughed, and in that moment Eleanor was struck by the bizarre ambiguity of the statement.

He turned up on time, though Eleanor was still towelling her hair upstairs. Mrs. Trent answered the door to him and beamed her most charming smile as she invited him in. Her opinion of him as 'a bright, intelligent, clean-cut boy' was one that Eleanor agreed with, although since both Rob Gill senior and Emily Trent were currently without partners, Eleanor suspected an ulterior motive in her mother's friendliness.

She hurried down the stairs, having chosen at the last moment her best tight white denims, a cotton blouse and her favourite mohair sweater in pale amber. Rob whistled when he saw her.

"Wow! I hope you look this good at the party."

"What party?" But Eleanor remembered as she said it, and frowned. "I haven't been invited."

Rob shrugged lightly. "Nobody's officially invited to Abe Craine's play party. You just go along if you *want* to go along."

"If you feel you've got to tug the forelock to the master, and save your immortal soul, right?"

Now it was Rob's turn to frown, and Mrs. Trent, coming through from the kitchen, thought it meant trouble between them.

"Are you two all right?"

"We're fine, Mum," Eleanor said and then, to Rob, "I won't know if I want to go along until nearer the time. I'll let you know later."

His puzzlement was obvious, and it got them off to a bad start as Rob, unsmiling, opened the front door and held it wide for Eleanor.

The porch light had winked on automatically as the darkness deepened. Eleanor squinted up at it and beyond it, looking south and west past the Mainland Road. The air smelled sweet, almost cloying, like honeysuckle.

"What's that?" She pointed.

"Hm?" Rob said a polite goodnight to Mrs. Trent, closed the door and followed Eleanor's finger. "Oh, it's Venus. It'll get higher and brighter towards Christmas, reaching opposition in early January."

Eleanor grinned and opened her eyes wider in surprise. "And is astronomy another of your talents?"

Rob smiled back. "Another of Dad's, actually. He likes to tie in celestial phenomena with folklore . . . oh, and sorry about last night. I should have been there when you met Dad: he can be a bit intimidating and intense."

"I didn't find him at all intimidating," Eleanor said, lying easily. "He was lovely. He promised me access to the library at Hawksted."

"Then you are favoured! I'll take you along sometime and show you. It's really impressive."

"I need to go back to collect my bike." She felt pleased to have eased Rob's mind away from the play party and her uncertainty about it. They both gazed up at Venus. Eleanor noticed a long bar of cloud lifting slowly out of the west, like a slick of pollution staining a clear blue sea. Venus, unwavering, hung like a splinter of quartz above it.

"It's a good omen," Rob said, sliding his arm around Eleanor's waist. He leaned close and kissed her ear, touching its inner curves with his tongue tip.

And then Eleanor, amazingly, was struggling away from him, squealing. Rob let her go with a look of shock and self-consciousness. She was waving her arms over her head, stumbling over her own feet as she bumped back into him.

"Rob! It's a bat — oh, it's in my hair!" The creature, no bigger than Rob's thumb, had been on the hunt for evening insects and was attracted by the moths gathering around the porch light. Eleanor's brushed-back hair tied in a ponytail had never been its target.

Rob swept the tiny bat away and watched it flicking about in the darkness until, with a sudden change of direction, it was gone.

He laughed and as Eleanor turned to him, hugged her tight and smelled the perfume she was wearing.

She snuggled close to Rob until her pulse and breathing had slowed, then eased away and looked over his shoulder. Venus had vanished now, covered by the cloud which was still rising.

It looks like rain, she thought.

5

"The first play party of the year will come on that Saturday evening which is nearest to Halloween," Eleanor read. "Beneath the general celebrations is the very serious purpose of ensuring the continued prosperity of the community, and the spiritual health of each of its members. Divination games are played, in hope of a secure future and with deference to the controlling forces of nature.

"The symbolic pinnacle of some play parties is the lighting of the Beacon Fire, a gesture meant to rekindle the dying winter sun, and the cooking of soul cakes on flat stones placed in and around the flames. Soul cakes are little pastries and breads, baked by townsfolk and offered in exchange for blessings. In days gone by, the soul cakes were given to the poor of the district. More recently, prosperous communities consigned the cakes to the Beacon Fire in honour of the dead and to appease the creatures of the night that abound in the countryside at Halloween. Frequently this ritual was combined with a masquerade, not to frighten away such spirits, but to —"

A shadow fell across the book. Eleanor, startled, glanced up to see Miss Ross standing there looking down at her . . . But then, she realised, not at *her*: the librarian was gazing intently at an illustration on the adjacent page, of a young woman staring by candlelight into a dresser mirror. A shadowy male figure loomed over her shoulder, though the young woman seemed to be alone in the room.

"Journeys end in lovers meeting," Miss Ross whispered. Her eyes were alight and sparkling, and Eleanor felt a little uncomfortable to recognise the light in them as lust.

The eyes moved marginally to look at Eleanor.

"Dreaming of a husband, eh?" Miss Ross wondered. "There are many ways to foresee . . . Mirror-gazing is just one of them . . . Sit outside on Halloween Eve with other boys and girls and peel corn husks from the harvest. The one who finds a red ear of corn can demand a kiss from anyone else in the group, and that's the person the husker is sure to marry!"

"It sounds like a strange custom," Eleanor said awkwardly as Miss Ross giggled. The woman leaned closer and flipped pages.

"Or," she went on, "you may throw a ball of yarn over your shoulder, keeping hold of the end, and recite this rhyme:
Whoever will my husband be
Come wind this ball behind of me.
"And the man you will marry is bound to walk up behind you, winding the yarn."

Eleanor smiled uneasily, thinking that maybe a dating agency would produce more reliable results these days. She looked at the clock on the wall. It was ten minutes to four. She'd agreed to meet Rob at five, and drive over to Hawksted with him to see the library there, as he'd promised. Then, if the weather held, they'd go for the walk that was cut short the evening before. It had rained, as Eleanor had expected.

"If these rituals work," Eleanor asked, keeping her tone polite and friendly, "why are there so many? Why isn't there just one *infallible* way of seeing the future?"

Miss Ross lifted her eyebrows and nodded. "That's a good question, dear. It's horses for courses — do you know that saying? You choose the method of foretelling that most suits your personality and circumstances. Why, if you grow fruit, you use apple parings to look forward. If you work in a kitchen, you prepare a silent supper on Halloween Eve . . . "

Eleanor was interested despite herself, because Miss Ross actually seemed to believe in this stuff, whereas Eleanor had treated it all as an intellectual exercise. Just words. She shrugged.

"I'm a student." She glanced at her books. "How do I do it?"

Miss Ross's face lit up, then her eyes narrowed as she considered Eleanor carefully. "You are an inward-looking girl, I feel. A reflective type. Try the mirror method. Or, if you want to know more than the identity of your future love — if you want to *see your destiny* — use the double mirror!"

"What's that?"

"Around Hallowtide, take a hand mirror to a pool of still water. Lie down on your back and hold the mirror above your head, facing the pool. You will see an image of your future and your fate . . . Don't disdain these things," Miss Ross added with a trace of her old severity. "If you do not keep an open mind, you're likely to suffer some unpleasant surprises."

"What method of foretelling do you use, Miss Ross?" Eleanor asked. She felt like adding, And why hasn't it worked? because Miss Ross, a librarian in Oxrun for forty years, had been a spinster just as long, though obviously she had the same needs and desires as any woman.

Now she looked at Eleanor darkly and wagged a warning finger. "Ah, that would be telling. Nor should you reveal to anyone what *you* see, for your future is a secret and precious thing."

"Well, I'll surely keep my business to myself," Eleanor said, turning away to gather up her notes. Miss Ross watched her for a few moments silently.

"Yes. As *Oxrun* keeps its business to itself," she said then, and as Eleanor paused to ask her what that meant, Miss Ross turned and walked away towards her desk.

6

Eleanor called home to freshen up, ousting David from the bathroom.

"You're going skateboarding, you don't need to shower," she argued reasonably. "Anyway, if you don't hurry you'll have no time for it. The dark falls early these days."

"All true," David said, dragging on a T-shirt. "Besides which, you need at least an hour to doll yourself up for darling Robert!" He ducked as he said it, avoiding Eleanor's swinging arm, then dodged out of the bathroom an instant ahead of the flying sponge.

Eleanor stripped, showered and towelled dry in record time. She sprayed conditioner in her hair and combed it through, looking meanwhile at her misty reflection in the mirror. There had been something about Miss Ross's manner that unnerved her a little, and still did. Not the fact that she believed all the stuff about divination (intelligence has nothing to do with gullibility, after all, she thought starchily), but the way her words had been accompanied by such a look of *hunger*. Miss Ross had, for years, found her life wanting. And now she'd been driven, through panic at the thought of a lonely old age, to the most desperate measures. Eleanor wondered with a flash of sympathy what the poor old soul would do once Halloween was passed and she still had no proposal of marriage.

I'm glad my life is ahead of me, Eleanor thought. I'm glad I'm independent. I'm glad I can make up my own mind about things . . . She planed her right hand across her body, then looked at her left hand crabbed in against her hip. That's the only thing I'd change about myself, she decided. If 'the controlling forces of nature' could help me, then that's what I'd ask them to cure. It would be worth baking a soul cake for . . .

The telephone rang downstairs. David was passing in the hall with his skateboard, but he ignored it. Mrs. Trent picked up the kitchen extension, and a few seconds later called Eleanor up the stairs.

"Eleanor! It's for you: Natalie."

"Okay, Mum. I'll take it in my room!"

Eleanor slipped on her underwear and her jeans, and walked through to her bedroom where her choice of sweaters was lying on the bed. She plumped down beside them and picked up the handset.

"Hi Nat. How's things?"

"Oh, fine. Hey, did you hear about SJ?"

Natalie's voice was bursting with excitement. Eleanor frowned. "She wasn't in school again today . . . "

"She's in hospital!"

"What?"

"An ambulance rushed her in about lunchtime. Abby Taschen told me — she lives three doors up from Sarah Jane and goes home for lunch."

"But what's wrong with her?"

"Well, I thought you might have known . . . Abby says they suspect glandular fever, but Mrs. Taschen reckons anaemia. She said that SJ looked so pale, she was white. Looked like death, Mrs. Taschen says . . ."

Eleanor sighed in sympathy for SJ and in annoyance at Natalie's gossipy tone.

"Nat, I don't know what—"

"Of course, it could be leukaemia or something else really serious . . . I've got some flowers and I thought we could drop by to cheer her up. Visiting goes on till eight, and—" Eleanor cut Natalie off mid-sentence. "Nat, I can't go, I can't really. Um, I'm seeing Rob and we're driving over to Hawksted . . ."

"Oh. Well I know you don't get on with SJ, but she is one of us. I mean, you're standing next to her in the yearbook photograph . . ."

That made Eleanor laugh, and what stopped the laughter was the conviction that Natalie's sole motive in visiting SJ was idle curiosity or, even worse, maybe just to gloat.

Natalie persisted for a few seconds longer, but they both knew she was fighting a lost cause.

"I'll go by myself, then . . . and I'll see you tomorrow, okay . . ."

"Yes. Give SJ my best wishes. Tell her I'm thinking of her."

Before Natalie replied, Eleanor dropped the handset back into its cradle. She chose her red turtleneck sweater because there was a chill in the air, and as an afterthought put her hand mirror in her bag before leaving to rendezvous with Robert.

7

"What would happen if you looked into the future and saw nothing . . . or worse, you saw your own death . . . ?"

"What's that?"

Rob glanced over and smiled. The car was warm, a little too warm for Eleanor's comfort, and the air was heavy with the smell of Rob's aftershave. Eleanor smiled wanly at the way he was trying so hard to be a man: aftershave; his right arm draped casually across the back of Eleanor's shoulder; the big fuel-hungry Buick he'd bought from the autoshop for a song (and was now discovering why); the way he over-revved the engine at traffic lights . . .

He interpreted her smile as an intimate one, and twisted a strand of her hair in his fingers. Eleanor could tell he was turned on to her tonight, but she felt aloof and vaguely troubled, by SJ and by Miss Ross.

"I was just thinking aloud . . ." She was wondering if SJ had tried foretelling, and had seen something dreadful in her mirror . . . but she told Rob about Miss Ross instead.

"Ha! She's right off the wall, I'm telling you. Don't listen to her, Eleanor, not for a second."

"Why?" Eleanor asked, her quietness in contrast to Rob's loud sarcasm. Rob shrugged.

"Three hundred years ago she'd have been burned as a witch!"

"And maybe three *thousand* years ago she'd have been consulted as an oracle."

Rob's smile turned down at the edges. She had irritated him somehow. Just ahead, a cyclist was slanting across the lane to turn left. Rob undercut him with a raucous blaring of horns, dropping down a gear and powering away with a wheel-spinning screech of tyres.

Eleanor sighed audibly. "For goodness sakes, what's wrong with you tonight?"

Rob made to snap back, then blew his breath out in a gush. He withdrew his arm from Eleanor's shoulder and gripped the wheel.

"There's something going on around here . . ."

"Around where?" She was being deliberately picky, needling him more, pushing him.

"Around Oxrun . . . I mean, it simply feels strange to me . . ."

"Go on."

"The people, the time of year . . . I don't know: nothing I can put my finger on. It's getting to me. And this stuff about spinster Ross; it just adds to the weirdness."

"She was only telling me about some old Halloween customs. She knows I'm doing a project . . ."

"Yeah," Rob said heavily, "but she's so damned *intense* about it. Most people are around here. It's like Halloween is built into their bones; wired into their collective unconscious."

"A lot of folks take it seriously . . . part of the culture."

"Sure."

They had left Oxrun now. It was no more than a sprinkling of lights in Rob's rearview mirror. And, as the car cruised effortlessly along the slightly upsloping two-lane east towards Hawksted and swung a leisurely corner, even they disappeared into the darkness.

Rob and Eleanor fell silent for a few moments, as though mesmerised by the steady, ceaseless looming of trees in the headlight beams. The oaks and maples were past the best of their glorious fall colours; blood reds and chestnut browns were giving way to dull rusty tans on increasingly skeletal branches. Deeper off the road to right and left, pinewoods tangled into the night.

"I mean," Rob repeated, startling Eleanor, "I mean, it's like the Twilight Zone around here. There's Miss Ross staring into looking-glasses and hurling balls of twine, there're students at the College preparing their costumes and pumpkins for the weekend, as though they were kids again . . . Even Dad's caught up in the madness!"

Eleanor took Rob's anger lightly. "He *is* a leading authority on Halloween," she pointed out.

"There's a difference between knowing and doing."

"What do you mean?"

Rob eased his foot off the accelerator and the big Buick engine gentled to a purr, the car slowing.

"All this stuff about stars and planets . . . You remember Venus?"

Eleanor laughed at her panic over a two-inch bat. "How could I forget?"

"Well, Dad explained that it's coming into close conjunction with both Mars and Saturn — a very rare alignment, apparently."

"So what?"

"And Saturday night will see a full moon . . . and we're at the height of the sunspot cycle . . . "

"Now who's in the Twilight Zone?" Eleanor teased, but she could see from the tightness around Rob's mouth that he was taking it all seriously.

"My father," he said softly, like a confession, "is convinced that these celestial alignments, reaching their peak on October thirty-first, will have important consequences when people perform their silly rituals. So when Miss Ross winds-in her twine, she'll have the stars behind her."

"How do you know about her antics, anyway?" Eleanor wondered. Rob made a sneery sound.

"Because it's public knowledge, and she does nothing to hide it. Pathetic, really . . . but Dad thinks this year will be different."

"What do *you* think?" Eleanor had seen a notch in the darkness ahead, and a rickety wooden signpost pointing like a bony finger.

"It's all rubbish."

"Let's prove it then — take that turn."

"Say what?"

Rob slowed the car further, trickling it level with the sign indicating a one-lane dirt track through the trees. A back road to Beacon Hill and the Craine House.

"It's private land," he told her.

"Who's going to be about?"

"Abe Craine employs gamekeepers, and they're very stupid and they're very mean . . . "

But Eleanor persisted. "Take the turn anyway. We can always say we got lost—"

"Oh yeah. 'Sorry officer'," Rob mimicked. "'I took the wrong road . . . Well, I've only lived here for five years . . . '"

But he took the turn anyway, easing the car carefully along the rutted track, tutting when pine branches whipped at the paintwork.

"Reversing's going to be a whole bundle of fun . . ." A thought struck him. "Hey, I know what: you've brought me here to seduce me, right? You just want to rip off my clothes and—"

"Down, boy." Eleanor said, laughing. "Let me have my way before you have yours—"

Rob looked at her oddly.

"I mean," she said, "I'm as curious and as troubled as you are about what's going on. And if something is, I want to know what, so's I can meet it on my own terms."

"Brave talk, when you're safe inside an automobile," Rob said. He sounded nervous. "Look, I really think—"

"OK, stop here, at that passing point. We can turn and go back. But not before I've tested the waters . . ."

Rob's sigh of relief tailed off into one of frustration. He stopped the car but kept the engine running.

"Over there, beyond those trees," he said, "is Beacon Hill, where old man Craine holds his stupid play parties." Rob's finger swung round to the north. "And about a mile that way is the Craine house . . . You think Hawksted looks like something out of Fright Night? Wait till you see that pile!"

"Don't go," Eleanor said, needlessly, as she opened the passenger door, grabbed her bag and eased herself out into the lane.

"I just want to . . ."

"Want to what?" he asked, as she started walking away.

"Feel the night . . ."

Ten steps out, and Eleanor felt more alone than she had ever done before. Last evening's rain had given the land a damp smell. Tonight there was a chill in the air, thin cloud and hazy stars like smeared chalk dots on the dark. Through the trees eastward the rising moon cast a pale glow, very indistinct. That moon would be full on Saturday, but right now, Eleanor thought from somewhere deep in her mind, its power was not so strong.

She walked on, her shoes crunching on stones, her eyes slowly adjusting to the dimness. The lie of the land emerged vaguely around her. She sensed the bulking mass of Beacon Hill close by, a focus for her apprehensions.

And I still don't know if I'm spooking myself, or if what I'm feeling is real . . . Behind her, the Buick's idling engine was a soft whisper. She turned around and was shocked to see how far she'd come, the car's headlights lost around a long bend in the track. The countryside seemed absolutely still.

And now the moment came when childish fears tilted over into something else, becoming an older, greater fear that what we see is balanced on the brink of some endless otherwhere; that our power, in the larger scheme of things, vanishes away into an unimaginable gulf.

" . . . And that's what neither of us knows. So we should all beware . . . "

But Eleanor *had* to know, not wanting to submit to her racing pulse or the urge to run squealing back to Rob.

A couple of yards away on the roadside was a puddle. Eleanor gritted her teeth, delved in her bag and pulled out her hand mirror. She thought briefly about her clothes getting soiled, but the experiment would be worth it . . .

She lay down on the track so that the puddle was above her head, and angled the mirror to see the water's reflection.

That was the theory: but of course, she thought, how can there possibly be a reflection in such pitch blackness . . . ?

Yet there was — incredibly, a swirl of opalescence and then, rising upward, a pale and terrified face, like the face of a drowned corpse.

"Oh — my — God . . . " Eleanor whispered, as the terror started to tear at her resolve.

It was Sarah Jane's face, lost, doomed, sinking back to the depths.

To be replaced an instant later by the dark and twisted features of a bat.

8

The wind rose with Eleanor's scream as she dropped the mirror and left it lying face down in the dirt. She knew she was running; knew that her body was carrying her away from whatever awful unknown she'd encountered. But there was no purpose in her beyond that, and no fear, because she'd gone past both. She felt a cold numbness like winter slush in her stomach, yet her bowels felt hot as acid. Eleanor ran, so consumed by dread that in the end she forgot *why*, she ran, and started stumbling about pointlessly in the darkness.

There were no lights — and that thought brought her back to reality. There were no lights showing from Rob's car!

She picked up speed around the long curve of the dirt track; the suddenly gusting wind seeming to push her forward. It sang in the trees, little howls and whistlings, stirring the great masses of shadow that made up the woodlands. Those shadows were now cast against the palest silver as the moon rose higher, a glinting coin, on the edge of the world.

"Rob!"

Then there was a swirling whiplash of air that staggered Eleanor sideways, and a loud bang — followed by a mouthful of cursing as Rob twisted the ignition key. The starter motor hacksawed briefly; the engine cleared its throat, faded, then fired. The Buick's headlights sprang on, full beam, dazzlingly, trapping Eleanor like a moth.

Rob scrambled out and ran to her, hugging her tightly, crushing her into his chest. She pushed him away, gulped air in a sob, calmer now as she saw that he was shaking.

"Rob — what happened?"

"Something came by me," he said without hesitation, and in no doubt at all. "Something . . . " He stared at her steadily from arm's-length, looking for disdain or disbelief.

"Go on," she said softly.

"I heard you scream . . . I thought it would be better, safer, to get the car up there. If there was someone, an attacker, I could've

"... Anyway, the engine cut out and the lights died. I mean, no warning. All the power just died ... I began to turn the key, and then — Godammit! — something swept past and hit the hood with an almighty wallop. I saw you running — I didn't know what to do!"

"Calm, Rob, be calm," Eleanor said. She knew no more than he did, but deep down inside herself she recognised a certain strange inevitability in all of this: everything felt oddly right. "Did it pass you on the ground, this thing?"

"On the ground. In the air. Everywhere. I didn't see it properly. The wind came up from somewhere, and there was a spray of raindrops and blowing leaves ... But whatever struck the car was powerful, and vicious."

Rob turned from her and swept his hand over the hood, finding the six-inch dent immediately. He clenched his fist and pressed it in the metal. Whatever fist had caused this damage was twice the size and incalculably stronger.

"Best get back," he said, businesslike now. "Maybe I can run you over to Hawksted tomorrow. Dad'll be there then, anyway."

"He isn't there tonight?"

"He has some things to do in town. Besides—" He laughed suddenly and awkwardly, "I don't feel safe here now."

"I know what you mean." Eleanor gazed around, seeing little because of the car's lights. But once again, the land had settled and was millpond-still.

"Do you think it's all rubbish now?" she wondered, taunting gently.

Rob opened the passenger door for her like a gentleman.

"I think, maybe, it's not."

Something had happened in the town too, they found as Rob took them up King Street and then, on a whim, right along Centre Street.

"There's been a power-cut here, as well," he noted, "and a twister, by the looks of it!"

That comment was intended to be flippant, but Eleanor could see what he meant. Only a few random street lamps were shining to illuminate the chaos: snapped telephone lines, smashed-in windows, trash and litter and toppled dustbins scattered over the road, the few cars out on the streets avoiding them carefully. There were even fewer pedestrians, although Eleanor did notice what looked like a struggle of kids running across the street about a hundred yards away, disappearing around the corner of the block, heading, it seemed, towards the park.

"They're trick-or-treating early!" she said and then, less in surprise and more subdued: "What are their parents thinking of . . . ?" The figures had been squat and hunched, draped in black, hurrying with purpose. It had been the fleeting glimpse of their faces that had given Eleanor the notion of trick-or-treaters . . . *Those horrible masks . . .*

"Heads up, it's the cops," Rob said, so that Eleanor put her doubt to the back of her mind.

The police car was parked on Centre Street opposite The Brass Rail. The bar's windows had gone: glass lay strewn like a diamond field across the blacktop. Rob pulled over and stopped as the officer gave a warning red/blue flicker of lights, then stepped out of the car and approached.

Rob wound down his window. The cop looked in, neither recognising the other.

"We were out on a date," Rob explained, keeping his voice steady. Eleanor smiled thinly, very aware of her mussed hair and grimy clothes. "Um, here's my driver's licence," Rob added.

The officer took the document and glanced at it and handed it back. Rob wondered if his purpose was simply to keep people away from the damage. He felt confident enough to ask: "What's been happening?"

"Well . . . " The cop pushed his hat a little further back and looked down the street as he leaned against the Buick's roof. Rob noted the man's short-cropped reddish hair and moustache, and the angry shaving rash on his neck: it was a skinny neck, and his shirt collar looked one size too big.

"Seems like we've had a windstorm or something blow through here. About twenty minutes ago. The damage is sporadic, but it's affected the whole of Oxrun. Chief Stockton thinks it best if people stayed indoors tonight."

"Sounds like good advice." Rob tried to sound friendly and accommodating. "I'll just run my girl home."

"And then go home yourself. You never know with these freak weather conditions . . . and at this time of year you might get hail, or a downpour, flash floods, who knows?"

"Yeah. Who knows?" Rob engaged the gear shift. The officer didn't move away.

"So who took a grudge against your auto?" the cop said idly.

"Oh, I think some kid must've thrown a stone or something. That hood's going to take some beating-out . . ."

"Sure will . . . and it looks like the same kid took a garden rake to your side panels here . . ." He tapped on the roof. "Okay, safe home, son."

"Thanks," Rob said, winding up the window.

He made a U-turn, drove to the end of Centre Street and turned right into Thorn, stopping a couple of blocks short of Eleanor's house to check out the officer's comment.

"What the hell is going on?" Rob said. Eleanor got out and walked round the rear of the car, frowning as she caught sight of the jagged score marks running from nose to tail on the driver's side. There was no doubt in either of their minds that whatever had caused the dent in the hood had caused these deep gouges also. Even so, Rob scratched his head in puzzlement. "Must've been branches whipping by on that narrow track . . ."

"Must have been," Eleanor said, getting back into the car without further comment.

They drove to the far end of Thorn. Rob flipped on his fullbeams as they drew near to Eleanor's house.

"Looks like Dad's car parked outside — that must be my father at your door now."

Two figures — Eleanor assumed her mother and Robert Gill senior — looked back, and Mrs. Trent waved. She was smiling as Eleanor and Rob walked up the drive. But Doctor Gill seemed shaken and on the edge of anger.

"When all this happened, I rang Hawksted," he said, glancing at his Saab, "on the carphone. You hadn't arrived there."

"Doctor Gill was worried," Mrs. Trent added. Eleanor smiled inwardly at the way her mother was trying surreptitiously to tidy her hair and smooth her skirt. Admiration fairly glowed from her eyes. "I mean, we both were . . . "

"We motored a couple of miles, but the sudden gale made me decide to turn back," Rob said, improvising quickly. "Um, there was a tree down on the road. We tried to move it . . . " He cast a glance at Eleanor's grubby clothes.

"And across the railway tracks, in several places I understand. I called Chief Stockton—" Gill gave a flashing, scornful smile. "He put it down to freak weather between here and Harley."

"Maybe it's celestial alignments," Eleanor came back mischievously. Mrs. Trent shivered.

"It's chilly out here. Why don't we go inside for some hot chocolate, or perhaps, Doctor Gill, a glass of wine?"

Eleanor looked away, grinning at her mother's shameless flirting. At forty-two, she was still an attractive woman, very independent and capable; but Eleanor knew she got lonely sometimes. She had a fleeting, flash image of her mother hurling Kay Ross's yarn-ball over her shoulder, and felt saddened that Rob Gill seemed uninterested.

"Um, no, thank you, Mrs. Trent," Gill said. He looked distracted and momentarily confused as his eyes fixed on Eleanor's face for a second. Rob junior moved his hands in negation and shook his head warningly behind his father's back. "I'll go on to the house to see that everything's all right. Then I really must reach the college, tree-fall or no tree-fall."

"Well," Mrs. Trent hid her disappointment smoothly. "Take care then. I hope you'll call on us again soon."

"I'll see you tomorrow, Eleanor," Rob added.

Eleanor and her mother watched the Gills walk to their respective cars, Rob pausing once more to gaze at the damage inflicted on his. His father got inside the Saab, turned on the engine and lights, and looked around at the rear seats . . .

And for a startling, frightening second, Eleanor was convinced that she saw a passenger there: tall and sinister, leaning back out of sight, his glimmering eyes being the last thing to fade away into the darkness.

David had come home long before, when the impossible wind started. He'd spent his evening playing computer games by way of consolation. He paused in his space invading and made sloppy kissing noises as Eleanor walked into the lounge, followed by their mother. Mrs. Trent switched on the TV: David tutted at the empty glitzy show that was playing, packed up his kit and said he was going up to his room.

"We've been lucky," Mrs. Trent told Eleanor, indicating TV, lights and radiator. "Our electricity was only off for an hour or so."

"Some parts of the town are still blacked out."

"Well, I'll just watch this and then put the kettle on . . . Unless you want to make some tea, honey?"

Eleanor, slumped on the sofa opposite the stone fireplace, was staring into space, her eyes half-hooded with weariness. Mrs. Trent put it all down to the rigours of the day and because Eleanor was working so hard at school. She smiled, began watching the quiz show, and was herself asleep within five minutes . . .

Eleanor had not intended to doze off. The shock of what she'd seen in the mirror had drained her, but temporarily of emotion, not of energy. She could hear the TV far away; canned laughter, tinned excitement, meaning nothing. David was upstairs, Rob would be home safely. Everything was okay . . . So calm, be calm now, Eleanor . . .

She wondered what the creature was. Not a bat. It was huge, for one thing. Man-sized. And its eyes had burned with a fierce red intelligence that set it apart from any animal . . . Maybe it was that which had damaged Rob's car. But how had she seen its reflection? And why had SJ's face appeared — so distorted by pain and desolation? And then these awful gusts that came screaming down the valley from Harley to Oxrun and out over the plains . . . How? Why?

These were puzzles that Eleanor felt she hadn't the wit to solve. The TV played on. She heard her mother breathing deeply, very deeply, in the chair nearby. And the room was so warm, so cosy, so sheltered from the sinister night outside

Eleanor felt unconsciousness encroaching on her mind. She remembered Venus, and how the rising cloud bank had enveloped it, enfolded it in darkness. Like the darkness of sleep, she thought: her last thought, before that darkness opened up and she found herself flying down the High Street.

Eleanor gasped with the sudden chill and rush of air past her face. Her eyes began to water and her head spun.

No sooner had she realised where she was (though not *how*) than the ground tilted madly to the left, she swooped and came zooming in at head height, straight towards the plate glass window of Richards' Haberdashery Store.

Eleanor screamed. Someone else's mouth took up the scream to an unbearable pitch, so that Eleanor's teeth burred in her head. The big shop window trembled, starred, hung suspended for an instant like the world's most complicated jigsaw puzzle, then exploded outwards into the street, showering crystal fragments.

Eleanor craned her neck towards the sky, streaked upwards trailing mad laughter; gathered herself above the town and fell like a white quartz pebble swathed in streaming black rags.

The familiar streets swung by at unfamiliar angles. Eleanor caught sight of the red-haired police officer she'd seen a while ago with Rob . . . She snarled, flicked her body towards his car, reached out with her cold left hand (Left hand! My left hand!), and smashed the silently glittering blue-red warning lights to pieces.

The cop flinched back, stumbling. He kicked his heel against the kerb and fell, sitting down heavily on the sidewalk. Eleanor saw his eyes widen and his expression stiffen towards an unbelieving terror.

With a hiss, she lunged at him and swept her black-fingernailed hand across his face. A rake of cuts opened up in his cheek. His features twisted as he rolled clear, struggling to draw his pistol from its holster.

Eleanor's glee came in an eruption of shrieks and giggles echoing out over the town. She flashed into Chancellor Avenue, and without slackening her speed, flicked a ninety degree turn down a side alley between shops . . .

She rushed, inches from the ground, scattering cats and trashcans, along the alley, her velocity decreasing. And at last she stopped, crouched by the wall, panting, energy surging through her like fire.

The mind that Eleanor occupied (or that occupied her) quietened until she was able to gather her thoughts.

"What's — happening? Who — are — you?"

"History calls me Tuggie Bannock," came the unexpected reply. The voice was calm and smooth as blue velvet. The voice of a temptress.

"Why are you — doing this to — me?"

"Because . . . " The voice paused, laughter stirring in a soft white throat. "Because, my child, your curiosity helped to open the door."

"Let me go."

"Do you really want to be free?" asked Tuggie Bannock. The creature moved. Eleanor's perspective changed. She was walking now, her eye level six feet above the ground, out of the alley and into Steuben Avenue, she realised. She watched through someone else's eyes as they passed Garland's Grocery Store on the corner of Fox Road . . . where Tuggie Bannock stopped and looked full face into the window.

It was the most beautiful face that Eleanor had ever seen. The thin white doe-eyed face of the heroine in a Gothic romance. She smiled for the benefit of the girl trapped within her, and Eleanor's guts stirred, envying this statuesque woman who owned the night to its far corners. Tuggie Bannock lifted her left hand, her perfect left hand, and drew it gently down her cheek. A single scalding tear gleamed on the lid of each eye, and fell. That same graceful hand wiped them away . . .

And now, down the street, came the wail of police sirens. Someone shouted, a hard male voice full of fear and rage.

The creature came out of her reverie as the moment trembled and vanished.

A shot cracked out.

Tuggie Bannock hissed and spat, catlike, her gums blood red, her teeth polished black. The angles changed again, so that the mirror-image was ancient and twisted, like the famous old hag/young girl illusion. She started to struggle.

The police sirens were coming closer and closer, their pitch and tone sliding into something else—

—Into the telephone ringing in the hall.

Eleanor woke with a grunt and stumbled, drugged by sleep, to answer the call.

It was Natalie, Eleanor knew that: but somehow she was different, her words disjointed and muffled by sobbing.

"What?" Eleanor lifted her hooked left hand and rubbed at her eyes with her knuckles. "Natalie, what are you saying?"

More garble, until it suddenly clicked in Eleanor's head like a jolt of electricity.

"E-Elean-nor it's S-Sarah-Jane . . . She . . . She . . . SJ is dead . . .

9

'A story is told that in 1792 in the Rhode Island coastal town of Narragansett, strange weather conditions made putting to sea impossible. For four days and three nights, from October 28th to midnight on Halloween Eve, lashing waves, frightful gales, thunder and lightnings and hailstones (some as big as hens' eggs) plagued the area. Most folk stayed in their houses and kept their doors and windows fast shut. The usual festivities of Hallowtide were abandoned that year, although friends and families gathered when they could to perform the traditional rituals, in honour of dead ancestors and to drive away the ghosts, spectres and strangers who walked abroad . . .

'It is hard to say so long afterwards where the line is to be drawn between fable and folklore, and folklore and reality. Certainly the people who lived in these and other isolated parts of the United States believed very firmly in goblins, imps, fairies and trolls — as well as the more familiar creatures of the dark; the ghosts, litches and vampires, who also have their origins in mediaeval Europe, and even further back in Ancient Greece and Mesopotamia, and on to the earliest centuries of human civilisation.

'Although this corpus of myth and legend shows enormous cultural diversity, it is possible to trace a few strands that span time and distance, linking many of the stories in a tantalising way. Many traditional tales tell of freak weather around the time of Halloween; caused, so it is said, by the weakening of barriers between this reality and another. When these barriers are at their weakest, so the beings of the other place cross over into our world. They come for many reasons, not all of them evil. But like the people of this earth, their aim is to survive and to flourish, and so they will do what they must to realise their purpose . . . '

A drop of water splashed down onto the page, and suddenly Eleanor found that she was unable to read the words, which blurred and swam before her eyes.

She wiped away her tears rather crossly, took a tissue from a box on her bedside table, and blew her nose. Her bed was littered with books, which lay, both open and closed, all around her as she sat with her back propped against the headboard. She set down the volume she'd been reading and selected another one, opened at a page she'd found earlier.

> 'Just as Man thinks himself above the lesser beasts, so in the lands of legend, other creatures put themselves above each other. Goblins, trolls, imps and woodland sprites assemble on the lower levels of importance. Above them one sees the Ancheri, Bassarab, and certain ghosts born under moonlight on nights of high magic . . .

'And beyond them all stand self-crowned nobles of the outer dark, beings of grandeur and majesty and power, that no human language has ever truly named. They stir base reality like water with their fingers, speak unknown words of such beauty and dread, that stones crumble to dust at the sound. They gaze at rosebuds, and those flowers flourish or die at their whim. They drink water touched by starlight, though history also records their taste for blood. Many of them aspire to such high purpose that they never take the trouble to cross the veil to our world. But some, in mischief perhaps, or for reasons beyond mortal understanding, come to earth at the time when the clockworks of the universe make this possible.

'At these times, the nameless assume human speech and can be identified. Two who visit often in the mythologies of Europe and early America are Tsepesh, whose body contains nothing but liquid ice, and who kills if scorned in love, and Tuggie Bannock, the vain and beautiful, who dreams of becoming perfect and locking herself inside that moment forever . . .

'These Returners are rarely seen, and should be avoided if possible, for they seek to tempt the wicked and the greedy like themselves. But if the lonely traveller or the simple peasant should encounter one or other, he should not run; but, rather, speak with kindness and respect. That might save his life — or else a weapon of unpolished iron, which the revenants abhor . . . "

There was a gentle knock at the door. Mrs. Trent eased it open and looked in on Eleanor, pressing her lips together on seeing her daughter sitting there, red-eyed and weary, yet unable to sleep. She pushed the door fully open and came through with a tray.

"Soup — chicken, your favourite — some tea, a couple of granary rolls . . . " Mrs. Trent put the tray down, "and something to help you sleep, Eleanor."

"Mum — I—"

Eleanor felt the grief rising again in a rush. She clenched her teeth and fists and fought it hard. Her mother watched the struggle.

"Let it out, honey. Don't keep such pain to yourself." Mrs. Trent was weeping too, at Natalie's unexpected and unwelcome news. She had not known Sarah Jane or her family very well, but any death in a small and close community touches every heart. She sat beside Eleanor and hugged her, while Eleanor turned the bright raw horror of SJ's death into rage against those who had caused it. But there was fear as well as fury, because Eleanor knew that she was probably the only one who had worked out, really worked out, what was happening. The uncanny weather, that strange feeling in the air, little coincidences that seemed like nothing; all gathered into the idea hanging like a stone in her mind . . . Together with her dream of Tuggie Bannock, which was surely much, much more than a normal nightmare.

"I wish," Eleanor said, gasping out each word because her chest was so tight, "I wish SJ and I had been friends . . . "

"You were friends deep down, baby,' Mrs. Trent assured her. "Sarah Jane knew you loved her dearly . . . All that silly rivalry — just teenage games . . . So cry it all out, and don't be ashamed. Never be ashamed, because this isn't weakness, it's strength . . . "

So they cried together, and soon afterwards Mrs. Trent made Eleanor sip her tea and sample the soup, then handed her the little Seconal tablet to help her sleep.

"Take tomorrow off school, if you like," Mrs. Trent counselled. "I'll ring in for you. They'll understand."

She picked up the tray as Eleanor cleared the bed of books and slipped under the blankets.

"Take the pill, darling. Rest is the best thing for you right now."

Eleanor nodded and offered a wan smile, and put the pill on her tongue. She snuggled down as her mother turned out the light and closed the door almost-to.

Then Eleanor spat the tablet into her hand, because turning your mind away from what was happening wasn't strength, it was weakness.

She slept on and off, dreaming broken dreams but normal ones. Except one, when some strange telepathy sent her soaring once more over the moonlit woodlands around Oxrun — a wide silvery circle that encompassed the high hills to the north and south, the old deserted farm two miles out on the western road, and as far as Hawksted to the east . . .

Then northward once more, so that the moon rode on Tuggie Bannock's shoulders and made the many windows of Abraham Craine's ancient mansion flash and glitter coldly in the distance.

Eleanor sat silently in an alien mind, just watching. Maybe Tuggie Bannock knew she was there, but the creature said nothing, did nothing, as she spun and spiralled above Beacon Hill, where heatless flames were shimmering about a ring of flat low stones.

And within the ring stood a stranger. Tall, statue-still, and clad all in black, moving slightly only when the shadow of his companion flickered across the grass as she settled close beside him. This, Eleanor knew, was the being known on earth as Tsepesh, the Returner.

"The circle is unbroken," Tuggie Bannock told him, running her long, long white fingers through her long, long dark hair. "Until the point of separation, they are ours — as many as will come willingly: but everyone else, if we choose."

Tsepesh smiled. And it was a staggeringly handsome smile, but one of such desolation that Eleanor jolted in her sleep, knowing then that the witch was aware of her.

"Send the moth away from the flame," Tsepesh whispered, gliding up to Tuggie Bannock and looking deep into her eyes, finding Eleanor out like a guilty secret.

"Yes, Magister—"

Then the words changed out of all recognition. Eleanor felt herself hurled back, as though she was a stone thrown high into the air, high and fast . . . Then falling, falling, falling — back into her own head.

She jumped awake in a tangle of blankets, and lay with her heart hammering.

Her bedside clock read eighteen minutes past five.

10

She let the phone ring a dozen times, and was about to give it up when Rob answered sleepily.

"Rob—"

"Huh . . . Eleanor, is that you?"

"I need a favour."

Rob chuckled and said that if she'd just give him time to iron his pyjamas . . . But Eleanor was in no mood for his humour and told him sharply that this was serious.

"I want you to drive me out of town—"

"And you said this was serious!"

"I want you to drive me out of town," Eleanor persisted, the fascination of her dream gripping her now, convincing her that it was the stuff reality is made of.

"Where to?"

"Anywhere, it doesn't matter. I need to see if we can do it."

"Well . . ."

He argued unconvincingly for another minute or so, before reluctantly agreeing. Eleanor said she'd meet him on the corner of Northland and Thorn, assuring him they should be back by around six-thirty, before her mother was awake.

She dressed quickly and was standing at the top of the stairs when Mrs. Trent stirred in her sleep and muttered Eleanor's name.

"Just using the bathroom," Eleanor whispered. She walked through to the bathroom, waited a minute and then flushed the lavatory, before hurrying down to the hallway and, carefully, out through the front door.

The night was chilly and early-hour still. The moon, a couple of days from full phase, hung bright and low beyond the Mainland Road. Higher up in the south, Jupiter shone with a white unwinking light. The constellations looked strange to Eleanor, but then she recognised Orion bleached by moonlight in the trees, and felt reassured that not everything was different.

She walked down the driveway and onto the sidewalk, enjoying the quietness and the empty feeling in her stomach, that reminded her of special days when excitement or nervousness had kept her awake; Christmas morning, her birthday, the eve of an important exam . . . That's what it felt like now, the eve of some hugely significant event that would come and go and leave Oxrun changed. It would leave *her* changed too, she knew that: for better or worse was up to her.

Across the way from the Jones's house on the corner of Thorn Road and Poplar stood an oak, its leaves rusting but plentiful. The tree would keep them far into the winter. Eleanor crossed and stood beneath it on its shadowed side, away from the street lamp, to wait for Rob.

Thorn Road looked odd from this angle, as so many things just lately had been tilted out of true. Her own house, its porch light a dazzling jewel, seemed unfamiliar. She felt like a stranger, newly arrived in town, wondering about the small and ordinary lives of the people who lived in these meagre dwellings . . .

Eleanor chuckled at the thought. Little people, hardly important at all, yet so concerned about the future that, for so many of them, would come to nothing. Didn't they ever dream about the stars? Didn't they ever realise their own ignorance: the tiny orbits within which they spun?

Something moved behind Eleanor in the hedgerow fringing the woodland. She jumped, but then thought it must be a mouse or a bank vole . . . seemed too small for a badger . . . But the owl would be waiting in the branch tops, ready to drop with its trap of claws . . . and in an hour or two the kestrel would be abroad, circling, caught on the hook of its hunger.

Eleanor felt tempted to go searching herself (for what, Eleanor? For what?), but then there came a flare of bright light and the silence broke and Rob came cruising down Northland, slowing and stopping as Eleanor stepped out to wave him down.

"This," he said as she slid in beside him, "had better be convincing."

As Rob turned down Fox Road and then left along King Street to reach the Mainland Road, Eleanor tried to explain; about her dreams, about all the research she'd done that had given her the clue to what was happening; about the old rituals of Halloween and how they echoed on through the centuries for a reason... About SJ's death, and the other deaths that were bound to follow.

Rob did not interrupt her. He drove on stony-faced, the corners of his mouth downturned. They passed the old apple orchard on Mainland, then the deserted farm, the remaining roof slates glowing with a slick of moonlight. And then the last building was behind them and they were moving through a landscape of hedges and trees sunk deep in the Connecticut night, miles away from anywhere...

Cut off, Eleanor reflected, lost and kept to itself, like Narragansett was... and how many other places, in how many other times?

"So," Rob said, that one syllable heavy with impatience and disbelief. "You're saying that on certain occasions — all to do with the time of year, the position of the stars, the geographical location — this world touches some other place. And that for a few days, as this happens, the things that live there can get to us?"

"And we could cross over into their world," Eleanor added, nodding. "You've summed it all up, Rob..." She watched his face, and saw the anger rising like a blush through his skin.

"This," he said tightly, "is just nuts!"

"But—" She could hardly believe his reaction. "But you saw the chaos caused in the town! Our universe and theirs are coming together. The barriers grow weak..."

"Yeah, and I'm a monkey's uncle!"

"You admitted it wasn't all rubbish when you saw the damage to your car: when you didn't feel safe out on the track to Beacon Hill!"

He smiled sheepishly. "Guess I spooked myself. I used to do it years ago, staying up to watch those old scary B-movies."

"It's more than that now," Eleanor said, choosing quiet confidence rather than sharp admonition. "Can't you feel it? The land is alive."

"Oh, quit it!" Rob said, his temper flaring. "If you could just see yourself now!"

"I know I'm right," she told him, and then realised that he knew it too. "Rob, what are you hiding from? Why won't you just let go and believe it?"

He drew in his breath very deeply, then let it out with a shudder.

"Don't you think," he said, his voice broken, "that if all of this was real, Dad would know all about it? He'd have seen it coming, maybe years ago, he — he'd h-have . . . "

Of course, Eleanor thought, that was it. That was why Rob was not allowing himself to see the truth. And it explained a lot . . .

Rob senior *did* know, and *had* seen it coming. That's why he had taken the lectureship at Hawksted. Halloween had always been a big thing in Oxrun Station. The lie of the land was just right, and the people went through the old rituals that ran in their blood, some in ignorance, but many, perhaps, with an inkling of understanding: like Kay Ross, who through superstition and blind belief was hoping to find her dream.

But what was Doctor Robert Gill hoping to find? That was the question that occurred now to Eleanor, as it must have occurred to Rob long ago.

"Rob," Eleanor said gently, "if we weren't fascinated by the unknown, we'd never bother to look there and add to what is known." She thought about the story of circles that Rob's father had told her. "Personally, I admire Robert Gill far more for daring to ask, and being prepared to accept the answers . . . "

Rob slammed on the brakes. Eleanor surged forward in her seatbelt, which locked and snapped her back.

She thought she'd offended him; provoked him beyond any anger he could control. He turned to look at her, and she could see the acceptance in his eyes.

"Okay." He turned off the engine. "Okay, it's pointless pretending. I know you're right, because I'd half worked it out for myself. All those hours I spent in Hawksted library, checking on what Dad told me, hoping and praying that his head was just full of nonsense. But it's not. Of course it's not. They visit us at Hallowtide... They come..."

They come to feed, Eleanor thought then, shivering. They come to take back. They are the kestrels. We are the mice.

"Oh, Rob, I'm so glad you told me this... We're going to need each other so much..."

She reached out and stroked Rob's face, her hand very pale against his skin. With her fingertips she stroked Rob's eyelids and touched the teardrops she found there, and brought them to her lips and tasted the salt.

Embarrassed perhaps, or still frightened, Rob turned back and reached for the ignition keys.

Then he frowned.

"Wait a minute. Where the hell are we?"

Eleanor followed his gaze through the windshield, to the trees, to the hills. They could not be more than a couple of miles out on the Mainland Road. Both of them knew exactly where they were, and yet driving on to any definite destination seemed impossible.

"Turn off the headlights," Eleanor told him. Rob did so, and the sky was hung with pale auroral curtains through which the stars gleamed faintly: the ring of confusion put there by Tuggie Bannock while she and Tsepesh went about their work.

"Well I'll be damned," Rob said. And beside him, lost in wonder and terror, Eleanor thought for the first time how that might just be true.

But at city bidding there be bound
To do all things that I bid them do
Starke be their sinewes therewith
And their lives mightless
And their eyes sightless!
Dread and doubt
Them enclose about . . .

The little riddle rhyme circled in Eleanor's thoughts like a fading song of childhood. She was about to whisper it, but Rob leaned over and kissed her. He kissed her deep, his tongue pushing past her lips.

Eleanor groaned, licked his mouth and kissed him, lips, cheek and neck, drawing back and smiling as the heat rose in her.

Smiling at the healthy heartbeat that was pulsing in his throat.

11

The spark did not light to a fire. From the outset, Eleanor knew this wasn't right. She was very fond of Rob, maybe too fond for her own good, and sometimes she thought there was nothing more she would like than to make love with him.

But now, as he fumbled for her buttons, she saw what was wrong, as someone inside her smiled and licked its lips, and a black fingernail trailed along the line of Rob's carotid artery.

"Send the moth," Eleanor said, slowly and distinctly, "away from the flame."

There was a sudden change of pressure within the car, as though a hurricane was blowing by outside. The temperature dropped to zero and the windshield crusted instantly with frost.

"Holy shit!" Rob yelped as Eleanor pushed him away and focused her mind on banishing Tuggie Bannock.

The Buick bucked and rocked, its dashboard lights glowing dangerously bright, then fading. It grew darker, so dark that for a moment or two Eleanor couldn't see a hand in front of her face. And while Rob was starting to panic, she remained steady and strong.

She reached for his hands and grabbed them. Held them.

"Rob, stay calm. It'll pass. It'll pass."

The noise and movement lifted to a crescendo. All around the car the air howled and swirled, spinning leaves, twigs and small stones into the windshield like hail. The night swarmed with half-seen figures and faces, among which were some that Eleanor thought she recognised.

Then with a final bang it was over. The presence left them and went screaming off into the distance, leaving Rob, white-faced, locked in his seat; and Eleanor grinning fiercely as she realised that she'd defeated Tuggie Bannock. Whatever it was, and wherever it had come from, the bitch was not unbeatable.

"We can go home now," Eleanor said calmly. "We're safe for a while. Call me tomorrow . . . and — I love you, Rob . . ."

She kissed him lightly on the lips. Without a word Rob started the car, turned it and drove back to Oxrun; while Eleanor gazed out at the sky draped with the lovely aurora that, for the next two days and nights, would keep the town hidden away from the rest of the world.

She slept until ten a.m., and woke when her mother looked in with a cup of tea.

"I called the school," Mrs. Trent explained, "and I spoke with Mrs. Wallace. She told me that a number of pupils are absent. Some, obviously, because of Sarah Jane's death and that of another girl, Ursula Strong. There's also a flu virus going around . . . Apparently it's affecting the whole town, children and adults alike. Mrs. Duffey next door was telling me that her husband Jack has been off work since Monday . . . the school's letting everyone go home if they want."

Mrs. Trent put the tea on Eleanor's bedside table, then walked over to swish open the curtains, still talking. Eleanor was only half listening. The virus story was a good one. It would help people to come to terms with their weakness and confusion, and would explain away the nightmares they would be suffering — the proud pale faces that visited them in the dark.

" . . . so you just rest, my love, and—"

"Oh," Eleanor said, "I'll need to go into school . . . some things I must do." And, before her mother could put up an argument, "The fresh air will do me good, Mom. I won't stay the whole day. And I do feel much better. I had a really good rest."

Mrs. Trent smiled, giving up because she knew that Eleanor would not.

"Well you make sure you don't overtax yourself . . . But I must say, it is good to see you looking so cheerful." Eleanor sipped her tea, then gulped it with relish.

"Did Mrs. Duffey say anything about the weather damage?"

"The electricity seems to be restored most everywhere. But the phones are still out, apart from local services . . . Oh, and the TV and radio are affected. There's no signal at all from the radio station at Harley—"

"Makes sense," Eleanor muttered. Then, as her mother's eyebrows knitted. "I mean, makes sense that the lightning would have interfered with TV signals."

"Yes, I suppose it does," Mrs. Trent said, coming over to plump Eleanor's pillow and straighten her blankets. She looked pained. "But I hope it clears soon. I don't want to miss the next episode of *Dude Ranch Farm* . . ."

The atmosphere at the High School was strange, a mixture of tension, sadness and excitement. A lot of kids had taken advantage of the unexpected holidays. Eleanor felt it as soon as she stepped over the threshold. She knew she could not linger here for long, nor would she want to.

She went to her locker to collect the notes that would have provided the final touches to her project: would have done, if the whole thing had been no more than a mid-term assignment. But as things stood, the project could never truly be finished. There was still a great deal she didn't know, and a lot that had not yet happened, and much that went beyond simple words.

These few days would surely haunt her forever. And no matter what she wrote, who afterwards would believe her, or even understand?

A sudden commotion made Eleanor turn around, as a bunch of sixth graders came streaming down the corridor, raggedy gowns flapping, papier mâché masks waving madly, empty-eyed and grimacing. They made spook noises as they rushed past, and two leaped at Eleanor and yelled "Boo!". She ignored them, watching them out of sight to their art class . . .

Moments later, their high singsong voices echoed back down the empty corridor: "Halloween, Halloween, strangest sights I've ever seen . . . "

Maybe, she thought, it's a meaningless rhyme to them, part of the ritual to get candy and run wild for a few hours . . . But how do I know? Who, amongst the population of Oxrun Station, has made it more than a holiday festival? Who knows of the arrival of Tsepesh and Tuggie Bannock . . . and is allowing it to happen?

On her way out, Eleanor dropped by at the office to register her visit and to say she was keeping a doctor's appointment. Mrs. Brannigan, the school secretary, thanked her for that courtesy and hoped she'd be feeling better again soon.

"I don't know what it is, but I've never seen so many absences before . . . all week long — and now today—" She waved a well-manicured hand at the day books on her desk. "This flu bug is a nuisance too — adds to my paperwork, anyway!" Mrs. Brannigan laughed, then became serious and leaned closer. "But I reckon no small number of these are because of Halloween."

"Oh?" Eleanor felt a shiver ripple down her neck.

Mrs. Brannigan nodded. "Kids getting ready for their trick-or-treating; making their costumes, carving out their pumpkin lanterns . . . I blame the TV myself, putting all these ideas into kids' heads. You'd think a good education would be more important to them, wouldn't you?"

"Yes," Eleanor said automatically. "You would."

"It's all too commercialised for me," Mrs. Brannigan continued, as Eleanor took a pace backward and half turned.

"Well, I really must be—"

"It's Halloween this and Halloween that—"

"I'm going to be late . . . "

"Halloween, Halloween," Mrs. Brannigan chuckled, as Eleanor made her way to the main doors, the woman's voice echoing behind her: "Strangest sights I've ever seen . . . "

She walked along Steuben Avenue and turned left on to Centre Street to reach the library. Council workmen were clearing up the last of the damage and stretching lines of bunting between the street lamps, and many individual shop owners were arranging window displays, or putting up signs announcing weekend special offers.

Eleanor stopped in front of the Playland toy store, its big front window crammed with Halloween merchandise: ghostly shrouds, plastic bats, little devil figures on sticks, skeleton puppets, witches' costumes . . . and tucked down beside a pyramid of orange sponge jack-o-lanterns, a pile of little wicker boxes containing 'promise dolls'.

Eleanor was intrigued, but at the same time she felt pressured to move on. She wanted to find out more about what was happening, realising now that the creatures who had stepped over into our world would be stronger tonight — and increasingly so until the break of All Hallows on November 1st. If something wasn't done quickly, then goodness knows what Tsepesh and Tuggie Bannock would get up to . . .

Eleanor looked at herself in the window glass, and for the first time wondered if she would survive. Poor Sarah Jane had been taken away so quickly, so easily . . . and now Tsepesh knew her name too, and might want from her what SJ had given him, at the cost of her life.

But at the same time, Eleanor understood the truth behind the outwardly absurd little superstitions she had read about, and so with that thought in mind, she walked into Playland.

She visited the shop occasionally, and usually with David, who came in to buy computer games; she knew Mr. Mabey, who was standing behind the counter now, arranging a display of grotesque rubber creatures, all leering.

He turned to smile at Eleanor.

"Good morning — Eleanor Trent, isn't it?"

"That's right, sir, yes. Good morning." She pointed at the window. "I noticed your promise dolls, and—"

"Ah!" Mr. Mabey beamed. "It's the best dollar's-worth you'll spend this side of Christmastide. And I'm running a special offer on them for Halloween: two for $1.75, four for $3.50."

"It sounds like a bargain — but what do they do?"

"Well . . . " Mr. Mabey was tall and lean, painfully thin. The pose he struck now reminded Eleanor of a contemplative scarecrow, one bony hand on hip, the other lifted to stroke his chin.

"Well, promise dolls," he said slowly, "can be used in various ways. At certain special times — and Halloween is definitely one of those! — you can exchange a doll for a promise from whoever receives it. They are also used in place of lost souls."

"What do you mean?" Eleanor wondered. Mr. Mabey shrugged and scratched his head, which was bald save for a white cobwebby fringe at the back and sides.

"I mean that if a soul needs to be saved, then you offer the doll in its place—"

"Who do you give it to?" There was a slight urgency in Eleanor's voice that caused Mr. Mabey to look at her oddly.

"Traditionally, to whoever has come to take that soul away. These days," Mr. Mabey said, looking mildly disapproving, "young people tend to pass them to each other. There's a little game kids play: if you can sneak a doll into someone's clothing, then they owe you a promise."

Eleanor thought it was a good game, but didn't dare say so, because she knew what kind of promises Mr. Mabey had in mind.

She dug in her jeans pocket. "I'll take — oh, I only have $2.75 . . ."

"Hmm." Mr. Mabey looked at the single bill and spill of coins in Eleanor's hand. "Well, since your brother is a good customer, I'll let you have three for $2.50 . . . "

He reached into a bag on the countertop and counted out three tiny dolls; just flicks of straw wound with bright cotton, with dots for eyes, nose and mouth. He dropped them into a wicker box which reminded Eleanor of a coffin, and passed them across.

She gave Mr. Mabey all of her money. He smiled and handed her a quarter back. "The box," he told her, "always comes free."

She spent the next two hours in the library, at first aware of Miss Ross's frequent suspicious glances, but then she became so absorbed in her studying that she ceased to notice or care.

Eleanor dipped into a world of dark mythology and tangled folklore, where scattered stories and vague references gradually gathered to form a picture that made sense.

She knew now, and believed, that the great seasonal festivals existed for a real and very practical purpose. Halloween embodied the rites of passage where worlds touched, and wove protections around those who wanted nothing of it. Some were content with what they had, and waited fearfully for Hallowtide to pass. Others tried as far as they could to take advantage of the situation for their personal gain, on both sides of the divide . . . So, Eleanor reasoned, when the Returners arrived, then they were *expected*. And more than that, they were allowed to take back what they wanted, in exchange for certain gifts—

Nearby, a browsing customer, Rena Viser, who was in Eleanor's history class, dropped a book. The loud *clap!* as it hit the floor flat startled Eleanor back to reality. She rubbed her eyes, gathered up her own selection and walked over to the issuing desk.

Miss Ross sniffed rather censorially as she stamped the books and slid them back to Eleanor.

"Much good they'll do you, I'm sure," she said. "Simple knowledge is never enough!"

"What are *you* hoping for, Miss Ross?" Eleanor asked, with no challenge in her voice, just curiosity. For a moment the woman said nothing. Then she gave a splintered laugh full of envy and pain. One or two people reading in armchairs near the window looked up.

Miss Ross's eyes were bright and glittering as she ran them over Eleanor's body.

"When I was young, I was beautiful — can you believe that?"

Eleanor nodded. "Yes, Miss Ross, I can . . . "

"All the boys courted me, and all the girls envied me. My hair was black as midnight, and I wore it long — all the way down to my waist. Ah, the times I could have offered my favours to the handsome young men who walked me home from school! But I was saving them for one boy, for one special boy who loved me, I was sure of it. But he was shy, and his parents dreamed of great things for him, and they did not entirely approve of me, the daughter of a shopkeeper . . . "

The woman's tone became wistful as her eyes, sparkling with tears, gazed back into the past.

"I made so many plans in my head! And once, Timothy took me out to dinner. It was like a dream come true. I couldn't tell him just how I felt, of course. That wasn't appropriate. But he said that he found me very attractive, and that one day he'd be free of his parents and then . . . Well, it's not important. They were dark days. The war began and Timothy started college, and then, I heard, he received his draft papers and went out to fight . . . "

Miss Ross smiled bleakly, as Eleanor guessed the rest.

"And you never married? Even when you knew he was not coming back?"

"Oh, I waited, hoping that in the confusion of war there'd been a mistake. There had not. And I might even have come to terms with it all, if his mother — his evil, spiteful mother! — had not sent me a photograph of Timothy . . . A keepsake, she said in her first and only letter . . . "

An elderly couple had come up behind Eleanor to have their books stamped. Miss Ross ignored them as she fumbled in her handbag, took out her wallet and slipped a photograph from it to show Eleanor.

It was a small black-and-white snapshot, creased along one corner, of a young man, smiling and handsome, with his arm around a pretty blonde girl who was looking coyly at the camera.

On an impulse, Eleanor turned the snap over. There was a brief message written in a neat and precise hand, in faded ink. Eleanor recognised the quote from Shakespeare:

> *Hereafter, in a better world than this,*
> *I shall desire more love and knowledge of you.*
>   *Till then, take care, Tim. All my love, Annette*

The elderly gentleman standing behind Eleanor coughed impatiently. Eleanor handed back the photograph. "I'm sorry," she said. "I'm terribly sorry."

Miss Ross's expression became distant.

"Everything's possible. You've read the books, my dear:
> *And beyond them all . . . stand beings of grandeur and*
> *majesty and power . . . Who stir reality like water with*
> *their fingers . . .*

I have not given up hope."

"I almost have," the old gentleman said irritably.

Miss Ross smiled thinly with her lips, turned her attention to the waiting couple and did not look at Eleanor again.

The street seemed close and rather humid after the dry, cool atmosphere of the library, and the sun shone with a brassy and quite painful light between gathering rain clouds, black and silver tumbled together in chaos. Just a few hours earlier it had been bright and clear . . .

It was approaching two p.m. Eleanor decided that she would call Rob: they'd meet later and together they'd work out what to do for the best. She knew it was quite pointless to go to the police. And escape was impossible. Anyone who tried to leave or enter Oxrun Station would become hopelessly lost, until they turned around and headed back to town. The most that could be done would be to gather together the people who mattered to her and keep them safe — or at least warn them of the danger they were in.

With that in mind, as Eleanor saw the callbox ahead, she thought she'd phone Natalie first, who would probably appreciate some cheering up.

She tapped out the number and waited, listening to the distant burring of the ring-tone through heavy static on the line. Then a voice said hello and some other words that were lost in the flare and crackle of interference.

"Oh, hi, Mrs. Dayne. This is Eleanor. I wondered, could I talk to Nat, if she—"

Mrs. Dayne interrupted her, speaking quickly and, Eleanor thought, sounding in some distress. If anything the static was growing worse, as the first fat drops of rain began to fall on the glass of the telephone booth.

"Mrs. Dayne — hello, can you hear me? I can't quite make out—"

Thunder boomed overhead. Eleanor flinched. People were hurrying into shop doorways, and the council workers were climbing quickly down off their ladders. The wind was gathering, spitting rain across the yellow-bricked roadway on Centre Street.

"Mrs. Dayne—"

" . . . Natalie's very ill, she . . . "

More thunder, and some tines of white lightning stabbing at the hills beyond the town.

"Can I speak to her!" Eleanor shouted. And the thin, torn voice came back:

" . . . very ill. She's in hospital, Eleanor. I don't know what to do . . . "

12

Eleanor ran, careless of the rain, down Centre Street and right into King Street. Increasingly heavy thunder and strobelight flickers of lightning accompanied her dash towards the hospital, three blocks down. Very soon the storm was so intense that she could see just a few yards ahead, as the slashing sheets of water whipped and stung her face and hands.

An ambulance sluiced past her, heading into town, its wheels displacing spray in a graceful cascade. The driver flicked on the whooping alarm klaxon and the sound made Eleanor jump. She stopped to catch her breath, bent over, hands on her knees, while water trickled from her hair and down over her already sodden jeans.

She reached her destination dizzy and exhausted, like a bedraggled kitten seeking shelter. The receptionist looked at her with a mixed smile of amusement and sympathy, while a passing porter took pity. "Here, hen," he called, and offered her a white ward-issue towel.

"I've come to visit a friend," Eleanor said, her gasping easing off now. "Natalie Dayne. She was brought in a short while ago, I understand . . ."

"I'll check," the receptionist said, as Eleanor contrasted the woman's prim and efficient manner with her own state of disarray and, she feared, her growing loss of control over the situation.

The woman glanced up from her computer screen. "Yes. Room E3. We're keeping her in for observation and to run some tests."

"What's wrong with her?" Eleanor felt she already knew, and that all she would be given was a logical, medical opinion, based on the limitations of human misunderstanding.

"Well, I'm not sure I should say, miss. Are you related at all?"

"I'm a school friend," Eleanor said, her patience worn thin by fear and helplessness. "I'm her best friend. My name is Eleanor Trent, I live at—"

Eleanor paused as the receptionist reacted to the name.

"I see. Well, Miss Dayne was admitted in a state of shock, and very enervated. She was quite confused. Doctor Collett, our resident consultant, suspects incipient anaemia, but—"

"*Then can I go see her.*" Eleanor made the question sound like a demand. The receptionist's eyes flashed, for she was not used to being challenged. But she nodded and offered a tightly controlled smile.

"Certainly, Miss Trent. Take the elevator to the first floor, then turn left and it's the third room along."

"Thanks," Eleanor said without meaning it, glancing back with a grin as the prim woman leaned over her desk to look at the puddle of rainwater she had left behind.

Eleanor was surprised to note, upon leaving the elevator, that all of the rooms along this corridor were private. She had no doubt that the Daynes had medical insurance, but nothing substantial enough to warrant this degree of luxury. She wondered who would be paying the bill . . .

But her surprise turned to confusion, and then, darkly, into suspicion as she entered . . .

She saw Natalie, as pale as her pillow, lying in a bed opposite the window. There was a tube feeding blood into her arm from a bag hung on the wall. Her biomonitor bleeped weakly with a slow, languid pulse. She hardly seemed to be breathing.

A man was stooping over her. For an instant Eleanor thought this was Doctor Collett. But then he stood and Eleanor recognised Robert Gill. He turned on hearing her.

"Eleanor. Come in. I had a feeling you'd find your way here . . . Um, I'd like to introduce you—"

There was someone else standing away from the door. He was tall, his white skin marbled with veins, his hair seeming so glossy black that Eleanor felt sure he must be using a dye. He watched Eleanor with eyes so cold and passionless that she was automatically revolted. But at least he was merely a man, when her fears right now were of things that were not even human.

"This is Abraham Craine," Gill said quietly. The man was wearing a dark astrakhan coat and black kid-leather gloves. His hands were resting on the globed silver top of an ebony cane that reached to the floor. Delicately, Abraham Craine leant the stick against a chair and plucked his glove from his left hand, which he extended. Eleanor, embarrassed and at a loss, offered her own left hand, its wrist twisted, the fingers curled. Craine took it and held it for several silent seconds, while Eleanor squirmed inwardly and wanted only to run.

"So," Craine said at last. "This is the resourceful Miss Trent. I'm delighted to meet you."

The words, like the man, held the coldness of a lizard on a moonlit rock. Eleanor neither trusted him nor believed him. She was instinctively repelled and frightened by him. But she said, politely, as she had been taught:

"Delighted to meet you too, sir. I, er, I didn't realise you knew Natalie."

"Natalie?" Craine replied. He slid his gaze to look at the girl in the bed.

"Mr. Craine happened to be in the hospital," Gill interrupted. "He's naturally been worried by this, urn, spate of mystery illnesses."

"The flu virus," Eleanor said flatly, meeting Gill's gaze steadily, "or the anaemia?" She did not trust him for a minute. Craine was here for other reasons, all of these excuses as blatantly artificial as his hair colour.

Gill didn't answer, but looked away so that Craine could take the lead.

He smiled, glancing first at Gill, then at Eleanor.

"I think we'd better — what's the phrase? — come clean, eh, Robert? Otherwise I can see that this young lady is going to upset some rather fine balances. Sit down," he told Eleanor.

There was a small round glass coffee table by the window, and two chairs. Eleanor sat in one. Craine took the other.

"I'll come straight to the point," Craine said, as Eleanor stared him out with the angry, defiant expression she kept reserved for unjust schoolteachers and, sometimes, for when she quarrelled badly with her mother. If Craine was affected by the insolent look, he kept his irritation well hidden.

"Let me say firstly that all you have learned is true. Doctor Gill here has been telling me about your project. Very enterprising,

Miss Trent. But dangerously naïve."

"I don't know what you mean—" Eleanor began.

"You know exactly what I mean!" Craine hissed, his spittle speckling Eleanor's face. She flinched away from him.

He said, more quietly, but with no less menace, "What you have discovered really happens. Here at Oxrun Station, the fabric of the cosmos unweaves from time to time. It doesn't occur every year: it hasn't happened, in fact, for nearly a lifetime. But the people in their simple routines keep the rituals alive, for when the Returners come again."

"But why?" Eleanor wanted to know, expecting Craine to laugh at her. He didn't.

"Because the creatures you have seen possess powers beyond our understanding. Their knowledge is not the knowledge of physics and chemistry, but of enchantment. Their bodies and lifeblood owe nothing to earthly biology . . . "

"What they can give us," Gill added, "is beyond worth or description. They can end hunger and war. They have the ability to confer eternal life . . . "

"So then," Eleanor asked quietly, "after all these centuries — why haven't they done it?"

Craine chuckled softly in his throat. "They have, my girl, to those who respect their ways."

Something clicked in Eleanor's mind, a tiny circuit of understanding. She looked at Abraham Craine anew, and with a rising horror; at those unnatural hands, the face that looked like moulded plastic, the overtinted hair that, nevertheless, seemed leached of all vigour.

And Craine watched her dawning realisation with a gleam in his eyes. "But you get nothing for nothing, child. To get, you must give . . . "

"What do you give?"

"Easy access," Gill said. "We let them in, the beings you call Tsepesh and Tuggie Bannock, and their retinue of lesser creatures. We give them Oxrun Station for the three days leading up to Halloween. The people practise their rituals, follow the old folklore. In return, they see the future and receive other personal gifts."

"Will Miss Ross the librarian find a husband?"

"She will find an end to her pain," Craine answered ambiguously.

"Will you grow young again, Mr. Craine?" Eleanor asked. And he smiled, and nodded. "But what price do you pay . . . ?"

Without wanting to — because admitting it was an agony — Eleanor stared across at Natalie, whose life had all but been sucked away by a single kiss . . . just as Tsepesh had destroyed SJ, and how many others, as though they were cattle.

"No . . . Oh no . . . "

"Eleanor." Gill's voice sounded sharp and commanding. "Be sensible about this. We can not only survive the encounter — we can profit from it!"

"You bastards," Eleanor whispered in return. Then her anger gathered like a wave and crashed through her. "You filthy, murdering bastards!"

She made to stand up. Craine moved in a flash and grabbed her hand, holding it trembling in front of her face.

"Look at this! It's a deformity! But it can be cured . . . "

He pushed Eleanor back into her seat, and settled again himself.

"You are a pretty girl. And you'll live to be a beautiful woman, having all you ever wanted: a fine husband, bonny children, a wonderful house filled with possessions — a splendid career, if you want it . . . "

"Will they make me happy?"

Craine laughed sneeringly and pointed at her hooked left hand. "Will that?"

A silence fell between them. Outside, the storm was abating and the flat expanse of hospital roofs lay gleaming in fitful sunshine, reflecting a picture of quickly dispersing clouds.

"I have a feeling the weather will hold for the street celebrations," Craine said mock-cheerfully. "And tomorrow, the night of the party. You'll be there my dear, of course . . . "

"Of course," Eleanor said. Gill breathed a deep sigh of relief.

"Good girl. Let's, uh, let's take you home, Eleanor. You must stop worrying. I'm sure we can do something to help your friend Natalie."

Eleanor nodded and stood up slowly, as though terribly tired. She went over to Natalie and leaned across her. It seemed that her life had shrunk down to a tiny spark, flickering on the edge of extinction. Tsepesh, Eleanor remembered, was the creature whose blood was liquid ice, and who killed if scorned in love. Perhaps he would visit Natalie once more, to offer her a final chance . . . Unless, Eleanor thought deep in her secret heart, I can get to him first.

She dug in her pocket and found the flimsy box holding the three promise dolls. She took one, a little girl of straw with an orange cotton dress, and wound it into Natalie's hair.

"Eleanor?" Gill said, lifting his coat from a side chair.

"Just a keepsake. To show her I won't forget her."

Craine reached the door first and politely held it open for Eleanor, who smiled graciously at him — before slamming it back in his face and sprinting down the corridor.

She heard Craine bellowing in rage, and Gill's accompanying yell of alarm. Both men came pounding after her, but she was fast, and she was desperate.

She reached the elevator just as the doors were beginning to close, and laughed aloud because that only happened in the movies. But, rather than enter the elevator, she pressed for the fourth floor, then ducked away through the nearby swing door for the emergency stairs.

It was a simple strategy that she didn't expect to work, so she was surprised when she reached a rear exit to the hospital unchallenged. She walked past a delivery bay and a row of huge industrial trashcans, leaving through the wide-open security gates as a van from a linen supplier drove by in the other direction. From Devon Street she circled round to Chancellor Avenue, then away from the centre and through suburban streets where there were hedges to hide behind and, if necessary, the woods to the south of the town just a few minutes' walk away.

Eleanor remembered there was a callbox on the corner of Western Road. She used her last quarter to phone home, explaining to her mother that Rob had invited her out for a meal; that she was feeling much better for her walk; and that she'd be home late, so not to worry. Mrs. Trent swallowed the lie whole, and Eleanor blessed her for it.

Then she dialled the operator and asked for a collect call to be put through to Rob Gill junior at Hawksted College. Eleanor said she'd wait while he was found.

She realised the chance she was taking, not knowing how much Rob knew about his father: not knowing if he, too, was co-operating with Abraham Craine's foul plans... Not knowing even if she was important enough to Rob for him to risk his life in this, her bid to fight back.

The line, which had been crackling faintly like a distant fire, went dead for a few moments — then Rob's voice was there, clear and close. He sounded very concerned.

"Eleanor!"

"Rob, I need your help..." Her plea was brushed aside by his excitement and horror.

"Eleanor, listen. I've been checking up on some of the things you've been telling me, and—"

"Rob, you must help me!"

"Narragansett suffered a forty-four per cent population drop in the autumn of 1792," Rob went on. "And again in 1842, and 1896... I've been checking the census for Oxrun Station. The same thing happened here in 1873: a massive, sudden drop in population in the autumn of that year... What do you mean, I must help you?"

Eleanor explained quickly and briefly, leaving out Robert Gill's complicity with Craine. Nor did she go into detail right then about her wish to retaliate. Rob listened, then told her to stay calm.

"Where are you now?"

Eleanor opened her mouth to say, then thought better of it.

"Rob, I'll meet you where we drove to last night — you remember where we watched the moonlight on the roof."

"I remember. How long?"

"Um, thirty minutes. And take care," she advised, though without saying exactly why.

She replaced the handset and left the callbox, doubling back down Quentin Avenue and King Street to reach the Mainland Road. It was thickly lined with trees, from the edge of the town onwards, and where the trees thinned the hedgerows gave ample cover.

Eleanor set off towards the deserted farmhouse at a jog, which became a more leisurely walk as she realised she'd reach her destination in plenty of time.

There were, in fact, ten minutes to go before Rob was due to rendezvous. Eleanor turned off the highway and walked down the grassy track towards the farm.

The time was a little past 3.30 p.m. and the afternoon was advancing. Yet the sunlight was unseasonably strong and the air rather damp after the downpour.

Eleanor reached the crumbling hull of the old farmhouse and sat in the shade of the east wall, where she could look back towards the town and see any approaching traffic. But the road looked deserted and the quietness was complete, and for the first time that day Eleanor felt relaxed; because, she reasoned, she had taken a stand and was doing something positive.

She thought fiercely: I won't be herded and slaughtered like cattle, by the creatures of the night!

A field away was the abandoned apple orchard, its trees long untended, its fruit now maggoty and neglected. Eleanor's eyes had been focused there as her thoughts wandered, but now she paid more attention . . .

One of the trees was moving, of that there could be no doubt. Its branches twisted and swayed, and a little flurry of dust and grass and leaves was spinning about the trunk.

A faint unease clenched in Eleanor's stomach. Because now the tree had turned to face her and seemed somehow to be moving closer amidst its gowns of whirling litter.

She stood up, preparing to run. Maybe it was someone in a jeep hurrying nearer. Or a spooked horse from the meadow. Or more freak weather. Or . . .

Or none of these, as Eleanor now realised.

The tumbling mass hurtled towards her, and the air was pierced through by a scream, as thin and keen as a needle.

Eleanor flung her hands up to protect her face and eyes.

The madness was all around her.

Then a hand settled softly on her shoulder.

"The moth," said the voice of Tuggie Bannock, "has returned to the flame."

13

She was an ancient witch, Eleanor understood just then: a haunter of quiet places and lonely souls. Summoned by the forlorn and the lost, she preyed upon their weakness to find her own perfection. How long this must have gone on! And yet how fruitlessly. Tuggie Bannock had nothing that Eleanor wanted. She was a sad, spent force, a creature to be pitied rather than hated and destroyed.

Sensing this, Tuggie Bannock stepped beside Eleanor and held her crippled left hand. Eleanor was no longer afraid, because now she divined something of this predator's purpose, and knew she was strong enough to resist it.

> *Eleanor, I've seen you where you never was,*
> *And where one day you'll be:*
> *And yet you in that very same place*
> *May still be seen by me . . .*

It was a human riddle, written long ago and learned by children in kindergarten through the generations. Eleanor recognised the puzzle and the solution, as Tuggie Bannock waved her right hand in the air, and the horizon shimmered, and in front of Eleanor's face a mirror appeared of quivering mercury, hanging there by itself, its ripples ebbing.

"Gaze into the eye of time. Look the future in the face. Find the way your life will rhyme—"

"And cause no-one disgrace . . . " Eleanor smiled as her mirror image changed, her hair growing even longer and more luxurious, her figure filling out, her face reflecting the strength and beauty of her years — and her left hand melting like mist, the fingers uncurling, the locked bones righting themselves. She felt an exquisite pain, and a longing so intense that she almost — she almost — reached out to the illusion and accepted it, taking it to her heart and so falling under Tuggie Bannock's power.

"Honour the authors of thy being, daughter; thy mother and father, and thy perfector . . . "

It was the kind of thing the enchantress would have said back in 1873, Eleanor mused, when she was last here. What happened to her victims then? How many of them discovered the happiness that the witch could never find?

Eleanor shook her head as her throat tightened and hot tears squeezed into her eyes. Years ago her father had left the family: walked out with no warning to live with a much younger woman, a beautiful woman who would, no doubt, work him like a puppet until a more suitable man came along. Eleanor had never lost the sense of betrayal, or the knowledge that beauty was not truth. That was all she had known, and all she needed to know.

She waved the image away with her left hand, and with her right broke open the little box in her pocket and offered a promise doll to the dark figure at her side.

For a moment or two, Tuggie Bannock said nothing. Then her fine and sensual mouth began to open, wider and wider, until it was cavernous: a cavern lined with nails and blades and blood.

She roared, and it was the thunder of the waterfall and the avalanche of rocks: it was the height of a storm, the fastest hurricane that ever blew across the prairie. It was a sound of pure desolation and of utter defeat.

She staggered away from Eleanor, her ragged gowns whirling, her long hair whipped by elemental forces. Eleanor closed her eyes in terror, but kept her hand open.

Slowly the turmoil faded, the sagging door of the farmhouse stopped banging in its frame, and when Eleanor looked again, she was alone.

And her palm was empty.

Rob and Eleanor listened to each other quietly, each feeling numbed by the magnitude of the truth. Rob looked tired, admitting he had been at Hawksted library since the early morning, finding evidence to back the theory that had been forming in his head, and which Eleanor had more or less confirmed.

Eleanor, for her part, seemed livelier and stronger than Rob had ever seen her. He asked her why, but she refused to answer: it was a private and intimate thing.

They had steered clear of the town, but were careful not to stray too close to the circle of confusion in the countryside around. Eleanor suspected that Tuggie Bannock, having failed to win her over, would try to prevent any further interference. She suggested to Rob that they return to Oxrun.

"There are people in danger. People I care about . . . Natalie, David and Mom, your father . . . "

Rob gave a hoot of laughter. "I think my father can look after himself! From what you've told me, and from what I've learned, I reckon he's gone along with Abe Craine so that he . . . "

"What, Rob?"

"So that he can go with Tsepesh and Tuggie Bannock into their world, when the time comes. He's always been an explorer, usually through books. But now he has a chance to *go there*, to *see* for himself . . . " Rob checked his watch. "And that's what he'll do, some time in the next eight hours."

"By then," Eleanor added, "it'll all be over. One way or another."

They decided to look in on Natalie first, partly because the hospital was close to the western edge of town, but more importantly because of the condition she'd been in. And because of a growing conviction in Eleanor's mind that Natalie had been deliberately put into a quiet private room, paid for probably by Craine. He had arranged it all. Natalie was an offering to Tsepesh: the gift of a life in return for the endless life that Abraham Craine so desperately sought.

There was every chance, of course, that Craine himself would still be searching for Eleanor, maybe in the vicinity of the hospital. Or he might have spoken with Chief Stockton, who'd put out an alert. Rob's battered Buick was rather conspicuous, so they left it on some waste ground south of Chancellor Avenue and walked the short way to the hospital.

Darkness was coming on, the evening of Halloween.

There were more people in the streets now. Some of them, red-faced and laughing, had already hit the bars to drink the night away, either in celebration or in trepidation, Eleanor wasn't sure. Children were out in the costumes they'd prepared, dropping tiny flashbangs on the sidewalk, looming and leering at those who went by, running off screeching down alleys and cut-throughs . . . these crowds of ghosts and witches, skeletons and sinister clowns gave Oxrun a strange, unearthly look. Eleanor wondered fleetingly if this was a reflection of Tuggie Bannock's world; a place of monsters and prisoned mischief . . . And now, beyond the town, the tumble of dark clouds was lined with silver as the full moon rose and the wind lifted. A paper cup went tumbling past Eleanor and on down the street.

She shivered. "Come on, Rob. Let's hurry."

There was, luckily, another receptionist on desk duty, who did not recognise Eleanor. She and Rob walked confidently by, as though making for the hospital shop, but then veered off and took the stairs to the first floor and Natalie's room.

They went in without knocking. Neither Gill senior nor Abraham Craine was there. But Natalie was not alone.

And now Tsepesh mantled over her, but paused and looked round at the disturbance. When he saw Rob and Eleanor, he hissed, and the smell of acid filled the room.

"Oh God," Rob said flatly, hesitating at the threshold. But Eleanor stepped forward with her fists clenched and determination stamped powerfully on her face.

"Get away from her!"

The creature stood, his handsome face shrouded in shadow, his head almost touching the ceiling.

"You call me 'Magister', child. The Master . . . "

"Get away from her — ghoul," Eleanor breathed. And Tsepesh shuddered, his body changing beneath his clothes.

"I think you annoyed him," Rob said.

"She scorned me in love, so she must die."

"So do I scorn you, monster. And I deny you . . . "

"Eleanor, don't!"

"Therefore," Tsepesh told her, "you must die also . . . "

He started to move, but Eleanor moved faster, sweeping her hand across the dresser-top and hurling its contents up towards Tsepesh's face: a cup, a clock, get-well cards, a mirror. Tsepesh flicked them aside and they clattered to the floor. His arm, growing longer, swung out towards Eleanor, the hand becoming as big as a shovel-blade, hooked wickedly with claws.

"Get out of his way!" Rob screamed, but Eleanor needed no telling. She ducked and flung herself backwards out of reach, noticing as she fell a fire-alarm button on the wall nearby.

Tsepesh pushed the bed aside and came closer. Just as Tuggie Bannock had shown her true self, so now did the Returner. His face, bulging out, swirled with waves of colour like a chameleon's skin. His eyes reddened. His mouth enlarged and bellowed, making the air tremble.

Rob, in a panic, grabbed an extinguisher off its wall bracket and sent a hissing gush of dry ice gouting over the creature. Tsepesh laughed, for his blood was colder yet, and moved in towards Rob.

But then he drew back, and Eleanor knew why.

"Rob, it's not the dry ice, but the iron extinguisher Tsepesh is frightened of!"

Rob understood. Instead of discharging the extinguisher, he hefted it high and hurled it right at the monster's head. It struck Tsepesh full in the face, disintegrating with a bang that sent needles of pain through Eleanor's ears.

Dizzily, she scrambled to the wall and smacked the heel of her hand on the alarm button.

The strident clanging of the fire bell was drowned out by the sound of Tsepesh's agonised roaring. He thrashed about in pain, staggering towards the window. His impossibly distorted body was swelling even further. Eleanor threw herself to the ground, and hoped that Rob had the sense to do the same.

Tsepesh hit the window and the surrounding wall like a runaway juggernaut, exploding it outwards. A great cascade of bricks and rubble flew far out over the hospital roofs, while inside, the room was filled with dust.

Eleanor picked herself up, rubbed at her eyes and spat dust from her mouth. She stumbled over to Natalie's bedside, where Rob joined her.

Natalie was still breathing, still alive. And the brightly coloured promise doll was still woven into her hair. Eleanor did not believe for a moment that the token had saved her, but she was glad she'd given it anyway.

"She'll be safe now," Eleanor said with quiet confidence. "Tsepesh will not trouble her again." Her face assumed a serious look. "There'll be others he can woo."

"So what now?" Rob asked.

Eleanor looked at him and gave a grim smile.

"Let's party."

Oxrun Station Fire Department responded to the alarm within five minutes. There was no panic. Most of the hospital staff, and the patients, thought it must be some Halloween prank, though a stupid one to be sure.

"But they'll get one heck of a surprise when they go into Natalie's room," Eleanor commented as she walked with Rob towards the town centre.

Her plan, and Rob agreed with it, was to join the crowds who would soon be making their way to Beacon Hill. The chances of destroying Tsepesh or Tuggie Bannock were remote, they both knew. But if they could somehow prevent their human hosts from completing the ceremony of baking the soul cakes, then perhaps the Returners might be stopped.

"Even if it means tying Abe Craine up in his own house, and suffering the consequences tomorrow, we should do it," Eleanor said determinedly.

"Yeah." Rob nodded. "And I may just be able to persuade my father to give it up. Too many people have been hurt or killed already."

"Folks do crazy things sometimes, Rob." Eleanor took his hand and squeezed it. "Don't hate your father for what he's doing. He was tempted and he weakened."

Some of the shops on Centre Street were still open, taking advantage of the festival. The sidewalks were busier than a market day morning and street stalls were doing brisk business.

Eleanor was broke, but Rob had enough money to buy them both costumes of sorts, that they could use as disguises. Eleanor picked a witch's mask in grotesque green rubber and a pointed hat to wear on top. Rob chose a pumpkin head made of sponge. Eleanor glanced at him and giggled.

"Gosh, but you're sexy!"

Rob waggled the head about. "How about a cuddle, honey?" he teased.

They walked on along Centre Street towards Williamston Pike. All around them, people swarmed, in families or larger groups, in pairs or alone. She recognised a few: Theo Bronson and his sidekick Zack Skelton, Theo all in black, as always, and Zack's scarred face looking even uglier than usual. And was that Chuck Antrim's little sister Nicole and her best friend Merrilee?

At first Eleanor paid little attention to individuals: she was too wrapped up in the carnival atmosphere, in the singing, in the glowing jack-o-lanterns hanging from lampposts and shop fronts, in the rich smells of toffee-popcorn and cinnamon, hot apple cider, roasted nuts and ham-and-bean suppers that you could buy in a tray for a dollar. Part of her warmed to this gathering of local people, continuing a tradition that had gone on for so many centuries. And most of them knew nothing different. They had no idea of the dark undercurrents of evil moving invisibly beneath this night of bright festivities.

But some, Eleanor suspected, knew exactly what was going on. She saw one reveller whose pumpkin-head was just a little too real for comfort, and she dreaded reaching out to touch it and finding it flesh. Another figure, dressed as a ghost, glided by on a gust of wind, which lifted the hem of his sheet and revealed no feet beneath. And in a dark doorway, a skeleton stood watching as Rob and Eleanor passed by . . . and Eleanor could clearly see the blue painted door and small glass panels through the empty cage of his ribs.

She hurried Rob onwards, because now there was a general drifting of the crowds towards Park Street, which ran between the town park and the cemetery, and out towards Beacon Hill. People were chattering and laughing; kids were whirling rattles and blowing whistles. Many of the adults carried pumpkin-lanterns or torches. Snatches of song and fragments of rhyme scattered like paper downwind, as half the population of Oxrun congregated at the intersection of Park Street and the Pike, and moved north.

"I'm worrying about my father," Rob confessed to Eleanor twenty minutes later, leaning close and speaking quietly, because behind them strode a huge square-shouldered figure in a ragged black frock coat, tall stovepipe hat, and a grinning skull mask: at least, they had assumed it was a mask. But Eleanor now strongly suspected that Tsepesh and Tuggie Bannock had brought a retinue of lesser creatures with them, to ensure that enough people were taken in the Ritual of Exchange: one man, woman or child for every soul cake burned on the Fire Stones.

"I thought," Eleanor said, "you told me he could look after himself . . ."

"That was before you thwarted Tuggie Bannock and I found Tsepesh's weakness at the hospital. They may be out for revenge, and it may be on my father."

"So what do you want to do?"

They were following the crowd along a wide public path that ran out of Oxrun almost to Beacon Hill. A few hundred yards from the hill was a fence and a stile, where the Craine estate began. Smaller pathways struck off into the trees here and there, and Rob now pointed down one of these that vanished into the dark woods.

"Hawksted is only about a mile away. I think my father will be there, making his final preparations to . . . to leave with Tsepesh."

"He might still be with Craine, though," Eleanor said. Rob shrugged.

"In which case, we have time to check at the College, then get back before the play party ends. It'll go on until midnight, when Tsepesh and Tuggie Bannock will make their move and the doorway between the worlds closes for another lifetime!"

Eleanor glanced down the woodland path, which dwindled into darkness.

"The moon will light our way," Rob said, guessing her expression behind the mask. "It's now or never . . ."

Eleanor thought about it, then nodded and grabbed Rob's hand. They slipped away from the stream of people and ducked down behind bushes. Within a few minutes the chattering laughter and the swaying Halloween lanterns had faded and they were alone, save for the night owls' cries, and the sighing wind in the trees, and the moonlight.

"Okay, let's do it." Eleanor began walking with Rob coming up at her side. "But if I get grey hair because of all this," she added, "you're in trouble."

As their eyes adjusted to the gloom, the sense of the woodland around them grew stronger. Actually it was more than just a woodland, Eleanor thought: the huge stands of pines and occasional oaks and impenetrable undergrowth seemed undisturbed and ancient, these few paths being the only impression made upon them. An idea came to her, that she immediately felt sure was right . . . That this swathe of woodland draping the hills around Oxrun was virgin territory, wild woods dating back at least to the last ice age: a place where Man did not often tread, and thus a place where enchantment had time to take root and grow. A natural doorway to elsewhere.

Thinking this, Eleanor quickened her pace. Rob lengthened his stride to keep up with her.

"Hey, slow down. No need to hurry — look, I can see lights ahead. It's the College."

Eleanor reasoned that there was every need to hurry. They had no power here, and the magic was high tonight, and chance was stacked against them. It would be wise to get to Hawksted quickly, find Robert Gill and use his car to reach Beacon Hill by a better route. Eleanor found the prospect of walking this lonely path unnerving.

She said nothing to Rob, but her unease increased as freshening gusts of wind blew across the hillsides and the vast leaf canopy whispered and moaned, ancient branches creaking. Far off, something fell with a crack in the trees.

"Dead branch blown down," Rob said, uncertainly.

Now they were fifty yards from the tree line, and no more than two hundred from Hawksted's trim lawns and neat herbaceous borders.

"Come on, Rob!" Eleanor said urgently. She heard a muffled gasp behind her and thought Rob had stumbled and fallen.

She turned to help him, and screamed.

The skull-faced creature stood behind them, a thing of towering blackness, the moonlight glinting on its cheekbones. It had Rob clamped helplessly against its vast body. He was struggling weakly, as the beast's other massive arm reached for Eleanor.

She leaped backwards, caught her heel on a root and fell heavily, winding herself.

The huge being stooped. Eleanor rolled desperately aside, tangling in the undergrowth and scrambling away. She heard the thing give a rumbling grunt of frustration, and then its heavy lumbering tread as it turned and walked back along the path.

14

"Rob!" The scream echoed, fading, from tree to tree, to the depths of the woodland. But there was no-one to help. Eleanor knew that her only possibility lay at the College, where perhaps Robert Gill was waiting to start out on his journey. And he was the only one with the knowledge to help: these creatures were too powerful to fight by normal means, but they too must obey the laws of their universe, and discovering those laws had been Gill's life's work.

So instead of running blindly and foolishly after Rob, Eleanor hurried in the other direction. She guessed that the skull-faced monster wouldn't kill him, because his blood needed to be warm and his soul needed to be willing. Tsepesh was an overlord, not of the dead, but of the doomed.

Seconds later Eleanor burst from the trees into moonlight and lawns laid so heavily with dew they looked like beads of shattered crystal.

She followed the cinder path round the side of the main College building to the quadrangle, noticing that barely a light was shining inside. From here she could see that the car park was virtually empty. Gill's Saab was gone, and it was likely that the rest of Hawksted's population were either at the play party, or had taken a weekend vacation.

And now, as she stood there, a wave of helplessness washed over her. She was truly alone, frightened of the journey back through the forest, and over an hour away from Beacon Hill by any other route. Unless . . .

The thought came like a photoflash in her head. Her eyes flicked to the lamppost where she'd parked her bicycle days ago — she suffered a moment's despair, then relief to see that it had been moved into a corner of the quadrangle, probably by a considerate gardener. Eleanor ran over to the bike, lifted it free of the leaf-drifts piled against the wheels, jumped astride the saddle and pedalled furiously down to the road.

She stopped once, to turn on her lights. They were not needed, of course, for now the moon was high and sailing in a sky largely clear of clouds. But an unwary motorist, or one drunk on the magic of the night, might not see her. And it was unthinkable that she should be stopped now by so mundane a mishap.

Very soon she came to the turn-off that she and Rob had followed two days earlier, when she had seen the hideous bat face in the mirror. Eleanor had no fears that it would return here, because she knew its earthly name now, and the purpose for which it had come.

The land sloped upwards more steeply. Eleanor stood on the pedals and struggled on, sweating. She came to a gate and a cattle-grid, hurled the bike across and climbed over, jumping down on the other side.

Now she was on Craine's land, and she could hear the sound of distant singing. Eleanor slowed, her lungs and legs burning. Above the hedges, high on the hill, she caught sight of a glow that mimicked the moonlight; the gleam of the beacon fire that was the exact point at which the two worlds touched. When the play party was at its height, people would be offered a handful of soul-cake dough. Some would refuse, for whatever reason, and would live to see another ordinary year. But others would accept and hope that the token of baked bread might bring their fondest wish.

Why, Eleanor asked herself silently, are people such fools? Don't they know the way of the world? There's the kestrel, and there are the mice. And rare indeed is the mouse who wins his survival with the lives of his kin . . . But that's what Craine has done, Eleanor mused. That's what he's always done. So he is the most contemptible of all . . .

There would be few people around the beacon fire as yet, because the time was not right; just some of Craine's staff making sure that all was as it should be. The play party itself would be taking place on the wide flat lawns near the Craine mansion. Eleanor recalled Gill senior mentioning a marquee, barbecues, side stalls — a very grand event indeed.

So it was here that Eleanor headed, hurrying again, but wondering what she could possibly do once she'd arrived.

Her witch's mask and cone hat were long gone, though it didn't matter. Many people had abandoned their disguises, so that their true faces were revealed. Eleanor left her bike at the rear of one of the tents, and walked among the revellers, marvelling as much at them as at the luxury of Abraham Craine's celebrations. On the far side of the lawn from the main marquee, in front of the house, a bandstand had been built and a string quartet was playing traditional melodies. Groups of people were dancing and spinning in circles nearby like whirling paper streamers. Eleanor passed a fortune-teller's tent, from which emerged the sweet smell of incense and promises. Seconds later, a man came out with greed burning brightly in his eyes. A young woman stood next in line. She was very plain, with stringy hair and a bad complexion. She glanced at Eleanor enviously as she passed, then lifted the flap of the tent and stepped inside, to be told that it wouldn't be long before she need never worry about her ugliness again.

Eleanor moved on, angered and saddened by the things she saw. Once or twice, she spotted beings from the other world, squat troll-like creatures moving amongst the crowds. They pretended to be children trick-or-treating. One man refused to give candy, and a troll ripped off its mask to reveal an identical face beneath. The man yelled in alarm and hurried off. The group of troll-things laughed, slack-jawed. Eleanor turned away.

She was working gradually towards the magnificent front façade of the Craine mansion. Lights were blazing in most of the windows, and two wide wings of stone steps rose from the lawn to converge on a large paved balcony, on to which the main doors opened. A constant stream of people moved in and out of the house, so it was easy for Eleanor to blend in and simply walk through into the grand vestibule.

Here, uniformed servants were offering glasses of ale mulled with apples and sugar to adults, while the children were given orange juice and a taffy pull. The servant nearest to Eleanor smiled and held out a glass of ale. "I'd prefer the taffy pull," Eleanor replied. And the servant, being a gentleman, obliged.

Now came the problem of finding not just Rob, but also his father. Eleanor had begun to think that Rob's capture was one way of preventing her from damaging the Ritual of Exchange, which was imminent. Abraham Craine would want everything to go smoothly, because otherwise he would not live to see the next occasion when Tsepesh came to Earth. And while Eleanor understood very little of how the festival fire ceremony might work, she guessed that the forces involved were finely balanced, and that a word or deed at the wrong moment could be disastrous — either for Craine, or for herself.

The crowds were allowed free access to several fine rooms on the ground floor. But Eleanor noticed that certain other rooms and corridors were roped off, as were the main stairs. Most likely, Craine would be keeping to a quieter part of the house. On the pretext of finding a washroom, Eleanor wandered close to several darkened rooms and, when no-one seemed to be watching, she stepped over the barrier ropes and hid herself in the shadows, sneaking down the corridor and deeper into the house a few seconds later.

The mansion was built in the Colonial style. Eleanor knew that there would probably be back stairs leading from the kitchens at the rear of the house to the servants' quarters tucked away on the top floor. The expensive carpeting gave way to quarry tiled floors, and then Eleanor found herself in the kitchen area, deserted because the hog roasts and the rest of the cooking was going on in the marquee. She risked switching on a light, and saw the stairs she was looking for. But first she went into the kitchen and selected the most robust knife she could find, before making her way to the first floor landing.

There was a closed door at the top. Eleanor opened it silently and peered through. Craine and Robert Gill senior were no more than ten yards away, turned in half-profile. Craine was speaking quickly, and Gill was earnestly nodding. Craine pointed towards a more distant doorway and began — not walking towards it — but hobbling, as though his years were weighing heavily upon him now . . . As indeed they must be, Eleanor thought, if Abraham Craine last made his bargain with Tsepesh on the occasion of his previous visit, in 1873.

Eleanor's body moved along the landing towards the room that Gill and Craine had just entered. She held the knife out in front of her, and was aware of a quickening heartbeat and a gloss of sweat on her forehead and face. She watched as her left hand reached out and awkwardly took hold of the gold-plated door handle to Craine's study. The hand paused before gripping the handle as best it could, then turning it. Eleanor's eyes took in the layout of the room and the position of the two men. Her legs walked her forward. Her throat worked and generated words . . . and all the while she was amazed to note her own reaction, as though this was happening to somebody else.

She registered Gill's wide-eyed shock, and Craine's reptilian smile of amusement. Then something clicked and she came back to herself, feeling the weight of the knife and the heat of its handle in her fist.

"You are happy to waste dozens of lives, Mr. Craine," Eleanor said stonily, but wanting to laugh at the absurd sense of melodrama. "So I am happy to waste one to stop you."

"You're making a big mistake, girl," Craine replied with absolute assurance.

"Eleanor," Gill added, "he's right. Put the knife down and walk away from here. You don't know what you're meddling with."

"*Somebody's* got to meddle, Doctor Gill," Eleanor lifted the knife higher, as though to demonstrate her determination.

Gill's face was white, his eyes full of pleading. "You don't understand — they've got my son."

"And Tsepesh will keep him and suck his soul dry unless we do something!"

"Eleanor — please!"

As Gill spoke the word, he moved, not towards Eleanor, but away. He leaped at Craine's desk, snatched up a heavy glass paperweight and hurled it at the knife in Eleanor's hand.

Eleanor watched it coming, and knew she could dodge it in time. But as that certainty occurred to her, Craine slipped his hand smoothly into his jacket and took out a gun.

The momentary distraction turned success into failure. Eleanor started to scream Gill's name, because Craine was pointing the gun at him—

The paperweight hit her, smashing into her temple with a burst of light and pain as the gun went off with, Eleanor thought, a surprisingly puny 'crack', as she toppled backwards, ever backwards, into warm blackness empty of any care or concern.

She woke slowly. It felt like the aftermath of drunkenness, and Eleanor was reminded of the end-of-semester party last summer when the boys had played midnight baseball and the girls stood on the bleachers jumping and cheering and singing stupid ra-ra songs . . .

Then Eleanor realised where she was, and sat up. A feeling of sickness stirred like oil in her stomach, and her throbbing head was an agony. Her eyes started to focus . . .

Robert Gill lay face down a few yards away, his shoulder and the side of his head soaked in blood. Eleanor's guts clenched as she crawled over to him to see if he was dead.

Gill groaned when Eleanor touched him. He eased himself over, winced at the pain of his wounded shoulder. His face looked grey, but the colour came back quickly, together with the look of despair Eleanor had recognised earlier.

Gill sat against Craine's desk, shaking his head slowly.

"I tried to warn you—"

"I had to do something!" Eleanor replied hotly, casting around for her knife. Having revived Gill, she now needed to prevent him from helping Craine finalise his plan.

She saw the knife a few feet away and moved to retrieve it. Gill grabbed her arm with a bloodstained hand.

"I was trying to stop him, Eleanor." It was the quiet sincerity in his voice that made her believe him. "You can't just go in with all guns blazing: the moment has to he right."

"Doctor Gill — I didn't realise—"

"No, I guess not. Ever since I came to Oxrun Station I've been learning all I could about Craine's history, and the nature of the beast with whom he bargains. Know your enemy, Eleanor . . . By now, I know Abraham Craine and Tsepesh all too well."

"I thought you were *helping* him — Rob thought so too."

Gill smiled weakly. "Rob got it into his head I was mounting an expedition, as though the region where Tsepesh dwells was on some kind of safari trail! Of course, I couldn't tell him the truth because, as the saying goes, the night has a thousand eyes."

"Do you know where Rob is now?" Eleanor asked. Gill shrugged, and gasped at the pain of it.

"In Tsepesh's power. He would have taken you too, Eleanor, if he could."

"There's still time . . . " Eleanor looked at her watch, and frowned to see that her fall had stopped it.

"I hope so." Gill wiped blood from the dial of his own wristwatch. "Oh my God," he said softly. "We've been out longer than I thought."

The time was ten minutes to midnight.

They made their way downstairs to the front of the house, and walked out on to the balustrade. The wide front lawns were deserted, the only movement being the drift of litter in the breeze, and shadows leaping from the light of the few torches left burning. Eleanor looked up into the moon-soaked sky. The full moon itself was surrounded by haloes, spun of the subtlest light. They reminded her of the story of the circles.

Gill startled her by speaking.

"Eleanor, Beacon Hill is half a mile away. We'll have to drive there—"

"Okay."

"That is, *you'll* have to drive there . . . my shoulder's stiffened up, I can't move it."

Gill hurried with her around to the side of the house, where the Saab and one or two other cars were parked. Eleanor climbed in on the driver's side; Gill sat beside her in the passenger seat.

"Now, it's not an automatic, so—"

"Rob's let me drive his Buick a couple of times," Eleanor pointed out. "So I know what to do."

Rather than argue or fret, Gill sighed quietly and closed his eyes.

Eleanor found that the Saab was easier to handle than the Buick; smoother and more responsive. She eased it carefully on to the gravelled driveway and started following the track that led away from the house, skirting woodlands towards Beacon Hill. From this position she could see the Hill clearly, a paper cutout shadow, its summit alight and burning with silvery flames. It was no more than a few minutes away.

Eleanor dipped the throttle and the Saab picked up speed — but then she slowed again, filled with a sudden anxiety.

Two hundred yards away, streaming across the sloping rear lawns, a weave of darkness and lightning was forming. It snapped and sparked with energy as it grew, twisting within itself and around, leaving the grass scorched where it passed. On its present track it would intercept the Saab before it reached the foot of the hill.

"Doctor Gill," Eleanor said calmly. She flicked on the car's main beams, and groaned at the horror. The writhing shadow looked more solid now, a thing of whirling, mouldering rags and wild black hair. Tuggie Bannock fixed her fearsome red eyes on Eleanor, and began to run at them. Her face changed moment by moment, reflecting the dozens of victims she had destroyed over the long, long centuries of her unhallowed life.

"Faster, Eleanor!" Gill snapped in alarm. "You can outrun her!"

Eleanor clenched her jaw. "Like hell I will!" She spun the steering wheel, corrected the backsliding rear wheels, and eased the throttle down so that the Saab picked up speed in a controlled way. While Gill gripped his seat and held his breath, Eleanor kept her mind steady and her intention focused with the sharpness of a laser beam. Not for an instant did she take her gaze from the lamia's face; both women caught fast in the spell of the other's eyes. For as long as she lived, Eleanor would never understand the futility of craving perfection, as this witch did in her madness, chanting her gibberish charms: while Eleanor, a jewel flawed, would forever remain a mystery to the sorceress known as Tuggie Bannock.

At the final moment, like the lifting of a veil, Tuggie Bannock's transformation became complete. She was Eleanor in every detail; but Eleanor perfected, a grown woman, her face aglow with happiness, reaching out her slender left hand in an offering of friendship and love.

Something wrenched in Eleanor's heart. She would never be the same again, she knew that, as she slammed the Saab into the monster at over sixty miles an hour.

The windshield cracked across and one headlight was smashed out. There was a dreadful bang and a withering scream. Behind the speeding car, a black whirlwind caught light and flew into the sky, leaping towards the safety of Beacon Hill in a fiery arc.

Eleanor paid little heed. Midnight was a few brief minutes away now, and she was thinking of the poor trapped souls within the Circle of Stones; Miss Ross and all the others. The Saab took the hill without slowing and, also without slowing, raced towards the cold blue flames of the festival fire.

It seemed like several hundred people had gathered on Beacon Hill. As Eleanor caught sight of them, she jammed her hand on the Saab's horn and kept it there, and watched them scatter.

"There may be others inside the ring of stones," Gill warned. "They'll be harder to frighten away."

"I'm looking for Rob!" Eleanor yelled, feeling her self-control going at last. "Where is he — for God's sake where is he?"

She saw him then, hanging limply like a doll in the grip of the thing that stood within the circle of fire.

It was a night of true faces, not of masquerade, and Tsepesh stood revealed at last. What by normal moonlight might have been mistaken for a cloak or ceremonial gown, Eleanor now recognised as wings, membranous and black, that spread in a terrible magnificence as the car's one remaining headlight beam swept across. And the being's cold handsomeness was gone like a distant memory. Tsepesh now showed an alien face, monstrous, with tiny black lips drawn back from needle teeth, a squashed pug nose sniffing the air for meanings, spike-haired ears alert for danger. This was the source of the ancient legend: the fearful beast that drank the blood of the world.

Eleanor was set to repeat her success with Tuggie Bannock. The ring of fire stones was complete, but for one wide space where people entered. The quivering headlight beam showed the ring deserted now, but for Tsepesh and Rob. Eleanor was counting on the creature dropping Rob in its startlement, and on her grinding the demon down beneath her wheels in a final act of defiance.

Gill guessed her intention, but knew not to panic her.

"Eleanor, this won't destroy him. He cannot be destroyed by brute force . . . Eleanor, in the trunk I have weapons — unpolished iron, which the revenants abhor . . . "

Eleanor recognised the quote from Gill's own book, and lifted her foot from the throttle.

But before she could touch the brakes, the side window shattered. Another shot a split second later blew the offside front tyre. The steering went instantly as Eleanor felt the change from a precision machine to a ton of hurtling metal.

"Get out, Eleanor!" Gill yelled at her. "Get out now!"

He snapped his seatbelt, loose, pushed open the passenger door and was gone. Eleanor tried to follow his example, but her crippled left hand did not possess the strength or dexterity to lift up the door handle.

She was still struggling desperately when the Saab entered the ring of flames. Its passenger side was stoved-in against one of the fire stones; the car slewed to the left, hitting Tsepesh a glancing blow—

And the moonlight turned off, the engine died, the flames vanished, and sudden heavy rain slashed and hammered on the roof.

Though there was chaos outside, Eleanor became very still. She understood what had happened. By a sheer accident — or perhaps it was part of the clockworks of heaven — the Saab had come to rest on the boundary between worlds. It was a precarious situation, one that could last for only a few seconds. Eleanor knew she needed to act immediately.

Glancing back, she saw Robert Gill heaving at the lid of the trunk. Out through the front windshield, smudged by veils of rain, unbelievable things were gathering: a graceless assembly of gargoyles, deathsheads, ogres and raw-boned skeletons, brought by the blood-smell of the girl.

Eleanor felt too scared to scream. She saw Rob's body just ahead, lying in the stinking mud, and getting to him was all that mattered. She wrenched the handle and half-fell out of the car.

She took three stumbling steps and splashed down next to Rob, turned him over and saw his eyes rolling upwards, his mouth moving as black filthy water spilled from his lips.

A slime-covered tentacle slithered bonelessly out of the bleached grass nearby and slid over Rob's chest. Others, dozens more, were following.

Eleanor groaned in disgust, scrambled up and began dragging him the few yards to relative safety; pausing only once, in wonder, as an animal with the body of a squat ape and the face of a sweet and smiling child hopped onto the hood of the

Saab and began to sing in what Eleanor would later recognise as Latin.

The singing was drowned out by a growing commotion in the air above; by the heavy flapping of wings, and a thin piping squeal that opened out into a horrifying roar of frustration and rage: Tsepesh returning to feed.

With a last effort that drained Eleanor of strength, she hauled Rob through the divide, feeling the brief and scalding ecstasy of the flames before the cool night air of New England surrounded and soothed her.

Eleanor lowered Rob to the ground — then gasped and fell backwards as Tsepesh loomed out of the fire curtain and reached for her.

She heard Robert Gill shouting close by. The creature's ugly head flicked up. And a spear of unpolished iron whispered through the air and lodged in Tsepesh's heart.

The sound that followed was indescribable; partly of pain, partly of an all-consuming hate. But other emotions were expressed that Eleanor's human heart could never feel, and that went beyond all naming or sanity.

Blood spouted from his wound, as his huge wings flapped in agony. Even so, Tsepesh stood to his full height, gripped the haft of the spear and ripped it free.

Then, with a final look of glittering fury, but also one of acquiescence, he stepped back into his own domain and disappeared.

The circle of flames flared more brightly, whipped like flags in a gale, tore loose from the stones and swirled together into the dwindling doorway between worlds. Gill watched the back end of the Saab shear off and drop with a crash to the ground.

"I think," he said to Eleanor, "it's a write-off."

But she was too tired to laugh.

There was a silence that all three of them could have curled up and slept in. But the quiet was disturbed by the sound of dust settling, and the ghost of a voice struggling up from a crumbling throat.

Something that had once been alive walked jerkily into the ring of stones. It held a gun in the bones of its right hand, but the weight of metal unravelled the tendons, and gun and fingers fell in a scatter of wristbones to the ground.

"I — wanted it — all . . . " said Abraham Craine, as the last of his hair came free and his grinning skull smile widened.

October had moved into November now. An owl hooted in a tree far away. But Craine failed to hear it. He had no life left in him, and no purpose, so his pitiful remains crumpled like a structure of sticks, fell to the dirt and lay still.

They buried him in the family vault in Oxrun Memorial Park, together with the three iron railings that Gill had removed for the purpose of destroying Tsepesh's threat.

The service was a modest one. There were only a few mourners gathered there among the grey condolences and white snow.

Eleanor was not one of them. She left Rob and his father and walked to the other side of the cemetery, to Sarah Jane's grave.

With tears running down her face, Eleanor picked out the wilted flowers from an earlier arrangement and replaced them with sprigs of holly, heavy with blood-red berries. Christmas was a few weeks away, but in Eleanor's mind holly had more ancient meanings; as a symbol of luck and enduring life. It seemed very appropriate. And among the holly twigs she placed her third and final promise doll, a dark-haired girl in a yellow skirt, with spots of paint for eyes and a smile.

"Fly free, SJ," Eleanor whispered. "Fly free."

She stood up, shrugged her coat collar higher and breathed in the clean, cold air.

Across the way, the funeral service had come to an end and people were moving slowly back towards the cortege. Eleanor watched the little figures go, and made no move to follow them.

Here, high above Oxrun, the silence was a splendid and delicate thing. There wasn't a breath of wind, and the snow made not the slightest sound as it fell. Eleanor thought that perhaps winter really had begun.

Meanwhile, among the roots of the nearby yew tree, mice were moving in their endless search for buried seeds, while above, circling slowly, was the kestrel, caught on the hook of its hunger.

TINA

WHEN TINA BROADBENT GOT HOME FROM school, her dad was making breakfast. Well, breakfast was what he called it, it being his first meal of the day: but her dad was not the bacon-and-eggs type. Breakfast today, she could tell as she swung in the front door and dropped her book-backpack on the chair in the front hall, was going to be some kind of noodle with — she sniffed — probably that weird Thai hot sauce again, the one made out of pickled fish and hyper-hot chillies. Sometimes she would have agreed with the other kids' assessment that her dad was slightly crazy . . . except that (as Tina occasionally felt forced to remind them) it was her father who took care of the crazies, and therefore had the next thing to paperwork stating that he was sane. In the status-conscious world of senior year in Oxrun Station, this peculiarity counted for something . . . if not as much as money, the older, the better.

She wandered down the hall, pulling her sweatshirt off over her head as she went, and came into the kitchen, dropping the sweatshirt over the back of the nearest kitchen chair; then paused and looked around her with a sigh. Tina occasionally felt annoyed that her dad couldn't afford as big a house as some of the other kids at school had. But his pay cheque — none too big to start with — was raided every week by what he called "the Alimony Fairy", so that Tina and her dad had to make do with a little two-bedroom clapboard house, hardly more than a cottage, on Thorn Road. The situation was not exactly comfortable when you had to deal every day with kids who lived in big old Colonials and Victorians, and whose parents seemed to effortlessly exude money from all their orifices. The kitchen in particular was not as cool as, say, Chuck Antrim's mother's, all stainless steel and shining granite worktops; *this* kitchen was resolutely stuck in the Formica Age, with a fridge that had trouble making ice cubes at all, let alone dispensing them from the door, and linoleum that must have seen better days once . . . possibly when dinosaurs walked the earth. Tina did not bring many people home, at least not the ones that cared a lot about such things. This limited her social life: but limitations were something she had got used to since her mom and dad broke up, and Tina had learned to deal with it... for the time being.

"Two heavy sighs in half a minute," said her dad. He was over by the stove, bending over a pot and favouring it with a critical expression. "Bad day at the madhouse?"

She pulled out one of the chairs around the old scrubbed-wood kitchen table and flopped down in it. "I don't want to talk about it."

"Sure you do, when you make noises like that."

He looked over his shoulder, and Tina hurriedly bowed her head over the table, fiddling with one of the beige woven-linen placemats, so that her dad wouldn't see her grin. It could be a real pain in the butt having a psychiatric nurse for a father. Not that he wasn't occasionally wrong about what was going on in your head... but he was too good at being right and at the same time not pissing you off, which was simply unfair when all you wanted was a good fight. "Noises?" Tina said, and made another one: *sppllppppllllttt*, a prolonged raspberry.

Her dad went over to one of the cupboards and started rummaging around for a colander. "Maths teacher or science teacher?"

It really *wasn't* fair. Tina would have given anything sometimes to be able to scream "You don't understand me!", except that in her father's case it would have been so blatantly untrue. "Maths," Tina said. "She keeps calling me 'innumerate' in front of everybody."

Her dad put the colander down in the sink, got the pot off the stove and drained his pasta, then started to shake it around. "Unimaginative," he said. "You can count all right."

"Oh, if it were counting, I'd graduate tomorrow," Tina said, starting to pull apart the fringe on the placemat. "The problem's the calculus."

Her dad moaned softly. "I thought we were done with that unit."

"Not yet," Tina said. Her dad insisted with "helping with her homework": mostly what it helped Tina with was her sense of being the most hopeless person in the world as far as calculus was concerned, for her dad was worse.

"I don't know," he said as he came over to the table with a plate with the drained pasta on it, and sat down, reaching for the jar of weird Thai sauce that was already sitting there waiting for him. "Maybe we should see about getting you some tutoring. SATs are coming up . . . and if you're going to take that advanced placement one . . ."

"I've been studying with some of the other kids in free period," Tina said. "It'll probably be okay."

"Which others?" her father said. "Not that Antrim kid, I hope."

"There's nothing wrong with him!"

Her father reached for his fork. "I think we've discussed this already."

"You mean you've told me what you think about him. That's not a discussion."

Her father raised his eyebrows. "Tina," he said, "leaving out the fact that the kid has a nose for trouble, and a gift for following his nose . . . he's even more innumerate than I am." He tested a bite of the pasta, then reached for another bottle: hot sauce this time. "He's not going to do you any good with your calc."

Tina made a face, since he was right again, and she hated it when he was right in this reasonable tone of voice, without yelling or making a scene. She opened her mouth. "Maybe he's the life of the party," her dad continued, "but try to find other help, for the maths anyway. Tell me what you've sorted out at the end of the week, okay?"

And he *would* wait for her to sort something out, too, and ask her then, and not nag her about it. Tina's dad could be really annoying sometimes, and not in the usual ways. She watched him put the hot sauce on his pasta and dig in enthusiastically. He was a big, dark-haired man, broad across the shoulders, going a little thick around the waist now, and continually complaining that he didn't have enough time to exercise; though Tina privately considered that a little less pasta wouldn't hurt him. "You're going to give yourself ulcers, eating that stuff," she said.

Her dad shook his head as he chewed, swallowed. "No medical effect whatever," he said. "More likely to kill the bugs that cause ulcers than to cause new ones." The sweat popped out on his forehead.

Tina shook her head and got up to make herself a sandwich. "How long are they gonna leave you on evenings, Daddy?"

"Another month or so," he said. "Then Norma and I switch shifts."

"I wish it was sooner," Tina said. It wasn't that she disliked being alone at night: she wasn't the panicky kind. But she saw less of her father when he was on evening shift, between four and midnight, than at any other time, and she didn't much care for never having him to talk to, even when he was annoying.

"Yeah," he said, "so do I. Wouldn't mind changing over right now." He wiped his forehead.

Tina was unwrapping the bread, and she stopped; his tone of voice wasn't usually quite so revealing. "You got some bad patients now?"

He would never discuss this with her in any detail. "No worse than usual," he said. "It's just . . . the time of the month."

"Uh oh," Tina said. "Well, you'll be okay. You always are."

He grinned at her. "Yeah, "he said.

"It's not like they turn into wolves or anything," Tina said, getting a knife out of the knife drawer and then rummaging around in the cupboard for the peanut butter. "They're just crazies."

"Oh, they turn into things, all right," said her dad. "Pains in the butt, mostly . . . "

Tina laughed out loud. "Not as big a pain as Cerise, I bet!"

Her dad laughed too. "And what has the divine Miss C. come up with this week?"

"Same as last week, but worse." Cerise Fallon was one of Tina's better friends at school, partly because Cerise was another of those kids who were relatively new to town and having trouble "breaking in" to the circles of those kids whose families had been here for a long time, and didn't mind letting you know it. Cerise went out of her way to be different at a time when this was usually fatal. Her hair was never the same colour two days in a row, her clothes were always one shade or another of black, and her constant discovery of newer and weirder forms of "spirituality" had caused Chuck Antrim to claim that the initials C.F. should actually stand for Colossal Flake. "The Flake" Cerise had indeed become to most of the school, and she wore the title like a banner, looking down with what seemed like good-natured scorn on the rest of the school that scorned her.

"It was astrology, wasn't it?"

"It's always been astrology with her, more or less," Tina said, spreading the peanut butter on thick. "At least, that's the first thing I remember her really being interested in, when we first moved in. But she's got this really detailed book on it out of the library, and now you can't tell what she's talking about half the time. Half of it is maths, and the rest of it, I don't know *what* it is, angles and crap like that: she keeps saying that now she knows what trigonometry is for." Tina grimaced: her own experience led her to believe that trig had been invented purposely to frustrate her attempts to get into college. "And then she went into some Web site on the Internet and downloaded all these bizarre charts and tables and stuff, and today she actually got up in civics, when she was supposed to be doing a report on Oxrun in the 19th century, and she started warning everybody that there was an awful 'conjunction of the stars', and the earth was going to open and everything." Tina rolled her eyes, brought the plate over to the table and sat down.

"Was she serious?" Tina's dad said, finishing his pasta and wiping his forehead with his napkin. "I mean, does she really believe it?"

"This week, I think so. Last week she really believed that there were spirits in trees. Last *month* she really believed in the Norse gods, all this Asatru stuff, and she told Angie Hanover about the horse sacrifices they used to do, and Angie nearly decked her right there in the cafeteria: she's a pony freak. . ." Tina bit into her sandwich. "When Cerise picks up on this stuff," she said after the bite went down, "she's so . . . enthusiastic. A week later, two weeks maybe . . . poof. It's gone."

"Well, at least she's interested in things," Tina's dad said. "It's the ones who don't get interested in anything that worry me." He took his bowl to the sink and spent a couple of moments with the sponge and the dishwashing liquid. "Listen, do I look okay?"

As far as Tina could tell, her dad always looked okay when he went to work; today, a casual blue shirt, dark trousers, dark shoes — psych nurses didn't have to wear uniforms. But the question was traditional — Tina suspected it was because her dad knew he had put on weight over the summer. "You look fine, she said. "They letting you off the usual time tonight?"

"As far as I know." Her dad ducked out into the hallway from the kitchen and came back shrugging into his favourite leather jacket. "Assuming no-one gets sick all of a sudden — sicker, anyway. Or drops dead, or runs off, or jumps out a window. . ."

Tina made a face. "I thought you said they couldn't."

"The windows are built that way," her dad said, "but what human ingenuity can devise . . ." He came over to her, kissed her, gave her a hug. "Get that homework done first, okay? I'll 'help' you with it when I get home."

"I may not be awake that long," Tina said.

"Okay. Make sure you lock up, then. Is Cerise going to come over and help you?"

"She said she might."

"Make sure her folks come and get her when you're done, then. I don't care how safe she thinks it is: not all the crazies around here are locked up, and the ones from outside have cars." He waved and headed out the back door.

It shut softly behind him. Tina sat there chewing another bite of her peanut butter sandwich, considering how very quiet the house got, these October afternoons, when her dad went off and didn't come back until midnight, long after the dark crept over everything . . .

Tina made herself hold still and finish her sandwich. Then she got straight up and went to call Cerise.

Tom Broadbent, by and large, was happy with his work: as happy as any nurse could be, in this time in which nurses were chronically underpaid, malpractice insurance was desperately overpriced, doctors produced by the local medical schools were not up to the standards of even ten years ago, let alone fifteen, and hospitals considered psychiatric units necessary, but only when run at the lowest possible cost.

Tom had always wanted to do psychiatry, though not at the medical level. His discovery that you could be a nurse and do psych had filled him with joy, and his family with an embarrassment that they found very difficult to voice, since they had immediately assumed any male who wanted to be a nurse had something, well, *wrong* with him, mentally if not also sexually. There were moods in which Tom would have agreed with them about the 'mentally' side of it; male nurses, in an overwhelmingly female profession, very soon found that nursing had its own glass ceiling that they might never completely succeed in breaking. He hadn't argued that particular point with his family, and instead contented himself several times during his training with telling them the story of the one "rogue" nursing school in upstate New York in the 1800s which had by itself produced all the stories about gay male nurses. His family, horrified that he had met their concerns unafraid and face on, backed away and stopped mentioning the issue.

His birth family, that is. Candace, Tom's wife, had been happy enough to use the excuse about "what everybody thinks about you" to end their marriage — though she had never minded spending the money that his work brought them, while they were still married, and she didn't seem to mind spending the alimony money now. Tom sighed as he swung down the street towards the hospital in the slanting late-October sunlight. The real cause of their marriage's end lay elsewhere, several different kinds of elsewhere, and Tom was still analysing it. But that was his nature, and one of the things that made Tom good at his chosen profession: that ability to quietly nibble away at a problem until he found its underlying cause. In the meantime, Tom had found himself a single father — for Tina had been vocal about which of her parents she wanted to stay with, and the courts had agreed with her. For his sake as much as hers, Tom had looked for a placement well out of the City, somewhere upstate in a quieter, greener place, less pressured for both of them, where he would have less trouble keeping an eye on Tina while still making enough of a living to send his daughter to a decent college.

The perfect spot had opened up right in front of him, it seemed, when he started jobhunting. Oxrun Station's small hospital, ready to expand in several directions, had decided to stop farming the area's psychiatric admissions out to larger, more impersonal and more remote facilities in Hartford or New Haven. Tom had grown up in this area: not Oxrun Station itself, but about twenty miles south, and he knew the relaxed feel of the region — the sense of a slight displacement in time, of things moving at a gentler pace. He also had heard some of the odd rumours surrounding the Oxrun area, but any place where people have been living as long as they had in Oxrun Station acquires some bloom of legend about it; it was all part of the cachet, as far as Tom was concerned. His interview with the hospital had been uneventful, in fact slightly frantic: their new psych wing — all six beds of it — was built, ready to open, but staff applications had been few. Tom suspected the problem was something to do with the shortage of housing stock in the area. But he had lucked into a small house which had gone up for sale in the week of his interview, its owners wanting to exchange small-town life for something busier and more impersonal; the day after he accepted the job offer from Oxrun Station Hospital, he had exchanged contracts with the owners of the house on Thorn Street. A month later he and Tina were moving in.

Two years ago, Tom thought as he turned into King Street, where the hospital was. Seems like about ten minutes, some ways. A new psych unit always brought its own problems with it: staff problems, as people working on the unit settled in and got used to each other, and as other hospital staff got used to having psychiatric patients in-house for prolonged periods; community problems, as the people around the hospital got used to the idea that there was more than one kind of illness being treated there; budget problems, logistics problems, God knew what else. It had all sorted itself out eventually.

Well, most of it . . . Tom headed in through the front doors of the hospital, waved at Mike, the security guard, and made for the new wing, feeling in his pocket for the keys that were chained to his belt. With Tom, there were five nurses now: Carol, the head nurse, who worked days when she was here — though she was on vacation at the moment; Norma, the night nurse, who was presently working days; Laura, normally evenings, who was working nights; and Ginger, the LVN, graduate of a two-year course but working on her third year in night school at the state college extension down in Torrington. Ginger was floating between days and nights at the moment, "on demand" as patient load required, and Tom occasionally wondered when she found time to sleep. But taken all together, it was actually a very good setup as far as staffing went: a far cry from the days just after Tom graduated, when he might find himself all alone on nights with twenty or thirty patients who were both seriously medically ill and as crazy as bedbugs.

He walked down the hallway through the hospital's oldest med-surg ward, which was presently closed for renovation, stripped bare of beds and equipment and at the moment a shadowy, bare-bulb-lit welter of paint cans, plasterers' equipment and plastic and cloth sheeting, the tall old windows partly blacked out with masking gunk. This was one of those handsome old buildings which looked elegant, even noble from the outside, but which over many years had become, not exactly decrepit, but certainly run-down. It was a credit to the trustees that they were finally doing something about it, modernising the place in stages while maintaining unbroken service to the local community. He admired even more that the trustees had resisted the temptation to sell the place off as a going concern to some moneygrubbing HMO, as so many owners of other old hospitals in the area had done, washing their hands of the problems and taking the money, then running. But apparently Oxrun Station people conducted matters differently; tradition counted for something here. Tom approved.

He pulled his keys out as he came to the locked door which was the "front door" of the psych ward; checked through the window to see who might be nearby, saw no-one. Tom unlocked the door and stepped through, locking it again behind him. The question of whether to go "locked" or "unlocked", when the unit had been opened, had apparently been slightly controversial in the area: finally the trustees decided "locked" would be smarter until the unit's intake patterns stabilised and the staff got some sense on the volatility or dangerousness of a "typical" Oxrun admission. Though, Tom thought, this time of month, there's no such thing as typical . . .

He headed down the carpeted hall, looking into the various open doorways on either side as he passed. Most of these were bedrooms, most of which were empty, for the unit wasn't busy at the moment. There had been only four patients in place when Tom went off shift last night, two of them relatively new admissions, one of them scheduled for discharge, and one about to be discharged "against advice", having started the seventy-two hour process two days ago.

One room halfway down the hall, close to the nursing station, was closed and locked; Tom knew who would be there, and paused to look through the window, seeing what he expected to — a tall, blond, blank-eyed man, seated on the floor and keeping very still, dressed in grey sweatshirt and sweatpants. Tom sighed and went on down the hall.

Then he paused, hearing what sounded like a faint crunching sound. He stopped, wondering, and listened.

Nothing: it was gone. From further down the hall, he heard a yell: "I heard the door! Is that you, Tom honey?"

He raised his eyebrows slightly at the familiar screech, and for the moment he didn't answer, since he didn't know "which" Andrea Gabrieli he was talking to, and even someone as floridly nuts as Andrea deserved the courtesy of being addressed by the name she claimed to be using at the moment — though Tom had his doubts about the real reasons for the multiplicity of names. He would sort Andrea out shortly, when he made his checks.

He went past the door to the meeting room/coffee room and turned in at the one windowed door which had a curtain across the window on the inside. Norma Gaines was there, sitting at the long desk that ran down one side of the room towards the windows, doing charting. She looked up as he came in, and smiled at him. "You're early, 'Tom honey'," she said.

He grinned. Norma, "Miss Norma" as everyone called her, was a big, statuesque Jamaican lady with close-cropped hair and a voice like melted caramel running down the side of a chocolate ice-cream sundae. Today she was wearing a silk dress in a bright Caribbean print that somewhat recalled the startling colours of the turning leaves outside. "Call me a glutton for punishment," Tom said. "Quiet today?"

"'Nothing significant to report'," she said, quoting the line that would usually be put in a patient's chart on such a shift. "Truth , for once."

"No new admissions?"

"Nobody scheduled, anyway. Had a call from the University clinic at Hartford, something about checking into available beds for the next few days, but they didn't call back. Nothing urgent, it looks like."

Tom suspected he knew why they were checking: they sometimes did, at this time of month. But he didn't say anything. "You in a hurry to get out?" he said.

"No, I've got a few things to finish up here."

"Andrea?"

"Miss Andrea has been most naughty today," Norma said, wrinkling her face up. "I'll tell you when we go through the charts. Go get yourself some coffee, I'll be done in a minute."

Tom nodded and turned. In the doorway he paused, listening. "You hear me?" Andrea hollered. "When you gonna come talk to me, I'm gonna die of boredom in here!"

"Huh," Tom said. "Are they drilling in those walls again?"

"Where?" Norma said.

"Next door." The construction workers had been breaking through walls in the older part of the building, and sound travelled through them oddly sometimes, while the crowbars and drills were working, making you think the work was closer than it actually was.

"Not so much today," Norma said. "A little this morning, but I haven't noticed anything since." She sighed and nodded towards the hall. "With her commenting on everything all day, even the crowbars have trouble being heard."

Tom chuckled. "Back in a moment," he said, and headed down the hall, the way he had come, towards the coffee room.

Crunch . . . crunch . . .

Tom paused: listened—

"She won't talk to me any more, the stuck-up bitch," yelled Andrea, "she stuck me in here and left me all day since breakfast, what the hell kind of two-bit psychiatric clinic is this?"

Any crunching noise that followed was lost in the ensuing tide of complaint. Tom remembered Laura muttering ruefully under her breath one day: "Why is it the Medicare patients are always the ones who complain loudest about the service?"

Tom smiled as ruefully. Your tax dollars at work, he thought, and went for a cup of coffee to have with the shift-change report.

Tina sat at the kitchen table with a second sandwich and a paperback book with the wildly misleading title *Calculus Made Easy*. Symbols and numbers and letters swam in front of her eyes on the printed page and made no sense whatever: they might as well have been in Linear A, which she knew more about and understood better than this stuff. That's because the inventors of linear A were Cretans, Tina thought regretfully, and I'm a cretin. That's what old Johnson would say...

The "doorbell" rang, actually a horrifically nasal and insistent buzzer that brought Tina up and out of the chair as if someone had stuck a cherry bomb underneath her. "Coming," she yelled, and headed for the door. She opened it.

There, silhouetted against the resplendent October sunshine that flooded this side of the house this time of day, and against the paintspatter background of the leaves of the trees in their street, all scarlet and gold, stood a dark shadow: Cerise. Her hair was blue today, mostly, and she was wearing black leggings and black sneakers and a black lace leotard top and a black denim jacket and black lipstick. Tina regarded this last with open admiration. "Your mother," she said, "must be from another culture or something. My dad would never let me get away with that."

"My mom is very *counter*cultural," Cerise said, slipping in past Tina as Tina held the screen door open for her.

"Yeah, well, she must want another kid," Tina said, "and be counting on your dress sense to help her out by giving you pneumonia. Aren't you freezing in that, this time of year?"

Cerise glanced down at the black lace top. "It's thermal," she said absently. "I wouldn't give her the satisfaction of seeing me shiver." She grinned and dropped her bookbag (black) on the kitchen table. "Your dad gone?"

"Yeah."

"Shame. He's cute."

This was such a completely unexpected sentiment that Tina wasn't sure what to make of it. "Uh, I guess so," she said.

"No, really," Cerise said. "Pudgy guys can be cool."

"My dad," Tina said, trying to keep any edge out of her voice, "is not pudgy."

"Oh, I didn't mean as in 'obese'," Cerise said casually, flopping down in the kitchen chair opposite Tina. "Pudge in the sense of 'cuddly' is what I meant."

"Yeah, well he's a little old for you," Tina said. "Besides, I thought you were more interested in Chuck Antrim. Where is he, by the way?"

"Couldn't come," Cerise said. Tina's heart fell a little: she was more than a little interested in Chuck herself, though Tina considered that Cerise had "First claim", and was not going to be mentioning anything about her own feelings. And anyway, Chuck was showing more than a little interest in Beth these days. "Thought you said your dad was down on him, anyway."

"Yeah," Tina said.

"Shame," Cerise said, and reached for her bookbag. She began rummaging in it, pulling out notebooks and printed-out papers from her computer printer, as well as a big old book in shiny buckram library binding with 855.33J written on the bottom of the spine in white ink: the title, higher up on the spine, was rubbed away by years of use, and nearly invisible. "I understand he tee-peed his maths teacher's house last night."

"He *what*?" Tina said, completely delighted. She had been run over old Johnson's coals twice last year, once when she took trig as an "early" junior subject and flunked it, and once during summer school when the whole course had been concentrated into four weeks, this last summer, and she passed it in desperation and loathing, intent on never having to see Johnson's nasty face again. "All *right*!"

"Apparently Johnson just about busted a gut, screaming and yelling and dancing around outside his house," Cerise said, opening the big book up and paging through it absently. "A pity no-one got any videotape of it. You could make a lot duping and selling it to people."

"There's a thought," Tina said. Her dad had a videotape recorder, and she found herself wondering how she would have finessed such a thing even if she had known it was going to happen. The trouble was, she hadn't known. No-one at school told Tina about any of the really interesting things that went on . . . and Cerise was also far outside those circles, though it seemed this was as much out of her own choice as because of the other kids' preferences. "Sorry I missed it, though. Must have been super."

"Yeah, but it won't be winning Chuck any friends among the 'responsible adult community'," Cerise said dryly, "so if I were you I would put him on the Subjects To Avoid With Your Dad list for a few days, until the heat's off. After Halloween, maybe things will quiet down. You know how this place always gets. . . " Odd, though: as she said it, Cerise looked somewhat uncertain.

"A little tense," Tina said, remembering last year and the year before. It wasn't as if the usual trick-or-treating didn't go on: it did. But there was always a sense in Oxrun that people were waiting for something to happen . . . something not very good. No-one ever seemed terribly willing to talk about it, either. "Nervous . . . "

"And I think I may have stumbled onto one of the reasons why," Cerise said. "Wait till you see. Of course, half the people around here are too busy to listen at the moment." She sounded scornful as she started going through the things from her bag. "A lot of them are wasting their time getting all excited about that big Craine thing on Halloween." Cerise rolled her eyes. "The 'play party' or whatever."

"Oh, C'mon, Cerise, is it really that bad?" Tina was surprised to find herself sounding slightly wistful. "I mean, I was thinking about going." After all, there had been moments lately when being "the nut nurse's" daughter had not exactly been the most wonderful thing in the world. Tina had been thinking that going a little way to meet these kids might not be such a bad idea.

There would be some of them up there: though there had been kids at school who weren't interested, others were . . .

"Oh, Tina!" Cerise sounded genuinely shocked. "What *century* is this?! Promise dolls? Telling the future by looking at apple peelings? Or whether or not nuts float? Cut me a couple feet of slack!"

Tina put her eyebrows up. "It's just traditional stuff," she said. "I thought you liked traditions. Dancing around trees . . ." She grinned.

"That's just honest animism," Cerise said, and actually sniffed. "This superstitious stuff is different."

"Oh," said Tina, and closed her mouth before anything more cutting came out of it.

"This is more than just that kind of *dumb* thing," Cerise said, loftily. "The ancient Egyptians did astrology. So did the Greeks. Even the Babylonians and Mesopotamians did it. Without the research they did to support their astrology, we wouldn't know anything like as much astronomy as we do, especially about eclipses."

"Oh," said Tina.

"So stop giving me a hard time, and pay attention!!" Cerise practically hollered. "I mean, really, Teenz, you were the only one I thought had enough sense to *listen* to me about this stuff!"

"I had a lapse," Tina said, doing her best not to sound *too* contrite. "But the Craine thing . . . I thought it might be, you know, a way to meet new people."

Cerise rolled her eyes expressively. "There is nothing 'new' about anyone in Oxrun. The money is old, the buildings are old, the cars are old, the ideas are old . . . the kids in our class are old, half of them, even if they're barely eighteen yet. I cannot wait to graduate and get *out* of this place."

It was an idea which had occurred to Tina on more than one occasion . . . except that her dad plainly intended to be here for a while, which meant it was going to be her home for a while too, unless she managed to get accepted by a college far enough away from home that she would have to board there. And right now, with calculus looming as the Great Insoluble in front of her, it looked seriously unlikely that Tina was going to manage SAT scores which would even faintly interest CalTech. And then there was always the matter of her dad's salary, and even with all the student loans she could swing, Tina did not see herself going anywhere Ivy-Leaguish. "Well," she said, "someday . . ."

"Not if things keep going the way they're going," Cerise said, looking up, and the expression in her blue eyes was unusually intense.

Tina slumped back in her chair. "Okay," she said. "Things got a little exciting in civics today, especially after your shouting match with Miss Alopecia started." The civics teacher's name was actually Miss Pastizia, but these days no-one could fail to notice the way her cherry-red hair was thinning out, and someone had discovered the medical word for this — not Tina: she was denying it constantly. Shortly thereafter the nickname had become unmovably attached. "What did they do to you in the principal's office?"

"Oh, the usual . . . nothing much." Cerise leaned her chin on one hand, propped up by the elbow. "Yelled at me some, told me my bad attitude was going to hamper me in the future, and if I wasn't careful a report of my 'repeated antisocial behaviour' was going to have to go on my permanent record. What are they going to do, send it to the FBI?" She snickered. "If my SATs are good, no-one will care."

Tina raised her eyebrows. "Probably you're right. But what was it about, anyway? You sounded more upset than usual."

Now it was Cerise's turn to raise her eyebrows. "'Than usual'? Thanks so much for the vote of confidence."

"Cerise," Tina said patiently, "tell me what's on your mind before I expire of suspense, here."

"Well." Cerise laid out the papers she had unloaded, very orderly, and opened the big book to a spot marked with a torn-off piece of Post-It note. "Did you know," she said, "that *places* can have horoscopes?"

"It hadn't occurred to me," Tina said. "Mostly I barely notice the 'people' one in the paper. And if I do, I usually just look at it, and if it's good and anything like it happens I say 'That's nice, it was right', and if it's bad and it doesn't happen, I say 'See that, what kind of accuracy can you expect from someone who's not only a franchise, but dead.'" It was something she had heard her father say.

"Huh? Oh, yeah, that guy's horoscopes weren't worth much even when he was still breathing. What can you expect when he gives you two sentences and they're supposed to apply to one twelfth of the human race?" Cerise smiled a superior smile. "But personal horoscopes, done with the hour and place of your birth, and the year . . . that's different. You can get really good results out of those. I did mine on the computer last night. You want me to do yours?"

"Cerise," Tina said, "what I want is for you to tell me what the heck this has to do with you yelling at the teacher and getting sent to the principal's office!"

"Yeah, I'm getting to that. Look, here's mine." Cerise pushed one of the computer-printed sheets of paper at Tina, and Tina turned it right side up and looked at it. The pattern printed on it looked like a spoked wheel, and inside the twelve 'compartments' of the wheel, symbols and numbers were printed here and there. Some of the symbols Tina recognised as those of the inner planets, Venus and Mars and so forth: others were less recognisable. The whole thing reminded her entirely too much of some of the calculus equations she had been fighting with for the past hour or so, nasty complex things that made her rue the day she had decided to go for 'advanced placement', a phrase which she now realised was code for "giving yourself grey hair before your time".

She looked up at the top of the paper. "Libra," she said. "Scorpio rising."

"Yeah. And you're what?"

"Taurus. May 18."

"Yeah, that's why we're friends. See, we're opposite signs, and at least one of us has her Moon on the other one's Sun: that makes people like each other a lot of the time." Cerise pulled the sheet of paper back to her. "See how this is set up? It has the time I was born, and the place, and that way the computer was able to tell what constellations were rising and which ones were setting, and what planets were up then and where they were. Then you can tell how they aspect each other, and all kinds of things. It makes the horoscope a lot more accurate, a map or a plan instead of just a guessing game."

Tina wasn't sure she bought into any of this, but Cerise's interest was slightly catching. "So fine," she said. "But this wasn't what was making you scream at Miss Alopecia."

"No," Cerise said. "This was." She pushed another sheet of paper at Tina.

Tina looked at it curiously. It said OXRUN STATION, 73 degree sign 05" 06' W 41 degree sign 52" 46' N. "The latitude and longitude."

"You got it backwards, but yeah. Then factor in when Oxrun was founded, in the seventeenth century. For some reason it doesn't matter which year you pick: it always comes out the same. Look, I did several, based on what that odd librarian in the local history section told me."

They leaned over the sheet of paper together. "There are some relationships among the planets that repeat," Cerise said. "Some of them are good ones . . . some aren't so good. Some are pretty awful. See this one?" She pointed to the paper. "And this, and this . . . "

Cerise was indicating three symbols; the circle-and-downward cross for Venus, a crescent, and a thing that looked like a backwards small H. "Is that one the Moon?" she said.

"Yup. And that other one's Saturn." Cerise was looking at them uneasily. "When they're in an evenly spaced triangle like that, it's usually not very good. Saturn is a problem . . . "

"And Saturn means what, usually?"

"Age," Cerise said. "Old age . . . time passing . . . cold . . . winter . . . darkness . . . pain . . . death. The end of things.

Everything running down. Entropy . . . " She looked sidewise at Cerise. "You know, if you watched more *Sailor Moon*, you'd know all this stuff already."

"Spare me," Tina said. "I graduated to *X-Men* some time ago."

"Patriarchalist myth," said Cerise archly. "Never mind, it's a stage, you'll get over it. But Teenz, never mind that. The problem is that Saturn affects any other sign in trine with it — that's what this relationship is called: a Grand Trine. Venus can be nice; but not in this aspect. Here all that strength gets corrupted. So does the Moon until she's at midheaven, and the trine starts to break. Saturn is worst: it's in its exaltation, now at its strongest. And here's the *really* creepy part. This particular Grand Trine happens in Oxrun Station's horoscope every seventy-three years. And it's happening *this* year."

"And just what happens when this trine thing sets in?"

Cerise sounded more uneasy yet, if that was possible. "I wasn't sure at first, so I did a little research," she said. "There are a lot of old newspapers in the town library. I didn't want to be obvious about it. And I didn't want to say anything until I was sure. I know everybody thinks I'm a witless pseudogothic geek with no fashion sense." That bitter tone almost made Tina start: it was very unlike Cerise. "I wanted to have my facts in place before I opened my mouth. And now I'm almost sorry, because the facts are that a lot of people *die* here, all of a sudden, when that trine happens. Mostly young people, children, teenagers, kids our age. Something happens that's old age's revenge on youth, in one way." Her face set grim. "Or if you want to look at it another way — the powers that 'live behind' that trine come out, get loose and have themselves a little party. Venus and Saturn and the Moon. And not the good sides of them, either! I know Saturn's not all bad, Teenz; there has to be painful learning, and age and death, or everything just stands still — jeez, even Walt Disney knows about the Great Circle of Life these days." The bitterness got into her laugh now. "But this isn't *normal* death. Venus in this aspect isn't just *normal* love or lust: it's lust *against* life, not *for* it. Hunger . . . the Devourer who gnaws the bones. And it's not the nicey-nice virgin or good-mommy mother-goddess parts of the Moon that get involved here; it's the Barren One, the Hag, the Old Lady with the Shears who cuts your life-thread short, who cuts you off at the knees . . . Until it changes. And before it changes, more people are going to die, and some of them are going to be some of *us*, unless we do something to stop it!"

"Like what?"

At that Cerise looked at Tina, and ran out of steam. "I don't know," she whispered. "Calling Civil Defense seems kind of useless at this point."

Tina felt inclined to agree. And bringing this up at school was likely to have little effect except to get Cerise sent to the school psychiatrist, which definitely *would* go on her permanent record. "But something's got to be done," Cerise muttered. "Some kind of ceremony, maybe. A church service — the new gods against the old ones, maybe. Or maybe something invoking the good sides of the planets, I don't know . . . But we're going to need some kind of help, something really strong. Saturn's in his exaltation, and there's no way to defeat his malign influence until the Moon hits midheaven, and shifts the rest of the trine towards detriment—"

All of a sudden it all got to be just too much, too fast. "Cerise," Tina said, "*what century is this?*"

Cerise stopped in mid-sentence, blinked at Tina, then closed her open mouth.

"This is *Saturn* we're talking about, for cripesake," Tina said. "It's umpty thousand million miles away."

"Nine," Cerise said, with rather injured dignity.

"Nine, thank you. But I have to ask: how can something nine thousand million miles away really affect us like this? The Moon, that I can buy, it's practically in the Earth's back yard. The Sun, yes, turn it off and see what happens to us! And it's got a huge magnetic field that makes a difference to our own, and to the world's weather and whatever. Fine! But Saturn? Gimme a break. Magnetism's too weak at a distance like that. So is gravity. Light doesn't matter. What's Saturn going to *do* to Earth to affect it? Make faces at it?"

"You're not taking this seriously," Cerise said.

"Cerise. *Hello*?!" Tina waved at her friend in an attempt to get the attention of some more reasonable part of her brain. "I'm bad at maths, but not this bad! This makes no sense in terms of science . . . even I know that much. Can't you give me some reason that makes sense?"

"No," Cerise said mournfully. "It's just transcendental, or something: that's what I think. Science won't explain it. But if you have any explanation for all those kids dying seventy-three years ago, when the Grand Trine happened last, I'd be glad to hear it. And SJ's in the hospital already, did you hear? And so is Ursula, but in her case it's just broken bones. SJ's in a coma."

Tina covered her mouth, shocked.

"My God," she said, when she could talk again. Cerise was watching her. "My God. I didn't know."

"I'm a long way out of the loop," Cerise said, rather bitterly again, "but I do hear some things, even if I have to eavesdrop. It's started already, Teenz. And if it's all the same to you, I'd really like to find a way not to be part of it. I wear black for fashion reasons, not because I intend to be buried in it any time soon."

Tina sighed. "Look," she said, rather more softly, into the heavy-hanging atmosphere. "Want some iced tea?"

"You make your own," Cerise said, "or is it out of a can?"

"Please," Tina said. "The canned stuff has aspartame and weird chemicals in it. My dad says he has to put enough chemicals into people in the line of business, as it is: he doesn't like to do it on his time off. Caffeine, yeah, but nothing stronger."

"I'll get a glass."

There was that comfort between them, at least: they both knew the contents of each other's kitchens, though Tina's was considered slightly superior because of a lack of siblings to eat everything in it while no-one was looking. Brothers, in particular. Cerise had two, one who was incredibly studious and normal and one who was a couch potato of the most highly developed kind, and Cerise was convinced that they were both the result of reverse alien abductions. Tina was glad there were no such annoyances to deal with in her life; she had more interesting ones, though the present one was a lot more interesting than she liked.

They sat at the table and drank the iced tea in silence for a while. Finally Tina said, "We could tell my dad. He believes a lot of crazy things."

"I can see why he would," Cerise said bleakly, and started to get up. "You think that I'm—"

"*I think that I'm going to whack you right between the ears if you don't stop interrupting me!*" Tina hollered, slamming her iced tea down on the table. It slopped around.

Her eyes wide, Cerise subsided.

"We have to at least try telling him," Tina said. "The worst that can happen is he'll tell us we're both nuts. But he's going to want to see some proof. One of the things they taught him in nursing school, he told me, was never to accept third-hand evidence. You're going to have to go get Xeroxes of those newspaper stories or something."

"I have some at home. I can't dig around for them tonight, though . . . my folks would strip the flesh off my bones if I didn't go straight to bed."

It had never occurred to Tina that Cerise was even slightly concerned about what her parents thought. "Okay, that can probably wait for tomorrow, she said. "But, Cerise, the other thing is that we've got to make some headway on this calculus. Do all these trines and angles give you a better leg up on it than I've got? Because if I don't have this stuff done before my dad gets back, he won't want to hear anything else we have to say, not even if we can show him Godzilla is standing in the back yard holding a sign saying THE END OF THE WORLD IS NIGH."

"Integrals," Cerise said. "I can do integrals . . . some. My brother taught me."

"You can?" Tina said in astonishment. "Your brother?"

"He did it to win a bet," Cerise said, sounding extremely annoyed. "Don't expect me to tell you the details. Gimme the book and let's see what we can do."

She reached for the paperback. Tina sighed and looked out the window. Dusk was falling: and high up in the window, in the burning blue above the tattered gold of the trees in Thorn Street, she could see Venus in the sky, a small hot white light that at any other time she might have mistaken for the landing lights of an aeroplane. Tonight, though, it looked nothing like that. Dazzling, remote, brilliant, it looked like an eye, looking down at the world, at Oxrun Station, and at Tina, amused, malicious, and unblinking.

Tina blinked first, looking away to the calculus book with a completely bizarre sense of weariness and relief.

Tom and Norma sat in the coffee room with charts out on the desk in front of them, doing what for Norma was the end-of-shift report and what was for Tom the signing-in one. "So our wandering boy," Norma was saying, "came to the end of his seventy-two hours and waltzed out the door with hardly a word for me." She sounded amused, but Tom knew she was covering up a certain amount of irritation. "I spent all this morning trying to contact someone from his family, but I couldn't reach anything but their answering machines . . . and I think I know why. They've finally washed their hands of him."

"Where did he go?"

"I have no idea," Norma said. "I was hardly in a position to be able to follow him down the street. All I could do was call the police and let them know he was going to be out on the street again, which seemed a courtesy, since they're probably going to find themselves picking him up again in a few days or a week."

Tom sighed. Harry Pelsen had been officially homeless for months now, but refused to stay in any halfway house or other facility where he was placed for longer than a few good meals. After that he homesteaded under bridges or in run-down properties in neighbouring towns before being picked up, usually dehydrated and malnourished, and brought back to Oxrun. He would stay long enough to get rehydrated, clean and deloused, then sign himself out again . . . and there was nothing anyone could do about it, for State law said you needed two qualified physicians to jointly certify a person as sufficiently insane to be kept against his will; and Harry was just too sane to be 2PCd. In a less enlightened and better budgeted era, he would have been committed to a big State asylum without a second thought, but those times were not these times.

"Okay," Tom said. "So much for him, until next time. Michelle Warkins, though, she was discharged as scheduled?"

"No problems . . . her mother and her therapist came to pick her up." Michelle was a local woman who had had a psychotic break, possibly secondary to an ongoing divorce: a week or so of medication, and another couple of weeks of nearly nonstop talking, had pushed her through the crisis of the "break" and out the other side to a state that looked a lot more like normalcy. She still had a lot of issues to resolve, but Michelle's therapist had been working closely with the staff on the unit, and he was a careful, thoughtful sort who would keep her talking and off the drugs through the uncomfortable time that would follow. Tom had high hopes that the nursing staff here would never need to see her again. "How did she seem when she left?"

"Tired. But game. She has that kind of spirit," Norma said, "that flashes out at you sometimes; makes it plain she's not going to let this beat her. I think she's one of the winners."

Tom nodded. "Meantime. . . "

"Meantime," Norma said wearily, and picked up Andrea Gabrieli's chart, flipped through it. "Andrea has not had the best day. She was quiet enough at breakfast, and after her shower we sat down and started chatting about her mother . . . but that didn't last."

"Does it ever?" Tom said. Andrea was in her mid-twenties, an Oxrun native who had been suffering from one form or another of schizophrenia since her teens. For a long time she had been shuttled from one State facility to another by doctors and therapists who had been unable to get any kind of handle on exactly what her trouble was, and had tried every possible intervention, from ten different kinds of psychotherapeutic drugs right down to electroshock, without any significant result. Sometimes Andrea was very crazy indeed; sometimes she was less so; sometimes she could be quite sane . . . for a few days at a time, until everything seemed to come undone. Tom's opinion was that she was thoroughly institutionalised — so used to life in one kind or another of hospital that normal home life was now alien and terrifying to her, so much so that she had no particular interest in getting better, since doing so would mean being sent home to the mother with whom she had had such a problematic relationship all her life.

At the moment it seemed to be manifesting itself in the form of wildly inappropriate seductiveness and other sexual behaviour: shameless flirting, exposing herself, sexually explicit language, endless innuendo. Dr. Masham, the third-year resident presently taking care of her, was of the opinion that Andrea was suffering from multiple personality disorder, and that these behaviours were the expression of "Marcie", Andrea's name for one of her alternate personalities. Tom's opinion was that Dr. Masham was succumbing to the popular fad for diagnosing this particular disorder, and that Andrea, far from expressing some aspect of one of her multiple personalities, was simply acting out the more uncontrolled side of her particular brand of schizophrenia, and preferred to use the sexual idiom because she had noticed it both freaked out and fascinated her therapist.

"Andrea," said Miss Norma, looking resignedly at today's notes on Andrea's chart, "has spent all day in and out of her clothes. She put them on herself, all right. But then after lunchtime I found her out in the hall in her underwear, or rather about half her underwear, yelling that she was the Great Sex Goddess and that we would all bow down before her and worship. 'Not in that outfit,' I said, and put her clothes back on her again. That lasted about ten minutes. The third time, I told her she could just stay in her room until she agreed to keep her clothes on. No agreement was forthcoming . . . and there we stand at the moment. Maybe you will do better. She likes *you*."

Tom's grin was wry. "I suppose I should be grateful. No other interesting conversations?"

"Nothing at all. This has not been one of her better days, therapeutically speaking."

"Okay," Tom said, and Norma put aside Andrea's chart. "And last of all, our John. . . "

"*Him* I wouldn't mind some yelling and physical activity from," Norma said sorrowfully. "No sign, though." She flipped through this chart as well. "His doctor suggested we change him over to trizelanepam . . . I agreed; it seemed like a possibility. I gave him the first dose this morning, intramuscular, and another after lunch."

"He ate?"

"He chews, sort of. I keep worrying that he's going to aspirate, but eventually the food goes down. A little, anyway . . . I gave him oatmeal for breakfast, again for lunch, with the vitamin supplement in it. He drinks all right, from the squeeze bottle; at least we don't have to worry about dehydration yet."

Tom sighed again. John Doe 14 had been brought in a week ago by Chief Stockton — found sitting on a bench in the Park, having been reported to have been seen sitting there, immobile, unspeaking, for hours. When the cops brought him in, the immediate diagnosis, even by the occasionally relatively clueless types in the main hospital's ER, had been catatonia, classic type, with the tall fair-haired man showing every symptom including the classic "waxy flexibility" that kept his limbs in one position until you forcibly moved them. They would then resist you ever so slightly as you made them move, and after reaching the position you were trying for, there they would stay, like those of a wax doll or an effigy. Back at the State hospital where he had trained, Tom had seen bored staff on nights play some cruel jokes with such people, forcing them into "funny" positions, using them (on a couple of occasions he remembered with particular loathing) as coatstands or tray-holders.

Tom had always hated such games, and he felt for catatonics, very ill people trapped in one of the most vulnerable states in which a human being can find himself. He knew how that seeming immobility could belie a terrible rush of mental activity — not stillness nor unconsciousness, but an awful inturned activity so frenetic that the body was literally frozen stiff by it, nerves overloaded with too much interior "business" to allow any normal physical movement. Medication might help . . . sometimes. Mostly there was nothing you could do but wait, and that was what he and Norma and Laura had been doing, for days now. "What's the estimate of how long the triz will take to hit therapeutic levels?" Tom said. "Three days?"

"So the book says, though serum cholesterol levels can make it shorter or longer, apparently. We'll see."

They put the charts aside. "So that's everything," Norma said. "Med cabinet's in order, count's done on the controlled substances cabinet. Oh, and I tried out the new coffeepot."

"I saw it." The old one had expired untimely because of repeated abuse by third-year residents who thought the way to make coffee was to put in a whole pound of the stuff at once. "Coffee's good."

"At least *something* works around here," Miss Norma said, and got up and stretched. "Though some would say things are running a lot more smoothly than they are in the Big House." This was unit "code" for the rest of the hospital.

"Oh?" Tom stood up too, and started putting the charts back in their rack. "What's wrong?"

"A lot of admissions all of a sudden," Norma said, reaching into the closet for her jacket. "Mostly trauma — seems a lot of people are having one of those accident-prone weeks: falling down stairs, broken bones, things like that. But one of the admissions might need a psych evaluation: Rick Collett wasn't sure of the aetiology — she came in confused and disoriented, went shocky, and collapsed. No-one qualified was available this afternoon, but it doesn't seem to be a priority: we can get Rob Millman over to have a look at the kid tomorrow when he comes down to the unit to check on Andrea, since her therapist's away."

"All right. What's the new admission's name?"

"Natalie Dayne."

Tom nodded. "Okay. Maybe I can scare her up someone tonight. What else is the matter with her?"

"Comatose," Norma said, "so Eleanor on Med-Surg told me... that's why I said there was no rush: can't do a full evaluation till she's conscious. Might be a neuropsychiatric problem, but they're ruling out medical and organic causes first. Private patient," Norma added. "Craine's paying, apparently."

"Huh," Tom said. "Really." The Craine family fortune was part of the foundation of the hospital's trusteeship. You didn't see Abraham Craine often — just his car, sometimes, big and black, coasting around Oxrun — but the sense of his money and influence were everywhere in this part of the world, and his personal involvement in anything made people pay attention. "Interesting. She a relative?"

"Don't know," Norma said, shrugging into her jacket. "Though gossip over in the Big House may suggest something." She rooted around in one of the file cabinets for her purse. "You're all by yourself here tonight," she said. "Can I bring you something in for your break?"

"Naah, I'll send out for some sandwiches from The Luncheonette."

"Okay." They went out into the hall together; Tom locked the nursing station behind him. "You have a good one, Tommie..."

"Do my best," Tom said as Norma headed down towards the locked door.

"You come on down here, honey!" Andrea shrieked from her room. "I want to talk to you!"

Norma threw Tom an amused look as she unlocked the door. "I told you," she said, slipped through it, and locked it behind her. Tom just grinned.

"We can talk in a while," Tom called to Andrea, suspecting exactly what the talk was going to sound like. Not that he would refuse her: listening to patients talk out their problems was nine-tenths of what a good psych nurse did, and nine-tenths of the way you ever did your patients any good. But in Andrea's case, Tom much doubted he was going to hear much more than an hour or so of smutty chatter, having nothing whatever to do with Andrea getting better, and mostly probably suggesting at the end of it that she needed her medication adjusted again. Probably upwards, Tom thought, and then felt faintly guilty at the thought.

He paused before the doorway of the one 'secure room' on the floor. It was not the padded cell of legend: good clinics didn't have such things, using pre-emptive care to make sure their patients didn't get to the point where they hurled themselves into things. If they started to do so, they were usually sedated and restrained in bed until the right combination of drugs and other interventions could be found to keep them from bashing themselves up; and then the therapy, the talking, would begin in earnest. Tom had not seen a straitjacket since he graduated from nursing school, thirty years ago, and he shuddered at the thought of such things. At least psych had got past that.

But for all the progress that had been made, there were still the people you couldn't do anything about, you couldn't help: and here was one. Tom could only begin to imagine what might be going on inside the man who, as he peered through the small square window in the door, was sitting on a foam weight-distribution pad on the bare floor, his hands clenched together in his lap, his legs straight out in front of him like those of a child. The blue eyes, surprisingly intense in their blueness, stared at the wall, seemingly sightless — though Tom knew that the blind expression was an illusion, and that John Doe 14 here probably knew every paint fleck and bump on that wall better than any other human being would. The sharp-cheekboned face was slack and expressionless, but that would be illusion too: a storm of emotion would be rushing through the mind behind the face, so virulent that it was holding the muscles paralysed. There was no telling what those emotions were, and until the man's medication "mix" was got right, right enough at least to break the catatonia and allow some motion — including speech — there would be no way to find out. For the moment, "John" had to be checked every fifteen minutes, as if he were a suicide risk — for there was no telling, he might be suicidal as well, and catatonia did sometimes break without warning — and turned and shifted like someone comatose, to prevent pressure sores forming, and cleaned and changed like a baby, for he had no sphincter control.

Tom looked him over carefully. He was still dry — Norma had changed his incontinence "pants" an hour ago — and he did not need to be moved for another fifteen minutes, since Norma had come in to move him just before Tom arrived; next time he would ease John down and turn him on his side. It bothered him that there was so little else that could be done for him now. *But until the meds take* . . . Tom thought. And the room itself could help: bleak though it seemed, the mild sensory deprivation of being in such a plain and unstimulating place could itself help ease someone out of catatonia, giving less stimulus to keep the rushing torrent of thought going than even the quiet unit outside would.

He gave John one last look. *Who are you, buddy?* No-one in Oxrun knew him, which in itself was mildly unusual. The hospital didn't usually get 'wander-ins' from outside, either medical or psychiatric. But it was always possible that John wasn't so much a wander-in as a drive-through: a relative of someone from some neighbouring state, driven in and dumped here as casually as someone might dump a cat they didn't want to keep any more. Tom had seen a lot of that kind of thing while the big State hospitals were still open — elderly relatives, not even mentally ill, simply shoved into the State hospital system by relatives who found them too expensive or too much trouble to take care of. Now, though, in these days of community care, people got dumped even more callously; their relatives seemed not to care whether anyone took care of them at all . . . for all too often there wouldn't be enough money or facilities to care for severely ill patients, and they would wind up in B&Bs or bedsit apartments somewhere, "fallen between the cracks", forgotten, eventually usually homeless . . . often, later, the victims of robbery, even murder.

Tom sighed. At least John Doe 14 here was all right for the moment. Later, in a couple or a few weeks, would come the time when the money would run out, and he would probably have to leave here. *And where will he go then . . . ?*

He stepped away from the door and went down to look through the window of Andrea's room. Rather to Tom's surprise, she was mostly dressed, and as she saw him come to the window, she jumped up off her rather disordered bed, buttoning her dress up, and hurried over to the door. "You going to let me out, Tom sweetie?" she said, squirming herself at him lasciviously.

Tom didn't react, for the effect was ridiculous. Andrea was not a bad-looking woman, really — dark-haired and rather on the plump side, though Tom for his own part was not going to be running anyone down for that. But her illness caused her to twist her face into bizarre expressions, which were usually capable of instantly ruining any fleeting attractiveness that might manifest itself, and this kind of behaviour only made her less attractive still. "Andrea," he said, "I don't feel like playing this game today. If you'll promise to keep your clothes on, you can come out and sit, and watch TV if you like. Or we can talk." He half wished she would opt for the TV, and condemned himself for cowardice as he wished it. But Andrea's conversation wasn't usually terribly revealing of anything but a continuing desire to be in people's faces. Or in their pants, Tom thought with a grimace.

"Come on, Tommie, let me out!"

"And you'll keep your clothes on?" Tom said. "Because if you don't, you're going straight back in here. You know it's not appropriate to just strip off every time you feel like it."

"But there's no-one here but you! And you're a nurse. You're *professional. You* don't care about seeing people naked." She put a spin on the word that made Tom have to control himself to keep from rolling his eyes at her in annoyance.

"Flattery will get you nowhere," Tom said, "and as for being naked, there's a time and a place for everything, and this isn't it. You keep your clothes on, you stay in. You start taking your dress off, and you go straight back in again. I am not up for limits-testing tonight."

There was a sullen and rather prolonged silence at that. Tom waited, while Andrea squirmed herself at him. Finally she said, "All right, I promise."

For once she seemed to mean it. "Okay," Tom said.

He unlocked the door, and she undulated out past him. There was no other word for it: and again Tom had to strictly control himself to keep from laughing, since such a walk and demeanour in a woman wearing a tired-looking cotton housedress and bedroom slippers, was not only wildly inappropriate in itself, but verged on the grotesque.

Andrea undulated right on past him and down to one of the two chairs that sat on either side of a table and table lamp a little way down the hall. There she enthroned herself with a grand air, like a dowager duchess, and waited for Tom to join her.

He kept his face straight and sat down in the other chair. "So what's going on today?" he asked.

"I," Andrea said, "am the Queen of the Sky."

"Oh yeah?" Tom said. This kind of opening gambit, phrased to shock, he was used to: but this one was a little more creative than usual. "Since when?"

"Early this week," she said, and grinned at him. It was not a pleasant grin, but then most of Andrea's expressions had a feral or angry cast to them, which was also no particular surprise.

"This is the first I've heard of it," Tom said. "Is this something you've felt you had to keep secret?"

"For a little while," she said, "but not much longer." Briefly she squirmed in the chair, and this time the squirming was more like that of an excited child, sitting on a secret that it was having trouble keeping. "Pretty soon everybody will know."

"Interesting," Tom said, and nodded thoughtfully. "What does this mean, exactly?"

"That I'll be able to have anything I want."

Oh boy, Tom thought, here it comes. "And what does that look like to you, at the moment?"

"The world," she said calmly, "and all the men in it; to devour."

Boy, would her therapist love to hear this one, Tom thought. Is this too Freudian, or what? But then, so's her therapist. "That would take you a while," Tom said, "even if it was a reasonable goal."

"It'll take just the blink of an eye," she said, "one way." Andrea giggled, and smiled a very knowing smile. "Time is relative . . . Other ways, it'll take a long, long time. Forever, or better. . . "

"I see," Tom said. "Why would you want to devour a whole world, anyway?"

She looked at him with slight surprise. "Because it's *there*," she said.

"Aha, the Edmund Hillary approach," Tom said. "A big job for just one woman, though."

"Not a woman," said Andrea calmly. "Or not *just* a woman. And I am not alone. There are others."

"Oh," Tom said, thinking that this was an interesting change from the usual veiled or non-veiled smut, and wondering where it was all coming from all of a sudden. "Such as?"

She only smiled that uncomfortable, knowing smile again: and from down the hall, Tom thought he heard something go *crunch . . . crunch . . . crunch.*

"I'd tell you," Andrea said, "but I don't think you're listening, and I hate not being listened to. I think I'll watch TV instead."

"I'm listening to you, Andrea," Tom said, "but I'm not sure I understand what you're getting at."

"You're hearing, maybe," Andrea said, getting up and smoothing her housedress down. "It's not at all the same thing." She headed on down towards the TV room. "Is this the day for the new TV guide?"

"Yesterday," Tom said, bemused, getting up and watching her go. "It should be down there on top of the TV, as usual. But if you want to talk—"

He heard the TV come on in a rush of laughter, some afternoon talk show. Well, that's worth putting down in her chart, whatever brought it on, Tom thought. Unusually weird, even for Andrea.

He made his way back up to the nursing station, unlocked it, went in, and pulled Andrea's chart out. And as he stared at it, a sudden and surprising weariness came down on him. *I can't wait to go home . . .*

But it would be a while before he could do that. He pulled a pen out of the pen canister, flipped Andrea's chart open to the page where Norma had made her last notes, and then paused.

Crunch . . . crunch . . . crunch . . . crunch.

Tom stood up, his curiosity seriously piqued now, and as he did, the sound stopped. He stood there listening hard for a moment. But no other sound came but that of an audience on the TV saying "Whoooaaaaaa!" in the interested tone of voice of people who suspected that one of the guests on the talk show was about to get up and punch another one in the eye.

Tom raised his eyebrows, sat down again and went back to starting his notes. "*I am the Queen!*" Andrea yelled then from the TV room. "*I'm the Queen of the World! Why don't you get it?!*"

Tom smiled wryly and turned a little in his chair... then was suddenly distracted by something bright out the window. He glanced that way. High in the sky of early sunset, burning ridiculously bright, Venus looked in the window: like an eye, lingering on him, bright, silent and amused.

He turned back to his writing. *First conversation with the patient today suggests she may be exhibiting ideation indicating a new delusional system,* Tom wrote. *Classical delusions of grandeur seem to form some part of it, but a certain sexual component is still evident—*

The eye did not blink.

Tina was sitting hunched over the sheet of paper, staring at it. "I'm supposed to do what with the integral?"

"You don't *do* anything with it," Cerise said, sounding slightly exasperated. Well, maybe she had reason: they had been at this for hours, now, even counting the time they'd taken off to take a break, have a few snacks, and gossip. "It just sits there. What you do is—"

The sound of a key turning in the front door brought Tina's head up. A moment or so later her dad came in. "My God," he said, taking his jacket off as he came in and glanced around the kitchen, "what's been going on in here? You guys planning to open a Pizza Hut? Hi, Cerise."

"Hi, Mr. Broadbent," Cerise said, very proper. Tina strangled a laugh.

"We only had two pizzas, Dad, honest," Tina said. "I was saving one for you."

Her father smiled a little tiredly and sat down in the chair at the end of the table, glancing down at the welter of paperwork, most of which was covered with Tina's attempts to translate into execution the mathematical exercises Cerise was explaining to her. "Looks like you two've been hard at it."

"Mostly her," Cerise said. "We're helping each other. I know a little about this, but Tina's been working real hard..."

Tina saw the look on her father's face, and recognised it; he plainly suspected he was being sweet-talked for some reason.

"Cerise," he said, "did your folks know you were going to be out this late?"

"Yeah," she said.

"You won't mind if I call them and check?"

"Nope," Cerise said. Tina threw a quick glance at her, but Cerise was not wearing that 'armourproof', slightly challenging look that she wore when she was brazening something out. She was casual.

"Okay, then," he said. "You did leave me *one* pizza?"

"I'll put it in the oven for you," Tina offered.

"No, it's okay, I can wait a while," her dad said. She looked at him curiously: he sounded unusually tired.

"You have a bad day?" Tina said.

"No more than usual," he said. But his voice was making a liar out of him — there was something on his mind. Tina hated to even mention what she and Cerise had been talking about earlier, but she had to do it. If Cerise was right, it was really important . . . *If she's right*, said a suddenly sceptical part of Tina's mind.

She kicked that thought back where she wouldn't have to look at it. "Dad," Tina said, "how are you at problem-solving?"

"That's what I'm here for," her father said, "so they tell me. Except," and he looked rather morosely at the torn-out pages of lined spiral notebook paper lying all over the table, "where *this* kind is concerned. I was kind of hoping you had this under control."

Tina looked at him and realised that those were bags under his eyes. He looked really pooped. After only eight hours? she thought. Is he coming down with something?

"Oh, *this*," Tina said, as if it wasn't the barbed-wire tangle of maths that it was, with shreds of her mangled brains hung off every barb of it. "No, this isn't the problem we were worried about."

"Oh? Then what?"

"Maybe you should give him the pizza first," Cerise said, sounding unusually nervous. "Brain food. Protein."

"Poppycock," he said in a good-natured way. "And other substances. What's the matter with you two? You look like you've seen a ghost. And you're three days early."

"Two," Cerise said, sounding hushed now. "It's after midnight."

"Pedant," Tina said under her breath, and nudged Cerise's leg with her foot, under the table.

"Ow!"

"Lay off that," Tina's father said leaning back in the chair, "and tell me what's eating the two of you."

"Okay," Tina said. "But, Daddy, promise you won't laugh."

He raised his eyebrows. "I promise," he said.

So Tina told him what Cerise had told her. It took a while. Tina had made Cerise promise to stick to the technical part of the astrology, and the part about what she had found in the old newspapers. Tina's dad, to do him credit, sat quiet during most of it, looked attentively at the diagrams Cerise showed him, and asked a question here and there.

Finally they both ran down. "We have to do something," Tina said at last. "We had to tell somebody. You seemed like a good bet."

They both looked at him, waiting to see how he would react.

Tina's dad sat quiet for a few moments, then ran his hands through his hair and leaned on his forearms on the table. "Saturn," he muttered. "And Venus."

"I know how weird it must sound . . ." Tina said.

"No weirder than a lot of things I've heard at work," he said.

"I was afraid he was going to say that," Cerise muttered.

Tina's dad shot Cerise a look which, if it had been directed at Tina, would have kept her quiet for some minutes, wondering if there was going to be an explosion. Cerise went a little wide-eyed, and said nothing further.

Then her dad sighed, the old familiar sound of a man putting up with one more annoying but interesting thing in his life, and some of the tension went out of the situation for Tina. "I have to tell you from the git-go," her dad said after a moment, "that I don't believe in this kind of thing." He reached out and tapped the horoscope for Oxrun Station with one finger. "It's absolutely the *worst* kind of anti-science. It's got all the mistakes we ever made about the universe, all the ones we were supposed to have grown out of, rolled up and concentrated into one place, so that we can make them all over again."

Cerise flushed a shade of crimson that clashed emphatically with her hair.

"And that said," he said, "what I can't argue about is that there are a lot of trauma admissions to the hospital all of a sudden. And a lot of them have been young people. And a couple of them are severe. And this progression of events kind of bucks the odds, though God knows there are times when you seem to get a whole year's worth of some kind of admission at once."

"And the Moon—" Tina said.

"I don't want to get into that right now," Tina's father said very quietly, and Tina backed away from the subject immediately: she knew that tone of voice.

Her dad made a wry face. "My problem," he said, "is that I want to see proof before I throw something out of court. Otherwise I would throw all this out right now, and suggest very strongly that you two stick strictly to calculus. Which I thank you for helping Tina with," he added to Cerise, "no matter what else we do about this stuff, or don't do about it. But mostly I want to see those newspaper articles you were telling me about first, before I make any decisions about anything. What you're talking about here may simply be some kind of coincidence. Or alternatively it may be a clue to some weird kind of public-health crisis that recurs around here on a cyclic basis: something strictly natural. Though that would not be nearly as *interesting* as Saturn coming down from heaven on a bicycle to make people have accidents and behave badly, and then having it do a hornpipe with Venus and the Moon in the middle of Oxrun Memorial Cemetery, it would still definitely be worth knowing about, and people would thank you afterwards for helping people get to work explaining it. So what about it? This is a put-up or shut-up issue. Can you put up?"

He said it all mildly, and with some humour, but there was no mistaking that he was being deadly serious about this. Cerise bobbed her head "yes", surprisingly meekly for her, and continued, "I can bring the copies tomorrow night."

"Okay," he said. "It's a date, then, and we'll look at them when I get back from work, assuming it's okay with your folks for you to stay out so late another night."

"They won't mind," Cerise said. "They don't, when they know I'm studying."

"Which obviously you have been. I take it," he said, picking up one of the much-scribbled-over pages of calculus and holding it up between thumb and forefinger as if it was something dead and icky, "that you haven't quite mastered this art as yet." He looked at Tina.

"Uh," she said, "no."

"Good, then you can spend tomorrow evening working on it, and when I get home, before the newspaper clippings come out, you can explain it to me. Or as much of it as you've figured out by then." He dropped the paper on the table. "And now I will put that pizza in the oven, and drive Cerise home. And if you need me to make any excuses to your folks so that you can come and study tomorrow night," he said to Cerise, "I'll do that. Got your jacket? Good, then get your things together and let's go."

Cerise gathered her paperwork together and began stuffing it hastily into her bookbag. Tina's dad headed for the front door, and got the car keys off the hook.

"What's a hornpipe?" Cerise whispered.

"You got me," Tina said. She got up and followed her dad to the door, and as he turned to open the door, she grabbed him and hugged him.

"You're not bad," she said.

"Not bad," said her father. "Higher praise there cannot be. I think." He hugged her back. "You know," he said very softly, "that this is likely to turn out to be a great big heap of adolescent overcompensation for something or other."

"Hey, big words," Tina muttered.

"Politer than some short ones I can think of," her father said mildly. "Lock up behind me. I'll be back in a few. Ready, Cerise?"

"Ready," said Cerise, and there she was. "See you in school tomorrow, Teenz."

"Yeah, see ya," Tina said, as her dad and Cerise went out. She waited until they got into the car, a ten-year-old Volvo sedan that her father loved too much to trade in just yet, and watched them drive away, pools of light preceding the car, swinging around the corner of Thorn onto Centre Street, and out of sight. Tina looked up then, seeing a light up among the trees down the road and thinking it was a plane. But it was the wrong colour for that; yellowish rather than white.

Tina craned her neck to see the light better through the flutter and rustle of the drying leaves on the trees, pallid gold and orange in the light from the streetlights nearby. It flickered dim, and she realised it was something moving very very slowly over the low hills to the west of town: not a plane, but something much further away in the sky. Saturn: westering slowly, brighter than she had thought. Suddenly, when you really looked at it, it was like something watching; brighter than any star, more knowing . . . and even here, with the streetlights theoretically so bright they should have washed it out, the shadows behind things were a little odd for that extra fraction of light falling on them, that splinter of brilliance. Shapes did not look quite as solid, somehow, with that light on them. You began to think, somehow, that things looked a little soft around the edges, that they might, if you looked sideways at the right moment, actually start to *run* . . .

Tina blinked at the sound of her dad's car coming back already, and the streetlights looked normal again then. *Already, though*? Tina thought, a little dazed. Cerise's house was three minutes' drive or so from here, and here he was back already. She couldn't have been standing here six minutes? ten maybe? *Daydreaming? Or what?*

Tina swallowed, and shut the door and locked it, and went upstairs to avoid further explanations . . . she had already made enough of those for one night.

She did not go immediately to sleep: the memory of that long frozen moment in the doorway was too much with her. Tina was going to be glad enough to get into bed and pull the covers up tonight. But first she padded softly out into the hallway where her dad's "reference" bookshelves were, and got down one of his books on mythology, an old paperback with beautiful scratchboard engravings in it, taking it back to bed with her. It's not like I don't trust Cerise, Tina thought, or the spin she puts on things . . . but checking out for myself some of this stuff she's been talking about doesn't seem like a bad idea.

With the book in her hand, Tina paused for a moment at the head of the stairs, looking down them at the light from the living room. Her dad was still up, finishing the last of his pizza, watching late TV — or rather trying to, surfing rather hopelessly from cable channel to cable channel in search of something that was not an infomercial featuring someone setting the hood of a car on fire, or someone else sucking the air out of a plastic bag with blankets in it.

Tina slipped quietly back into her bedroom, shut the door, undressed and got into a long nightshirt, and shut off everything but the small reading light by her bed, before climbing in and getting comfortable. The mythology book was a big heavy one, and the rustle of the pages as she turned them sorted agreeably with the dry rustle and whisper of the leaves out on the trees in the back yard.

Saturn . . . It was not a Greek name, but Latinate, the book said: a name for a being who wasn't one of the better-known pantheon of twelve Greek gods, but a member of an earlier group. They were the Titans, the gods before the Gods: grandchildren of Chaos, born from Earth's darkness and the destroying fire of

Heaven — a turbulent brood, dangerous and wild. The king of them was Saturn, though Cronos was his name to the Greeks, the god of Time and Death, who devours everything. The stories about him were creepy; images of scythes and blood and chopped-off bits kept coming up, and he was probably the source of the modern images of the Grim Reaper. The book said it had been prophesied by the forces that dwelt in darkness above the world that Saturn's son would kill him. So when Saturn married another Titan, Rhea, every time she bore a child, he would snatch it up and devour it. Eleven children of Rhea were eaten this way, and finally, having reached the end of her rope (kind of late, Tina thought dryly, but maybe better late than never), Rhea bore her last child, a boy, but hid it and gave Saturn a rock wrapped in swaddling clothes instead. Saturn ate the rock, and was satisfied. But the baby was raised far away, in secret, in a cave, and grew up quickly to be a powerful god, and a cranky one when his mother filled him in on what his father had done with his brothers and sisters. This young god was Zeus or Jupiter, and he did not let his siblings stay where they were for long. He got another Titan, Metis, to give Saturn an emetic that made him throw up all the swallowed gods and goddesses; and then Jupiter himself went after Saturn with his new-forged weapon, the lightning-bolt, and fried him.

Tina lay there in bed, propped up on one elbow, and grimaced in distaste at all this. There were aspects of it that were pure fairy-tale stuff, like the rougher versions of the Little Red Riding Hood story. But the parts she suspected of being the oldest ones, the cannibal images of jealous gods devouring their children, somehow rang uncomfortably true. Tina shuddered, though she was warm enough under the covers. If this was what religion looked like in the really old days, she thought, I won't make fun of Cerise for dancing around the occasional tree. It's definitely preferable . . .

She turned the pages. Of Venus, Tina had some vague pink-tinted image of a negligée-clad goddess who made people fall in love with each other: and indeed there were some fairy-tale type stories of this sort about her among the Greeks, involving guys falling in love with statues and getting Venus to bring them to life. But the book suggested that Venus, or Aphrodite if you used the Greek name, was a dumbed-down or cuted-down version of a much nastier, much older goddess, Mesopotamian or Babylonian: a bloodthirsty type whose story routinely got tangled up with those of other goddesses with names like Tanit or Astarte or Tiamat. They were all ostensibly goddesses of love or fertility, but all their stories got bloody in places, reflecting the habits of this older, meaner goddess who routinely demanded human sacrifices to distract her from her intention to turn into a dragon and eat the world and everything in it, or to break Hell open and let all the dead people out to eat the living. Beautiful she might be, but she was also ravenous, and needed occasional killing. The Assyrian version of the story got pretty gory about it, splitting her open like a flounder and plastering her bloody body all over the sky.

And as for the Moon, not even she was entirely what you would call normal, though it was becoming plain to Tina that what might pass for normal among gods and goddesses was plainly up for grabs. She was apparently good at helping women in childbirth — unusual work, Tina thought, for a virgin — and protecting the young and innocent. But she also had her bad days. Even the Greek version of her suggested that Artemis the moon goddess was a killer with her silver bow, though mostly a merciful one. Tina wondered at *that* description of her when contrasted against the story of how she shot one of her boyfriends in the head, on a bet. Sure, he got turned into the constellation Orion afterwards, but Tina was sceptical about exactly what that was worth as compensation. And then there was the poor hunter who accidentally came across her while she was skinny-dipping, and she got so annoyed that she turned him into a deer and had him ripped to pieces by his own dogs. Talk about your basic overreaction, Tina thought.

And this goddess too looked to have been even more dangerous once, more bloodthirsty: "The Moon, who makes men mad," Shakespeare had said. *And it looks like she was the* best *of this bunch*, Tina thought after a while, and closed the book. *Wonderful.*

She put the book over on her bedside table and frowned. *Maybe Dad is right. Maybe all this is just craziness on Cerise's part.*

But if it's not . . .

Tina didn't know quite what to think if it wasn't. If some horrible thing was about to start happening here, if it had happened before and no-one had been smart enough to see it coming, or to stop it . . . what chance did people have to stop it *now*? People believed *less* in this kind of thing than they used to in the old days. Just being modern, and having all kinds of information handy in books and on television and in the computer networks, didn't guarantee that things were going to go differently this century. If what Cerise had told her about SJ and Ursula was true, it seemed like it was happening again already.

Boy, I hope not . . .

She leaned over from the side of her bed and pulled aside the drapes of the nearby window. The waxing moon, two days off full, was already high. Away southwards, Saturn was still there, a little lower in the sky now; yellowish in colour, and dull compared to Venus, especially in the moonlight. It would not set until after dawn. She looked up at it . . .

. . . and could not quite get rid of the feeling that it was looking at her.

I am seriously *weirded out tonight*, Tina thought. She shivered, suddenly cold. The sensible part of her mind insisted that there was something wrong with the weatherstripping on this window: her dad kept meaning to fix it, and kept forgetting. But some less sensible part of her mind identified the source of the cold as that dull, faint light in the sky, eight billion miles away.

Such a distance away. Not even a star. But still it shines, still we can see it . . .

She shivered again. A cloud slipped across that part of the sky, hiding the stars, and Saturn. It made no sense for Tina to feel warmer, but she did.

She pulled the curtain back, turned over, turned out the light, and pulled the covers up high, cuddling down into her pillow and hoping she would not dream.

As usual, when Tina got up her dad was in bed. She showered and dressed quietly, made breakfast, checked around the kitchen to see if he'd left any notes for her — he hadn't — and locked up the house. The walk to school was only a short one, a few blocks.

The morning was grey and cloudy, and Tina hurried to get into school before it started raining in earnest, rather than the present "spits and spots", stinging cold water borne on a cold wind, and usually right into your face. She barely noticed homeroom, still being somewhat preoccupied by the reading she had done the night before, and Tina went through her first and second period classes, even the third period maths class, more or less on automatic pilot, grateful afterwards that her maths teacher had for some reason ignored her today. Just when I'm ready for you, Tina thought, annoyed, as she headed out to fourth period study hall. There's no justice . . .

In study hall, Cerise was waiting for her with a triumphant and expectant expression. "You got the clippings?" Tina said quietly to her, as they sat down at adjoining desks to work.

"Yup. Not here," Cerise said, glancing around at the others in the room, some of whom were acquaintances or friends, but not all. "Wait till after lunch."

Lunch was the next period, and since they were going to be spending extra time on calc that evening, Tina didn't bother with it, concentrating instead on the civics unit they were working on. Suddenly local history seemed a lot more interesting to her than it had previously: but unfortunately the teacher was presently concentrating on late nineteenth century stuff instead of what would have interested Tina more: early twentieth century Oxrun material, especially the period which would coincide with seventy-three years ago. *Never mind. She's got the clippings . . .*

Then it was lunch: uninspired, something claiming to be meatloaf, but the looks of which made both Tina and Cerise profoundly suspicious. Instead they grabbed a packet of potato chips, an apple and a fruit juice each, and sat down with Beth and some of the other kids.

There was some talk of the 'play party', as had been inevitable for most of the week, and some jokes about trick-or-treating among those with younger brothers or sisters who were going to have to be escorted through the town on their 'rounds'. "The old atmosphere's really building up out there now," Chuck said, and sang, "It's beginning to look a lot like Halloween . . . "

There were groans at the bad scansion and at Chuck's singing, which took place in no known key; but there was general agreement about the serious onset of the season. Halloween decorations had begun appearing in force over the last couple of days. Pumpkins were manifesting themselves on doorstep after doorstep; bound-up pale-beige cornsheaves with bright ornamental corn in the ears were appearing tied to the posts of people's mailboxes; corn- and wheat-sheaf wreaths were popping up on front doors here and there, and some windows and porches had orange and black streamers or bunting draped or wound around them. Mr. Robson's gravestones had sprouted in his front yard as they had for as long as anyone could remember, and the kids were already making bets on whose name was going to appear on the black middle one *this* year.

"The pumpkins are best, though," Sam Jones said. "Poor butchered things . . . "

"Oh, come on," Chuck said, "you have pumpkins in England!"

"We do now," Sam said, "but in the old days we used to do the same thing, carving faces on them, with turnips." Then suddenly he burst out laughing.

"What's so funny?"

"Well, think about it," Sam said. "They were to scare away demons."

"Yeah, well, so are the pumpkins, supposedly," Tina said.

"But *think* about it." Sam laughed harder. "Seriously. What kind of demon is going to be scared away by a face carved on a *turnip*?"

"A fairly useless one," Cerise said, amused.

Chuck laughed too. "Either your ancestors were wusses," he said, "or the demons were. Why even bother wasting perfectly good turnips on them? You could probably have chased them down the road and squashed them like cockroaches."

This produced a lot of snickering. "Or run them over with cars," someone else said.

"Yeah! As soon as there were cars, anyway. Now, demons that would be frightened by pumpkins," Chuck said, "all right, those might be a little bigger. But still not what you would call exactly life-threatening—"

The discussion went on in this vein for some while Tina excused herself to get rid of her trash from lunch, and when she did, Cerise came quietly over and joined her.

"Come on," Tina said softly, "let's have a look at what you've got." They slipped out the side door of the cafeteria. Smoking had been banned on campus, but there were nonetheless a few nicotine-desperate idiots sneaking a smoke out in a sheltered cul-de-sac near the cafeteria doorway: Tina and Cerise slipped past Theo Bronson and Zack Skelton and around a corner, where they were out of view of both the cul-de-sac and the windows of the school on that side.

Cerise dug into her bag and pulled out a bunch of Xeroxes. The first one was dated October 29, 1926, and was a story from the *Station Herald* about the death of someone called Lucinda Jacobs, of a fever, in Oxrun Station Hospital. The second one, dated October 30, told how a girl of five, Mary Wesley, had fallen down a hillside the day before while walking with her brother and broken a leg; while in the hospital, she had had "a fit" and died. Then followed two more clippings dated October 31, one telling of an accident on the Turnpike in which a mother and her two children aged twelve and sixteen had been mown down by an automobile which had missed a curve, supposedly because of brakes failure. And then one for November 1st describing the death the evening before of a young man of eighteen, apparently due to a "heart seizure", even though he had otherwise seemed to be in the best of health—

Tina read all these hurriedly, with an increasing sense of tension, as if someone or something was looking over her shoulder, watching her read, with ill intent. "This is really weird," she said. "All of these at once, just like that, in such a small town. . . "

"I don't think your dad's going to be able to write these off to a 'public health problem'," Cerise said. "Public *lack* of health, maybe. Everyone dropping dead at once. . . "

Tina handed the copies back. "My dad's got to be impressed by this," she said. "But look . . . assuming that he is . . . we'd better come up with some suggestions for what to *do*."

Cerise looked slightly crestfallen. "I was kind of hoping *he*'d do that," she said.

"It would be nice," Tina said. "But all bets are off on this one, Cerise. Let's get our brains in gear, and not just on the calc."

The bell rang for the end of lunch. "Come on," Tina said, and ducked back into the cafeteria. She could not now get rid of that sense of something looking over her shoulder, something inimical, now that she had actually read the clippings. If this kind of feeling was what was driving Cerise, then Tina could understand her friend's nervousness. Dad, Tina thought as she parted company with Cerise and each of them headed off to her next class, boy, I hope you can come up with an answer for this one . . .

The phone went off and woke Tom up an hour before his alarm was due to wake him, which surprised him slightly. He fumbled for it on the bedside table, found the receiver. "Yeah?"

"Tom?" It was Norma's voice. "Oh, gosh, I woke you, I am sorry."

"Just an hour early," he said; "don't worry about it."

"Look, I had to check something with you," she said. "Ginger's called in sick for tonight. Can you do a double? Otherwise we'll have to call the temp agency in Hartford, and you know how Admin is about that."

Tom knew: there would be screaming, since the temp agency's rates were, by hospital administration's standards, extortionate. He lay there on his back, rubbing his face. "The timing's not great," he said, and thought for a moment. "But I can do it. A little overtime never killed anybody."

"You are a tower of strength," Norma said. "Thanks." She sounded relieved, which Tom could understand. With Laura on vacation, staff assignment and scheduling were Norma's job, one which Tom did not envy her, since someone always lost out somehow — and the scheduling nurse who did the 'time sheets' was assumed to be the one to blame.

"No problem. How's it been today?"

"Hectic," Norma said, and that deep rich voice of hers was closer to a growl than Tom had heard for a while. "I'll fill you in when you get here."

"Right," he said. "See you in a couple of hours."

He hung up, then got up and had his shower. Half an hour later he was having breakfast — honest bacon and eggs for once, if at the slightly odd hour of two in the afternoon. It was grey outside, though the weather looked as if it might break and try to clear up later in the day, and Tom looked out at the wet golden leaves whirling past on the wind and sighed. This could be a pretty time of year, if he ever had time to get out and enjoy it. The minimal staffing at the clinic meant that he and all the other nurses did ten days on, four days off, and you were so tired at the end of those ten days that you tended to lie around for most of the four, recovering, rather than getting out and enjoying yourself.

As he ate Tom mulled over in his mind the strange performance from Tina and Cerise the night before, with all the crazy old pseudoscience they'd trotted out. He would normally have thought Tina was too hardheaded to buy into that kind of thing. But something about Cerise's manner or approach must have convinced her there was something worth being worried about, he thought. And then there were the newspaper clippings Cerise had been talking about: surely she would know better than to make stuff like that up. She could be a quirky kid, but she wasn't a liar, as far as Tom knew: she was straightforward, and she stayed out of trouble — insofar as anyone who chose to be so different in her late teens could manage that trick in a peer culture which valued being the same as everyone else so highly.

He sighed. Whatever was going on with Cerise, and to a lesser degree with Tina, he wasn't going to be able to deal with it tonight. He found a Post-It pad in the kitchen and a pen, and scribbled: *Honey — can't meet with you and Cerise tonight, have to work a double shift, sorry. Please postpone our little get-together till tomorrow afternoon after school, we'll talk then. No late night here for Cerise tonight, you lock up early and I'll see you at breakfast for once, Okay? Love you! Dad.*

He finished dressing, then had a fast look at the TV news, and made himself a few sandwiches to take to work with him — there was no way to tell whether he would be able to finesse a break between shifts to go get anything. After that, there was nothing to do but head for work, walking, as he usually did — with the hospital so close, the thought of driving was idiotic. Tom had to grin a little at the pumpkins he saw on doorsteps on his way; some of them artistically done and perfect, some of them plainly the efforts of very young children or adults rather challenged in the handling of sharp knives. One of them, as he turned the corner into King Street, made him laugh out loud: it had a jagged, toothy grin and a single eye in the middle of its 'forehead'. *Some people*, he thought.

He went on into the hospital and met Mike the security guy leaving the chair that sat outside the locked door. "Hey Mike," Tom said, and Mike said, "Might be a lively one tonight, Tom . . . "

"Oh?"

"George said there was a lot of banging around inside today." George was the day security guard; he and Mike split the day into twelve-hour shifts between them.

"Andrea?"

"*Someone* female," Mike said over his shoulder, on the way down to the coffee machine, "and George said he didn't think Norma usually used language like that."

"Uh oh," Tom said. "Thanks . . . "

"Don't mention it. Yell if you need help."

"Will do . . . "

Tom let himself in and locked up behind him. Everything seemed quiet enough at the moment, but he knew from long experience that that could be deceptive. He went on past Andrea's room without looking in, not wanting to rouse her if she had only recently quieted down, and paused only for a quick glance in at John Doe 14. He was lying on one side on his mat, a pillow under his head, eyes open, staring at the wall.

Tom shook his head and went on down to the nursing station. There he found Miss Norma writing notes, her chin propped on one hand. She looked weary. As he came in she glanced up at him and said, "Boy, am I glad to see *you*."

"A long day, huh?"

"Get your coffee and I'll tell you."

He got the coffee, and when he came back Norma was stacking one of the two active charts on top of the other on the desk and flexing her hand as if suffering from incipient writer's cramp. "So what's the story?" Tom said.

"Let me start with the easy one," Norma said, leaning back in her chair. "Our John Doe has had a completely uneventful day. Nothing significant to report. He ate a little, he drank enough, he's voiding normally. He's dry, now, by the way. Miss Andrea, however, has spent nearly the whole day screaming that no-one respects her — either as Andrea, or as 'Marcie', who has been very much in evidence today, yelling that she is tired of us 'institutional bitches' keeping her away from your body—"

"Oh boy," Tom said.

"Yes. And also as her new persona as the Queen of the Universe, or the Galaxy, or whatever it is. It changes from hour to hour." Norma looked wry. "She broke a lamp, for which she got put in her room to think things over after lunch."

"Any undressing?"

"Oh, every now and then, but she seems to keep getting distracted. Very labile today, a lot of flights of ideas, a lot of weird ideation. But she keeps coming back to this 'Queen' thing, persevering at it. She may be working out the details of this new personality."

"Consciously or unconsciously?"

"How do you tell with that one? I think her medication needs to be looked at. I know she got her last two doses of CPZ, but before that? Sometimes I wonder if Ginger watches her as closely as she should to make sure she's not ditching them."

"We could ask the doctor to give us orders for the liquid again, rather than the tabs. She has more trouble ditching the elixir."

Norma sighed. "Better you than me, sunshine. I remember how she loved spraypainting me with it the last time we tried it. I wish they'd take the red colouring out of that stuff."

Tom half smiled: he had been 'ornamented' with the sticky chlorpromazine liquid by reluctant patients all too often in his career. "Maybe somebody better explain to her that if she doesn't get it by mouth, she's going to start getting it with a needle in the butt."

"I leave that entirely to you," Norma said, getting up wearily, "assuming you can convince Bob Millman, and assuming he ever turns up."

"He didn't show up today?"

"No, they had him over in the Big House all day, and I don't know if we'll see him tonight, either. Three more trauma admissions, two with very odd aetiologies, both needing NP evaluations." She got her jacket out of the closet. "I would think something was going around, except I don't know any viruses that make kids fall downstairs and go into comas. The Big House staff are getting a little creeped out."

Tom thought briefly of what Tina and Cerise had been telling him last night . . . then dismissed it. "So Andrea is where now?"

"Out of her room, sitting down in the TV room at the moment. She got fairly quiet when she came out. Either she was tired, or the dose of CPZ I got into her at lunch quieted her down, or she's preparing to be a good innocent girl for when you show up, now that the 'institutional bitch' is going home." Norma smiled, a dry look. "Which she is very glad to do. All the rest of the sordid details about what she was screaming are in the chart: you can read them at your leisure. Listen, you want somebody from the Big House to spell you for an hour tonight between shifts so you can go get something to eat?"

"Naah, I brought a bag with me, I'm okay. Thanks, though."

"All right," Norma said, picking up her handbag and heading for the door. "You be careful tonight, then."

"Will do."

Norma went out. Tom heard her call "Goodbye!" to Andrea, in the TV room, but there was no response; her key turned in the lock, turned again: she was gone.

Tom hung his jacket up and went out to check on things. The table down the hall was now minus its lamp, and Heaven knew when there would be a new one: the hospital could be slow about replacing what it considered 'nonessential equipment'. *Maybe I'll move one out of the TV room . . . there are two in there anyway*, he thought.

He glanced into Andrea's room, which was open. Messy bed, bedstand and possessions tidier than they usually were . . . which suggested that they had been tossed around, and that Miss Norma had cleaned them up. *Hokay* . . . Tom thought, and made his way down the hall towards John Doe's room. Then, there in the middle of the hallway, suddenly he stopped. *There it is again*, Tom thought, shocked at the loudness of the sound.

Crunch, crunch . . . crunch, crunch, crunch . . .

And now he knew what it was. It was the sound of teeth grinding.

Tom went to look through the quiet room's window. John Doe was lying there, 'bruxing' hard: you could hear it right through the door, an appalling sound, like someone chewing rocks, as his lower jaw gritted and ground against the upper like that of someone chewing gum.

The thought that he might have got hold of something and be chewing it up occurred to Tom immediately, and he unlocked the door, slipped in, locked it behind him again, and went over to John to have a look. "John," he said, "do you mind if I take a look at what you might be chewing?" No response there, not that he had been expecting any, but it was common courtesy to ask anyway, even when he knew that John wouldn't answer; he knew the man could hear him.

Tom knelt down and carefully lifted the man's upper lip a little. He couldn't see anything in the mouth; the teeth were gritted together. He couldn't hear anything but the sound of them grinding. Hard.

How would he have got at anything in here, anyway? Tom wondered. *There's not even a doorknob on this side for him to have pulled off. And nothing else, not so much as a paint chip . . .*

Grind, grind, grind went the teeth. Tom sat back on his heels, looked into John Doe's eyes — if 'into' was the word when they were so very blank-seeming, so lacking in any sense of someone looking out. Yet someone *was*: and this bruxing was the first independent movement that John had made since he had been brought in from that park bench. *I wonder what it means. Except for the obvious, that the meds are starting to take. Good . . .*

"John, you look okay," Tom said. "If you want me, you just give a yell, if you can, all right? I'll be around every fifteen minutes anyway."

No answer, none expected. Tom got up, checking John to see if he was still dry — he was. "You want to talk, any time," Tom said, "I'm here, buddy. Just let me know. See you later."

He came out of the room and locked it up again, and walked away, though not without a long last look through the window.

Grind, grind, grind. Crunch, crunch...

To think he was doing that so loudly that I thought he was someone ripping up the plaster in the walls, Tom thought. How is he making that much noise and not splintering his teeth, for pete's sake? I'm going to see about getting the guy a dental consult today. Either he's got skull bones that're as sound-conductive as the outside of a grand piano, or he's got to be damaging himself somehow...

From just behind him, a voice spoke. "He does not move."

Tom looked over his shoulder and saw Andrea standing there, dressed in the usual housedress and peering past him through the window.

"He moves his jaws pretty good," Tom said, "but that's about it at the moment."

"He will move soon enough," said Andrea.

Tom looked at her. "Just who is this," he said, "telling me this? The classical turn of phrase is kind of a new sound for you."

"I am the Queen of Heaven," said Andrea calmly, "and the Queen of Earth. All things are under my dominion."

"Ah," Tom said, "so that's how it looks to you today?" He walked away from the room, back towards the TV room. "Including the furniture and the lamps, huh?" He paused by the table between the two chairs and touched the long scratch over the table's top where the lamp had hit it. "I hate to tell you, but the furniture is under my dominion, not to mention Laura's and Norma's, and we'd appreciate you not smashing it up."

"That is of little account," Andrea said, brushing past Tom and walking first into the TV room, where she sat down in the chair in the corner, furthest from the TV, enthroning herself rather the way she had done the day before. "All things are mine. I can have anything, and anybody, I want. Even you."

"I think I'm the one who would get to decide that," Tom said, unplugging the spare lamp.

"Not once I speak and make my will known," Andrea said. "What Marcie wants, Marcie gets ... now that the Queen is here."

Tom wondered as he coiled the lamp's cord up whether this was supposed to be a new distinct personality, or just a new 'crazy game' that Andrea was playing. She had occasional fits of normalcy, mostly when she slipped and took her medication steadily without managing or bothering to conceal it or spit it out unnoticed. But Tom's experience of her suggested that Andrea didn't much care for feeling sane, and usually moved quickly to sabotage her medication schedule so that she could get uncontrolled again . . . meanwhile playing 'games' in which she tried her best to act crazy, with very uneven results. And through it all the ancillary personalities, like "Marcie", the sexpot, would sometimes put their heads up and complicate the picture. "Oh yeah," Tom said, "the Queen. Is this another 'you', or something else we should be told about?"

"Not a 'me'," Andrea said, sounding mysterious, and then grinning. "I'm another *her*."

This was a new approach. "She's bigger than me," Andrea said. "Older. She promised to do me a favour, if I did her a favour. I said, why not? Don't have anything else to do." She started plucking at the collar of her dress, fiddling with the buttons, preparing to unbutton the top one.

"Don't start," Tom said.

"I didn't promise you anything today," Andrea said, with a smirk.

"Doesn't matter," Tom said. "You know what's appropriate behaviour and what's not."

She kept smirking, apparently unconcerned. "And after tomorrow, I won't have to promise anybody anything."

"Oh really. What's tomorrow, then?"

"The end of the world."

"You know," Tom said, "people keep predicting that, but the world keeps not seeming to hear about it. You think there's any chance you might be mistaken?"

"Not today," Andrea said, with that mysterious smile again. "And not tomorrow. For there will *be* no more tomorrows, after tomorrow. The Queen will come in her power, and all will tremble before her, and all will fall."

"Fall where?" Tom said.

"From the Great Above, to the Great Below," said Andrea, as if reciting a poem. "And from the Below, to here in the world. This is the time when the door is opened. And if the door is not opened willingly for her to enter, it will yet be opened regardless: I will go forth! I will smash the door, I will break the lock; I will smash the door-posts, I will force the doors!" That smile was going distinctly triumphant now. "I will bring up the dead to eat the living, and the dead will outnumber the living!"

Tom raised his eyebrows. "The last bit I wouldn't argue, in an abstract sense," he said, "but the first part sounds kind of undesirable, if you know what I mean."

"Since you're the living," Andrea said, "I can understand that." She shrugged. "It's just tough on you, I guess."

Tom blinked at that. "Oh. And what happens to you, after all of this?"

"Oh, nothing can stop it. Except her, the bitch. White bitch," Andrea muttered, her face suddenly twisting, going ugly. "*Bitch!* But after that, I will go on, and on . . . " She rested her arms on the arms of the chair in that queenly pose again. "Forever and ever, like him, like the others, my brothers and sisters, the ancient ones, the gods before the Gods. Until the next time, until the door opens again . . . "

"Uh huh," Tom said. "Andrea, would you excuse me for a moment? I want to go plug this in."

"*I AM THE QUEEN!*" Andrea shrieked. Tom did not jump: he had heard the intake of breath that preceded it. He simply walked out with the lamp and left Andrea sitting in her chair, watching the TV, which was now showing some children's afternoon special about Halloween; Tom got a glimpse of small children in ghost costumes running down some autumn street in a small town, yelling happily.

The laughter that followed him out into the hall had a slightly unsettling quality to it. "You'll find out," Tom heard

Andrea say, to him or to the TV, it was uncertain which. He went out to the table with the lamp, plugged the lamp in, checked it: it lit all right. Tom turned it off and walked on down to the nursing station to add a few notes to Norma's. 'White bitch?' he thought as he sat down and reached for the chart. Whoever that is, it isn't Norma. Does she mean Ginger? Or someone she saw on TV, maybe?

It might have been the latter, for Ginger reported that Andrea had slept almost all night, and had hardly spoken to her except at breakfast. "Nothing significant to report," said the chart: yet once again Tom was wondering if Ginger had missed something, or noticed it but neglected to chart it. Oh well. No-one really works nights well, and when the fatigue really hits you around six, it's so easy to miss small details of the previous hours . . .

Never mind. Tom did his nursing notes on the conversation with Andrea, and then went on to take care of the other routine start-of-shift things. He called the Big House about a dental consult for John Doe, and was told (as he'd half expected) that it would have to wait a day or two: things were busy over there right now. And the first hour's work passed into the second and third and fourth, the usual checks, the usual routine; and things stayed quiet. Andrea sat in the TV room, seemingly absorbed by what was on TV, with that odd, apparently unremovable, smile on her face. John Doe lay in the quiet room, or sat there when Tom sat him up, and ground his teeth, loud as a man chewing stones.

Dinnertime passed, and darkness fell, and the hours continued to slide by. Once as Tom was walking down the hall to make his checks, he stopped still, hardly knowing why he did it, except that it seemed abruptly imperative that he do so, as if he had seen something on the floor that he was going to trip over. But there was nothing there. He found himself looking out the west-facing window of one of the empty patient rooms, and through it he could see Venus, clear, bright and high in the sky, visible through a blown tatter of clouds; looking down, looking like an eye, looking at him.

Tom shivered all over. It was a funny feeling, that sense of being looked at. *Impossible. It's just a planet.* But again he thought abruptly of what Cerise had been talking about, the night before . . .

He went on down the hall. It almost cost him an effort to do so, and he actually stopped again and looked behind him at the carpet, as if to see if there was something that had made him stop there. There was nothing. But, very faintly, he could see the light of Venus on the rug. The thing was *astonishingly* bright tonight; even the dim light in the hallway should have washed its light out.

"Huh," Tom said softly. He went on down past the TV room. Andrea had not turned on the other lamp; she sat illuminated only by the TV's bluish glare, and on this room's floor too the faint light of Venus shone, despite the TV. "You okay?" Tom said.

She looked up at him slowly. In this light there was something odd about her face. Normally he would not have described Andrea's face as anything extraordinary. She could be pretty, in a vapid kind of way, when she wasn't twisting her face out of shape. But tonight she looked . . . almost handsome: somehow a little thinner, a little harder; the cheekbones looked higher, the face looked more . . . classical, somehow. *A statuesque face*, Tom thought, bemused. It was very strange; he'd seen her by TV-light often enough, and never noticed this before. *Maybe she's losing weight.* There was definitely something more attractive than usual about her. *If she weren't crazy . . .* he thought.

Then he rejected the thought immediately. And his attention was drawn again to the light of Venus on the floor, shining through the uncurtained window, impossibly bright; an eye in the sky, unblinking, looking at him, looking at her . . .

"The promise," Andrea said, "is kept."

Tom, not wanting to possibly provoke another outburst when Andrea might be shaking down to go to sleep, merely said "Okay" and passed on.

And nothing else of interest happened, and he was doing the change-of-shift notes in the charts, when he heard a key in the lock down at the end of the hall, and looked up. He got up to look out of the nursing station, and was surprised to see Ginger coming down the hall towards him, shrugging out of her Burberry.

"What're you doing here?" Tom said. "I thought you weren't coming in!"

"I felt better," Ginger said. "I couldn't reach Norma this afternoon: I assumed she was busy, but I left a message on the unit voicemail and then called Admin to let them know. Didn't they tell you?"

"No," Tom said. This was unusual: it wasn't like Admin to fail to pass on a message about staffing. Still, sometimes these hiccoughs happened, and if what Norma had told him was anything to go by, there had been reason. Norma had probably been busy dealing with Andrea, and might have missed picking up the voicemail entirely. "I think it just got lost in the shuffle," Tom said. "Things have been a little broken loose here today . . . and over in the Big House as well."

"So I heard," Ginger said. "Well, come on, I bet you'd like to get out of here."

"Wouldn't mind a bit," Tom said. He shut the office door and gave her the change-of-shift report; it didn't take long. About twenty minutes later he had put his own jacket on and was heading down towards the door, with one last look in at John Doe, still grinding away, and one look into the TV room, where Andrea still sat. "Good night," Tom said.

She looked up at him, and her eyes were very dark in the pale light; they glittered. "For some," she said.

He went out, and as he locked himself out he shook his head. Mike the security guard, sitting there for a few minutes between tours of duty in this part of the hospital, looked at Tom and said, "Tough one?"

"Quiet," Tom said. "But weird."

"Hey, it's Halloween," Mike said. "Time of the year for it."

"Mike my man, in there it's Halloween all year round," Tom said with feeling. "See you tomorrow."

"Right . . ."

The distant sound of knocking was what alerted Mike McGregor to the fact that something was amiss, there in the quiet of the new wing of the hospital at three in the morning. He was making his usual rounds with the keys for the Detex watchclock system, which logged his presence at each of the Detex stations as he reached it and turned his key in it. It was just another of management's ways to make sure that you didn't fall asleep on the job; but Mike took it in good part. He was clear enough that this place needed security. There were too many nasty people out in the world who came into hospitals and did evil things like steal babies from nursery units and assault the staff, who had other more important things to do than be attacked. Mike was glad enough to keep that kind of thing from happening, and more than prepared to act if he caught anyone trying anything funny.

What he was not prepared for was the sight of the extremely good-looking woman looking at him through the window of the psych wing's door. He didn't recognise her at all. She was tall, and had a spectacular mane of black hair on her, shining black, falling in waves down beside her face and down her back; her face was simply beautiful, with high cheekbones, big dark eyes, a gorgeous red mouth that suggested all kinds of nice things that might happen to you if you were the lucky guy she got interested in. "Hey, guy," she called, "you can let me out, I'm done with my visit now . . ."

Mike blinked at this. He knew all the patients in there by sight — not that there were ever so many of them that this was a problem — and this wasn't one of them. *Visit?* said some part of Mike's mind. *The middle of the night isn't visiting hours!* — But that part of his mind seemed dulled and far away, somehow, a little voice there was no need to pay attention to . . . especially when an amazing-looking woman like this was gazing through the window at him, smiling. Such an inviting smile. Impossible to think it wasn't him she was interested in . . .

Mike swallowed. "How'd you get locked in, lady?" he said, reaching for his keys.

She shrugged. "Door's always locked, I thought. I came to see my daughter, late, but she's not too talkative tonight . . . and what's her name, the nurse, she's busy with the quiet guy, the one who sits on the floor all the time, she didn't have time to let me out just now . . . "

"Yeah," Mike said. He could believe it: that Ginger could be kind of curt sometimes. She didn't really like working nights, he knew that. "Half a minute," Mike said.

He unlocked the door. She slipped out, and with her came a wave of dizzying perfume. Mike locked the door again behind her, and actually had to brace himself against it as it locked, the perfume and another scent, the scent of her, got so powerfully into his nose, up into his head. He blinked: it was like there was smoke in his eyes, it was hard to see, almost a haze. Suddenly there was a touch on his arm, he turned, saw her leaning towards him, her mouth parted a little, breathing soft and warm.

Closer she leaned, and Mike realised what she wanted, it was *him, oh God what luck, but not here, I . . . I . . .*

Her hand slipped behind his head, caressing. All the strength, all the will, went out of him in a rush, like blood, like . . . All he wanted was to feel those lips on his, let them do to him whatever they wanted to. They brushed his lips, now, tempting, promising. *Yes*, she said, though somehow he couldn't actually hear her say it; *yes, I am your Queen, you are my slave, your body and your soul are mine now and forever, the first but not the last . . .* He closed his eyes like a girl, overwhelmed by the sweetness and the lush moist promise of her, by the overpowering desire rising at the centre of him. He opened his mouth, breathing out a last breath before it happened; drew her close , let himself be drawn close, closer, unable to resist . . .

And then, just once, he screamed.

"Look," Cerise said to Tina as they walked to school together the next morning, "we've got to do something."

"You said that before. And I said, *Like what*?" Tina said. She was worried enough about things in general. She had come close enough to getting in trouble yesterday; knowing her dad was going to do a double shift, she had invited Cerise over and they had spent half the evening talking, not about calculus, but about the Grand Trine, and had resolved nothing. Something, though, had made Tina insist on Cerise going home early . . . and it was just as well, because at midnight, much to her surprise, her father had come in the door, to find her (belatedly) struggling with the calculus again. The thought of what he would have done if she'd let Cerise stay overnight still made her come out in a hot flush of fear. Well, it hadn't happened . . . But Tina was feeling guilty, and on top of that, was getting more nervous about the whole trine thing. She had looked at Venus and Saturn again, last night . . . and had seen them looking back at her. It was not a nice feeling, and not one she could have explained to her father at the best of times. *He's super . . . he really is. But this time he just won't understand . . .*

Cerise was brooding. "I'm not sure what you would call it," she said. "Is it religion, what's happening, or magic?"

"*Old* religion, maybe," Tina said. "Not the kind I like a whole lot. I was doing some reading . . ." She shuddered.

"I know," Cerise said, somber. "They were really screwed up about blood and stuff back then. And now it's like it's trying to come back."

"I'm not sure it ever left," Tina said. Her reading had left her thinking there was still a fair amount of blood left in modern religion, though it had mostly been reduced to symbolism, sanitised.

"I know what you mean. But look. If this is all . . . old stuff . . . but evil . . . then there must be something we can use against it. Old stuff, but good."

"Such as?"

"I have some books about it at home," Cerise said, her voice very low. "Stuff I mail-ordered. My folks don't know about it. New Age stuff, it says on the covers . . . but I don't think it's so new. It's about people trying to bring back the good parts of the old religions, the idea that you should be part of the world, not simply trying to make it do what you want by twisting it out of shape, unnaturally. Working with the natural forces that are here to make things work right."

"Witchcraft," Tina whispered.

"The patriarchalist name for it," Cerise said.

"Give me a break," Tina said, annoyed. "I don't automatically think all witches are bad, and not all males are bad, either."

"But you can't argue that in the past males haven't—"

"If we don't stop arguing about doesn't-matter stuff in the past, maybe we're not going to have much of a future!!" Tina said.

Cerise opened her mouth, then shut it again.

"Sorry," Tina said. "But we have to stay focused here." It was one of her dad's favourite sayings, and she was clinging to the reasonableness of it now as if to a liferaft; if she had to be crazy, she was going to be *sane* about it. "So what do these books say about the good stuff?"

"Well . . . " They were getting close to school, and other kids were beginning to pass them by now. They waved at Sam Jones, walking with Penny Galbraith and Jeff Dacre. Cerise paused under one of the biggest old maples. "There are things that evil doesn't like — the old spirits and demons, anyway. Silver. Iron. Running water. Some kinds of tree."

"What kind?"

"Oak. And especially rowan — I think we call that white ash now. You know, the one with the red berries, the birds go crazy for it."

"I guess demons don't like birds crapping on them or something," Tina said. "But the iron thing I've heard about."

"Yeah, it's a symbol of industrialisation — made things and built things: seems like demons, and gods for that matter, didn't care much for civilisation when it got started. They liked it better when people were separate and scared than when they started living together and talking each other out of being scared so much. Silver . . . I don't know. I think it has to do with the Moon."

Tina nodded. "When I was reading," she said, "the Moon looked like the least nutso of the . . . powers . . . we're dealing with."

"The Old Gods," Cerise said.

A cold wind breathed by them: they both shuddered and went silent. *Oh, come on, it's five minutes to November,* Tina thought, annoyed at herself, *and this is New England: what do you expect the weather to be like right now, the Caribbean?* But the wind still seemed to have more than the usual hiss to it this morning; and last night, too, Tina had thought she heard mutterings in it, voices . . . until she had got annoyed at herself then too, and turned the TV up in defiance.

She breathed out. "Silver and iron," she said softly. "And running water. Is this going to be enough against, well, gods?"

"It will if we don't start giving them credit for more power than they've got," Cerise said promptly. "The thing about old gods is, well, they're *old*, aren't they? If *everybody* still believed in them, we'd be screwed. But everybody doesn't. Maybe two people believing really hard in the opposite direction is enough to tip the balance at a time like this." She looked unusually intense. "And look, Teenz, there's one thing that helps. The Moon's always changing . . . and she changes sides tonight, at midnight. Once she hits midheaven, she's back in 'her dignity', and the balance shifts . . ."

"It says in the book." Tina swallowed hard. "Cerise . . . has it ever occurred to you that the book . . ."

Cerise held up her hand. "*Don't say it!* I don't want to hear it. Look," she said, and frowned, and the intense expression got even more intense. "We can either try to do something, and be wrong, and get swallowed by the Earth or whatever, or we can just stand around wringing our hands and going 'Oh woe is me' and not do anything, and get swallowed anyway. I'd rather *do* something, if it's all the same to you. So let's meet tonight, when it gets dark, and get it sorted out."

Tina looked at her friend and allowed herself about half a smile. "Yeah," she said. And then the other half of the smile manifested itself, worried and scared as she was. "How do you wring your hands, exactly?"

Cerise's eyes went wide with surprise. "You know," she said, slinging her backpack so as to leave both hands free, "I'm not sure."

"Oh woe is me! . . . "

"'Oh woe!'"

Laughing rather hysterically, they practised wringing their hands all the rest of the way to school, with only limited success.

Tom got up at the usual time, showered and shaved and dressed and ate, had a 'hot sauce' accident with his pasta and had to eat about half a tub of sour cream to put the fire out — which left him looking woefully at his calorie count for the day — and then walked in to work. Rather to his surprise, he found the chair outside the unit empty; when he went in, Miss Norma was already done with her note-making for the unit, and talking on the phone. She put it down after a moment and said, "Andrea's eloped."

"*Eloped*?" Tom said. "Shit. How? When?"

"On nights. The other details we're unsure about," Norma said. "And it gets more interesting. Mike McGregor's gone missing, too."

"Jeez, what *else* is going to happen? He didn't let her out, did he?"

"No-one knows. But when George came on shift to relieve him, he was gone."

She looked furious. Tom could understand why, and suspected that Ginger the night nurse was even more so — not to mention upset, since this could mean her job if Andrea wasn't found. It wasn't exactly wonderful to have a patient elope on your shift. You signed for them, as it were, when you came on shift and made your checks: if one was gone when the next shift came on . . . ! And then Mike. Tom didn't know what to make of that. Losing a security guard as well could be seen as downright careless — the security guards were theoretically supposed to be taking care of themselves as well as everybody else.

And there was another possible twist to this elopement, one closer to the way the layman might use the word. "Was she being Andrea today? Or was she more Marcie-ish?"

"If you mean, was she flaunting her body around here," Norma said, "apparently she was. Ginger says Andrea was awake when she came on shift, wouldn't go to sleep, wouldn't take the sleep medication prescribed for her when she gets restless like this . . . and she started taking her clothes off immediately. Finally Ginger had enough of it, about two, and locked her in. Not too much argument about that, apparently. And then—" Miss Norma waved one hand in the air "—poof, she was gone when Ginger went to do her checks. No signs of a break-out. Nothing messed up in her room . . . "

"Damn," Tom said. "Tonight of all nights. The streets are going to be full of little kids . . . all they need is a nude crazy lady wandering around in the middle of it. And God forbid she should get crazy enough to hurt somebody. Ginger make out an elopement report?"

"First thing. Hospital general security's been notified as well. I would have let them know anyway, since Mike went south."

"Okay. We'll need someone else assigned on the outside door. Last thing I need is for someone else to bust out of here."

"Not our John, surely," Norma said, sounding dry.

"Listen, the kind of night this is shaping up to be . . . " Tom said. "And the moon's full tonight. . . "

Miss Norma breathed out, a sceptical noise — though not the slightly disgusted one that Tom had heard some nurses make. Norma had been observant enough to make the connection between the full moon and 'general trouble' on her own. "Good thing Laura's not here to hear that," she said.

"No," Tom said, "if she were, it wouldn't have been on my mind to mention it..."

Norma went off to sign off on the controlled meds-cabinet book. Tom sighed and looked out the window.

It would be coming up pretty soon, now, out there, past the trees: *I see a full moon rising*... Tom rarely heard the song now without a slight pang of annoyance at what it tended to mean in his work. Everyone who worked psych noticed the connection, sooner or later... that crazy patients got crazier, psychoses more florid, acting out more histrionic, with a moon full or just past it. But no-one talked about it. It seemed too much like superstition, in this time of hard-edged medicine and advanced dual-track therapies. The one or two times Tom had tried to discuss it seriously with one or another of his superiors, in other hospitals, he had been either laughed out of the office or warned, quite severely, to watch his mouth.

It did not change the facts. Back at the big State hospital where he had trained, back when dinosaurs walked the earth, Tom and his fellow students had known what time of month it was getting to be just by the much-increased sound of shrieking and hooting that came floating out of the big brick buildings of The Place. It was always worse then, no matter what their instructors had said. It had given some of his fellow students the shivers. The rest of them had pretended to ignore it... but ignoring it had actually been impossible. Everyone knew.

And Tom knew now. Whatever the reasons might be for it, Andrea had got enough worse to go a-wandering; someone would have to find her, bring her back. It would not be fun for the Oxrun police, as she could be violent without apparent provocation. She would certainly resist being returned to the unit, and would kick up an incredible stink...

Norma came back, having finished the last of her paperwork. "I take it," Tom said, "that John Doe is the same as always?"

"The same, except for that bruxing you noticed," Norma said. "I managed to get the dental consult in, anyway. Not that John cooperated at all, just kept on grinding away."

"And?"

She shrugged. "The dentist, what was his name? Dr. Lazarus — he said the guy must have teeth of stone, because they seem all right. He left us an anti-bruxing appliance, but first somebody has to get poor John's jaws open enough to get it in."

"You couldn't do it after you fed him?"

"He wouldn't eat today. Or drink. I couldn't get his meds in him, either; we may have to go IM on those."

"How's his urinary output?"

"No change in that. But that won't last, if he gets dehydrated."

"No kidding. I'll see what I can do."

Norma got her jacket, and sighed. "Not the best day around here," she said. "I was amazed to get the dentist, with all the madness in the Big House."

"Why, what's happened now?"

"Little Ursula what's her name, you remember, the one with the broken bones? Fell downstairs? She died, poor thing."

"Died?" Tom said in astonishment. "Of *what*?"

Miss Norma shook her head. "You got me," she said. "The county coroner is going crazy. Ron told me that Helen told her that he was muttering about 'potassium leap' and hormonal storm and about six other things to explain the sudden mortality."

"Potassium leap would have worked fine if she'd been buried under a building for eight hours and then dug out all of a sudden," Tom said, "but not unless. 'Hormonal storm'? Sounds like the man's grabbing for straws, here."

"You wouldn't be the first one to think that," Miss Norma said darkly. It was the considered opinion of various hospital staff that the county coroner's office had been in need of change for some months, if not years; there were too many death certificates that had had easy answers written on them when much harder or more suspicious answers were thought to be the proper ones. Unfortunately, in Oxrun County the coroner was a political appointee, and until the next election when some party other than the usual one won, there would be no changes.

"General opinion is that maybe one of the bones was mis-set, and she threw a blood clot from the bone marrow," Norma said. "It went to her lungs, or her brain . . . " She shrugged, frowning.

"Shit," Tom said with feeling. And the thought came back to him: *a lot of young people dying* . . . He shook his head.

"So if you have any trouble tonight," Norma said, getting her purse, "and I hope you don't . . . don't expect the Big House to be able to react all that quickly. They're in a mess over there, and if they feel as tired as I do, I would absolutely understand why."

"I'll make a note," Tom said.

"You want me to drop something by for you for your break?" Norma asked, heading out the door.

"No, thanks, Miss Norma, I'm all set up. You have a quiet one."

"Don't know how quiet it'll be, since I'm gonna be answering the doorbell mostly," she said, "dressed up as a witch."

Tom chuckled at the thought, and wished he had the leisure to do something like that . . . though dressing up as a witch, in his case, would probably be excessive. Tina would be handling the trick-or-treaters tonight, and guarding the house against being tee-peed or having other mild outrages perpetrated against it. *But maybe I should call her,* he thought, *and let her know that one of our less sane citizens is out walking the street tonight . . . After I make checks.*

"I'd give money to see that," Tom said as Norma headed down the hall. "You have fun, now."

"Do my best. Good night, John . . . " Norma said to the window of the quiet-room door. A few moments later her key turned in the lock.

He checked out those things he needed to have a look at in the nursing station, then went on down the hall to have a look at John Doe. Norma had left him sitting upright on his pad after his last change-and-turn, leaning against the right-hand wall. He was grinding his teeth hard: Tom could see the big muscles jumping and working in his jaw.

You poor guy, Tom thought. What are we going to do with you? The thought of Andrea running around uncontrolled all over the landscape was annoying, but it would give Tom a chance, until she was found again, to try something else he had been thinking about. Leaving this guy alone seemed to be having little effect. Maybe someone talking to him, carefully, quietly, so as not to overstimulate him, was what he needed — or just someone to be with him. There would be leisure tonight to find out whether that made any difference at all. It's worth trying, anyway. And what else is there for me to do? Sitting in the station all evening isn't going to help him . . .

Yet as he looked through the window, slowly a feeling came down over him as if a great weight were bearing down on him . . . a sense of great age, inertia, weariness. It came so completely out of nowhere that Tom was astonished; he felt his shoulders sagging under it, his bones going cold . . .

Cold. Tom shivered, looked around him to see if a window was open within sight. None was. Am I having a blood sugar crisis or something? he thought. But I just ate, that's not it . . .

John Doe sat there, grinding his teeth, chewing nothing. Nothing. A sound like chewing rocks.

The hair abruptly stood up on the back of Tom's neck as an image surfaced, an old memory, provoked by Cerise's odd little performance the other night. *Saturn.* The old god of Time and Death, the god who devoured his children, the younger gods. Until finally the mother of those baby-gods, desperate to save at least one, fed him a rock, which he swallowed . . .

A sound like chewing rocks . . .

Tom breathed in and out a few times, still feeling the cold, though now it was receding. Weird, he thought. Weird with a capital W. Good thing I know I'm sane, or I'd start to wonder . . .

But as he made his way back to the nursing station to lock its door, Tom was wondering: and he was still cold.

An Oxrun Police cruiser was cruising slowly down Northland Street as dusk drew on. Officer Jacobsen had his eye on the kids who were already being taken trick-or-treating by their parents or older siblings, the usual welter of fluorescent orange or dayglo green and black costumes: witches and ghosts, but also Jedi knights and Stormtroopers and any number of young heroes escaped from Greek mythology, along with warrior princesses, Power Rangers, and double-ponytailed blondes in schoolgirl skirts and high boots.

What he was not seeing was what he most wanted to: a white female, twenty-six years old, five foot seven and about a hundred and fifty pounds, dark hair, dressed in a pink housedress and bedroom slippers — or not: the hospital said she liked to take off the housedress whenever possible, and the thought made Deke Jacobsen chuckle a little, though probably it wasn't really that funny. Not for the hospital staff, that was for sure: they had warned that she was schizophrenic and might have had some kind of psychotic break, possibly involving assaulting one of the hospital security staff, who couldn't be found either. *Wonder if they ran off together*, Deke thought, and found that idea decidedly unfunny. You couldn't tell, these days, though, with the kind of people who turned up working with private security firms. Background checks just weren't what they used to be . . .

Officer Jacobsen turned right at the corner and drove slowly down Park Street, pulling over and stopping by the park entrance. The street was quiet today: most of the action in town was elsewhere, as the first wave of trick-or-treaters with their candy bags and their plastic jack-o-lanterns hit the houses to get the best of the night's haul. Jacobsen smiled slightly as he got out of the car and locked it up, remembering nights from his own childhood when he had rolled home close to midnight with two, maybe three huge paper bags full of every possible kind of candy, and had made sure he stashed at least one of them somewhere undetectable before his folks took the rest of it off him so that they could let him have it 'a little at a time'. Ah, those nights under the covers, gorging on candy corn and marshmallow peanuts without his mom and dad knowing. *Those were the days*, he thought. God, he had been sick afterwards, but mostly what he remembered now was the taste of the marshmallow peanuts. They just don't make 'em like that any more. All these chemicals and artificial flavourings, that's the problem . . .

Meanwhile, if there was any place a crazy person who knew this area might think about going to hide, Deke suspected this area would be high on the list. The park would be quiet tonight; all the shrubbery and trees would give a fugitive plenty of cover. He stepped quietly through the gate and made his way along the blacktop path that ran eastwards through a belt of trees and shrubs. Deke walked quietly, listening. At first he heard nothing but the wind rustling in the leaves which were in the process of coming off the trees; little papery whirlwinds of yellow and yellow-brown maple leaves blew across his path, danced whispering around him briefly as he made his way towards the open space in the middle of the park, where the ball field and bandstand were.

There he stood and listened. The wind dropped off for a moment, and the silence that fell was profound. A breath, two breaths, three, he stood there, listening—

A rustle. It wasn't an animal, he didn't think: it sounded too big. *Aha*, Deke thought, and very quietly made his way towards the rustling as it continued over by the trees between the ball field and the pond.

On the way he paused once, listening again. The rustling was definitely there, definitely stronger. Yup, Deke thought, I bet you anything . . . that's our girl.

He slipped into the wooded area and held still again, listening.

Rustle . . .

He saw a flash of colour. Pink?

Very quietly he made his way over to the shrubs . . . but it was hard to walk quietly here. There were too many twigs and little branches underfoot, too many dry leaves. However, it wouldn't matter—

He got close enough to see clearly. Yes, it was her. Crouching there. No dress. Bare naked as the day she was born, crouched down, and eating; gnawing on something, delicately, like buffalo wings down at the Brass Rail, or chicken fingers.

"Come on, lady," the cop said. "Time to go back—"

She smiled and looked up at him, pausing in her chewing. *She's no five seven. How tall is she? And God, what a looker, no-one told me she was—* And suddenly Deke saw what she was eating, saw her blood-smeared mouth, the seductive smile it wore.

Fingers, yes, he thought, as the hair stood up all over him and his stomach turned over inside him. *But not chicken—*!

Horrified, Deke stared at the body lying beside her, even though he desperately did not want to. She had not started with the fingers. She had gone first for a more tender bit, a bit that had no bone.

He would have thrown up, or run away, or shrieked, when he saw that . . . except that he found, suddenly, that he could not move. Couldn't stir a limb. She got up, slowly. "I have eaten once," she said, "and rested. But after rest, fresher meat is sweeter." Slowly, she came towards him; and through the fear, through the horror, still he felt himself aroused, arousing, by the sheer unmitigated femaleness of her, all against his will.

"Twice I will now have eaten today," she said. "Once more only is needed for the great Devouring to begin. But how sweet even this small titbit will be. . . " Already enslaved, unable even to manage to struggle out a scream, Deke watched her come, saw the curves and shape of her seemingly now burning with a terrible lust-red light; and she reached out to him, slowly, smiling with blood-red lips, reaching out with hands tipped with nails now dark at the ends.

"Sloppy seconds?" she said softly: and drew close, and closer . . . and sank into him.

He could not even scream as her teeth closed on him.

Tom sat on the floor in the quiet room, next to John Doe, watching him, and wondering.

It was cold in here. It was cold enough that when Tom had come in the first time, he had had to go out and get his jacket;

and the oppressive sense of weariness that had hit him when he stood in front of the door before was there again, so that he had to resist the urge to sit bent like an old man, the muscles twitching and shivering on his bones. John seemed not to notice it at all: he appeared impervious, and when Tom checked his skin temperature, it was perfectly warm. It was as if the cold were radiating from him, though he took no part in it. And always his jaws kept working, the teeth kept grinding . . .

Saturn . . .

Channelling, Tom thought. He remembered how hard he had laughed, a few months ago, when he heard about the big company Mattel suing some woman who claimed to be 'channelling for Barbie'. The idea that a plastic doll could be channelled for had been hysterical.

But the concept itself . . . Often enough, fragmented egostates used human beings, more or less against their will, to talk through: that was 'channelling' of a kind. Could other kinds of life get fragmented and use human beings to 'channel' through? Evil powers?

Gods . . . ?

Tom cursed softly under his breath. It was superstition, that was all. Yet at the same time, much old history rose up in the back of his mind, reminding him that the ancient Greeks and Romans had routinely used crazy people, and people in drug-induced states of madness when they couldn't get genuine crazies, as 'channels' for what they felt the gods had to tell them. The 'Pythia', the most famous of the old Greek prophetesses, had been one of these. And crazy people themselves had been thought, in most of these cultures, to be under the protection of the gods, likely to speak their will at unpredictable intervals. A weak mind, a mind not fully in possession of itself, was thought to be the perfect vessel for a god who wanted to speak and act in the world. And some of the advice that had come through such channels had appeared, in later analysis, 'inspired': the advice, for example, that had saved the Greeks at the sea-battle at Salamis, to depend on their 'wooden walls' to protect them — meaning their fleet of ships, which won the day against terrible odds. Was it just possible that, instead of mere human intuition, something older, stranger, stronger, sometimes spoke through human minds?

"John," Tom said. "If that's even your name, which it probably isn't. John, what's going on with you, guy? What's this all about?"

No answer, not that he was expecting any. The teeth ground on. The air seemed, if Tom was any judge of it, to be getting colder; you could actually see your breath on the air now. "Boy," Tom said softly, "you would be popular around here in the summer, John, when the air conditioning gets out of whack. Brand new system, and the thing still doesn't work in the really hot weather. You could show them a trick or two."

Nothing, no answer.

"John," Tom said, "or whatever your name is." He felt stupid saying what he was going to say, but hey, if this was just a crazy person, he might not even remember it later. If ever. And if it wasn't. . . "If you're trying to communicate with us," Tom said, "this is not exactly a great way to do it. By and large, talking works better. And it's all I've got to work with for the moment, not being anything but human."

No answer, nothing.

"So if you've got anything to pass on to us," Tom said, "talking is simply what you're going to have to resign yourself to. I don't do mental telepathy: it makes my brains hurt. You're just going to have to come down to my level and tell me what's going on with you. I can't help you otherwise."

Nothing. Tom hugged himself with the cold. *I really should get him out of here*, he thought, *just for experiment's sake, and see what happens. If it follows him, then I know I have a real supernatural problem on my hands.* There, he had said it, the *S* word. He didn't mind thinking about the Moon having an effect on crazy people . . . but not like this.

Tom got up and unlocked the door. "Come on, John," he said, "this is doing neither of us any good. Let's get you out of here and sit you in a chair and see what happens." He bent down to John, taking him briefly by the wrist to check his pulse before he moved him.

"Death," John said. It was a more a croak than a normal voice, but the word was clear.

Tom swallowed. "That's a concept, all right," he said. "Thanks for saying something, John. I'm going to take you out of here, in the hall, where we can sit in chairs and talk like normal people, okay?"

It took some doing to stand John up, the waxy flexibility making matters more difficult than Tom liked. But he was strong for his size, and expert in moving people who were unconscious or unresponsive. He got John more or less upright and moved him out of the quiet room as quickly as he could, into the biggest of the chairs that were out in the hall.

"I am Death," John said, as Tom settled him in the chair. "I am the Lord of Death."

"Okay," Tom said. "And this means that *what* is going to happen, exactly?"

"The doors are open," said the voice, and indeed it sounded enough like Death to give Tom the shivers by itself, without the cold, which had indeed followed them out into the hallway. "At this time, as before, they open for us. And once again we may pass to and fro."

"We've had a little of that today," Tom said. "Door-opening. You wouldn't know anything about that, would you?"

"Lust was here," said the voice. "I swallowed her, once."

"Uh huh," Tom said, finishing the business of sitting John securely in the chair. He didn't want Death, or whoever or whatever this was, failing on the floor in the middle of a sentence: that might make It cranky, and besides, John could get hurt.

"I vomited her up," said the voice. "I would have kept her forever inside, safe. But she was spewed up — lust, the uncontrollable, that makes new life. I would have made this earth safe from life, but it was not to be."

"Mmm, I could see how you might have found that to be a disappointment," Tom said, that being the most nonjudgmental thing he could find to say on the subject at the moment, with the cold growing all around him.

"All would have been cold," said the voice. It sounded like cold itself, like ice breaking, like the particular way snow crunches when the temperature is below -30 Fahrenheit, that weird low squeak. "A cold world, a clean world, clean of life's infection, the purulent spreading growth of it. But the cloud fell about this world, and the Fire was too close, and life grew. Lust grew, and multiplied itself, creeping from the slime, like slime itself, and it overthrew me."

"Well, life is here now," Tom said, "and has it occurred to you that it might have thoughts of its own on the topic? Like it would like to stay here, having managed to get here in the first place?"

"Life will fail," said the voice. John's face was still as a corpse's. "Lust too will fail. I will prevail again, now that the doors are open."

Now that would be a bad thing, Tom thought. And how exactly am I planning to stop it?

"Yet she grows," said the cold voice. Was that the slightest element of alarm?

Tom looked up and saw, out the window at the end of the unit, the Moon, rising. *Bitch*, something said in his mind, a memory. *White bitch!*

Definitely not Miss Norma, Tom thought. And not Ginger, either. It was the Moon Andrea was cursing out.

What was it Cerise said? It gets to midheaven . . .

. . . when? At midnight?

Could it actually be a help for once?

Come on, Moon, Tom thought. Get up there! Give me a hand here for once!

But in the hallway, the cold continued to grow . . .

"Death," said the cold, cold voice. "She may grow, but it will not avail her. I put forth my power now. Death . . . "

Tom swallowed. "We'll see about that," he said.

The dark had fallen some hours before, and now, around ten o'clock, strange hoots and yells were coming out of Oxrun Station. Most of them were from human beings, Tina thought . . . though how long that was likely to be the case, she wasn't sure. Here over by the park it was quieter: most of the kids were busy on streets with more houses. Cerise had insisted this would be a good place to do what they had to do. "It's got water," she said, "to mirror the Moon. That's good. Not running water, maybe, but it'll do. We can bring the other things, and I've got a good book . . . "

Tina was wondering whether it would be good enough. Now, as she saw Cerise hurrying towards her, she looked up at the sky and saw Venus definitely watching her, an eye: and Saturn there too, yellower, colder, less immediate-looking, but somehow more sinister. She felt cold looking at it.

"You got what you were looking for?" Cerise asked, coming up to her.

"Here," Tina said, holding out what she had brought and looking nervously over her shoulder. The Moon was rising, and Tina was absolutely sure that the face on it, which she had noted only in passing for all the rest of her life, was now looking at her too. It gave her the creeps. *No-one told me astronomy was going to be an interactive subject . . .*

"A crowbar?" Cerise said, looking doubtful.

"It's iron," Tina said. "It's old . . . my dad found it in the garage when we moved in. God, you wouldn't believe the junk that was in there. He found a—"

"Never *mind*," Cerise said, "let's stay focused, that's the motto for tonight, isn't it?"

Tina grinned; she was flustered, no use trying to pretend otherwise. "Yeah, okay. What have you got?"

Cerise produced a large silver salad spoon and fork set.

Tina blinked.

"Yeah, okay, so it's not a crucifix or anything cool like that," Cerise said, sounding annoyed. "My folks are big believers in stainless, what can I tell you? This was the best I could do. Our aunt with all the money gave it to my mom last Christmas, and Mom never uses it: I bet you if it gets melted or something, she won't even care. It doesn't match anything my mom has, and she hates that aunt anyway." She looked at the crowbar, took it from Tina for a moment, hefted it. "Not bad," she said. "You smack even a god in the kneecap with that, I bet it'll at least sting."

"I hope so," Tina muttered, taking it back. "Now what?"

"We go in there and enact a Strengthening of the Moon," Cerise said.

"Is that in the book?" Tina said.

"Well, sort of," Cerise said. "I expanded it a little." She produced another printed-out computer sheet. "We have to set the wards — that means going around and making a circle around what we're doing, so that the bad things can't get in at us. And then we stay in the middle and do our thing once an hour until midnight."

"And after that?"

"If the Earth hasn't swallowed us by midnight, it won't do it at all," Cerise said.

"Good. My dad may have a few choice words for me," Tina muttered, "but maybe we can work out something separate so that I can survive that."

"Come on," Cerise said.

As they went into the park, Tina threw a curious look at the Oxrun Police car sitting there by itself, empty. "Wonder what's going on?" she said.

Cerise shrugged as they headed in towards the centre. "Probably nothing. We'd better think of something to tell him if we run into him, though."

Tina snickered. "Yeah. Two teenagers with a crowbar and a salad set. Like he's going to worry."

"Hide the crowbar," Cerise said, and laughed too. Then she got a little more sober as they headed forward into the moonlit darkness under the trees, and all the leaves hissed and rustled in the wind at them.

"What if this doesn't work?" Tina said softly. "Venus and Saturn . . . " She thought of what she had read about the two bloody Old Gods, and shivered.

"It better," Cerise said. "Saturn . . . well, it's not great. But at least as far as Venus goes, we have an advantage."

"And that is?"

"We're virgins."

Tina stared at her as they walked.

Cerise stared back, looking somewhat nonplussed. "Well, you are, aren't you?"

Tina gave her a cock-eyed look, somewhat embarrassed. "Not from lack of trying," she muttered. "How is this supposed to help us, exactly? Regardless of what most of the grownups here probably think of kids these days, I suspect this place is littered with virgins. Doesn't seem like it's going to stop Venus one way or the other."

"Yeah, but the other virgins don't know what's going on. We do."

They made their way towards the pond, and Tina thought, Boy, I hope she's right about this. If not . . .

The leaves hissed, and the wind was cold: and from somewhere in the trees between them and the pond, Tina thought she could hear soft laughter, and something else . . . a wet noise. She stopped.

"What's that?" she whispered, and her heart began to hammer.

Cerise stopped too. For a moment the wind kept on rustling, then dropped off.

The laughter was more audible. It sounded nasty . . . and also rather as if someone was doing it with their mouth full.

"Midnight picnic?" Cerise said, suddenly sounding very uncertain.

"I don't know," Tina whispered. "Let's get over to the pond."

They hurried through the darkness, trying to ignore the things they heard the leaves whispering . . .

Tom sat there in the hall, in the chair next to John Doe 14, talking . . . trying to pace himself, trying not to talk himself hoarse: he was getting an increasingly unsettling feeling that, once he fell silent for more than a few breaths, he would not be able to speak again. He was not sure how long he had been doing this — an eternity, it felt like, of sitting here, trying to keep himself going, trying to give John a chance to break out and say something. The cold was trying to take him by the throat: the cold, the overwhelming sense of age and weariness, a great heaviness settling over everything, as if the planet itself were weighing down on the spot; or worse, a kind of apotheosis of everything Saturn meant — vast pressure terrible enough to turn gas to metal, massive weight, millions of years' worth of age, an unbelievable bitter cold; darkness, remoteness from light. All of life and light seemed as remote to Tom, now, as the Sun must look from Jupiter.

"Come on, guy," Tom said, softly, trying to keep his teeth from chattering so much he couldn't speak. "Don't check out on me here. I know you're still in there. We call you John, though we don't know what your name is, and Old Father Time here couldn't be speaking if it weren't for you letting him borrow your skin. I want to hear something from you now. This is your body, you get a vote. Talk to me, John. Tell me what your name is, anyway, before icicles start forming on both of us."

No answer. Tom kept talking, inconsequential things, the recent weather — the real weather, not this bizarre indoors winter — the fortunes of the local baseball teams, the big stories in the news this past week. But his mind kept coming back again and again to what Cerise had been talking about.

Venus and Saturn in trine. But not the new versions of them. The old ones. The Venus who devoured men. The Saturn who devoured children. Gods from a time when man often had other uses for his fellow man than mere companionship. Prey . . . food. And after such feasts, who got the souls? Gods who learned to appreciate this particular hunger in man . . . encouraged it when they could. Gods forgotten except at times like this, when they might slip through... *What was it Andrea said? I will loose the dead upon the living to eat the living... or something like that. Nasty.*

If only Cerise was right, Tom thought, his teeth chattering. The Moon reaches midheaven... and things change. Tom never thought he would be so eager to see the Moon reach zenith, the time when things were usually worst... Now he was praying for it, for her, to hurry up...

He was running out of things to say. "Let's sing something," Tom said. *God, I'm really at the end of my rope here...* He looked down the hallway, where the moonlight was shining in from a different window now. Suddenly something came to him, something completely inane:

"Shine on,

shine on Harvest Moon,

up in the sky—"

A strange, sudden silence. John had stopped bruxing, which threw Tom off his stride for a moment. Then John hiccoughed, which was stranger still. Some blood electrolyte problem, Tom thought. Or maybe just my singing. Certainly the latter had occasionally produced strange neuropsychiatric symptoms in his last wife, like her throwing things at him.

"I ain't had no lovin'

since January, February,

June or July—"

"Shine on," John said suddenly, somewhere in the key of M. It was the best sound that Tom had heard in years. Shivering, he realised that he couldn't remember the rest of the verse, and so he started the first one again. "Shine on, shine on Harvest Moon—"

"Shine on, shine on," John sang, and this time it was genuinely John, a human voice and not that voice hewn from methane ice millions of miles deep in space or years deep in time. Tom thought of something he had heard one morning in report from one of the other nurses, about an aphasic who couldn't talk but could sing, and once the staff realised that, they sang everything to the patient and got all their answers back in song, and the place started to sound like an opera written by Schoenberg while drunk, but at least therapy got done. "Shine on, shine on Harvest Moon," Tom sang, and John sang it with him. It was a change, at least: it meant something, it must mean something, oh please let it be something good!

And the Moon's light crept across the floor, and from down the hall, Venus's light came in another window, bright, too bright, dazzling—

Tom turned his eyes away from it, to the blank eyes of John Doe 14, and kept singing.

Tina and Cerise stood by the pond, in the middle of a circle that only they could see, and the Moon shone down on the water . . . and Saturn and Venus looked at them, from either side of the sky. Venus was bright as a plane's landing lights, and threw shadows of its own; and even Saturn was bright enough to cast shadows, but the ones it cast had that weird runny look around the edges. Tina was shivering, but trying hard not to show it, for it was feeling unusually cold, and she had only her fall jacket on. How Cerise was holding up — she was wearing the black lace and black denim again — Tina couldn't imagine. She doubted the black lace thing was thermal enough to deal with *this*.

"Is the circle going to be big enough?" Tina whispered. She had watched Cerise drawing it in the grass with a steak knife, and was half disappointed not to see magic fire come up from where the knife had passed.

"It should be," Cerise said, somewhat muffled, as she was holding a mini-Maglite in her mouth while sitting cross-legged on the ground, paging through her book.

"How will we know something's happening?" Tina said.

Cerise took the Maglite out of her mouth. "I'm kind of new at this myself," she said, "so you'll forgive me if I say *I don't know, will you stop joggling my elbow, Teenz?!*"

Tina sat down beside her and breathed out. It was getting unusually quiet out there, for Halloween night at least. She found herself wondering what was going on at home. Please God, she thought, or Goddess or whoever, please don't let Chuck Antrim tee-pee our house while I'm not there to stop him. Dad will hit the roof. And please don't let—

CRASH! went something over on the edge of the little field where the pond lay. Tina's and Cerise's heads both jerked up.

That was when they saw the woman.

"*Showtime*," Cerise whispered, and stood up. Tina did too, if only because it was easier to run standing up than sitting down.

She was huge. She was about twenty feet tall, and she had no clothes on whatsoever, and she glowed with an odd light which was not strictly visible, but somehow still manifested itself as red. The crash appeared to have come from a small tree, which she had just brushed out of her path and knocked over as she came slowly towards them. "Daughters of men," the woman said, "have you come to worship me? How wise you are.

"Of course it would be so, here at the opening of doors, here at the beginning of my new day among men. I will accept your worship."

With the crowbar in her hand, Tina watched her come, and started to forget the crowbar... started to forget everything. The woman was beautiful.

There was absolutely no doubt of that. Tina looked at her and her heart went cold, colder than it did even when she looked at the pictures of the supermodels in the magazines and knew beyond all possible doubt that she would never, never look that good in her life, no matter what she did to herself, no matter what she did to her hair or her skin or her teeth or her nose. This was what women are supposed to look like, she thought. But we miss it somehow. We all miss it. And the feeling began to creep up on her: Nothing will ever go right unless we look like this. Maybe... if we were her friends... maybe...

"I will accept your worship, if you fall down before me now," she said. "And yours, young priestess. Why do you carry silver?

Why do you bother with the Moon? She has no power. Turn away from her, and turn to me now, and I will teach all men who see you to love you. They will have no power to resist you: they will fall at your feet and worship you, seeing me in you, knowing my power in you . . ."

Her beautiful soft voice crooned smooth and low as she slowly drew closer to them. Tina felt everything start to go strange and slow around her. The woman, the Goddess, increasingly looked more real than everything around her, and the trees wavered in the light of Saturn and Venus like seaweed in water. Not even the Moon was as bright, and its light seemed washed out, somehow, in the brilliance of the two eyes that looked down from the sky, the hot bright one low in the western sky and the cold one, higher up, more pallid, old and strong.

"Turn to me now," the Goddess said. It was Venus, Venus herself, and she was strong, stronger than Tina had thought she could be. *Yes, let's be hers*, something was saying in her head, *let's do what she says, she's powerful, what does the Moon matter?* "You shall have all power over men. Perhaps you shall even learn to do as I do, who have all power over them, and they are meat and drink to me . . ." She smiled, and though she was still beautiful, the smile was not. "And if they resist me, they are meat and drink indeed; to me and my servants. Twice they have been so already tonight. . ."

The smile. The smile. It was red, Tina saw, red, and not from lipstick, not because the lips were normally that way. She was coming closer, and Tina could see what it was. Blood. *What does it matter? She is a Goddess, anything she wants is right*, said that lulling crooning something that was down inside Tina's head now. *Worship her and anything you want will be right too. Have anything you want, do anything you want . . .*

Tina swayed. But *Blood*, said another voice in her head, harder, angry; and the iron in her hand suddenly started to feel cold as the Goddess came closer.

"And there will be a third time," said the Goddess, the monster-Venus. "And with the third time, nothing will be able to stop me ever again, and I shall free my servants from the darkness, and they too shall feast." Yet she stopped, then, and came no further forward — and Tina realised that she had stopped where Cerise had drawn the circle with the steak knife.

"Cerise," Tina whispered. "Cerise!"

No answer.

Tina gulped. The iron was burning in her hand. "You've got blood on your mouth," she said to the Goddess.

"The blood of men," the monster-Venus said softly. "If they will not give me their bodies one way . . . I take them another."

Cerise looked up. She too, like Tina, had been wavering in the spell of the low soft voice. But now she stood there with the silver spoon in one hand and the steak knife in the other, and she held herself straight and tall.

"You," Cerise said, severe, "are a complete slut and cow."

The woman smiled at her, the way you smile at an ugly bug you intend to step on. "It is not wise to speak so to a Goddess, to the Queen of Heaven and Earth," she said. She tried to move forward towards them, and could not.

"Uh huh," Cerise said.

"Uh huh what?" Tina whispered, terrified. "Thanks so much for pissing her off. *Now* what do we do?"

"I'm thinking," Cerise said. But she glanced sideways as she said it, and Tina followed her glance. Venus was setting . . .

. . . and the Moon was very close to midheaven . . .

Tom's voice was starting to give out. Don't think about that, he thought desperately. Think of this as just another of those long nights when you have to keep talking to keep someone from suiciding, or noticing that their medication's working at last.

"The doors are opening," said the cold voice. "The doors are open!"

"Shine on, shine on Harvest Moon — come on, John! — up in the sky—"

"The Moon is weak, she has no power like mine! I swallowed her too, once, at the beginning of things: I shall swallow her again, devour her again, at the beginning of the end—"

Not if I have anything to say about it, buddy. Come on, Moon! "I ain't had no loving since January, February, June or July—"

The whole park was wavering in the light of the setting Venus and Saturn sliding towards the west, baleful, the yellow eye and the white one. Cerise glanced at Tina and said under her breath, "I'm going to release the wards."

"*Are you out of your mind?*"

"There's two of us, Teenz, and there's only one of her. It's got to be worth something. You run one way, I'll run the other, only one of us has to hit her with what we've got—"

Tina had the strong feeling that something was going to go wrong with this. "You cannot defy me!" the monster-Venus cried. "No matter what you do, I shall feed again and become great as I once was. Worship me now, or I will turn against you—"

"Oh great Goddess, forgive your servants," Cerise said, and knelt down, and elbowed Tina. Tina glowered at her, but did it too, for the look of the thing.

Cerise elbowed her again. "We will worship you!" Tina said loudly, adding under her breath, "Like hell!"

The Goddess's aspect softened somewhat. "You are wise," she purred. "Swear me now that you will be my servants—"

Tina watched Cerise's hand, the one with the steak knife in it, slowly come up . . .

. . . and Cerise threw it away from her, over the boundary of the circle.

The monster-Venus stumbled forward. Cerise sprang up and darted off eastwards; Tina did the same and headed west. The Goddess recovered herself, and shrieked once, terribly, in rage; the sound went through Tina like a spear, struck her still for a moment. "Stupid creatures!" the monster-Venus cried. "Do you mock me? You will not do so for long. With you or without you I will feed again, and those who loved me and died will walk the earth again and feast on the flesh of men as I do!"

She went after Cerise, but Cerise was out of her reach, and staying that way, holding the silver salad servers up in front of her. The Goddess seemed to be trying to get close to her, and could not. She turned, started coming after Tina. "And because you defy me," she said, smiling that terrible red smile again, "blood of your blood, flesh of your flesh, shall be the one I devour next, the one who sets me free. The one in the place of the sick, who mocked me night by night while I grew in strength. He shall know what that strength is worth now. Your father—"

She turned away from them, headed towards the park entrance.

Tina's whole body went hot and cold in one terrible flash. *Dad*—!

She ran up behind the Goddess, blazing with fury: ran right up behind her, and clubbed her behind her Titanic knees with the crowbar.

The shriek that tore the air then was so terrible that Tina collapsed, her hands over her ears. A moment later the earth shuddered as that huge form went down, just missing Tina. Stunned, blind with the shock, Tina tried to crawl out of the way. She managed to get her eyes open, looked up—

Standing over the Goddess's supine head, as the monster-Venus struggled to get up and could not, with the fork and spoon raised high, was Cerise. The Moon stood on high, behind her head, like a halo.

"Nice try," she said.

Then she plunged the fork and spoon down, and in the rending scream that followed, the fabric of reality parted and left them in the dark.

"Shine on Tom coughed: he was losing it. "Shine on, Harvest Moon . . . "

He glanced at his watch as he had not dared to for a long time. *Seven minutes to midnight.* Is this watch fast or slow? He didn't remember having checked it, the last couple of days. "Come on, John, don't make me sing solo here—"

But it was the cold voice that spoke to him now. "The doors are open, this is my time, I must go forth, all things shall again be swallowed, life and lust and all else shall die—"

"Sorry, buddy, you may think this is your time but John gets equal time now, you're going to have to take it up with him. *Shine on, shine on Harvest Moon!*"

"Up in the sky—"

Tom was hanging onto John by the shoulders with both hands, now, shaking him in time with the music, reinforcing the lyric, the circumstance, this moment of the present, this reality, as best he could. The cold voice broke in, regardless. "*It is my time, death is all, all things will be swallowed—*"

A tremor went right through the building. In the nursing station, there was a crash as something fell off the windowsill onto the floor. Tom hung onto John as everything swayed, abruptly going heavy, a vast weight pressing down onto both their shoulders and the two of them bowing under it, under the cold, the massive numbing, flattening force, irresistible. "*Shine on, shine on Harvest Moon—*"

The pressure increased terribly, pushed them both down and down: Tom croaked the words out, fought the air out of his lungs, choked, saw bright phosphene-spots start to dance in front of his eyes, saw it all start to dim out. *I tried. Oh, I tried. It's not fair! Shine—*

—and all the pressure suddenly eased.

Tom blinked and shook his head. Very, very slowly his vision cleared; he looked at John.

John was staring at the wall across from him. He opened his mouth.

"This song is desperately stupid," John said. "Can we please sing something else?"

Tom slumped sideways. At almost exactly the same moment, there was a distant jangling: the fire alarm going off in the main building. *Like I need this!* Tom thought. *Is anything else going to happen tonight? They're going to have to handle it: I have my own problems.*

"Absolutely," Tom said. His eyes were watering with the return of warmth in the hallway . . . or the sight of moonlight that looked normal . . . or something else. "We'll take your requests in just a moment. But first of all . . . just what is your name?"

In the park, Tina and Cerise picked themselves up off the ground and looked around them in disbelief . . . for everything seemed terribly normal, except for the faint Halloween noises still coming from other parts of Oxrun. There was a steak knife on the ground, and a silver fork and spoon stuck into the wet turf; and the crowbar lay where Tina had dropped it.

"Nasty bitch," Tina said softly, picking it up. It no longer burned in her hand. She looked up at Venus, which had almost set now: it no longer seemed to be looking at her. Saturn too looked faint and far, and no longer even slightly interactive.

"Such language," Cerise said, walking off to retrieve the steak knife. "What did she say there that made you lose it? That was terrific, by the way."

"She was threatening to eat my dad," Tina said. "I could see what she was going to do to him." She shuddered.

"She won't do it now," Cerise said, bending over to pull the fork and spoon out of the grass. "Huh. Look at the tarnish."

"Let's go to my house," Tina said, "and see if we can get it off before you get home. I have to get back before Dad does anyway. If he finds out what we've been doing . . ."

"You want to bet he knows?" Cerise said, dry. "Or he'll guess. This is your dad we're talking about . . ."

Very quietly, so as not to attract attention, they walked out of the park and made their way back towards Thorn Street.

Change of shift report that night took nearly half an hour, since Ginger had been trying unsuccessfully to get into the unit for some fifteen minutes: the door had seemed to be frozen shut. She and Tom had spent the next fifteen minutes or so making Richard Mullion — that was his name — comfortable in a more normal room than the quiet room. He had fallen asleep, as if exhausted, almost immediately. Tom had left him with Ginger readily enough, suspecting that Andrea's elopement had possibly had more behind it than carelessness on Ginger's part. He suspected it would take days to sort things out, and in that he was later proved right. He also suspected that they would not be seeing Andrea again . . . and in that too, he was right, though he would not learn the truth about that for some hours.

He walked home gratefully. The night, which would normally have seemed cold to him, now, after the last couple of hours, seemed positively balmy. "Shine on, shine on Harvest Moon," he sang, and looked up at the big, full, yellow Moon with much more affection than usual.

As he turned into Thorn Street he saw two slim young forms coming towards him: not costumed, not trick-or-treaters. One of them broke into a run at the sight of him. She met him halfway, threw her arms around him, laughing, even crying a little. Tom put his head down against her shoulder and hugged her back. "What the hell are you doing out?" he said. And added, "Hello, Cerise . . ."

"I'll tell you," Tina said. "But let's just please go in . . ."

They turned towards their house, and paused for just a moment, noticing that the front of it had been most thoroughly tee-peed.

Then the three of them laughed, and went in, and turned on all the lights. What spilled out onto the toilet-paper-striped lawn was a plain light, electric and homely, which washed out the now-faint gleam of Saturn: and which sorted very well indeed with the light of the Moon.

CHUCK

1

MAYBE, KENNY THOUGHT, HE SHOULDN'T BE here after all.

He especially didn't want to be here alone. He didn't even see a sign of this old house they were supposed to be exploring. It was so dark out here in the woods that he could barely even see the trees. To heck with being quiet and secretive. He wanted to know where the three other guys had gone.

"Sammy?" he called out in the darkness. "Where are you? Nick? Jim? Come on, Sammy!"

Nobody answered. Unless that faint sound he heard was laughter. That was it, Sammy and the boys, playing one more joke on old Kenny.

Sammy, Jim, Nick and Kenny, the four track stars of Oxrun High, and the school's four best practical jokers. Or so they were always trying to prove, especially with each other. And all Kenny had done was fill Sammy's underwear with shaving cream after their last track practice. Kenny guessed he deserved it. Except that he didn't find being left in the woods all that funny.

The woods were so thick here that they blotted out any light that might come from the moon and stars. The only way Kenny could walk around was with his arms outstretched, to feet for trees and bushes in the almost total dark. He wondered if he could find his way back to the car. They had parked up by the quarry, in the mouth of a dry stream bed. Sammy had led them up the stream for a hundred feet or so; then they began to climb. Since then, they had been walking uphill almost all the way. So, Kenny figured, if he just felt his way back down the slope, he should find the car sooner or later.

That is, if the car was still there. Kenny got a sinking feeling deep down in his stomach. Sammy and the others wouldn't take off on him, would they? Kenny could still remember how mad Sammy had been at the white foam filling his jockey shorts. Somehow, that little joke didn't seem quite so funny after all.

Where the heck had the other guys gone, and so fast, too? Sure, they were all pretty good at running the quarter mile, but at night, in the woods? He thought about calling out again, but decided he wouldn't give the others the satisfaction.

Instead, he decided to walk downhill. If he couldn't find the car, at least he could find the road back into town. He didn't think they could be more than five or six miles outside of Oxrun Station. Somebody was bound to recognise him on the road and give him a ride.

His sneaker caught a rock, almost tripping him. He stumbled away, twisting around to keep himself from falling. Ha ha, guys, he thought, when he finally managed to stop his staggering down the hill. He tested his weight to make sure he hadn't twisted his ankle. No, the ankle was a little sore but he was all right, no thanks to Sammy and the others. Ha ha, he thought again. He'd have to come up with something really good to get them all back for this.

He moved really slowly now, always heading down the hill, feeling both with his outstretched hands and the toes of his sneakers for anything that might get in his way. He couldn't hear any other sounds besides the noise of leaves and twigs beneath his feet. It sounded like Sammy and the others were long gone. Ha ha, guys, he thought again.

"Hey, you're just as bored as I am," Sammy had said, "sitting around boring Oxrun." He should have seen right through it. "We're seniors now. Isn't it time for a little excitement before we blow this town?" What a set-up. But Kenny was the perfect patsy. Oxrun Station was boring nine months of the year, and visited by nosy, noisy tourists the other three. And he *was* a high school senior, after all. It was time for a little excitement.

Or a little practical joke. Ha ha, Sammy.

The moon appeared between two of the trees above. It was almost full, and Kenny felt like he had suddenly stepped out into daylight. The woods were thinning here, and he could actually see where he was putting his feet. He hurried down the rest of the hill, and spotted the dry stream bed only a moment later.

He stopped when he stepped onto the dry shale of the stream bed and looked around to get his bearings. There, no more distance than the length of a football field, sat Sammy's car, at the edge of the moonlit lake within the quarry.

Kenny smiled. He had a better sense of direction than he'd thought. He didn't see any of the others, either. Maybe he'd somehow beaten the other three guys back. Maybe he could even play a little practical joke — payback time — on the others.

He jogged down the stream bed to Sammy's old Chevy. The door was open on the driver's side. Hadn't they closed and locked the doors when they went up the hill? Maybe Sammy and the others were around here after all.

"Sammy?" Kenny called softly as he approached the car. "Jim?" He circled around to the open driver's door, half expecting the other three to jump up with a yell to scare him.

But there was nobody inside. In fact, there wasn't even a front seat. He could see all of the car floor, a carpet with spaces where the seat had once been bolted to the frame. The worn carpet shone silver in the moonlight. The back seat was gone too, and he could see straight into the trunk.

It wasn't until he stuck his head into the car that he realised the steering wheel was also gone. It was as if somebody was taking the car apart, piece by piece.

Somehow, Kenny didn't think this could be part of the joke. Even Sammy wouldn't go this far, would he? To his own car?

He turned his head to look at the dashboard. Even half-lost in shadow, he could see that someone had smashed all the dials.

Someone was destroying Sammy's car, breaking it up and pulling it apart. Kenny didn't think they had been gone for much more than thirty minutes, and already the car was half gone.

And that probably meant that whoever was destroying it was still around.

Kenny pulled his head out of the car. He wondered now if any of his friends were in trouble. How could he find them?

Maybe, he thought, it would be better if he ran out to the main highway and flagged down someone to take him to the police.

"I should never have listened to you, Sammy," he said, half to himself.

Kenny heard an answering noise from down by the lake. Except this time it wasn't a laugh. It sounded more like a groan.

What if it was one of the other guys? Kenny knew he had to go and look. He was a track star, after all. If anything really bad was happening, he couldn't just run away.

"Sammy?" he called softly as he walked towards the noise. "Nick? Jim?"

"Kenny?" a hoarse voice called back. "Hey, Kenny. I'm so glad to hear your voice."

Kenny couldn't recognise the voice. "Who—" he began.

The voice groaned again. "It's Jim, man. Where'd you go? It was good you got away. They surprised the rest of us." A bush rustled in front of Kenny. Was that where Jim was?

"Don't know what happened to the others," Jim added, a second later. No, his voice was coming from a couple of trees by the rim of the quarry. "I never ran so fast in my — what? Oh, no, they're here again! I gotta get—"

Jim called out then, a sound that started low and hoarse but rose as high as a cheerleader's scream.

Kenny saw a flash of red light, silhouetting three figures. The one in the middle looked a lot like Jim. The other two held him, and were dragging him away.

The light was gone. Kenny blinked, trying to get his eyes used to the darkness. He didn't think he could help Jim by himself. He had to get out of here if he was going to find help for any of them.

He turned back towards the car and started to run. Bright light blinded him suddenly. He stumbled to a stop again, covering his eyes. Like a rabbit, he thought, caught in somebody's headlights.

"Poor Kenny," said a voice he recognised. "Sometimes you just can't run away."

2

Chuck Antrim didn't even realise his mother had come home. He looked up, startled from where he'd been staring at MTV.

"We're going out again tonight!" his mother yelled over the noise. She waved and disappeared from the doorway.

Chuck hit the remote button, silencing the screaming guitars. Up until now, it had been a typical Wednesday. His mother had just got home from shopping. In another half an hour, his father would show up from work. It was a light night for homework, and he had been just hanging around until dinner.

Speaking of dinner, his stomach was getting interested in being filled. He looked back to the still-silent TV. The guitars were gone, replaced by an ad for pimple cream. Chuck decided the TV could stay quiet a little longer. He pushed himself off the couch and headed for the kitchen.

"So what's cooking?"

"Oh dear." His mother gave him one of her tight-lipped smiles. "We won't have time to eat with you tonight. I made you and your sister something special."

"Special?" With his mother, that could mean anything from lobster to liver. Ugh. Liver. Mom was a big believer in the positive effects of organ meats on growing bodies. Still, if his parents weren't home, they could always feed their 'special' meal to the dog.

"The casserole's in the oven," she said as she pushed on past him out the door. "Excuse me, dear. I have to get ready."

Well, Chuck guessed he could figure out what was important around here. Not that he hadn't guessed that a thousand times already. At least he wouldn't have to put up with all that 'And how was your day?' stuff.

What was it his mother always used to say? "It's so important for the whole family to eat dinner together." They used to spend every week-night at the dining room table, both kids being grilled by their parents on their day at school. And their homework, and their friends, and what they were doing on the weekend.

Now the family hardly ever ate dinner together anymore. At least that meant his parents had to find other ways to nag him.

His kid sister Nicole banged her way in through the back door. She grinned up at Chuck as she tossed her baseball cap on the kitchen table. "So what's cooking?"

Chuck peered into the oven. "We're having mystery dinner."

"Huh?" she asked, not getting it.

"Some kind of casserole," Chuck replied. He frowned at the dim yellow light beyond the oven window. Was it chicken? Tuna fish? Ground beef? It could be anything. "Mom was too busy to let me know the details."

Nicole nodded. "Another big night out, huh?"

Chuck turned to his sister. "Well, you know our parents."

"I used to," Nicole replied, without even a smile. She marched by him into the living room, not saying another word. What could she say? They both knew what was going on around here.

Their parents would go out again, leaving them on their own until ten or eleven at night, sometimes even midnight. It was funny. The way most kids talked, they would jump at the chance for that kind of freedom from their parents.

Except, Chuck thought, it wasn't exactly like being free. The rules Mom and Dad laid down seemed even stricter than when they were around all the time. Chuck and Nicole had exact instructions for how far they could go from the house and when they had to be back. "We know you'll be good kids," they'd say, "not like some of the others." Their parents even told them exactly who they could and couldn't see!

His sister stepped back into the kitchen. "I can't wait for Halloween!" she announced. With that, she turned and marched back into the dining room.

For her, Chuck realised, Halloween meant a little bit of freedom. It was a little bit that he didn't share.

He was sixteen, his sister eleven. She could still go around the neighbourhood and collect candy. Sometimes, Chuck felt like he was either too young or too old to do anything.

The phone rang.

"Could you get—" Mom called down from upstairs. Chuck had picked up the phone before she could even finish the sentence.

"Hello?"

"Chuck." He recognised the voice at once. Todd Baker.

"Yeah?" Chuck asked.

"You're free tonight." It was not a question.

"Yeah," Chuck agreed anyway. Or at least he was free until nine, when his parents insisted he be home.

"This is the first night," Todd told him.

"Tonight?" Halloween was still four days away. "But—"

"When you're with the club," Todd interrupted him, almost as if he could read Chuck's mind, "Halloween goes on all week." Todd paused for a second. Chuck didn't know what to say in reply.

Todd broke the silence. "Your parents will be gone in an hour."

"Well — yeah," Chuck replied in surprise. Did Todd know everything?

"Good. We'll pick you up."

Todd hung up without even a goodbye.

The front door slammed.

"Hi, Nicole!" It was their father. "Sorry, I'm running late!"

"Hello, Chuck!" he called towards the back of the house.

Chuck heard his dad's heavy footsteps clumping up the stairs before he could even call a 'hello' back.

Somehow, though, he didn't want to think about talking to his father. He wanted to think about the Halloween Club.

Todd was the one who had got the seven of them together. Todd said seven was a lucky number; that was important with something like Halloween. And three days ago, seven days before Halloween, things had started to happen.

The first day it was just a note, written in red pen and shoved into his locker. The note showed a drawing of a human skull. Beneath that were four words:

WELCOME TO THE CLUB.

The second day, Chuck found something stuck in the pocket of his jacket. It was a tiny, plastic skull with a wind-up key which made the lower jaw chatter. The same sort of thing had happened to all the other club members, with plastic tarantulas and glow-in-the-dark snakes stuck in back packs and purses. All gifts from the Halloween Club, of course.

It got wilder on the third day. There, in the high school lunch room, Susan's milk had turned to blood.

It was the first time that the Halloween Club was all sitting together. Todd and Alex and Sue were on one side of the table, while Jake and Beth and Mitch sat next to Chuck.

Jake had noticed it first, pointing at Sue's milk container, and the clear straw now filled with red.

Sue spewed liquid across the table, spraying Jake and Beth on the other side.

"What was that?" Beth called out in disbelief.

"Did it taste funny?" Alex asked her.

Sue shook her head, not yet able to speak.

"Who?" she said at last.

But everybody already knew who was responsible, even as everybody started to laugh.

Todd was gone. Somehow, between Jake pointing out the red and Sue spewing her milk, he had left the table, and the lunchroom too.

That was the Halloween Club; funny and a little weird. And all run by Todd Baker, who'd showed up back in high school this fall after being gone from town for two years. Nobody knew quite where he'd been, since his parents hadn't moved away. Private school maybe, or military school, although the real rumour around town was that he'd been in reform school. Some of the other kids in the club thought that rumour was neat.

Now Todd was picking Chuck up, and probably the rest of the Halloween Club as well. Chuck grinned at the thought. This club thing was somehow both corny and cool at the same time.

Who needed stupid trick-or-treating anyway? Todd had promised to show the rest of them a Halloween they would never forget.

"Dinner's just about ready."

Chuck's mother appeared in the doorway, dressed to go out, hair combed, new make-up, tiny gold earrings. She had that smile on her face that said she was going to do something really special. She never got that smile when she hung around the house.

"Harold," she called over her shoulder, "get out the car. We're going to be late."

"Give me a second," their father protested as he walked up behind her. "Hey, Chuck." He nodded a greeting. "This weekend, we'll try out that new glove of yours, okay?"

Mom frowned. "We can't this weekend, honey. We promised the Andersons."

"Oh, that's right." Dad frowned, too. "Well, soon, Chuck, soon."

What was this about the Andersons? And why was it going to take the whole weekend? Chuck never knew exactly what his parents had promised to whom.

There was an up side to his parents' busy life. They hadn't even asked him what he planned to do tonight. He had come up with a story, of course. His parents knew Jake and Alex. He would have told them he was seeing one of them. He was seeing both of them, after all.

Of course, he was seeing a whole lot more. But Chuck didn't think his parents were ready to hear about the Halloween Club.

He had the feeling that if his parents knew half of what Todd was planning to do, they'd clamp down on their son in an instant. Chuck would probably get grounded for a month.

But with his parents' busy lives, there was no way they needed to know, *especially* if they didn't ask him. Besides, what did a little grounding matter, compared to the Halloween Club?

"Be good, kids!" their father called.

"We *know* you will be," their mother added.

The front door slammed shut. Chuck heard their father start the station wagon. Their parents were gone.

His sister pointed at the casserole placed on the kitchen table. "You want to eat some of this glop?"

He supposed he should have a little at least. He had no idea what Todd was planning.

Whatever it was, Chuck knew it would be cool.

3

Restaurants had Birthday Clubs, and banks had Christmas Clubs. But nobody in all of Oxrun Station had a Halloween Club. Until now.

Chuck didn't really want to eat. The casserole turned out to be a combination of minced beef, macaroni and tomato sauce. The small part of him that was paying attention to dinner thought it tasted pretty good. Another night he would have wolfed it down.

Tonight, though, was different. Tonight, the whole Halloween Club was going to be together, away from school, away from parents, even away from little sisters.

Nicole stood up abruptly and announced she was going over to Merrilee's. The other girl lived two doors down, and was Nicole's best friend, at least this week. So Chuck wouldn't have to worry about his sister being home alone. He wouldn't have to explain anything about what he was doing, either.

This was going almost too well.

He put the remains of the casserole in the refrigerator, rinsed off the plates and stuck them in the dishwasher. Better if he obeyed all the rules that he could so his parents wouldn't look to see the one big rule he was breaking.

He checked himself out in the hallway mirror. He wished his sandy blond hair was a little longer, maybe his arms a little less scrawny. Still, he looked okay in his torn jeans and T-shirt.

He heard the blare of Todd's horn. Chuck grabbed his denim jacket and opened the front door.

Six arms waved as Chuck closed and locked the door behind him. Todd had picked up everybody else first. All six of them yelled at Chuck to hurry up.

For a second, Chuck felt a little left out. Being the last one picked up felt sort of like getting picked last for the softball team. Oh, yeah, somebody's got to take Chuck too.

But that was silly, wasn't it? This wasn't school, and it certainly wasn't gym class. This was the Halloween Club. His sister always told him he worried too much. This just meant that he had less time to wait before they got into the action.

He walked out towards the car at the end of the front walk. Todd had this old purple Chrysler from the '60s. He referred to it as the Steamship, since the car was as big as a boat. Chuck jumped into the back with Sue, Alex and Jake. Beth and Mitch rode up front with Todd. The Steamship fitted all seven of them easily. There might even have been room in the back seat for a couple more.

He sat down next to Sue. She was a pretty brunette, her hair cut short on one side, long on the other. Still, everybody knew she really liked Todd. Chuck had been hoping to sit closer to Beth, but from here all he could see was the back of her head and her long, blonde hair. Maybe on the way back, he thought. But on the way back from where?

"Where are we going?" he called out to Todd.

"Revenge," was Todd's reply.

Revenge? Was he supposed to know what that meant?

Todd raised a single finger towards the night sky. "It's the first lesson of Halloween."

Oh, Chuck thought. Thanks for telling me nothing at all. He should have expected this sort of thing from the mysterious Todd.

"We don't have to go very far," Todd added a moment later. "Revenge is best when it's close to home." He smiled at that. "Our very happy homes."

Sue glanced over at Chuck with a grin, rolling her eyes skyward in a 'Can you believe this guy?' gesture. Chuck finally laughed. This could be a lot of fun, he thought, as long as they didn't get caught. Of course, he'd never say anything like that out loud. The other guys would call him a chicken, or something even worse.

This was the first time he could remember having fun since he entered the junior class. Whatever happened, Chuck didn't want to be kicked out of the club.

"After all," Todd added a moment later, "we can't do anything really serious yet. It's only the first night."

A couple of the other kids laughed, but the laughter was more nervous than anything else. Chuck guessed that the rest of them felt the same way he did. As exciting as all of this seemed to be, they really couldn't enjoy themselves until they knew what was going on. At least Todd was having a good time. It was a little like playing Dungeons and Dragons on the streets of the Station, with Todd acting like a real life Dungeonmaster.

They rode in silence, down Thorn Road to King Street, moving back towards the middle of town. This was the first time Chuck had ever known the whole club to be quiet. Chuck wondered if the others were having the same doubts about Todd.

"Maybe I'd better find us some music," Todd remarked, flicking on the radio in the middle of the Chrysler's giant dashboard. Chuck heard snatches of announcers' voices, ads, and maybe half a dozen tunes before Chuck pulled his hand back from the radio's controls.

"Ah," he said with a sigh. "Perfect."

"*I put a spell on you,*" an impossibly deep voice sang from the car speakers, "*because you're mine!*" The music behind the singer blared out a single repeated note, creating a strange spell of its own.

"Just what we need," Todd announced. "Halloween music."

The singer cackled as he continued to sing about how there was no way for his love to escape. But the music was heavy. If it wasn't so loud, the tune could have been used as back-up music for a funeral. Sue began to pound on the back of the front seat in time to the tune; a second later, Jake and Alex started pounding too.

Chuck just had to join in. "*I put a spell on you . . .*"

"Here we are," Todd announced abruptly. He killed the engine, the song vanishing mid-beat as it was fading out.

"Here?" It was Beth's turn to ask the question. "Where's here?"

"Wait a second," Jake added, looking speculatively up at the large house they had pulled in front of. The windows were dark, the street quiet. It looked like nobody was home.

"Isn't this Mr. Johnson's place?"

Todd's smile stretched across his face. "Could be."

"Mr. Johnson? Maths?" Sue screeched, as if the very idea that they could be outside their trigonometry teacher's house was more than she could stand.

Todd nodded with a deeply meaningful frown. "I can think of no-one who deserves it more."

"Deserves what?" Alex demanded.

"Come and behold," Todd announced, waving the rest of them to follow. He grabbed the keys from the ignition and marched down the length of the great purple car to the trunk as the others quickly joined him. Todd unlocked the large rear compartment and swung the trunk lid up over his head. There, in the huge orifice at the back of the Chrysler, were at least fifty rolls of toilet paper.

"Oh, wow," Beth whispered.

"Neat," Jake agreed.

Todd grabbed a couple of rolls. "It's time to decorate the Johnson home."

"Do we really dare?" Sue asked as she stared up at the house. It was an old Victorian place. Somehow, the fact that it was dark made it look even larger.

"Why not?" Todd insisted. "Think of what he does to us on those maths tests."

Chuck had to agree with Todd there. Mr. Johnson gave the toughest tests at Oxrun High. If he didn't grade on a curve, everybody in the class would fail.

"Considering the way he treats his students," Todd drawled, "I think it would be more of a crime *not* to give him this little — demonstration."

"So come on, dig in!" Todd waved the others forward with the rolls of paper he held in either hand. "Besides, what's a prank or two this time of year? After all, it's almost Halloween."

The others still hesitated. It was something about that house, Chuck thought. He didn't want to go near it.

Todd stepped away from the trunk to allow the others to take his place. "Gentle people, choose your weapons."

Jake was first, grabbing three rolls in his large hands. Then came Beth, who gave Chuck a wicked grin before she picked up two rolls of her own. Well, Chuck guessed, who was he to spoil the fun? He grabbed two rolls himself and walked over to join the others.

"Who's good at climbing trees?" Todd asked. "To honour Mr. Johnson properly, we have to do the yard and house, top to bottom."

Mitch stepped forward. "I've had a tree house since I was six. I'll get up there."

"Good," Todd agreed. "Jake, you're not bad at tossing things." Actually, Jake was the second-best pitcher on the high school baseball team. "Throw Mitch extra rolls when he needs them."

Beth and Sue started to giggle as they ran side-by-side towards the house.

"And not too much noise!" Todd added in a hoarse whisper. "We don't want anyone to notice us."

How could people not notice what they were doing? There were seven of them running back and forth in front of the house. And they were throwing around big white rolls of paper that showed up really well under the street lights.

But, Chuck reassured himself, it was late enough in the year, and there was a nip in the air. Most people were safe inside, watching their sitcoms on TV. Nobody had any reason to look outside.

Watching TV. That's where his parents would have been, too, if they hadn't joined that new club of their own.

Maybe, Chuck thought, he did worry too much. He joined the Halloween Club to have fun, didn't he?

The Club quickly completed their first assignment. In a matter of minutes, there was new, white frosting on all the hedges that fronted the house, and streamers went from branch to branch of the large maple by the front walk. Alex and Todd had gone around the back, too, to make sure that all four sides of the house were properly decorated.

It still took Chuck a couple of minutes to get into the spirit of the thing. He finally picked a large bush at the very front of the lawn, and totally wrapped it in white. All the toilet paper made it look like a mummy bush, escaped from some Egyptian tomb.

"That's more like it, Chuck. I was a little worried about you."

Chuck glanced back to see Todd smiling at his work.

"Hey, I can get into it," Chuck said defensively. Todd must have noticed how much Chuck had hesitated.

"I'm sure you can," Todd agreed. "That's why you're going to be the one to ring the doorbell."

Chuck stared back at the other boy. "What do you mean, ring the doorbell?"

Todd nodded as if it was all settled. "Ah, Chuck. Glad you volunteered."

Chuck had? Well, why couldn't he do something like that? Who cared if you rang the doorbell of an empty house?

Something had changed. A light had gone on in one of the upstairs rooms, all the way over in the right hand corner of the house.

There was someone home after all!

Chuck turned back to Todd. Todd only smiled.

Todd was testing him. Without even asking, Chuck knew he had to do it if he wanted to be part of the club.

"Come on, guys!" Todd called to the others. "As soon as Chuck does his little job here, we're going to have to burn rubber!"

Now Todd was announcing it to everybody, Chuck decided he'd better get it over with.

He walked quickly towards the front door as the other club members tossed the last of the toilet paper and headed for the car.

Mitch yelled suddenly. Chuck stopped and looked up at the tree where Mitch hung by one arm.

"Almost fell," Mitch called out softly. "Guess I'm not as good in trees as I thought." He started to climb the rest of the way down — very carefully.

Now whoever was in the house was sure to know someone was out here. Chuck almost turned back to Todd. But there was still only the one light on the second floor; maybe the person inside hadn't heard after all. Chuck should be able to ring the doorbell and get away in plenty of time.

So why didn't he just go ahead and do it?

He took a deep breath and ran towards the front door. He took all three steps to the house in a single leap, pressing the doorbell as soon as he landed.

Chuck heard bells sound deep within the house. There were three tones in a row, the last one lower than any doorbell Chuck had ever heard.

No other lights turned on in the house, but Chuck thought he heard another noise, like something bumping heavily down the stairs. The sound froze him on the front step.

"Chuck! Come on!"

Chuck's head snapped up at the sound of Todd's voice. He turned and ran for the car full of kids, moving as fast as he could, still imagining some shadowy figure behind him, marching towards the front door.

"Beautiful," Todd announced as Chuck jumped in the back. "Revenge is complete. Let's get out of here and get something to eat."

As the car sped around the corner, Chuck turned back to look at their handiwork.

The paper strewn across the lawn glowed like some crazy, intricate web. In the moonlight, it looked like the Johnson house had been overwhelmed by the work of a giant spider.

But Chuck was more interested in what was inside the house. There still was no light at the front door. But as they turned the corner and lost sight of the Johnson place behind a row of trees, somehow Chuck could swear that the door was opening.

4

As usual, they went to The Cock's Crow.

It was a burger joint; nothing fancy. In fact, it looked a lot older than all the chain restaurants down by the mall in Hanley. Actually, that feeling of age, of a place that had been around for a while, was one of the things that made it special. That, plus Sid, the new owner, would let you hang around, not like the 'no loitering' attitude of the new Kentucky Fried McBurger places.

Sid looked up from where he read the paper, his elbows propped up on the counter. He was totally bald, which made it hard to guess how old he was. Chuck guessed the owner had been around for a while, because Sid's face broke into a hundred different wrinkles when he smiled. The top of Sid's head gleamed under the fluorescent lights as he nodded to the newcomers.

"Hey, kids," Sid said as the seven of them piled in through the door. "Let me know when you want to order." He looked back down at the sports section.

"Was that a riot or—" Alex started as soon as they were all inside.

"I bet old Johnson's going to have a few problems he never thought about in class," Mitch agreed.

Todd put a finger to his lips.

"The Club's business should not be discussed in public," he announced, quietly but firmly. "Now let's get some burgers."

One look at the frown on Todd's face, and everyone shut up.

"We're ready, Sid," Todd called.

Sid glanced up again, folded his paper neatly on the counter and got ready to go to work.

"Shoot," he said.

Most of the others ordered food of one sort or another. Chuck just got something to drink. For some reason, he didn't feel very hungry.

It was only after they had all squeezed into one of the big corner booths, hamburgers, fries, chocolate shakes and all, that Todd started talking about what had happened earlier.

"We can't talk in public about what we do," he said in a loud whisper. "That's what a secret club is all about."

To keep secrets? Chuck thought their prank might be even funnier if the other students back at Oxrun High found out about it. But then again, how could you keep some people in the know and others in the dark? If they told some of the other kids what happened, someone was just as likely to tell Mr. Johnson, or the principal, or even one of their parents. Chuck guessed Todd was right. In this cases secrets were best.

Besides, it wasn't like they had to keep quiet about this to everyone. This first secret was shared by all seven of them. In fact, it was this secret that made it really seem like a club.

Todd sat back and grinned as the others whispered back and forth about their triumph.

"Whoa!" Chuck looked at his watch. It was after 8.30. "If I don't get home soon, my parents will know I'm up to something."

Todd nodded. "That's the last thing we want to happen. I think it's time we got out of here—" he grinned "—and back to our happy homes. The Halloween Club has had a more-than-successful first night. But there are three more nights to go."

They wolfed down the rest of their burgers and headed for the car, passing Cody Banning, sitting alone in a booth and looking miserable.

"What's up with him?" asked Alex, curiously. "Looks like he's been deserted by his group."

"His girlfriend's in the hospital in a coma," Chuck said. "Guess he's feeling pretty down right now."

As they headed for the car, Sid looked up from his paper and waved. Chuck thought the Club could be talking about bombing the school and Sid *still* wouldn't pay any attention.

"We'll get you home first," Todd said to Chuck as he started the Steamship.

Chuck nodded gratefully. His house was only a few blocks away. He should make it back with five minutes to spare.

"So, tonight the Club got revenge," Sue said when they stopped at a red light. "What happens tomorrow?"

"Oh, each night is better than the night before," Todd replied as the light turned green and he pulled into Chuck's street. "The first night is revenge. The second night is — suspense."

"Suspense?" Chuck asked. What did that mean?

"Here you go," Todd replied as he pulled in front of Chuck's house.

Chuck didn't want to get out of the car until he got some answers. But he also didn't think Todd was going to give them any answers, at least, not until tomorrow night.

"Later," he said as he got out of the car.

"See you tomorrow, Chuck!" Beth called. Now *that* was a good sign.

Todd honked as he revved the old Chrysler on down the street.

5

The Halloween Club didn't really change everything, after all.

The next day at school wasn't particularly different. At least it wasn't until it was almost time for fourth period and Mr. Johnson's maths class. Chuck found himself getting nervous in Miss Lance's history class he had just before maths. And it only got worse when the bell rang for the next period.

What if it had been Mr. Johnson inside the house? What if he had left the lights off so that he could peer through the windows and identify the kids in the glare of the street lights? Mr. Johnson might not have seen any of the other kids up close enough to tell who they were, but Chuck had been the one to ring the doorbell.

Chuck walked to maths class as these questions ran through his head, his feet taking him where the rest of him didn't want to go. Kids jostled in the halls around him, laughing, shouting, stopping to talk or to visit their lockers. Chuck heard Jeff Dacre and Sam Jones say hello to him as they hurried past. He was lucky to manage a half smile and a wave in return.

His feet slowed down as he approached his destination. Oh man, he thought. The Halloween Club was fun at night, but he might worry himself to death during the day.

He looked up from where he had watched his sneakers cross the linoleum. Maths class was right in front of him. And the halls were almost empty. He stepped inside the classroom just as the second bell announced the start of fourth period.

Jake, the one Halloween Club member who shared this particular class, grinned at Chuck as he entered the room.

He wanted to shake his head and yell at the other boy to keep quiet, even though Jake hadn't said anything.

Chuck took his seat as Mr. Johnson looked over the class. If anything, the teacher looked past Chuck, to the juvenile delinquents who always hung out at the back of the room.

Mr. Johnson looked away from the class, down at the book he held in his hand. "Today, we start looking at sines and cosines." He turned his back to the classroom, writing the two words, 'sine' and 'cosine', on the blackboard.

So it was going to be business as usual, even after what had happened? Chuck tried to listen to the new concepts the teacher was laying before him, but he found himself listening more for other things. Did Mr. Johnson sound a little angrier today than usual? Would he make any references to last night, even casually, say, using the cleaning of a yard as the basis for a problem? Chris realised he was having trouble paying attention. He felt like he was listening more to the spaces between the words rather than to the words themselves.

But no matter how hard Chuck listened, Mr. Johnson seemed to have no reaction to what had happened the night before. Formulae danced across the board as Johnson described these new bits of trigonometry. Half the class laughed at some joke Johnson told. Chuck wasn't in the mood for that at all.

Shouldn't he feel relieved that Johnson wasn't making a big deal about last night? Instead, he only got more worried.

Maybe it wasn't even Johnson's house they had draped with toilet paper. They really only had Todd's word on that.

Right now, this Halloween Club wasn't anywhere near as much fun as he thought it would be.

The bell rang at last. The class felt like it had lasted forever. Chuck gathered his books and stood up. He took a deep breath, half expecting Mr. Johnson to tell him to sit down again so that they could have a little talk.

"Mr. Antrim?" Johnson called.

Here it was. The maths teacher always used last names. Said it helped with the education process. Chuck felt like he was going to get an education right now.

Chuck swallowed and looked to where Johnson now sat behind his desk. "Yes, sir?"

"Did you have a question?"

What was that? Did *he* have a question? Chuck realised suddenly that all his classmates were gone. Mr. Johnson had only singled Chuck out because he was the last student left in the room.

"Uh, no, sir. Just thinking about my next class."

"Oh." Mr. Johnson looked back down at the papers on his desk. "See you tomorrow, then."

Chuck quickly left the room. It was only when he made it to the hallway that he realised he had stopped breathing.

"Hey, Chuckster!" someone called from across the corridor.

He knew who that was without even looking. Only one guy in this school dared to call him Chuckster.

"Hello, Joey," Chuck answered back.

Joey Viser was a tall and skinny guy with the biggest smile you'd ever see. Kids around here called him the School Mouth, and that wasn't just because of his smile. To say that Joey Viser liked to talk was the understatement of the year. Good old Joey was ten times better than the school newspaper for finding out what was really going on. His sister Rena was equally hot on the gossip front: between them they pretty much knew everything that was happening.

Chuck wondered how he could ask the Mouth about the Johnson place without tipping his hand about his part in it. But Joey told him what he wanted to know without even asking.

Joey winked at Chuck, his voice dropping to that conspiratorial whisper he used to pass on all his juiciest titbits. "Did you hear what happened over at Johnson's place last night?"

Wow, if Joey knew about it, and was having such fun spreading the news around, that meant the whole school knew about it, too, and was laughing along with them. Maybe, Chuck thought, all this Halloween Club stuff would turn out to be fun after all.

Joey told a very colourful, if not exactly accurate, version of what had happened the night before at the Johnson place, about how maybe a dozen kids had gone in and totally overwhelmed the place with toilet paper. 'Tee-peeing', he called it. Joey's version sounded even better than what had actually happened. Especially the part he saved until the very end, the part totally new to Chuck.

"And then Johnson went out on his front lawn," Joey announced, "and he started yelling! At the top of his lungs, wild stuff like, 'If I find out about who did this, I'll make them pay!'"

Make them pay? If Johnson ever did find out about this, Chuck could see some failing grades, or worse, in his future. He still managed to laugh at Joey's delivery.

"But that's nothing!" Joey went on, so excited that his voice started to squeak. "Did you hear the *real* news?"

Nothing? Everything the Halloween Club did was nothing? What could top tee-peeing a teacher's house?

Joey's whisper fell into a lower, super-secretive register. "Did you hear what happened to those guys on the track team?"

"Track team?" Chuck asked, interested despite himself. A lot of the jocks at school were always getting in some sort of trouble or other. But it was usually the guys on the football team, the ones who would crush your head if you looked at them funny. The track team was nowhere near as bad, though; you could even talk to some of the guys who ran and jumped for the school.

"Yeah," Joey added, "They must be clear into New York by now. Might have disappeared into Canada."

Chuck felt like he had come in on the middle of the story here. He wondered when the last time was that he'd talked to Joey. Maybe he missed a couple of the Mouth's daily updates.

"What are you talking about?" Chuck asked.

"Don't you know?" Joey started bouncing up and down in his sneakers, looking so excited that he might jump up and leave the ground at any moment. "There was a big liquor store robbery over on Centre Street. Four kids involved. Police think it's got to be the four guys from the track team, especially since no-one's seen them since the robbery."

"Four guys, what four guys?"

"Oh, Jim Matursky, Sammy O'Neil, Kenny Anderson—"

Kenny Anderson? He lived just up the street from Chuck. Kenny could be a jerk sometimes, but Chuck never thought he was a crook. Things were getting weirder and weirder around here.

The second bell rang. They should be getting down to the lunch room before the hall monitors got on their case. "Listen," Chuck said to Joey, "I gotta go."

"We both do," Joey agreed. "But I think this story's only going to get juicier. Let me know if you hear anything!"

So Joey could tell everyone else in school, Chuck thought. Still, that sort of messenger service might come in useful sometime.

Chuck took the stairs down to the cafeteria two at a time. He might want to talk to the Halloween Club about what Joey had told him.

He saw Todd in the lunch line outside the cafeteria door. Todd nodded as Chuck walked up to him. "Today," he said casually, "maybe the Club shouldn't sit together."

Chuck stared at the other boy. "Huh? Why not?"

Todd frowned at that. "Club? Did I say something about a club? I don't know anything about a club."

Oh. Chuck got it. He quickly looked away. It might be better if they didn't hang around together in school. That way, if one or two of them got caught at one of their pranks, the authorities couldn't link them up with the ones who got away. And people like Mr. Johnson would never find out just who really decorated their lawns.

It was Todd's turn to stare at Chuck. "Do I even know you?"

Chuck shook his head and turned towards the end of the lunch line. "See you around, Todd."

Todd grabbed Chuck's shoulder before he could leave. His voice fell to a whisper. "Hey, Chucko, tonight we leave at six."

"Six o'clock?" What was he talking about? "I don't know, Todd. My parents—"

"Don't worry about your parents. Todd takes care of everything."

Apparently Todd ran everything too, including Chuck's life.

Suspense, Todd had said. Tonight was suspense. Would it be even more suspenseful than Chuck had already felt today?

When, Chuck wondered, had he totally lost control?

6

Then again, maybe it would be fun to lose control.

Chuck was flat-out amazed. Todd had been so right about Chuck's parents. Both his mother and father had rushed in and out of the house so fast that they didn't have time to ask Chuck anything. And they didn't tell Chuck where they were going, or leave a phone number, or any of that.

Their mother was dressed even more nicely than the night before. She had on a new piece of jewellery, a ruby ring that Chuck had never seen before. Their father waved a quick goodbye as Mom instructed both her kids to pick out TV dinners from the freezer. It wasn't even 5.30 when the front door slammed behind them.

"What was that?" Chuck asked as their mother's voice, constantly shouting the usual instructions about how they should be good, suddenly ceased. He heard the car start up and their parents pull out of the driveway.

"Oh, it's that stupid club of theirs," Nicole replied. "Apparently, they got started on some stupid game yesterday, and they had to finish the stupid thing tonight."

Somehow, Nicole always knew things that Chuck didn't have a clue about. His mother and sister always talked when he was out of the room; he figured it was some kind of mother-daughter thing.

Still, Chuck wasn't complaining. It seemed like his parents were as involved in their club as he was in his.

Of course, their behaviour was also a little bit beyond weird. "But why did they have to leave so early?"

Nicole sighed as if the answer should be obvious. "I think it's because Halloween's almost here. This could be the last year I'm trick-or-treating, you know? Like, our parents want to spend the holiday with their families?"

Chuck had never thought of that. What if his parents had plans for both their kids on Halloween — some neighbourhood party or something. Would they stop him from going out on the last night of the Halloween Club?

"I suppose you want to get rid of me, too?" Nicole asked. "So you guys can run around town again?"

Sometimes Chuck thought his little sister was the only one who really knew what was going on around here.

Chuck grinned back at her, "Well, you don't have to get lost for another half-an-hour."

She gave a no-nonsense nod. "Then I think we should eat. Maybe there's stuff for sandwiches in here."

So Nicole was as enthusiastic as he was about those frozen dinners? Not that their parents would notice. The way their mother was flying around now, she'd never remember what she had told them about dinner, anyway.

Besides, things were looking good in the refrigerator. There was ham, turkey, American cheese and a couple of kinds of bread. They spread the stuff over the kitchen counter, making sandwiches as they talked.

"So what do you do with your friends out there?" Nicole asked innocently.

Chuck looked up from where he was pouring a glass of milk. He couldn't tell her about any of that. The members of the club were all sworn to silence. Heck, he was probably even sworn to silence about being sworn to silence.

Chuck didn't particularly want to lie to his sister. So how would he get out of telling her?

"You wouldn't understand," he said at last. "You're only a kid." Heck, that excuse worked for his parents all the time.

His little sister made a face. "You're awfully eager to go out with these guys every night," Nicole said as she took her first bite of her sandwich. "Or maybe—" She paused to swallow, "—it's the girls instead."

Chuck looked sharply over at his smiling sister. "You know I'm not going out with any girls."

Nicole looked surprised. "Not even girls named Beth?"

Chuck almost choked on his sandwich. Did his little sister know everything? She was almost as bad as Todd. Was there a book around someplace where everyone could look up Chuck's secrets?

A very smug smile wrapped itself around Nicole's face. It didn't go at all with her braces. "Don't look so surprised. I hear things, too. Didn't you know that Beth had a sister who was my age, who's friends with me and Merrilee and David Trent?"

Really? It was Chuck's turn to swallow. Maybe he could figure out how Beth really felt about him. It looked like little sisters could be good for something after all.

A horn blared outside.

"Well, I guess I'll have to tell you about that some other time." Nicole went back to eating, as if the subject was closed.

Chuck looked towards the front door. Was that Todd? He was more than a little early. Chuck wolfed down the rest of his sandwich and followed it with the end of his glass of milk, leaving both of his dishes in the kitchen sink.

He looked back at Nicole, who was still focusing all of her attention on what was left of her food. He wished he could find out more about Beth. But Nicole wouldn't tell him now, even if the explanation only took a few seconds. If there was a book about Chuck, little sisters would be a big problem on every page.

"I gotta go," he called as he hurried towards the front door. "You can tell me about that rest of that later, okay?"

"The rest of what? I don't know if I can remember. I'm only a little kid, aren't I?"

And far too smart for her own good, too. He'd get the information later, even if he had to promise her a ride to the mall or something.

The horn honked a second time.

"Sounds like it's time to go," Nicole said without looking up.

"See you later," Chuck called back.

"Chuckie's got a girl friend," Nicole sang as he opened the front door, "Chuckie's got a girl friend."

On the other hand, Chuck thought, maybe he'd take his sister out to the mall and leave her there — forever.

He grabbed his jacket as he headed out the door.

He almost stopped dead when he saw Todd and the Steamship. Beside the driver, the old Chrysler was empty.

He got in on the passenger side, across from Todd. The car seemed even bigger when there were only two people in it.

"This time, I decided to pick you up first," Todd announced. He glanced at Chuck as he pulled the car back into the street. "Fair's fair, especially when you're dealing with — suspense."

So Todd wasn't going to tell him anything that made any sense — again? Chuck had had enough of this. He didn't care if Todd got mad at him. At that moment, he didn't even care if he got kicked out of the club. "The Halloween Club is fun and all, but does it have to be so mysterious? You know, I'm a little worried about some of this."

Chuck was surprised when Todd smiled. "Chuck, you think before you do a lot of stuff. That's good. I don't want to have a bunch of blind followers in the Halloween Club. In fact, after Halloween's over, I think we should have a vote on what to do next. In the meantime, though, I am the grand dictator of all you survey. I've got great plans. And plans — especially Halloween plans — are best when everybody doesn't know about them. But I've also got a question for you, Chuck." He looked over at Chuck as he braked for a stop light. "How'd you like to be second-in-command?"

Second? Right after Todd? Chuck didn't know what to say.

"Like I said," Todd continued, "you think things through. You won't do something foolish." He urged the Steamship forward as the light turned green. "If we ever got into trouble, I'd be glad to have you backing me up."

"Trouble?" Chuck didn't like the sound of that. "What are you thinking about doing?"

"Oh, nothing that deadly. We're talking about having fun here, not raising the dead."

Well. Chuck guessed he was glad at least that was out of the question.

"Think about it," Todd urged. "We'll talk later."

They pulled up in front of Beth's place, a couple of blocks down the street from where Chuck lived. Todd tooted the horn one more time.

Beth opened the front door and waved. She disappeared inside for an instant, then came out wearing a leather jacket that looked really good with her long blonde hair. She half jogged, half skipped out to the car. Chuck did his best not to stare.

Beth climbed in the front seat so that she was sitting right next to him. Did her elbow touch his arm on purpose? He remembered what Nicole said — or maybe didn't say. But then again, his sister *had* been known to make things up, especially when it could get her big brother into trouble.

Todd quickly drove around the neighbourhood, picking up Alex, then Sue and Mitch.

As soon as others joined them, it seemed like the private conversation between Chuck and Todd was over. Chuck guessed their driver still needed to be the Mysterious Todd for everybody else. It was a part of the club atmosphere after all.

"We get Jake," Todd called as Mitch climbed in the car, "and then we head for the hills."

Jake was the furthest away from the centre of town, living in an old development on Mainland Road. It sounded like the Halloween Club was going to leave the Station completely behind this time.

Three curves and a right turn later they were in front of Jake's house.

Todd honked the horn.

They waited a minute. The house was silent.

Todd frowned. "Chuck, could you go and see what's keeping him?"

Well, Chuck thought, here's what happens to the guy who's second-in-command. Beth opened the passenger door and got out before he could say anything. He supposed he might as well go up to the front door. After all, they hadn't tee-peed Jake's house — yet.

He walked quickly to the door and reached for the bell.

The front door opened abruptly before Chuck had a chance to hit the doorbell.

A tall, thin woman looked down on him. Jake's mother, Chuck guessed. He realised he had never met either one of his friend's parents.

"Jake can't come out," she said curtly.

"Oh, gee, Mrs. Sumner?" Chuck asked tentatively. She didn't disagree, so she really was Jake's mother. "Is something wrong?"

"Wrong?" She pointed a disapproving hand at Chuck, as if he was to blame for everything. He looked away from her frowning face, his gaze shifting to a ruby ring she wore. It looked a little bit like the new ring his mother had. Weird. Maybe rubies were the big fashion this year.

"He was out past his curfew last night," she went on sternly. "He's grounded for the rest of the week." She stepped back and slammed the door abruptly.

Chuck stood on the step for a second, surprised by the suddenness of what had happened. Jake's mother was not a happy woman. Jake must have really got it in the neck for staying out too long. It was funny. When Chuck had seen Jake in maths class, everything seemed to be fine. Jake must not have found out about being grounded until he'd got home from school. It sounded like the sort of thing parents would do. But then, Chuck thought, with the way his parents were acting lately, how could you predict them doing anything?

Chuck jogged back to the Steamship and quickly explained what had happened to the rest of the club.

"Curfew?" Todd shook his head. "Jake didn't tell me anything about that."

So maybe Todd didn't know everything after all.

"Well, get in," Todd called. "Six of us still have work to do."

Chuck opened the passenger door while Beth scooted over into the middle of the long front seat.

"My parents almost kept me in, too," Mitch called from the back, "after all those scrapes I got climbing the tree. I lied, told them I'd fallen down riding my bike."

So they had almost lost Mitch, too? Chuck remembered his sister's remark about how their parents might have plans for Halloween. It looked like the real world was going to get in the way after all. Was the Halloween Club even going to make it to Halloween?

"This will require some minor adjustments," Todd announced as he drove on. "It looks like some of our homes are just a little bit too happy." He shook his head. "But now it's time for night number two, and Suspense!"

Todd turned on his radio. The song this time was about a 'Witchy Woman'. It seemed that even the radio was getting ready for Halloween.

A few moments later and they had left Oxrun Station behind, Todd guiding his huge car through the back roads that wound their way around the low hills to the south. There never seemed to be much on this side of town; at least not that much that Chuck knew about. He guessed that Todd knew better.

Todd slowed suddenly and turned onto a dirt road that Chuck didn't even know was there.

"It's an old fire road," Todd explained. "Goes along the ridge here in case there's ever a forest fire."

The car's headlights showed a path just wide enough for the car to travel down, with thick trees growing to either side, their branches spreading above them. The trees were so thick that they closed out much of the sky overhead, making the road seem more like a tunnel through the woods.

The 'Witchy Woman' song ended, replaced by an old-time, jazzy number. *"That old black magic's got me in your spell, that old black magic that you do so well."*

Todd spoke up a moment later. "But it's the other end of the fire road that's really impressive."

With that, the road opened up before them into a clearing. The near-full moon was directly ahead, as if Todd was really headed for that cold and craggy circle in the sky.

Todd drove to the middle of the clearing and stopped the car.

"This is the future of the Halloween Club."

"To come out to the middle of nowhere?" Alex asked.

"Oh, this isn't the middle of nowhere," Todd said as he opened the door and got out of the car. "Back in the sixties and seventies, this was the place people used to come to — well, spend some time together." He waved at the clearing around them. "Welcome to Lover's Lookout."

"What," Mitch asked as he left the car too, "is the suspense — who's gonna end up dating who?"

"Oh, no," Todd replied, waving for the others to follow him, "I brought you up here to look out!"

Chuck got out of the car with the others and walked across the clearing after Todd. This used to be a real hang-out, huh? Chuck wondered why people stopped coming here. Todd's car was the only one parked in the whole field. The only whole car, that is. Off on one side of the clearing was the stripped chassis of another vehicle. For that matter, Chuck wondered why someone would bother to come out all this way just to take a car apart?

Well, he supposed, no-one would bother you in a place like this, whether you wanted to take apart a car or do just about anything. Maybe that was why people didn't come here any more. Some places could just be *too* isolated.

"Take a look," Todd said, just ahead.

Chuck heard Beth call out in surprise and hurried to join her. There, at the top of a slight rise, was a sudden dropoff, maybe a hundred feet down. But beyond that dropoff, in the distance, you could see all of Oxrun Station, a thousand tiny lights shining in the chill October air.

"Wow," even Alex admitted. "This was worth the hike."

"Yeah," Todd agreed. "You can really see why people used to come up here."

"But why don't they come up here any more?" Sue asked.

"I don't know," Todd replied, "but it might have something to do with what I'm going to show you next." He waved for the others to follow.

"Come on. Stay close and watch out for the cliff." He laughed, as if falling a hundred feet was the greatest fun anyone could ever have. "The Halloween Club always goes together."

Beth turned around and looked straight at Chuck. "What the heck is going on?" It was hard to tell in the moonlight, but Chuck thought she looked a little scared.

"Come on, guys!" Todd called from where he marched along the edge of the cliff. "Chuck, Beth, stay together! This is going to be fun!"

Chuck and Beth fell into step next to each other. He glanced over at her. Her yellow hair looked almost white in the moonlight. She looked at him and smiled.

Chuck felt better already. As long as they were together, how could things go wrong?

7

"Watch it here!" Todd called to the others. "The path gets a little narrow up ahead. One wrong move, and you could fall all the way back into town."

Chuck could barely see the track in front of him. A cloud had rolled across the moon, turning their surroundings into little more than shadows. The other club members were only dark silhouettes against the bright lights of the town below.

"I think we need to go single file," Todd announced. "I've got a flashlight here. Mitch, you take it and lead the way. The path goes up that ridge." Todd bounced the beam of the flashlight over the dirt, tracing the trail until it disappeared between a pair of bushes. "Mitch first, then Sue, then Alex and Beth and Chuck. I'll take up the rear. That way I can talk you guys through it."

So now Todd had them holding hands, and walking as close to boy-girl-boy as he could manage. He'd stuck Chuck and Beth together. Beth held out her hand for him. Chuck felt her cool fingers intertwine with his own. This was the first time they had ever held hands. He never wanted to let go.

Chuck's other hand was still free. He looked back to the dark shape of Todd behind him.

"Nah," Todd replied before Chuck could ask the question. "Go ahead. I don't need to be part of the human chain. I already know the way."

So he was sending everybody else towards a cliff or who knew what. Todd was setting this up so that they all had to trust him, or else.

Everyone stood there for a long moment. Somebody laughed, Alex maybe, but the sound was more nervous than anything else.

"What are we waiting for, club?" Todd called at last. "We don't want to blow anybody else's curfew."

"What the heck," Mitch said. "It's for the Club."

Chuck heard Mitch's sneakers scuff along the path. Beth's hand tugged him forward as the others followed.

They moved slowly over the uneven ground as they traced the path up the hill. Chuck kept bumping his toes against rocks and half-buried roots. It was a miracle that none of them tripped.

"Onwards!" Mitch called. "Into the great unknown!" He was really getting into being their leader, even if it was only for a moment.

Chuck wondered, if he was second-in-command, why wasn't he leading the club? But Todd had talked about the narrowness of the path. The most likely person to fall would be their temporary leader. Maybe Mitch was leading because he was expendable.

Mitch's flashlight beam disappeared. It took Chuck a second to realise Mitch had only stepped over the top of the rise and had started down the other side. The group kept on moving.

"Oh, wow," Mitch said loudly.

Chuck heard Beth gasp as she reached the top of the hill before him.

The last cloud had moved off the moon, turning the world around them bright with moonlight. Chuck stepped to the top of the hill and saw a whole other world spread before them.

"Pretty dramatic, huh?" Todd asked from behind him. "You half feel like the moon planned it this way."

Maybe, Chuck thought, when it got this close to Halloween, the moon did make these sort of plans.

The hill rolled down to a little valley, like a small bowl between the surrounding ridges. But it was the two things in the bowl that made it interesting.

One was a huge house, so big that it made their maths teacher's Victorian home look like a shack down by the ocean. And the huge house glowed a spectral white, as if it had been painted by moonlight.

But standing behind the sprawling building was something even stranger.

It was a group of upright stones. Not gravestones, though. That's what Chuck had thought they were at first. But they were shaped all wrong, and they were much too tall, more like pillars than grave markings.

"Pillars?" he asked aloud.

"Hey," Todd answered him. "Pretty good. And you haven't been down there to study them close up. But they're not pillars exactly, anymore than what we've got down there is your average country graveyard. What we've got here, boys and girls, is our own miniature version of Stonehenge."

Alex laughed. "What are you trying to pull on us, Todd?"

"No," Sue objected. "Todd is right. My parents took me to see another one of these places when we were on vacation last year. It was up in Salem, New Hampshire." She turned away from the moonlit stones to look at the group. "There were supposed to be dozens of these places once, all over New England. A lot of them were destroyed. Farmers would carry off all but the biggest stones to build walls to mark the edges of their properties."

"But they didn't get all of them, did they?" Todd smiled at Sue. "Can I pick the members of the Halloween Club, or can I?"

"Can we go down and get a closer look?" Beth asked.

"We can," Todd agreed, "and we will. But we won't do it tonight. I don't want anybody else to be out past their curfew."

Chuck frowned. It wasn't that late, was it? How long had they been here?

"You see before you the future of the Halloween Club," Todd continued. "Tomorrow night, we visit the house."

"That's all?" Alex complained.

"That will be more than enough," Todd replied dramatically. "I call tomorrow night — danger."

So that was it. Their leaving didn't have anything to do with getting anybody home. Todd just didn't want to blow all his surprises at once.

"Danger?" Beth asked. "What kind of danger?"

"Oh, each of us has to visit that house," Todd said slowly, "alone."

"Cool," Beth whispered back.

"And then," Todd added, "on Halloween, we'll have a party amongst the stones." It was his turn to laugh. "They were meant for Halloween, after all."

Chuck always thought stones like this had more to do with the solstices, with the sun rising in just the right place, between the standing rocks. At least that's what he remembered about Stonehenge. There was no way to figure out if the stones down below had been set up for the same purpose, or for any purpose, no matter what Todd said. Except, Chuck guessed, that they could stand here on Halloween night and see just what happened.

But they were really only a bunch of old stones, weren't they? Why did Chuck keep feeling Todd was keeping something from them? Of course, there was all this mysterious business that Todd kept pulling — that was a big part of it. Chuck wondered if Todd really knew any more than the rest of them about that stuff in the valley.

"A party around the stones?" Beth asked with a grin. She was really getting into this. "And we can bring a boom box and dance?"

"What would Halloween be without a little dancing?" Todd asked back.

"Cool," Beth agreed.

Maybe, Chuck thought, he and Beth could dance together. If he could dance all right in the middle of this spooky place.

And maybe he was worrying about all this other stuff so he wouldn't have to think about stuff with Beth.

He needed to stick with what was real around here. Like all his new friends in the Halloween Club. And — even better — how close Beth had stayed to him the entire evening.

With any luck, this Halloween would be the beginning of a whole new world for Chuck.

"Hey!" Mitch called.

"What's the matter?" Sue asked.

The clouds chose that moment to once again cover the moon. The wind rose suddenly; it began to feel very cold.

Mitch pointed down to the valley, now half-lost in shadow. "I could have sworn I saw somebody moving down there."

"Wow," Alex asked. "In the house?"

"No, no. Back in the stones."

"Do you think the place belongs to anybody?" Sue asked quickly.

"I think Mitch is seeing things," Todd interrupted. "And I think it's time we got out of here so we can come back here tomorrow. Anyway, it looks like it's going to blow up a storm."

The others turned quickly to go, like they were eager to get away from the place.

Chuck, though, couldn't turn away just yet. He thought he might have seen something down there, too, just when the clouds snuffed out the moon; a dark shape moving between the stones.

But Chuck had seen another dark shape — at Mr. Johnson's house. He turned and hurried after the others. He didn't want to talk about any of this. The dark shapes could be anything. They'd make fun of him, tell him he was imagining things. He probably was, too. Like, who or what would be walking in the middle of nowhere in the middle of the night?

Chuck was still awfully glad to see the car.

8

Chuck didn't feel much like talking on the trip home. But the other guys in the club were doing so much talking that they didn't even notice that half the lights in the town seemed to be out, let alone Chuck's silence.

"Wow," Sue called up to Todd. "Where'd you ever find a place like that?"

Todd shrugged. "Oh, you know. I like to explore. Just get in my car and wander."

"You must know everything there is to know about Oxrun Station."

"Only the best roads out of town." Todd laughed. "I know there's more to life than Oxrun. I was out of town for a couple of years."

Todd glanced over at their mysterious leader. Were the stories about Todd true?

"So I felt I had to, you know, reacquaint myself with our fair city," Todd continued. "Since I hadn't seen anybody for years, I didn't really have any friends. Plus, I had my Steamship. What could I do but cruise?"

Beth turned to Chuck and whispered in his ear.

"Todd really overdoes this mystery stuff, doesn't he?"

Her voice felt like a breeze down the back of his neck. Chuck had to keep himself from shivering. He nodded.

Beth frowned at him. "You've been awfully quiet since we got back in the car. Are you thinking about something?"

"I don't know." What could Chuck say? Half of him wanted to get even closer to Beth. But he didn't know how to start without seeming pushy. The last thing he wanted to do was scare her away.

Then there was the other half of him, the half that worried about those shapes he'd seen the last two nights. Everybody around him was laughing now about some joke that Todd had made. What if the shapes were nothing to laugh about?

"I think," Beth whispered back to him a moment later, "that Todd isn't the only one having deep and mysterious thoughts around here."

"Whoops, fellow clubbers!" Todd called. "All good things must come to an end. We've got to drop off our first passenger."

Chuck looked up as Todd stopped the car. He had brought them to Beth's house first.

But Beth and Chuck had hardly even begun to talk! Chuck had been hoping Todd would take them back to the Cock's Crow. But maybe Todd really was afraid of blowing somebody else's curfew.

Chuck opened the door and stepped out to clear the way for Beth. He supposed there was always tomorrow. He wondered if there was any last thing he could say, to let Beth know that what was happening between them was really special.

"Hey, Beth," he began as she climbed out of the car.

"Oh, Chuck," Beth replied, throwing her arms around him. His breath went away completely as she gave him a big hug. "Don't worry about anything. I'll see you tomorrow, okay?"

Chuck stared after her as she disappeared into her house.

"Hey, Chuck, don't get blown away out there!" Todd called from the car. "We gotta get home some time in the near future so that we can go out again tomorrow night."

Chuck quickly got back in the passenger seat, slamming the door behind him.

"After all, Clubbers," Todd added, "it's almost Halloween!"

The radio started to play 'Purple People Eater' as Todd pulled away from the curb.

9

Beth had hugged him goodbye.

That's all he could really think about from the night before. And it got better than that, because tonight he was going to see her again.

She really did want to be near him, to spend time with him, to do the things he wanted to do. When Chuck thought about it, he realised that half the reason he had joined the Halloween Club was so he could be close to Beth. Had she joined to be around him too?

Whatever the reason, they'd spend the next two nights very close together. Oh, Todd would throw some stuff out for the Club to do. Actually, what had happened to the Club so far had been a lot of fun. Todd had a way of showing them things which made them more — important, maybe, almost more real, than they might be otherwise. Besides, it gave Chuck and Beth something to do while they got to know each other.

School was different that day. For the first couple of hours he paid attention and all, took some notes, even answered a teacher's question or two.

It seemed to go by like a dream, a dance of students and teachers and classroom bells.

Beth had hugged him and told him not to worry.

Chuck and Beth didn't share any classes. On other days, he'd sometimes catch a glimpse of her between periods or pass her in the hall. Today every girl with long blonde hair reminded him of Beth. But then, one after another, they'd turn around and they'd be Penny Galbraith or Eleanor Trent or someone else, and none of them had Beth's blue eyes, or upturned nose, or slightly crooked smile.

Then the principal announced that a couple of seniors had died. SJ — Sarah Jane — and Ursula Strong. Both deaths had been unexpected. And two more seniors were still in hospital: Natalie Dayne and Angie Hanover. Even he sounded shocked. He told everyone that if they wanted to go home, that was okay.

Chuck heard the speech, but it didn't really register. He had his own problems.

He did see Joey Viser, who began at once: "Isn't this crazy? Whaddya think's going on around here? Didja hear? They just found one of those guys on the track team — or at least, they found his body. It was Jim Matursky, they think."

Chuck stared at the Mouth. Joey grinned, delighted to be the centre of attention.

"The body was in pretty bad shape," his whispered report went on. "Maybe some animal had been at it. They say he lost a lot of blood."

Chuck shook his head. Some other time, he would have been glad to listen to the gory details. Right now, though, there was someone he wanted to see.

"Later, Joey." He turned towards the stairs that led to the lunchroom.

"You know, Chuck," Joey called, "they used to have human sacrifices around here!"

Chuck turned back, despite himself. "Human sacrifices? Where'd you hear that?"

Joey smiled in triumph. "Miss Lance's history class. There's supposed to be a bunch of old ruins, up in the hills. And now this. One body found, and three others — just gone!"

"Later," Chuck said, feeling like a sucker for being drawn back in. Joey could tell a good story. It was too bad he had to make so many of his stories up. Chuck turned back towards the lunchroom.

There, standing on the far side of the hall, was Jake.

"Oh, hey, Jake," Chuck started. "I'm sorry about what happened with your parents and—"

"Don't talk to me!" Jake said, his fists bailed at his sides. He took a step away from Chuck, like he didn't want to be there. "Stay away from me! I don't know anything about you!"

"Okay," Chuck said softly, circling around him to go to the stairs. What was the matter with him? Jake's parents must have doled out some awful punishment for him to be this upset. Or maybe he'd known those two girls who'd just died.

Chuck took the steps down two at a time. He'd worry about Jake and dead bodies some other time. He had other things to think about.

He finally saw Beth at lunch, eating at a table at the far end of the cafeteria with Tina Broadbent and Cerise Fallon — or Colossal Flake, as he'd nicknamed her, because of her weird hair colours and even weirder dress sense. Beth tossed her hair out of her face as he walked towards her. Then she raised her hand just above the table top and gave him a little wave. Tina and Cerise smiled at him too.

Chuck smiled back. He wanted to rush over there and spend the rest of lunchtime talking to Beth. But the Club wasn't supposed to hang out together. And Chuck didn't want everybody at school talking about the two of them like they were an item — well, at least not until they really were an item.

"Hey, Chuck!" Somebody tugged at his elbow. Chuck turned to see Alex, a look of concern spread across his face.

"Hey, Alex," Chuck whispered back, "we're not supposed to be—"

"I know, I know. But I had to talk to *somebody*. I mean, last night Todd said we were going to face danger. I mean, is this guy for real?"

"Sure he is, Alex, and he just wants to make things mysterious." Chuck hadn't realised he had thought this stuff through until he started to talk about it. "The first night was revenge, according to Todd. And what ended up happening? We tee-peed a maths teacher's house. I suppose we could have got into trouble for doing that, but there are a lot worse things you can do for revenge. The second night was suspense. And what did suspense turn out to be? It was Todd telling us what would happen tonight and tomorrow! I wouldn't worry, Alex. Todd just likes to run things in a dramatic way. It's more fun for him, and it's more fun for us, too."

"Fun?" Alex gave a little snort through his nose. "That's easy for you to say. It looks like you and Beth are having enough fun for all of us."

It was that obvious, then? Still, Chuck felt sort of happy that Alex knew.

"Chill out, Alex," he whispered back. "Everything's going to be fine."

Alex shrugged, his frown more confused than angry. "Yeah, probably," he said after a moment. "I guess that house was pretty cool."

Well, Chuck thought as Alex wandered away, I've managed to calm down the troops. Maybe Todd was right and I really do make a good second-in-command.

And he also realised that he didn't mind in the least if the rest of the Club guessed where his relationship with Beth was going.

He looked back at Beth's table. He thought Todd could be right about one other thing, too.

This was going to be the best Halloween Chuck had ever had.

* * * *

10

His mother had already left when Chuck got home.

"Gone?" he asked in amazement as his sister nodded her head.

"Yep. I'm old enough to take care of myself. At least during the day I am." Nicole stood up as tall as possible. She was still a shrimp. "I am almost a teenager, after all."

"What?" Chuck kidded. "You'll be thirteen in — six months? A year?"

Nicole frowned and made a fist.

"Two years?" Chuck asked.

He easily dodged her blow.

"Chuck!" Nicole protested. "I spend a lot of time around here by myself. Especially lately," she added, her voice rising with meaning. Chuck realised that Nicole could tell their parents about all the extra time he was spending out with the Halloween Club.

"You wouldn't tell!" he blurted before he could stop himself.

"I might." Nicole nodded smugly. "It would be awfully hard to see Beth if you were grounded. And think how tough it would be to talk to Beth with all your phone privileges taken away."

This was blackmail. Chuck stared at his little sister. She smiled sweetly back at him.

"What do you want?" Chuck asked.

"Hey, I like having the house to myself!" Nicole answered with a laugh. "Besides, after Halloween I'll need to go to the mall. At least three or four times."

Well, Chuck thought, at least he knew the price he was going to have to pay. Still, part of what his sister said had surprised him. "So you want the place to yourself?"

"Well, it's not like Mom and Dad aren't telling us what to do. They left one of their notes." She pointed to a message pinned to the refrigerator.

Chuck walked over and took a look. The note was in their mother's handwriting.

Dear Chuck and Nicole,

> Your father took off a little early from work so that we could do one last thing before Halloween. I'm sorry we've been so busy lately, but we've got something really special planned for tomorrow to make up for it.
>
> There's a casserole in the fridge for you to heat up.
>
> Have a good dinner and get your homework done. We know you'll be good kids.
>
> We'll see you around ten.
>
> Love,
>
> Mom and Dad

"So that tells us just what to do," Nicole announced as he glanced back at her. She grinned at her brother. "Not that you're going to do it."

Chuck ignored his sister's latest poke. He was a lot more worried about the note, and the way it mentioned 'something really special'. It really did sound like Mom and Dad wanted the whole family to spend Halloween together. And that was something Chuck wasn't ready to do.

A horn blared outside. Could that be Todd already? He was even earlier than the day before!

"Wow," Nicole said dreamily. "I'm going to have this place to myself the rest of the afternoon — and all evening, too. Maybe I'll invite all my girlfriends over. Maybe we'll play all your CDs and read your comic book collection."

Chuck grabbed for his jacket. "Don't do something you'll regret, Nicole."

She rolled her eyes. "You sound just like Mom and Dad, Chuck. Well, don't do something you'll regret, either." She took a step away, just out of striking distance. "Remember, I'll need to go to the mall a few times around Christmas, too."

So he'd never stop paying for this, then? He must have made an even worse face than usual, since his sister started to giggle. Chuck just waved Nicole out of the way as he ran for the front door.

He thought about slamming the door behind him, but that would just let his sister know how much she had annoyed him. That look on her face was already way too smug. He settled on closing the door firmly.

Todd leaned back in his car and grinned as Chuck jogged down the driveway.

It looked like Chuck was the first one to be picked up again. Maybe this was the main benefit of being second-in-command. He supposed he could always ask. But Chuck wanted to ask Todd something else first.

"How'd you know my parents weren't home?" he asked as he climbed into the front seat of the car.

Todd laughed. "Because mine aren't either. Whatever games our parents have been playing these past few weeks, they've been playing them together."

Wow, Chuck thought. The Halloween Club hadn't talked much about their parents, or about much of anything else that happened outside of the club.

"A couple of the others have parents in that bridge club, too," Todd added. "There are a dozen or so couples in it."

"How'd you find out about that?" Chuck asked. "Mom and Dad never talk about that sort of stuff." His parents had a lot of things in their lives like that. It was just that if they didn't feel the need to explain something to their kids, they just wouldn't bother.

"And mine do?" Todd answered. "But there are other ways to find things out. My parents are so uptight they keep lists of everything. And I just happen to know where to find the lists."

Todd turned the key in the ignition and the old Steamboat roared to life. "Enough about our parents. We've got places to go and things to do!"

He pulled away from the curve as he fiddled with the dial on the radio.

But something else had been bothering Chuck.

"What happens when Halloween is over?" he asked.

Todd glanced over at him for a second before looking back at the road. Their leader actually looked surprised for a change.

"I hadn't thought about it. Maybe the Club will take over some other holiday." He frowned and shook his head. "Not Christmas. Everybody does Christmas. Maybe something like, oh, Groundhog Day." He looked at Chuck again. "But *somebody* else in the Club will have to take over. This club leader stuff is a lot of work."

Chuck was surprised at that last part. "You mean you're not going to run the Halloween Club—"

But Todd was way ahead of him. "Oh, yeah, that's completely different. I've already got ideas for next year. Halloween is my kind of day."

Chuck laughed at that. But he was still upset, and, as he thought about it, he realised the real reason why.

"You know, I might have a problem," he said in a rush. "My parents left me a note. I think they want me to spend Halloween with them."

Todd shook his head like that wasn't any problem at all. "Yeah, my parents are always doing that sort of thing, too." He laughed. "Just because they're planning something doesn't mean we have to agree to go. Who do they think we are, after all? Another year of school, and I'm going to leave this place. Bye bye, Oxrun Station!"

Chuck could relate to that. There was a lot more to this world than tiny old Oxrun. It felt good to talk to somebody else about this kind of thing. Nicole said girls talked about everything, and guys talked about nothing at all. Well, maybe Chuck could change that, at least a little, by talking to someone like Todd, who seemed ready to listen.

Todd punched another button and the radio sprang to life. "*Got a black magic woman!*" the man's voice called from the speakers.

Chuck just had to know. "Where did you find that radio station?"

Todd laughed. "I'll tell you my secret if you promise not to blab it around."

Chuck said sure.

"It's a tape, Chuck. I just stuck some radio noise from an old sound effects record in between a couple of the songs, and since the same controls work both the radio and the tape deck down here — well. Instant spooky." He turned up the volume so that the music was really pumping. "Just messin' with your mind, bro. Everyone needs to freak out a little bit around Halloween."

They turned towards Beth's house.

Maybe, Chuck thought, there'd be an even better club after Halloween.

11

But even the Halloween Club had its problems.

They picked up Beth next. But Todd cleared his throat as she started to climb in the front seat of the car.

"Probably time for one of you to get in the back," their leader remarked. "We want equal front seat privileges for all members of the Halloween Club."

Beth volunteered to climb in the back, all too quickly for Chuck.

"All right!" Todd called as he threw the car back into drive. Beth's hand brushed against Chuck's shoulder as she settled into the back seat. He didn't think the touch was accidental.

They picked up Mitch, then Sue, then headed for Alex's place. Chuck kept wanting to turn around and talk to Beth. Why did Todd have to go and put her in the back seat? He thought he saw Todd grinning every time he tried to glance towards the back seat, like Todd was trying to make Chuck as uncomfortable as possible. It was like he told Chuck about his parents and the radio, got Chuck to trust him, then went on to a whole other level of game-playing.

Maybe, Chuck thought, Todd wasn't the best person to confide in after all. The 'radio' started to play the theme from 'The Addams Family'. Everybody else in the car started snapping their fingers along with the music, but Chuck didn't quite feel like it just then.

And then nobody came out of Alex's place when Todd honked the horn.

"I'll check," Chuck said, jumping out of the car before Todd could ask. After all, he had to fulfil those second-in-command duties. Besides, he felt like moving around a little.

Nobody came to the front door this time when he went up the steps. In fact, there didn't seem to be anybody home at all. The house looked dark and empty. Chuck hit the doorbell anyway, and waited for a full minute before he turned around and looked at the others in the car.

"Not Alex, too!" Todd groaned.

"We are a little earlier than usual," Sue volunteered. "Maybe he hasn't got home yet or something."

Todd shook his head. "No. He was home earlier. I called and told him when we were coming. He said he was really looking forward to it."

Mitch frowned at Chuck as he walked back to the car. "Something must have happened with Alex's parents."

Parents, Chuck thought, as he climbed back into the front seat. If they weren't careful, their parents would destroy the Halloween Club.

Sue had scooted over to be next to Todd. From the way they looked at each other, they were even more of an item than Chuck and Beth. Maybe, Chuck realised, Todd had other reasons for playing musical seats.

"Now we are five," Todd said with a sigh. "I hope we don't lose anybody else tonight."

Sue frowned over at their leader. "Lose anybody else? What do you mean, Todd?"

"You'll see," Todd replied. He nodded his head as that 'Witchdoctor' song came on:

"*Ohh eee ooo ahh ahh, ting tang walla walla bing bang . . .*"

"What do you mean?" Sue insisted.

But their leader just smiled and tapped on the steering wheel in time to the music.

Things were back to normal. It was just Todd messing with their minds again.

12

They reached the clearing just before sundown. 'Lover's Lookout', Todd had called it before. Now, Chuck could really see why it could get that kind of a name.

The colours up here were incredible. The leaves still on the trees looked brilliant in the late autumn light. Chuck didn't think he'd ever seen more vibrant reds and yellows. And because they were on a ridge overlooking the town, it somehow seemed like they could see even more of the sky, with a horizon that stretched for miles. The sky had already turned a deep blue back east, over the bay and ocean beyond. And over Oxrun Station itself was an enormous black cloud — Chuck could almost see torrential rain pouring down on the little town. How weird: it looked like its own little ecosystem!

But directly overhead the sky was turquoise, and as you looked westwards, the sun already hidden behind the trees, the puffy clouds over that edge of the world were a deep crimson, almost the colour of blood. It seemed to Chuck that nature was working overtime around them, giving up one last burst of beauty before winter turned everything grey and dead.

He was holding Beth's hand. He didn't exactly remember taking it, but he didn't want to let it go. He wanted the two of them to be able to stand here, forever, and look out over a world high above that old town they called home. At that moment he was convinced that if the two of them stayed together, nothing could ever go wrong.

"Okay, campers!" Todd called as he slammed the trunk shut. He swung a full backpack over his shoulder. "Let's get over to the house while it's still light."

Beth squeezed Chuck's hand. "I bet this is going to be fun."

"You and me, stuck together in a spooky old house?" Chuck replied. "Sounds terrible to me."

Todd took the lead this time, and all the others followed. As much as he worried about Todd, Chuck had to admit everything had been fun so far.

Todd led them over the hill and down the other side. There was a pretty clear path to the old house.

"Somebody's been here recently," Mitch said, pointing down at the weed-free dirt at their feet. So Chuck wasn't the only one who noticed about the path.

"Well, there was me, for one," Todd agreed. "Actually, this whole area was more overgrown in the middle of summer. I think we're walking on some kind of deer path. There's a big pond out beyond the house, a little bit further down the hill, and I bet animals come through here to get water."

"Wild animals?" Sue asked in a voice that sounded both scared and delighted at the same time.

"Well, yeah," Todd agreed. "At least whatever wild animals you get in Connecticut."

"Oh, no!" Mitch agreed. "Marauding chipmunks!"

Everybody laughed at that. Chuck knew from his history classes with Miss Lance that the Connecticut hills had once teemed with bears and wolves and all sorts of neat stuff. There still were supposed to be some Copperheads in the area, although nobody Chuck knew had ever seen one. The worst thing they'd have to worry about would be a rabid raccoon. And Chuck couldn't even remember a newspaper story about rabies for the last year or two.

"I don't think we'll have to worry about the chipmunks," Todd said as marched down the hill. "But the house here has some other interesting features."

Chuck looked up from where he had been watching the path. The house was much closer now, maybe only fifty feet away. This close, he could really see how run-down the old place was. A lot of the windows had been broken, and there were a couple of pretty big holes in the roof. The front porch looked like it had been supported by four columns at one time. Now only three were left, and one of those leaned at a crazy angle, with the porch roof starting to cave in above it.

"Cool," Beth whispered as she, too, took in the place.

Sue was not so impressed. "Is it, like, going to be safe to walk in there?"

Mitch laughed at that.

"Cool," Beth repeated.

Chuck looked over beyond the house, at the standing stones. They looked more irregular up close, like they had been hacked somehow out of a granite hillside and dragged here and put in very definite positions. Most of the stones were eight to ten feet high. Chuck could see now why nobody had ever tried to move them again. Those suckers had to be heavy.

The whole area around the stones appeared pretty wild and overgrown, even more so than the dying trees and weeds around the house. Chuck didn't really see how they could clear a path and have a party over there, but he imagined that Todd must have figured out a way.

"Well, let's get going," Todd called to the others. "We want to get set up before we really lose the light."

It was getting darker fast. The sun was completely gone, and only a third of the sky showed the red that seemed to be everywhere only a few minutes ago. Overhead, it was already midnight blue, and they could see the first stars shining in the east.

They quickly walked down the rest of the path. Chuck tried to get as much of a look around as he could before the light failed completely. Todd had done his job for the club. Between the rotting house and the deep grey stones, the place really did look like Halloween.

The trail snaked its way around in front of the porch.

"Now," Todd announced, "follow me." The last of the light seemed to fade from the sky, turning the colours around them into different shades of grey. "I've been through here before. I know the way that's safe."

He walked up the far right hand side of the front steps. The others followed, Chuck right after Beth, then Sue and Mitch.

Chuck saw a hole in the left-hand side of the third step up, but the boards beneath their feet seemed sturdy enough.

Todd waited for the rest of them to join him up on the porch. He had opened the top of his backpack and retrieved a major flashlight, one of those long, silver Maglites with a powerful beam, so powerful that Chuck had to shield his eyes when Todd turned it on.

Todd quickly turned the beam away from the Club members and shone it on the open front door of the house.

"Okay," he said. He stepped inside. His footsteps sounded hollow as he crossed the floor. His voice echoed when he added:

"It's time to come in and get our very own happy home!" He laughed. "This is what the Club is all about."

13

The sound of Todd's voice got the other club members moving.

Sue rushed to follow Todd inside. Mitch went right after her. Beth glanced up at Chuck. He could barely see her in the gloom, couldn't tell at all what she was feeling. He could feel himself start to worry again.

But what could go wrong? Todd hadn't let them down so far. And besides, it wasn't like they were stuck here all alone. All five of them were together.

Beth pulled him forward to follow. Just in time, too, as the flashlight beam grew faint in the doorway.

"Hey, you guys, hurry up!" Todd called as Beth and Chuck stepped inside. The beam swept through the entryway, which looked huge. There was a great staircase off to the right, and a hallway on the left, where Todd and the other two now stood.

"We're visiting the ground floor tonight," Todd announced. "I think it's safer."

Todd shone the flashlight beam so Beth and Chuck could make their way through the debris that littered the old wooden floor.

"Good," Todd added as Chuck and Beth approached. "Now, follow me."

He pushed open a door to his left. The others followed him, sticking close together. Chuck, for one, didn't want to get left behind in the dark.

"The rooms in this house never seem to end," Todd said as he led the way. "There're at least ten of them on this floor, and a bunch of stuff in the basement. I think this was some kind of sitting room. And one of us is going to sit here."

"One of us?" Beth asked.

"Yeah. This is the test of the third night. Each of us gets a room of his or her very own, to stay in, all by themselves, for an hour."

Todd swept the beam around the room. A pair of overstuffed chairs and an old couch loomed out of the darkness as the light slid past. The old rugs on the floor showed fancy designs where they were still whole. They had probably been worth something once, before big parts of them had been eaten away. Something made a high-pitched noise as the beam approached the corner, followed by the sound of tiny claws scrabbling across the wooden floor. But by the time the light had reached that corner, they saw nothing there.

"Each of you gets a room," Todd repeated.

Nobody said anything, but from the way the other club members shuffled around him, the rest had as many mixed feelings about this test as Chuck had. All alone for an hour in a place like this? That didn't seem particularly — safe. Which, Chuck guessed, was the point of what Todd was doing here.

"Mitch," Todd continued, "I think this will be your room. You get to sit in the sitting room." Todd chuckled. "Except I wouldn't try the chairs, they're pretty far gone. Last time I looked at one of the cushions, something inside it moved." He laughed again. At least Todd was having a good time.

"No," Todd said as he swung his pack away from his shoulder, "I think we'll all do better if we sit on the floor. In the middle of the room." He let the pack hit the floor with a thunk, then opened the top flap and pulled out a couple of long, narrow objects that Chuck couldn't quite make out. The flashlight beam swung up towards the ceiling. Chuck looked up in the light. The paint was peeling overhead, but that was all. What had he been expecting? Bats?

"Heck," Todd muttered. "I can't do all this and hold the light, too. Sue, could you give me a hand?"

He handed the flashlight over to Sue before she could even answer him.

"Could you shine the light at my hands?" he asked as soon as she gripped the metal cylinder. She did what he asked, and Chuck saw that the two things in Todd's hand were a candle and a candlestick holder.

"All right," Mitch said softly.

"You didn't think you were going to spend an hour here in the dark, did you?" Todd's voice sounded like that was the last thing he wanted. "Hey, we want a little danger here, but we're not crazy."

He stuck the candle in the holder then placed the whole thing on the ground. "The least we can do," he added as he fished a matchbook from his jacket pocket, "is provide a little light to help our members pass the hour peacefully."

He struck the match and quickly lit the candle. It gave off just enough light to turn the surrounding darkness into something that looked like a room, the flame illuminating everything nearby with a warm glow, but losing its strength as you looked ten or fifteen feet away, so that the far corners of this large room seemed to be only vague outlines and hulking shapes.

"Each one of us gets a candle," Todd said in a slight sing-song, as if he had memorised these words just so. "Each one of us must stay for an hour, all alone, with the spirits of this place."

"Cool," Beth agreed.

"I'll see you in an hour, Mitch," Todd added as he hoisted his pack back on to his shoulder. "Sue, if I could have the flashlight again?" Sue handed it back over. "Okay. On to the next room."

He turned towards the door, once again leading the way.

"See you, Mitch," Chuck called as he left the room.

"Sooner than you think!" Mitch called back, maybe a little too cheerfully. "Just a few minutes stuck in this musty old place, and then we party!"

Musty? Yeah, now that Mitch mentioned it, there was a vague sickly-sweet smell in the air. Chuck was pretty sure it was the smell of things rotting.

Todd waited for the rest of them to follow him out of the room. Once Chuck was out of the doorway, Todd reached behind him and shut the sitting room door securely.

"So he can be alone with his thoughts," Todd said softly to the others. "But come on. We've got other rooms to visit." Todd started back down the hallway, walking away from the entryway. They passed one doorway on the left side, and one doorway on the right. Todd stopped at the next door to the left, and pushed it open with his flashlight.

"This is the library," he said as he walked in. "Chuck, this room is for you."

He swung the flashlight beam around to reveal the details of this newest place. There were high, floor-to-ceiling shelves to either side. Some were empty, but quite a few still held books.

"Sue, if you would do the honours again?"

He handed her the flashlight and quickly reached into the pack to retrieve a candle and candleholder. He was getting better at this with practice.

"Each one of us gets a candle," Todd said again as he lit the candle, like it really was some sort of ritual. "Each one of us must stay for an hour, all alone, with the spirits of this place."

"Come on, Sue, Beth," he said as he took back the flashlight and headed for the door. "See you in an hour, Chuck."

Beth waited for Sue to turn and follow Todd before she leaned over and gave Chuck a quick kiss on the cheek.

"See you soon!" she called softly, and then she too was out the door.

Chuck remembered to breathe as soon as the door closed.

He was overwhelmed. Who cared about spooky old houses when you had a girl like that?

Chuck just wished he didn't have to wait an hour to kiss her back.

He heard their footsteps faintly for a moment, and then they were gone, beyond his hearing, down the hall. It was very quiet here, and, now that the sun was gone, it felt much colder. Chuck zipped up his jacket and stuffed his hands in his pockets. He could sit down by the candle, he guessed, but sitting down on all these rotting floorboards didn't sound like the best idea.

Besides, he was in the library. Not a bad place to be when you had an hour to kill. There might be some really interesting stuff here. He wandered over towards the nearest wall of books, but it was too dim to make out the titles.

Well, he had a portable light in here, didn't he? He walked back to where the candle flickered at the centre of the room. If he grabbed the candlestick and held it carefully, maybe he could explore this place a little.

The candle flame wavered as he lifted it up. Chuck realised he had to be extra careful. He didn't have any matches with him. If the candle went out, he'd have to spend the rest of the time in here in total darkness.

He walked slowly over to the books, holding the candle flame before him.

The first shelf held a lot of novels by Charles Dickens. The shelf just above that was full of books like *Modern Farming Techniques*, and *Fifty Ways to a Secure Future*. He half hoped that some of the books would deal with magic, or devils, or something like that. But they all appeared to be pretty ordinary, at least on this bookshelf. Of course, there were always the bookshelves on the other side of the room.

Chuck almost dropped the candle when the banging started.

It didn't come from the door, but from the other side of the wall, like somebody was trying to break through.

It really scared him, too, until he heard the groan, and the high-pitched laugh. All these things together were just too much. It had to be Todd, the same guy who made a tape that sounded like a radio show. Except now Todd was giving them spooky house noises. He should have known better than to think Todd would let them sit in silence for an hour.

Chuck half wanted to yell at Todd to stop. After all, he had some serious reading to do. But the banging stopped before Chuck had really decided to say something.

Somehow, the silence now seemed even more complete. There were no birds, no insects, not even the wind. Everything was perfectly still.

When the banging started up again, it was at the window.

Now Todd was outside? Well, their leader sure got around. Still holding his candle, Chuck walked towards the outside wall of the room.

But the voice that called his name didn't belong to Todd.

"Chuck?" The voice was somehow both higher and gruffer than Todd's. "Is that you, Chuck?"

Chuck thought about the shape he had seen out among the stones the night before.

Chuck approached the window cautiously. It was broken. That explained how he could hear the person on the other side so easily.

"Who is it?" Chuck demanded.

A face appeared at the window so suddenly that Chuck almost dropped his candle for a second time.

"God, am I glad to see you, Chuck!"

The speaker's face was so scratched and covered with grime that it took Chuck a second to recognise who it was.

"Kenny," Chuck said. "Kenny Anderson."

Kenny nodded. He managed a weak smile. "You shouldn't be out here, Chuck. But boy, am I glad you are!" Chuck frowned back at him. "What happened to you, Kenny? I heard at school that you guys held up some kind of store."

"Held up a store? That's crazy." Kenny made a strangled sound that might have been a laugh. "'course, everything's crazy around here."

Kenny certainly wasn't making any sense. He took a sharp breath and looked away from the window.

"They're after me!" he called to Chuck.

"Who? The police?"

Kenny shook his head wildly. "No, other people. My parents, maybe. Or people who look like my parents!"

"What?" Chuck asked, totally confused.

Kenny looked back, wide-eyed. "You've got to do something, tell somebody. They already got the others. You're the only one I can trust!"

Chuck heard other shouts, then, coming from a distance, both men's and women's voices, like some angry mob.

Chuck was still trying to make some sense of this. "Kenny, what should I tell them? Who are the others?"

Kenny groaned. "They're going to get me now. I just can't run anymore." He took a couple of stumbling steps away from the window. "I'll try to lead them away from here." He looked back to the window. "Get out of here, Chuck. Get out while they're after me."

Kenny ran from the house, crashing through the undergrowth. The shouts grew even louder then, like the mob knew they had Kenny cornered. The voices were quite close now. They must be just around the other side of the house. Chuck looked down at the candle in his hand. The mob would see the light. They'd know he was here, too.

Chuck blew out his candle.

Somebody screamed outside as the room was lost in darkness.

14

Everything was dark. Clouds must have covered the full moon. He couldn't even see Venus, which had been blazing away all week.

What was going on out there? Chuck didn't know what to do next. Did those voices belong to humans? Or were they the shapes, come to take Kenny away?

Well, Chuck knew something was out there. And he had been able to hide, at least for the moment. But what if they got some of the other members of the Club?

The sounds were moving closer again. Chuck held his breath, listening. The voices carried well in the darkness.

"We've got him," one of them said.

"He won't fight us anymore," another agreed.

The voices sounded cheerful, matter-of-fact, the kind of conversation his father might have with a neighbour over the back fence.

There was a moan that Chuck guessed had to come from Kenny. Chuck wished he could do something. But what could he do without being caught? Whatever was out there, shapes or men, he couldn't let fear overwhelm him. He had to think!

"It'll all be over in a second," another man's voice spoke almost reassuringly.

"Do we save this one, or is he a sacrifice?"

"He is pretty far gone."

"Kenny? Not my Kenny." A woman's voice this time, and the first to show any emotion. The other voices had all sounded so happily reasonable all the time.

"But look how long he resisted," one of the men responded, his voice still calm. "And we have all those fresh ones in the house."

Fresh ones? Oh, no. So they knew Chuck and the others were there.

"We don't want to hurt them. How do we do it?"

The voices were fading now, as if the cheerful mob was walking away.

"Let's talk about it. We've still got a few minutes before they come out."

There was another scream.

"That's good," a voice said faintly. "Get all the screaming out now. You won't have very long to wait before—"

333

The voice was lost beneath the sound of many feet tramping through the brush. But that noise too was moving away.

The voices had to be talking about the Halloween Club. How could they know when they were going to come out? Todd must be in on this, too. Who else could have told them? Maybe Todd had planned all of this, set them up for — what?

What was really going on behind the Halloween Club?

Chuck had to get out of here and find Beth and the others, get them all out of here before whoever was out there came back. But what would he do if he ran into Todd?

Not let on about what he heard, he guessed. After all, there might be some other reason those people knew. There might even be someone else who told those people outside about the Club, although at the moment Chuck had no idea who that could be.

He turned away from the window. He had no way to light the candle. He'd have to find his way out of here in the dark.

He put down the candlestick and started to walk away from the window, guiding himself along with his left hand brushing against the books. Some of them crumbled when he touched them. Others were moist and soft, as if they were covered with moss. He rubbed the slime off on his jeans, trying to ignore the way it felt. Maybe, Chuck thought, the books were rotting from the inside out.

He held his right hand out in front of him, finally feeling the firm plaster surface of the wall by the door. He felt along the wall with both hands now, until he found the raised wood of the door frame. A little further along, his left hand hit the cold brass of the doorknob. To his great relief, the knob turned easily, and he pulled the door inwards.

It was almost as dark out in the hall, a faint light coming from way in the back of the house.

Maybe that was where Todd was now, banging on someone else's walls. Chuck headed for the light. He had to let the others know that, one way or another, the fun and games were over.

Chuck moved more quickly as the light got better. He turned a corner and almost ran into Todd. Beth and Sue were right behind him.

Beth ran up and hugged him. "Oh, Chuck! I'm so glad you're safe!"

"Beth," he whispered back. He'd never been so glad to see anyone. He wanted to hold her for a very long time. But he couldn't, not now.

He stepped back and looked over at Todd.

"You heard the people outside?" Chuck demanded.

"Well, yeah," Todd replied in a whisper. "That's why I got Beth and Sue out of their rooms. We were coming back to get you."

"They knew we were here, Todd!" Chuck was surprised at how angry he was. "Somebody must have told them. Was this what the Halloween Club was all about? Did you set us up for this?"

Todd looked back at Chuck as if maybe Chuck was crazy. Todd shook his head. "No, I swear it, no. I don't even have any idea who these guys are."

Sue tugged at Todd's jacket. "Tell him!"

"It's worse than that," Todd added. "I think they got Mitch."

"Mitch? How?" Chuck turned to look back down the hall. What was he looking for? Did he expect the answer to jump out at him?

"He was back in the kitchen," Todd explained. "He freaked when he heard the screams and ran out the back door. I couldn't stop him."

Yeah, Chuck thought, and we only have Todd's word that the story was true. But there was no time to question the other boy. The four of them had to get out of here before they were caught like the others.

"I think they're still around back," Todd said as he began to move down the hallway. "Let's go out the front."

The other three followed him quickly to the entryway.

The front door was open. They could see it as they reached the end of the hall. Chuck thought Todd had closed it behind them before.

Someone stepped in from the outside, holding a big lantern that lit up the whole front room.

It was Jake.

"Jake!" Sue called. "You changed your mind! You've come to join us."

Chuck frowned. This didn't make any sense. Jake had left the group before they'd even seen this old house and the standing stones next door. How could Jake have figured out where they were?

"Join you?" Jake said with a frown. "I could never join you!"

He cupped a hand around his mouth and screamed, "They're in here!"

15

"Hurry!" Jake added, "get them before they get away!"

"Jake's working for them!" Todd called. He waved the others forward as he started towards the ex-Clubber. "We've got to get out of here."

"Oh, no!" Jake shook his head frantically. He tried to stand so that his body blocked the door. "I'm not going to let you pass me. You've got to stay!" His voice kept rising, sounding more hysterical with every word. "It's for your own good!"

"Sorry, Jake." Todd socked him in the jaw.

Jake crumpled to the floor.

Todd grinned back at the others. "I learned a few things while I was out of town." He walked quickly to the door and took a look outside. He stepped back in and waved the others forward.

"Like when to cut and run," he added.

There seemed to be no-one else around the front of the house. Chuck had a funny thought as they crept down the front steps and onto the overgrown lawn. He remembered how, earlier, he had felt that the moon had been a part of all this. The moon had been covered by clouds before, making it easy for the others to surround the house. Now it hung bright in the sky. To help them make their escape? Or to let them walk right into the arms of their pursuers? Somehow, on the night before Halloween, he felt like the moon knew everything.

The four of them tried to be as quiet as possible as they made their way through the scrub brush. There must have been a dozen people calling back and forth in the woods. Most of them, though, still sounded like they were far away at the back of the house.

"C'mon," Todd called to the rest of them as he followed the path up by the standing stones, "let's get back to the car."

"There they are!" It was Alex, standing in the middle of the upright stones. He jumped up and down in excitement.

Sue started to say something, but Todd tugged at her sleeve, pulling her along.

"I don't think that's the same Alex we knew," Todd said. "We've got to move."

"Mommy! Daddy!" Alex called. "I found them!"

"It's like he's a little kid," Beth said close by Chuck's ear.

"Yeah," Chuck agreed. Alex sounded more like he was six than sixteen.

"We have them now!" The new voice came from behind them, but it was much closer than the others. "Bring them to the stone!"

Todd looked back in the direction of the new voice. "Mom! Dad!"

"Yes, Todd," two voices said together. "We've been expecting you."

Chuck turned around and saw that the space behind them was filled with parents. His parents. Beth's parents. Todd's parents. He saw Mitch's mother, too, and a bunch of couples he didn't recognise.

None of the couples looked angry, though. Instead, all of them were smiling.

The couples were all perfectly dressed, too. Chuck remembered how each night, all this week, his mother's dress had always been fancier than the night before. The other adults looked the same, many of the women with pearl necklaces and gold earrings, the men in dark suits or tuxedos. It looked like they were all going to some upscale dinner somewhere. Except this dinner party was in the middle of the woods.

Chuck's parents started to walk towards him. They were smiling, too, but their smiles seemed sadder than the others.

"Dear Chuck," his mother said, "you didn't follow any of the instructions we left for you."

"If only you'd stayed home with your sister," his father added.

So he was in this mess because he didn't obey his parents? "Look, Mom, Dad," he began, searching for an explanation, "I didn't mean—"

"Nonsense!" Todd's father called. "All that is in the past, now. We're so glad that you could join us."

"Yes," his mother agreed. "But it would have been so much simpler to bring both you and your sister here at the same time."

So they would have brought him here no matter what? Chuck had to keep his mouth from hanging open.

Todd's mother walked towards her son. "You'll all have to be patient with us for a moment while we prepare the stone." Her son took a step away as he looked around, searching for a break in the crowd of parents. "Well, actually, Mom, we had other plans."

"Todd!" his father said sharply, although the smile never left his face. "You will obey us!"

Todd looked at the smiling adults as they moved forward to surround the four teenagers. "I guess we don't have much choice."

"No, Todd," his father insisted. "You will always be with us in our happy home."

Todd stiffened. "Happy," he said, and then, "Happy home." The wariness on his face dissolved, replaced by a perfect grin. He walked over to his father, and stood by him, smiling peacefully.

"You've done what we told you," his father said as he gripped Todd's shoulder. "I hope it wasn't too unpleasant. We had to leave the power of the stone hidden in you. Now we can join you, forever."

"Happy home," Todd agreed, as if there would never be another thought in his head.

Chuck looked over at Beth as she squeezed his hand. From her frown, he guessed she was thinking the same thing he was. Todd had mentioned 'happy homes' before. Was this all that it meant? It was like Todd had been hypnotised. Somehow, some way, Todd had become one of the crowd around them. Had everything that had happened in the club just been an excuse to bring them here?

"Now that Todd is where he belongs," his father continued, "we'll bring the rest of you along."

Chuck felt Beth's grip tighten on his hand again. He didn't want to lose Beth, and it felt like she didn't want to lose him either. More than anything, he knew they didn't want to end up like Todd.

"Let me take my Mitchy first," Mitch's mother announced as she pulled her stunned son along behind her. "He'll be so much nicer afterwards. We'll be together forever."

"But to get from the stone," Todd's father called, to everyone now, not just the teenagers, "we have to give to it!"

"To get we have to give!" the other parents called back, as if this was a ritual, just like Todd and his candles.

"We must give what we cherish most," Todd's father continued. "We give Kenny Anderson to the stone."

"No!" Kenny yelled from where he was held by a group of the smiling adults.

Except one of the parents didn't smile.

"No," Mrs. Anderson stepped forward. "Not my Kenny. I won't let you."

Todd's mother looked to her husband.

"She's not close enough to the stone."

Todd's dad nodded serenely. "Those that do not join together must fall by the wayside. We give Greta Anderson to the stone as well."

The other adults crowded around Mrs. Anderson, pinning her in place.

"To get we have to give!" the crowd agreed.

Todd's dad nodded, as if the matter was settled. "The rest of us will follow with our newest members." He smiled at his son. "Soon, you will join us forever!"

"Oh, wow," Sue wailed. "I don't think I want to do this. Mom? Dad? Make them stop?"

"Now, now, Suzy," her father replied gently. "It won't be so bad."

Her mother nodded pleasantly. "It'll only take a minute. And you'll feel so much better when it's over."

"They've all changed," Beth said quickly, as if she was the last regular voice in a world that had gone crazy. "And they're going to make us change, too."

The adults all nodded happily, as if they were glad Beth got the idea.

"To the stone!" Todd's father called.

"To the stone!" Todd agreed.

The whole crowd surged forward, pushing Chuck and the others before them. The Andersons, mother and son, were being forced into the lead. And all of them were walking towards the stones.

Chuck saw a light ahead of them. It was in the exact middle of the crowd of stones, where one of the tall rocks glowed faintly with a white light the colour of the moon.

"We give to the stones!" Todd's father called.

"No," Mrs. Anderson called. "Not me. Not my son." But her protests were quiet, more a whimper than a shout, as if she already knew there was no escape.

"Give to us! Give to us!" the crowd of adults called around Chuck.

The glow of the central stone grew stronger as Mrs. Anderson was pushed towards it. Then she was surrounded by that cold whiteness too. She moaned and shook, like some wild dancer underneath the stars.

Then she began to fade away. Chuck could swear he could see the other stones right through her.

"Give to us!" the crowd chanted. "Give to us!"

Chuck could feel a tingling, first in his fingers and his toes, then creeping up his arms and legs. The feeling was somehow both very cold and oddly pleasant at the same time. Chuck felt like giggling.

The stone was changing him too! He took a deep breath. He would have to keep his head clear, try to fight it. But how could he fight something he knew nothing about?

Mrs. Anderson, or what was left of her, stopped twitching, growing suddenly rigid. And then she faded away — completely. Nothing remained on the slab where they had placed her but a small pile of dust.

Another wave of the chill pleasure passed through Chuck. He had to ignore it, get away somehow.

He pulled away from the hands that held his shoulders. There was no resistance. Everyone else stared at the stone. It was like his parents, and all the other adults around them, were in some sort of trance.

But he lost Beth's hand too. The crowd surged forward like a wave, breaking the two of them apart. Those around Chuck were pushed to the side as the group crowding Beth rolled towards the stone.

Beth looked back at Chuck in panic as she was carried away. What could he do? If he moved back to get to her, he'd have to plunge back into the middle of the crowd. They'd both be trapped then.

Maybe, he thought, there was some way he could circle around the crowd.

He tried to find a way back through the people around him, to get past the collection of parents without jarring anyone too much. He didn't know how deep the trance was that held them all. He didn't want to push somebody and find himself pulled back towards the stone.

"Give to us," the crowd chanted. "Give to us." Chuck ducked low, under the last of the outstretched arms. He was free, in amongst the trees. But what could he do now? They were miles from town. Where could he find help? And what about Beth and the others, all still prisoners?

"Chuck!"

He looked around, and saw his mother pushing her way through the crowd towards him.

"He is resisting!" she called to the others. Some of them jerked their heads away from the stone to stare at Chuck.

Todd's father waved at the stone.

"It is not strong enough!"

Todd nodded happily. "We need another!"

Kenny was pushed into the spectral glow. He moaned, his feet jerking beneath him like he wanted to run away. But one foot pulled one way, the other foot another, while his hands and head seemed to want to go to three other places. The stone had Kenny in its power now.

The boy began to fade.

Chuck backed away from the crowd, still free for the moment. But he needed somewhere to run, or, better yet, some way to stop all this.

He turned around saw something in the moonlight, out beyond the house.

There were others moving further out in the woods, behind the crowd. Were these the real shapes he had seen before, at the maths teacher's house and at the edge of the woods? Or were they some new group of people, looking for the other kids who had disappeared?

Whatever they were, Chuck thought, they couldn't be worse than what was here already.

"Over here!" he called to the newcomers.

He turned and glanced back at the crowd.

"The child is taken into the light!" Todd's father called. The cold light surrounded Kenny. Kenny screamed. Kenny was fading away more quickly now, just like his mother.

Three men crashed out of the woods.

"Stop where you are!" one of them called.

Two of them wore police uniforms. Chuck recognised Chief Stockton and his deputy, Bradford Dodds. The one man not wearing a uniform was his maths teacher, Mr. Johnson.

"There they are, Chief," Mr. Johnson called. "The kids who defaced my house!"

"It sounds like they're hurting somebody!" one of the officers called.

Mr. Johnson looked right at Chuck, his face full of anger. "I've been following you, watching you, waiting for you to trip up." He smiled in triumph. "I thought you'd be doing some kind of vandalism down here."

But the policemen were both looking beyond Chuck, at the glowing stone.

"What are you doing down there?" Stockton called.

"Give to us," the crowd chanted. "Give to us."

"Tom? John?" he replied. "I know these people. We can talk to them."

But no-one seemed to notice that the policemen were there.

"We need another!" someone called.

Chuck's mother pushed her way towards him again.

"Give to us," the crowd intoned.

Todd's father towered over Beth. "Your parents resisted," he said to her with the softest of smiles. "They must be taught a lesson."

"Push her to the stone!" he called, tossing Beth forwards.

"They'll all join us now," Chuck's father agreed.

"Hey!" shouted Stockton. "I want everyone to calm down."

Everyone else stared at the stone. To the police, Chuck thought, it didn't look like they were doing much of anything. But in a minute Beth would be gone, just like the others. Chuck had to do something.

"They've got a girl up there!" he called to the cops.

"We don't want you messing with the kids," the Chief called.

"Give to us," the crowd called back.

"Fire a warning shot!" he ordered.

Deputy Dodds, looking hardly older than the Halloween Club members, pulled the gun from his holster and fired a shot into the air.

The stone in the centre grew whiter still, until it was almost unbearably bright. Beth stumbled towards the glow.

"There's something in there!" the deputy yelled.

Didn't the policemen understand? "They won't listen to you!" Chuck called. There was only one thing he could think of that might get the crowd's attention. "Shoot at that rock!"

"What?" Dodds asked, puzzled.

Beth moaned as the light bled over her hands and started to creep up her arms.

"The rock!" Chuck insisted. "It's what they're all here for! Shoot the rock!"

Beth screamed.

Deputy Dodds raised his gun and shot straight for the stone.

The bullet hit the great, pulsating rock.

The stone screamed. The whole forest seemed alive with light for an instant, like a thousand voices crying all at once. And then the scream rose, and turned from a sound of pain to a sound of joy, as if the owners of all the voices had been set free.

He saw Beth, still alive, huddled by the great stone, which exploded in a shower of sparks. The crowd of parents staggered back, as if each and everyone of them had been hit in the face.

There was an instant of silence, as if even the night birds and insects were shocked to silence.

Then everyone started to talk.

"Where are we?" Mitch's mother asked.

"What are we doing here?" Todd said.

"Todd!" His father frowned down at him. "Is this some kind of practical joke?"

"Wait!" Chuck's father called. "Weren't we taking some kind of nature walk?"

"All right!" Chief Stockton called. "Everybody quiet down here!"

Chuck looked back to his parents. They had lost their dazzling smiles, and now looked only confused. Once the glowing stone had been destroyed, the spell it held over everyone seemed to have vanished, too.

The two policemen started ordering everybody into a line. Maybe they'd find the bodies, if the living stone didn't do something with them, too. Chuck remembered how Kenny's mother had disappeared in the brilliant light. Maybe the stone just made the bodies fade away.

The Chief frowned at the crowd. "Deputy, get names, will you? I'll expect each and every one of you to come to the station and make a report."

"They've done something, can't you see?" Mr. Johnson demanded. "They're up to no good."

"Probably," Stockton agreed. "Except that for the life of me, I can't figure out what."

Chuck felt a hand on his shoulder. He turned around. It was his dad.

"I'm glad to see you, Chuck." His father smiled. "Whatever was happening around here, it's good that you're all right."

His mother shook her head as she walked up to join them. "It's like I just woke up. We went out for that hike with our neighbours, I remember that. But then . . . ?" She looked down at her dress. "And why am I wearing this?"

Chuck pointed at his mother's finger. "You should get rid of that ring."

"Why? It has something to do with all this, doesn't it?" She frowned down at it, but did not take it off her finger.

Chuck's father stared at the ring on his own hand. "Maybe these will remind us that we have to talk to each other."

"All right," Chief Stockton said, "I think it's time we all got out of here!" He walked back past the maths teacher, ignoring Mr. Johnson's pleas to arrest at least *some* of the teenagers.

Beth walked up to Chuck and took his hand.

"Is it over?"

"Who knows?" Chuck admitted.

"I hope so," added Sue, close by their side, "but it isn't even Halloween."

Chuck looked at his watch. "It almost is Halloween. We've been out here for a while."

Mitch shook his head and whistled. "Boy, I wonder how the Club's gonna top this next year!"

"I don't think I want to find out," Chuck replied. He turned, still hand in hand with Beth. They walked away from the stones, underneath the smiling full moon.

CODY

1

THE WEEK BEFORE HALLOWEEN, I DIDN'T believe in monsters. The week before Halloween, I didn't believe in ghosts.

I still wouldn't, tonight, if it hadn't been for Angie, and a kid all dressed in black.

There wasn't much light that Sunday, although it still wasn't quite five. The sun was already halfway below the trees, and sharp-edged shadows pointed the way from dusk to full dark. The street lamps were on, and the handful of cars that passed the house had their lights on too, glaring the way they do when it's not quite their time.

Late autumn hung over Oxrun Station, a reminder that winter was just a few weeks away.

If you didn't know that already, you could figure it by the signs — the last of the leaves slowly burning in trashcans and gutters, adding a sharp smell to the air you couldn't get any other time of the year; a feel to the air like thin ice on the park pond, brittle and cold; the way sound carried when a little kid yelled or a dog barked or a door slammed.

The way you took a deep breath and felt suddenly wide awake.

I was awake, but I was home, and feeling pretty miserable.

A single leaf lay on the front porch, serrated edges curled like the fingers of a dead man. Despite the breeze that once in a while skated across the lawn, it didn't move but for a single brief tremor, scratching at the air.

The dead man daring me to come over and have a look.

I watched it from the bench swing and had every intention of getting up, walking over there and crushing it beneath my shoe.

I didn't move, though.

I sat on the swing, pushing a little with my heels, and watched it.

Mainly, it was a way to kill time. Mom wasn't home from work yet, and wouldn't be for a couple of hours, and I didn't feel like getting the rake from the garage and clearing the leaves from the yard. I wasn't supposed to or anything. I mean, it wasn't like it was my job for the day. For a change, I didn't have one. Instead, Mom reminded me it would be Halloween in a few days, and she wanted me to get my homework done, then 'go out and have some fun.' Yeah.

Right.

To be honest, though, I hadn't told her I was a hunted man, soon to be wiped off the face of the earth by a guy who had muscles where muscles weren't supposed to exist.

A breeze touched the back of my neck then, and I zipped up my denim jacket, flipped up the collar, and figured that if I sat here much longer, I'd probably freeze to death.

When I stood, the chains creaked as the swing swung slowly back and forth. Ghost chains, my dad used to call them. When my dad was still alive. This was his favourite season, and even though it's been six years, I still feel a little down when October rolls around.

And you'd have to be dead not to know it was practically Halloween — carved pumpkins on just about every porch, cardboard witches and black cats and ghosts taped in some windows, stalks of maize and promise dolls tied to a few front doors, things like that.

And things like the tiny red lights buried in the hedges in front of the Oppermans' house, and the mechanical things Mr. Opperman put in the leaves to make them rustle when you walked by, making you think there was something in there, ready to jump out and tear your arm off.

Or the huge iron kettle on Mrs. Galbraith's stoop, with dry ice on the bottom to make it boil over with smoke that trailed down her walk to the curb.

Or Mr. Robson's front yard, three doors down from mine, where he had a scarecrow with a painted gourd-head, dressed in a tuxedo, hanging by the neck from a twisted, fat maple, swaying over a bunch of tombstones. They were on a long, narrow stretch of what, in spring, would be his front garden — five stones in front, four on the lawn behind. Weird, but no big deal, except that he puts names on them, too. Not fake ones; real ones. Kids, grownups, anyone he would think of. No dates, just names. Mostly, they were the same every year, but there was always a blank one, and at the last minute, he'd put something on it, just for the heck of it, I guess. Every year the little kids fought like crazy to get their name on that blank one, running errands for him, making sure his paper didn't get tossed anywhere but exactly at his door.

I used to do that. When I was little. It seems really dumb now, but I remember one year crying like a jerk when he put Angie's name on instead of mine.

Of course, I grew up.

So did Angie.

And thank God she doesn't remember, or she'd never let me live it down.

Things were bad enough the way they were, after today; I didn't need that, too.

When I passed his house — a big old thing, like all the others on the street, practically all the others in the Station — he was kneeling in the dirt, straightening one of the tombstones — the blank one, right in the middle of the first row — and shoving rocks around the base to keep it from falling. He's a skinny guy, arms and legs and not much else, wearing jeans and a plaid shirt and these really ugly heavy shoes.

Actually, he's pretty okay, all in all, even though he yells at practically everything that touches his precious grass and garden, squirrels and birds included. He lives alone, so I guess taking care of his lawn and those flowers is about all he has left to do. Mom says it keeps him young, but I don't know. It seems like he's been old and cranky for practically ever.

Still, it was a brave kid that stepped on one precious blade of his perfect grass, or tried to pick one of his flowers that always won awards at shows all over New England.

Ballistic, actually, is a pretty good way to describe how he usually reacts.

"Evening, Cody," he said, waving as I went by.

"Hi, Mr. Robson." I nodded at what he was doing, making sure it was clear I was on my way to someplace important. "Somebody knock it over again, huh?" They weren't cardboard, those tombstones; they were solid oak, and five feet high. Even a good kick wouldn't budge one.

You really had to make an effort just to tilt one, believe me.

He scowled as he rocked back on his heels, wiping his face with the back of a spotted hand in a work glove. He always wore gloves. Not because of the work, but because of his fingers — a couple had been mangled in an incident — that's what he called it — when he was overseas during World War II. I've seen them. On the right hand, he didn't have the fourth finger or pinky at all, and on the left, the same fingers had been cut off down to the first joint, which is too bad since he's a lefty. It was the same reason he limped.

I think that, more than the yelling, was what made kids avoid him.

He also didn't look so hot. He moved kind of jerky, and he looked like he could barely hold up his head.

He sneezed, and blew out a breath while he shook his head. "Yep. Seems like every night, one gets dumped. Ain't the same around here anymore, Cody. Maybe this'll be my last time. Getting a little old for this kind of crap."

I didn't say anything, because he said that every year, because every year those things became a dare, and he knew it. Some kid, out late with his friends, dares somebody to go over and tip one. Most don't; every so often, though, one does. The idea, see, is to see who's buried underneath. Nobody is, of course, but that doesn't stop it from happening year after year; and it doesn't stop Mr. Robson from complaining, calling the cops, waving his arms and yelling at the neighbours, and generally being a royal pain in the butt.

Mom says it's just part of the season's ritual.

I still think it's just a royal pain in the butt.

So the old man grunted and pushed and straightened and grunted, and even though I figured he had the flu or something, I kept moving, reaching Centre Street just about the time I heard my name, looked back, and grinned as Matt Barton chugged up, chubby face red, dark hair flying in every direction at the same time.

"You," he said, pulling up alongside me, "are one brave dork, you know that?"

I shrugged.

"No, really." He frowned solemnly. "I am honoured to have known you."

"I'm not dead yet," I muttered sourly.

"Yet," he repeated. "that's the operative word, don't you think?"

There was very little car traffic on Centre Street, this being Sunday night and all.

There wasn't much any other time, either, as a matter of fact, even when the shops and offices were closing down. Not too long ago, somebody got the bright idea of tearing up the blacktop and putting cobblestones down. I guess it looked okay, but people hated driving on it and so most of them parked on the side streets instead. Besides, the Station isn't all that big. Practically everybody but those who live out on the Pike or in the valley can walk home in a few minutes.

So we stood on the corner, checking things out, not bothering to admit we were really checking for Theo Bronson.

Theo wanted my head.

He wanted every other part of me, too, but mostly, he wanted my head.

Matt tucked his hands into his football jacket pockets. He didn't play, he hated the game, but he wore it anyway, just to tick the jocks off. He forced a shiver, making it seem as if it were colder than it really was. "So, your mom working weekends again?"

I nodded.

He kicked at a leaf crawling towards his shoe. "So, you gonna cook?"

353

I shook my head.

Even if I was, it would be stupid to admit it. Matt could eat a banquet by himself and still complain there wasn't enough for dessert. The weird thing was, he wasn't really gross. I figured him to be over two hundred pounds, but the only place he looked fat was in his face. The rest of him was pretty solid.

"So, you gonna starve, or what?"

I didn't answer. Across the street, just coming out of the corner newsstand, was the girl who just by breathing had signed my death warrant.

Angie Hanover.

Long brown hair topped with a red beret; long legs and torso, wearing a down parka; dark brown eyes that looked at you with eyelids almost always half-closed. They drove me crazy, and she knew it.

Before I could turn away, or figure out how to become invisible, she spotted us and waved, called something to someone still in the store, and hurried across the streets.

Matt whistled, and she made a face at him before looking up at me.

"Hi."

"Uh, hi."

She looked a little tired, kind of worn around the edges, but she smiled at my brilliance, just a twitch of her lips, and wanted to know if we were going to the Halloween dance at the high school on Friday.

She couldn't have been more obvious if she'd asked me straight out, and I couldn't for the life of me think of an answer that wouldn't either get me killed, or get me in so much trouble that I might as well be dead.

"Well?" Her voice was normally husky, but when she was annoyed, it deepened even more. That drove me crazy, too.

I kind of gave her a one-shoulder shrug — *maybe, maybe not, it all depends.*

For a moment she actually looked angry, but it passed before I could say a word.

"Your mother," she said knowingly. "Working again, huh?"

"Yes," I answered quickly. I lowered my head, regret practically dripping off my body. "I kind of promised her I'd give her a hand, you know?"

She nodded and touched my arm. "Well, maybe you could come after, huh?"

I couldn't resist: "Yeah." I grinned. "Yeah, I think so."

"Cody," Matt said quietly.

A gust fanned her hair in front of her eyes, and she slapped it away angrily. A sigh, and she squinted across the street towards the store. She needed glasses, but say something to her, and she'd cut you off at the knees. "I swear that girl is going to drive me up the wall."

"Who?"

She didn't need to answer. Rena Viser raced out to the corner, looked around frantically, and flapped her arms helplessly until Angie called her.

"Hey," Matt said, moving slightly behind me. "Cody."

I started to turn, but Rena had already arrived, her little girl voice making me smile automatically as she blurted out the latest news about Marley Hunt and her boyfriend.

In Oxrun Station, if you wanted to know the real story behind any story that appeared in the paper, all you had to do was ask Rena or her brother Joey. Their father was a reporter on the *Station Herald*, and their mother owned the village's most popular hair salon for women. Between the two of them, and their kids' own maddening curiosity, you couldn't whack a finger with a hammer in Alaska without them, and the whole town, knowing it before dawn.

Marley Hunt was different.

She and her out-of-town boyfriend had been cycling up Chancellor Avenue towards the railroad depot a month or so ago, and hadn't come back. For days, search parties combed the woods and hills, the farming valley beyond the tracks, even up to the old quarry.

Nothing.

Not a thing.

The word was, Chief Stockton believed they'd run away, because Marley's father hated every boy who even looked sideways at his daughter, and hardly ever let her out, even on group dates, even when she finally went to college. I didn't know her all that well, she's couple of years older, but I wouldn't be surprised if they had taken off. Casper Hunt was one real son of a bitch.

"So how's Ursula?" Angie asked then, looking at me sideways.

I shrugged. "I don't know. Didn't see her today."

Rena's eyes widened. "Oh . . . really?"

"For God's sake," I snapped, "we're not married, you know."

Problem Number Two: we're all part of the same group — me, Angie, Rena, Matt, and Ursula Strong. We grew up together, were always in the same classes, stuff like that. A few weeks ago, Rena got it into her head that me and Ursula would make the perfect couple. Nobody else did, but she wouldn't let it go, and drove us all nuts with her hints and stupid winks.

It had been funny at first; now, it was really getting old.

Anyway, Ursula took a fall down her cellar steps a couple of weeks ago and smashed up her left leg pretty good. She was in traction for a few days, and damn grumpy the last time I saw her. What with Theo and all, I didn't need that too.

"Dammit, Cody," Matt snapped, and punched my arm.

"What?"

I turned, looked over his shoulder, and saw Theo Bronson standing on the corner a block away.

It was full dark now, and he was under the corner light. Standing there.

Just standing there.

"Oh, man," I said. Ice settled in my stomach; my legs went a little weak. "Oh . . . man."

2

I am not what you'd call a physical kind of guy. Where Matt was thick, I was thin; where Matt could lift tons of cord wood without breaking a sweat, I had a hard time lifting myself out of bed in the morning.

Well, it's not that bad, I guess. I'm pretty much just ordinary, you know? Nothing special — dark blond hair, brown eyes, a face and physique that wouldn't turn any heads. Just ordinary.

Theo Bronson was anything but ordinary.

He was taller by a head than practically anyone in school. He worked out all the time, so he was big, too. No; he was huge. And he loved to wear black from his shirts to a pair of squared-off biker boots. I swear, when you saw him coming at you, striding like he does, arms barely moving, you couldn't help thinking about Frankenstein or something. I know it was deliberate, and I know it sounds really dumb, but damn, it sure worked.

With him, just on the edge of the light, was Zack Skelton, almost as tall and twice as ugly. He'd been in a car accident when he was in fifth grade, and it had really messed his face up. At least once a year, his mother took him down to New York for another round of plastic surgery, just to try and make him look a little more human.

It hadn't worked so far.

They stood there, not moving, but I knew they had seen me.

Rena, who had finally caught on why we weren't talking anymore, said, "Uh-oh, it's Creepzoid from the Deep."

"Hey," Angie scolded. "Come on, what's he ever done to you?"

"He breathes."

Matt snickered, but I couldn't take it anymore. I slapped my forehead and miraculously remembered an errand I was supposed to run for my mother. Angie seemed disappointed, but she didn't have a chance to say anything, because I started down Centre Street in a major hurry, Matt catching up after whispering something to Rena.

"I'm dead," I said, stepping around a couple coming out of a jewellery store. "Dead."

"You could tell him to blow off, you know."

I glared at him. "You're no help, you know that? What the hell am I going to do?"

He didn't know, and neither did I.

For some reason, right out of the clear blue, Theo had decided Angie couldn't do better than pick him for her boyfriend. And because Angie and I had known each other since we were in kindergarten, and were best friends — no more than that, through no fault of my own — he had also decided that she didn't need me anymore. Ever.

He told me so last week.

His exact words were, "Talk to her, touch her, look at her again, Banning, and I'll rip off your head."

I was mad, of course. Furious. But there was nothing I could do about it. Fighting Theo Bronson would be suicide, and complaining to Angie would mean I wasn't smart enough to figure out what the right thing was on my own. So while I did try, I also did my best to avoid her. And when I couldn't avoid her, I made damn sure there wasn't a giant in black anywhere in sight.

I punched a fist against my leg and swore, startling an old lady who had stepped out of my way. "You know," I said to Matt, "if I don't do something soon, Angie's never going to speak to me again."

She was already a little ticked anyway. She had found out about Theo — from Rena, naturally — and had yelled at him right there in the middle of the hall, right in front of the principal's office. I mean, if the whole school wasn't watching, it sure found out before the end of the day. Which had only made him worse.

He called me last night: "Banning, you're dead." Nothing more.

He meant it, too; even Matt realised that. Last summer, Bronson had beaten some boy so badly, he was, as far as I know, still in the hospital over in Hartford. All the guy had done was ask him why he wore such stupid boots. The odd thing was, no charges were ever filed. Bronson hadn't done a single minute behind bars.

Matt grabbed my arm then and pulled me to a halt. We were at the T-intersection where Centre Street meets Chancellor Avenue, a bank on one corner, and the police station right beside us. He pointed at it and said, "Look, this is dumb. We'll be running all night, for God's sake. Why don't we just go in and tell Stockton what's going on?"

Cars sped along the avenue, tyres hissing over the blacktop.

Diagonally across the street, a few people were checking out the posters at the Regency Theatre, a place that looks just like a big brick house — no marquee or anything, just glass doors and a ticket booth. Maybe, I thought, I could hide in there, sneak out the back and get home without being seen.

"Cody!"

I shook my head. "Yeah, sure, I'll walk right in and demand that the chief give me round-the-clock police protection." I looked at him and sighed. "Get real. What do you think they'll say?"

He didn't answer; he already knew. Kids our age, we don't count for much when it comes to the police. They don't bother us or anything, but . . . we're still kids. They'd tell us to grow up, act our age, or talk to Theo's parents.

Hopeless.

It was hopeless.

"Oh . . . screw it," I said wearily, and starting walked west, back towards my place. "Come on, we'll order pizza or something, watch something on the tube."

He didn't argue. Free food beat fear in his world any day of the week.

We were almost there when suddenly he slowed, almost stopped, and I was a couple of steps ahead before I realised it.

"What?" I looked around frantically in case Theo had found us, but for the moment, we were the only ones on the street. "What's up?"

"Nothing," he said, and started walking again. "It's nothing."

I almost pushed him, until I realised where we were; then I wanted to hit myself a good one, right between the eyes.

We had just passed Sara Carter's house, and I hadn't even noticed. It was, this year, the only place on the block that had no decorations, no lights. It looked empty, but it wasn't. Her parents just didn't go out much anymore.

Two years ago, just about this time, Sara and Matt were going together, about as tight as any couple I'd ever known. Then she woke up one morning not feeling very good.

Five days later, she was dead.

Her heart gave out.

Just like that.

I don't know how many days I spent with Matt after that, not saying much, just being there when he had to get mad at someone, when he had to throw things and hit things and once, while we were in the park, cry as if he'd never cried before.

Remembering that kind of made my own problem with Bronson seem a little small, so I started figuring out aloud what I'd have on my pizza. An old trick, but it worked:

"Anchoves? Anchoives? You gotta be kidding. Anchovies and black olives? Jesus, you trying to make me puke, Cody? Man, you don't know the first thing about blending foods, you know that? It's a wonder you can taste anything at all. Anchovies? Jeeze, gimme a break."

All the way to my house, with one stop at Robson's to see if he'd picked the lucky name yet.

He hadn't.

"Maybe it'll be Bronson," Matt grumbled as we climbed the porch steps. "With any kind of luck, they'll kill each other."

I laughed, chucked him one on the shoulder, and we spent the rest of the night watching TV and listening to my mother complain, not very seriously, about how loud it was.

The only bad part was when the idiot told my mother about Theo and me.

After he left, looking a zillion apologies at me — and laughing — she made me go through it step by step, then threatened to call Mrs. Bronson.

"No!" I said, a little too loudly. Her look made me look away. "I'm sorry, Mom, but no, okay? That'll only make it worse."

It took me an hour, but she finally agreed. But only after making me promise that if I hadn't cleared it up by Friday, I had to tell her, and let her take charge.

Humiliating, but I had no choice.

Big shot high school senior protected by his mom. Brother!

3

When I finally got to bed, I had a hard time finding sleep. I kept thinking about poor Ursula in the hospital, poor Matt and his memories, and poor me, flirting with true death.

I don't know what time it was, but it must have been after midnight when I sat up, frowning.

I had the absolute feeling someone was watching me.

My room isn't that big, and I could see, even in the dim dark, I was alone. But I couldn't shake that feeling, so I got out of bed and looked out the window, into the back yard.

As far as I could tell, it was empty.

Then I slipped down the hall, into the empty room that had once been my father's study. I peeked around the shade, but saw nothing but the street, deserted, the blacktop shifting a little as shadows from the street lamp moved with the wind.

I cursed myself for letting Theo get to me this way, heard Mom groan in her sleep . . . and saw him.

At first it just seemed like the oak at the curb was larger because of the shadows. Then I realised someone was there. Watching the house.

I stared as hard as I could, but couldn't make him out. The porch roof, and the moving leaves, made that impossible.

Theo, I thought, a fist bunching at my side; so what's he trying to prove?

I almost got mad enough to run downstairs, yank open the front door and call him out, but Mom groaned again, and I knew she was about to wake up. I rushed back to my room, seething, and closed my eyes, pretending to sleep just in case she decided to check up on me.

She still did that, even after all these years.

Weird, but somehow, I don't mind.

What I did mind was Theo Bronson watching my house. As soon as I knew Mom was asleep again, I was going out, death or no death, and I was going to mangle his ass.

An empty hallway with a bright white light from somewhere at the far end.

In the light was a giant.

Standing there.

Just . . . standing there.

In the distance I can hear the thud and rumble of a furnace, nothing else.

I can't even hear myself breathing.

But when the giant takes a step towards me, it's like a hammer slamming on rock.

The floor trembles, even though it's marble, and the lockers in the walls on either side rattle. When he takes another step, a door flies open, and something dark and shapeless slips to the floor.

I can't back away. There's something behind me. I can't even look around to see what it is.

A third step.

The light shifts in broad beams around him, nearly blinding me.

Hammer on rock.

Over and over.

And a voice, Zack Skelton's high raspy voice, says in my ear, "You're dead, Banning."

I don't scream, but I whirl to face him, and find myself lying flat on my back. The light, the giant, the hallway — everything is gone.

I'm in bed, and it's pitch dark in my room.

I laugh a little at the nightmare, and try to roll over on my side so I can get back to sleep.

I can't move.

That's when I realise I can't breathe either.

There's no air in the room.

I try to sit up so I can get to the window, and my head hits something hard and solid.

You're dead, Bahning.

I'm not.

But I'm in a coffin anyway.

I can't see it, but I know it.

And there are voices, muffled, only inches away. Some are crying, some are laughing, some are just talking and I can't understand a word.

I have enough air in my lungs for one scream, or enough air to pound on the lid for a few seconds, hoping that they'll hear me.

It's no contest.

I scream.

And sat up dripping sweat, smelling sour, and gasping as I nearly fell off the bed and yanked up the window sash and stuck my head outside. Breathing deeply. Shuddering.

Actually enjoying the cold that I could see had already scattered frost across the grass.

When I thought I could move without throwing up, I closed the window and fell back onto the bed, wondering what was going on.

I haven't had a nightmare since, forever, and the last one I remember because I had it all the time — my dad coming back from the dead to take me to a ball game. It sounds stupid; it's horrible, because everyone at the ballpark is dead too.

For a moment I wondered if it was seeing Theo outside that got me going, actually believing I'd try to fight him right there in the street, in the middle of the night.

I didn't think so. I saw him every day at school, and he'd never given me nightmares before.

A hard chill hit me then, nearly making my teeth chatter, and I wondered if I was getting sick. Not a bad thing, actually, since that would keep me out of Theo's way for a while. My luck, however, doesn't run that way. Angie never gets sick at all; neither does Matt. I mean, never. Not a cold, not a sneeze, not even a damn headache. I catch the usual stuff, but only when holidays come around, or when I want to go someplace extra special.

Something like a good case of the flu to keep Theo from tearing me apart wasn't in my stars.

So I decided to figure out what the nightmare meant. That didn't work, either.

I fell asleep.

4

Monday I was a zombie. That sleep hadn't been very restful, although I couldn't remember any more dreams. I nearly dozed off in history, blew a pop quiz in biology big time, and walked past Rena and Matt twice before I knew who they were.

I didn't see Angie at all.

Or Theo or Zack, thank God.

But I did collide with the principal and got a lecture about paying attention, right in front of his office, right in front of half the school. The kids thought it was funny; I prayed for it to end, and when it did, so did last class, and I was able to escape to the grocery store where my mom worked as assistant manager.

I helped her sometimes with the inventory, which is what we had to do on Halloween night; today, I hauled crates and straightened shelves and generally made everybody feel pretty miserable with my gloomy attitude. She chased me out of there just around five, and told me to take out whatever was bothering me on making dinner.

On the way home, I bumped into Mr. Robson, on his way back from the drug store. He didn't say hello or anything, just bitched about the weather, held up a bag of medicine and bitched some more.

"Rather get hit by a damn truck," he complained, laughed hoarsely, sneezed, coughed, and staggered up to his porch.

I couldn't help watching him, thinking he was going to fall over any second, but he made it inside, but not before he turned and yelled at me to get the hell out of his yard.

Great, I thought miserably. My mother, the principal, and Mr. Robson, all on the same day.

Maybe I was the one who should be hit by a truck.

Then I went into the Kaler house, right next to Robson's. It's a small place, and it's been empty since the beginning of summer. They moved, and when it was clear the place wasn't going to be sold anytime real soon, the real estate lady hired me, thanks to Mom, to go in once a week and check for stuff. You know, broken pipes, broken windows, dead bodies, stuff like that. Then I had to dust the floors and things — everything was gone, and I mean everything — and generally make it look presentable.

It was quick, boring, and a fast fifteen bucks every time I went through the door.

No cleaning this time; I had done that last week.

Twenty minutes later I was home. I made dinner, waited for Mom, and afterwards, went to my room, studied for a while, and fell asleep with my clothes on.

He was out there again.

I got hungry just about midnight and padded down to the kitchen, to find something I could eat without Mom knowing about it.

Fat chance.

Then I felt it, that same sharp, cold sensation.

This time I looked through the living room window, and saw him, standing almost behind that oak, just far enough away and just enough out of the street lamp's glow that I couldn't make out his face.

I didn't have to.

Theo; it was Theo.

This time I wasn't angry. This time I realised the guy was nuts, and going out there would not be the best idea in the world. I thought about calling the police, thought about Theo taking off before the cops arrived, thought about Mom trying to decide for how many years I should be grounded, and I went back to bed.

I don't know how long it took me to fall back to sleep. It was a long time.

A very long time.

It wasn't a coffin.

It was a trench in the cold earth, with something wide and hard keeping the dirt from burying me alive.

I *was* alive.

I knew I was alive.

I also knew I could hear the giant's footsteps walking towards me from below.

Hammer against rock.

All night long

5

"If you don't mind me saying so," Matt said in the school cafeteria the next day, "you look like stale road kill. No offence."

We sat at the back table, alone. I had hardly touched my lunch, such as it was — Tuesdays were always macaroni and cheese — and could barely keep my eyes open. They felt lined with sand, and my head felt like it was packed with lead.

"In fact," he said, checking out my tray hungrily, "I don't think you'll have to worry about Theo anymore. He'd only have to breathe on you, and you'd fall over."

"Thanks."

"Don't mention it. You gonna eat that tuna?"

I shook my head, leaned back in the chair, and closed my eyes.

"Hey," he said softly. "What's up?"

I wasn't sure what he'd say, but I told him about the nightmares anyway. When I started, he couldn't help turning around, checking the other kids scattered around the room; by the time I was done, he couldn't take his eyes off me.

"Man," he said, shaking his head in sympathy. "Man." He plucked a potato chip from my tray and popped it into his mouth. "It's like that guy, you know?"

"What guy?"

"That story in English last year. The Poe guy? He was buried alive?"

I remembered, vaguely, and didn't really think my nightmare was anything like that.

It was, for one thing, too damn real.

"Cody," he said then, "you're working too hard, you know that? You gotta give yourself a break, man, once in a while, or you'll never make it to Christmas."

I knew what he meant. What with helping Mom at the house and the store, and the increased school work this year, by the time it was nine o'clock I was practically asleep on my feet. The trouble was, I had no choice. I had to do it. Dad didn't leave us a whole lot of money except for a small insurance policy, and I needed every nickel, dime, and good grade I could get my hands on if I wanted to go to college next year.

Which I did. Badly. Even more than Mom wanted me to go.

"So, look," Matt said, scarfing down the last of my lunch, "the plan is, I sweet-talk your Mom into letting you out early on Halloween, we hit the dance, and—"

He never finished.

Rena rushed in and plopped down beside him. "Guys, you won't believe it!"

Matt grinned. "You've volunteered for a brain transplant."

She slapped his arm. Hard. "No, it's Angie."

I leaned forward. "What? What about her?"

"She's in hospital."

I refused to believe it. Sure, she looked a little under the weather on Sunday, but that didn't mean anything. She worked hard, too, and it was bound to catch up to her.

Matt wanted to know the details, but Rena, for the first time in memory, couldn't tell us. All she knew for sure was that Angie had collapsed at the breakfast table that morning, and her father had driven her right to the King Street hospital. The doctors didn't know what was wrong, although one of them said it looked like exhaustion.

Matt said nothing, but his face sobered instantly, and I knew exactly what he was thinking. I stood and said, "Let's go."

"But it's only one," Rena protested. Her eyes widened. "Cody, you've never cut school in your life."

"Always a first time," I told her, and said, "You coming?" to Matt when Rena said she wasn't going with me.

We hurried out the side entrance and took the long way around, just in case. By the time we got down to King Street, a half-hour had passed, and I had already run through a hundred different reasons why Angie, my Angie, was sick. Not a single one of them was less than life-threatening.

Matt didn't say a word the entire time.

I knew he was thinking about Sara Carter.

It was obvious from the second we walked in that the receptionist wasn't going to let us upstairs. We were out of breath, wind-tossed, and could barely put two words together. She sympathised, but ordered us to sit down near the entrance and wait for Angie's parents to come down.

I couldn't.

I sat for probably thirty seconds, and couldn't stay still. With a look at Matt, I went outside and paced the length of the block a few times, looking up at the windows, wishing I could see her face. Just once.

I said we were best friends, and that's true. I hinted I wished it were more than that, and that's true, too. I loved her. Sounds sappy, but I did. She was always there when I needed a shoulder to cry on or someone to yell at or just someone who didn't mind an hour or so of nothing but silence while I worked things out in my head.

I guess she wasn't the most beautiful girl in the world, but there were times, when I looked at her, when I could barely keep from yelling something, anything, just to let out the pressure I'd feel in my chest.

Now she was in there, behind all that brick and glass, and they wouldn't let me see her.

Matt finally came out, hands in his pockets. He waited for me to reach the entrance, and looked at me.

"You hear something?"

He shook his head.

"Then what?"

"Counting today," he said miserably, "it's five days to Halloween."

Then he walked away.

6

I tried again to see her.

The receptionist, her expression concerned, still wouldn't give me a break. Nobody but immediate family right now. Try again tonight. Visiting hours started at eight.

It wasn't raining as I walked home, but it sure felt like it.

The sun hadn't set yet, but it sure felt dark.

I walked through every room in the house about a zillion times, telling myself this wasn't the same as Sara. Angie had been working hard, just like me. More than once, hanging out in the park or something, we'd dozed off on a bench, or in the movies, and made fun of each other for not being more alert.

No big deal.

But, something kept saying, if it was only exhaustion, why wouldn't they let me see her?

It was nearly four when I finally had an idea, and swore loudly for not thinking of it sooner — I called Ursula's room at the hospital.

"Hey," I said when she answered.

"Cody, hi! What's up?"

She already knew about Theo's new obsession, but she didn't know about how he and Zack had taken to following me around. She thought it was funny, and teased me for a few minutes until I actually started to smile. So I told her about Angie, and asked if she was mobile.

"Sure. Got my crutches this morning. They're on at me forever about practising." She giggled. "Maybe I'll take a hike down the hall."

"You're sure it'll be all right?"

"No sweat. Give me a few minutes, though, okay? It's not like I can run with these things yet."

I thanked her, promised to buy her anything she wanted for a homecoming gift, and hung up.

Then I sat on the couch, listening to the hall clock drag its way round towards five.

For a minute I got angry, thinking she'd forgotten. Then I felt guilty, because maybe she'd fallen and hurt her leg again, and it was all my fault. Then I was angry for asking her to do that, especially when I knew damn well she had this thing for me. Then I was guilty. Then I was angry.

Then, suddenly, I was numb.

All I could do was sit there and stare out the front window, watching the leaves move, watching the cars go by, watching a few kids on skateboards chase each other up and down the sidewalk.

When the telephone finally rang, I dropped the receiver, picked it up, pulled the cord too tight and pulled the base off the side table. When I picked that up, yelling to whoever it was to hang on, I dropped the receiver again, swore, and closed my eyes as tight as I could until I felt ready to try again.

"Hello?"

Ursula was laughing so hard she couldn't speak. Then she got the hiccoughs, and that started me giggling.

It must have been five minutes before either of us could talk without hooting and setting the other one off again.

It was worth it.

"She's okay. Nothing more than exhaustion, like you heard. What they're doing is forcing her to rest, and taking a few routine tests. Hey, that rhymes! Anyway, before her father chased me out of the room — boy, is he a grouch! — she said to tell you not to worry, to tell Rena she has a big mouth, and to make sure you don't forget Mr. Johnson's trig test tomorrow." She giggled, hiccoughed, and said, "So don't forget Mr. Johnson's trig test tomorrow."

I thanked her, gossiped a little, and hung up.

Then I think I went numb again, this time with relief.

Thank you I said silently to the ceiling; thank you, thank you, thank you.

Then I sat up. "Trig test? Jesus!"

The rest of the night was a blur. All I could think of was Angie, floating around sines and cosines and right triangles and a formula of depth and volume that made absolutely no sense when I read it, or when I tried to work out a practice problem with it.

I gave up and fell on the bed.

Almost immediately, I began waiting for that feeling. It kept me awake until I heard the downstairs clock strike two.

After that . . . nothing but that stupid practice problem, dancing around and around in my head.

And sure enough, the next day it mocked me from the first question on the test.

I was pretty sure I passed it, though, and so felt pretty good, right up until the second I walked out the door and saw Theo and Zack waiting on the sidewalk.

The other kids didn't even look at them. They hurried off the way I had left Angie on Sunday — as if they had suddenly realised they had a meeting with the President or something. But I was still feeling good, and probably a little stupid, so I walked right up to him and said, "How's Angie today?" It startled him so much he couldn't answer.

Zack, however, suggested that her health was none of my business, and if I didn't want to be in the next room, in a body cast, I'd mind my own.

Again, feeling good equalled feeling stupid. I looked right at him and said, "Blow it out your ear, Skelton. She's a friend of mine, okay? I got a right."

That's about when I came to my senses, just as he snarled and reached for my throat.

Before I could react — either by shrieking or just plain running for my life — Theo stopped him by slapping the hand away, and punching his shoulder. Zack couldn't have been more surprised if I had hit him myself. He gaped at his friend, a storm raging in his eyes. But he didn't say anything.

"She's okay, Banning," Theo said, his voice coming from about ten miles inside his chest. He took a deep breath. "Thanks for asking."

"No problem." I smiled, smiled extra sweetly at Zack, and got out of there before my legs and my heart gave way.

I hadn't taken more than a dozen steps, though, when Theo added, "You ain't off the hook, Banning."

He didn't need to explain, and I didn't need to stop. I kept on moving, all the way to the store, where Mom sent me into the basement to stack crates of lettuce and carrots for the next hour.

Later, we went to the Wednesday buffet at the Mariner Cove, next to the theatre, which was a treat-and-a-half, since we hardly ever ate out. The occasion was the raise she had been given that afternoon, and for a while there, it was just like old times.

She's beautiful, my mother, but she hardly ever laughs anymore.

That night I tried to call Angie, but the operator refused to put me through; doctor's orders.

I tried Ursula, too, but no-one answered. I grinned. She'd been sprung. Now that she could get around on crutches, they probably figured she didn't need to hang around anymore. When no-one answered at her house, though, I checked the time — it was just after nine — and decided I might as well go upstairs, listen to some music, and hit the sack. It had been, all in all, a pretty good day, and maybe I wouldn't have the nightmare tonight.

I didn't have to.

I had no sooner climbed the stairs, when the telephone rang. Yelling to my mother that I'd get it, I took the steps back down two at a time, yanked up the receiver, and said, "Your dime, my time, speak fast."

"Cody?" It was Matt.

God, it sounded like he'd been crying.

"What's up?"

"She's . . ."

He choked, and I heard his hand scrape over the mouthpiece, too surprised to do anything but wait.

"Dead," he finally said. And before I could ask, he added, "Ursula."

7

The rain began a long time before dawn.

I know, because I was still awake and I heard it against the panes, like tiny ice pellets.

Later, when it rained harder, it sounded like claws.

Like something was out there.

Trying to get in.

School only lasted until 11:00 a.m. on Thursday.

The principal got on the PA and told everybody what I already knew. Ursula Strong had died the night before, in her sleep; she was to have come home this morning. As incredible as it seemed, it was a heart attack; unusual for someone her age, but not impossible. Apparently the shock of the accident and recovery had been, finally, too much for her system.

What I hadn't known was that SJ — that's Sarah Jane Smith, not one of our group, but we knew her, had also died — in the same hospital, the day before. I was sorry about SJ, of course, but I was too shocked about Ursula to take much notice. SJ could have been ill for weeks as far as I knew.

The counsellors, Mrs. Wallace for the girls, Mr. Evans for the boys, were in their offices in case anyone wanted to talk; the rest of us could go home if we wished and grieve in our own ways.

Strange, though. Oxrun High is a small school, barely six hundred kids, but there were still plenty who didn't know Ursula or SJ. While they weren't exactly dancing for joy, you could tell who they were by their expressions — a free half-day, just because some seniors had croaked.

Matt, Rena, and I wandered over to my house, and sat on the porch.

The wind had come up, but it blew north to south, so the rain hit the back of the house first, and only barely touched us.

They were on the bench swing, I was in an old wicker chair that was due any day now to be brought back inside for the winter. We didn't say anything for the longest time; we only watched the fall of water from the overflowing gutters, watched the mist rise from the street, and listened to the wind speak its mind in the eaves.

We had already been through the 'I don't believe it' stage, and were working our way through the 'why her?'

Matt, huddled in his jacket, shoulders hunched, jerked a thumb over his shoulder. "He'll do it, you know."

I didn't catch it. "What?"

"Robson. What do you bet he'll put her name on the tombstone."

"Oh, man, that's sick."

"Yeah, well, I wouldn't put it past him, the son of a bitch." He shifted, making the chains creak, and looked first to Rena, small and silent beside him. "You remember that time he nearly chased her to Hartford?"

I smiled, stopped because I thought it probably wasn't right, then smiled again. "Yeah. She'd picked one of his dumbass flowers, right? Something yellow or something. He was so mad, she didn't stop running for hours."

"You know, for an old guy who gimps like that, he moves pretty good."

I made a face: "For a guy that old, he ought to be dead."

Matt snickered, and nudged Rena with an elbow. She looked up, eyes puffy and cheeks flushed, and tried to say something, but her lower lip trembled too much.

I hadn't known she and Ursula were that close.

Then I realised she wasn't trying not to cry at all; she was scared.

Matt saw it, too, and put an arm around her shoulder. "What?" he asked softly, with a puzzled glance at me.

"He is," she answered, so quietly I almost didn't hear her.

Matt frowned. "What are you talking about?"

"Robson."

"What about him?"

"He is."

Matt's patience was just about gone. "Is what, Rena?"

"Is dead."

Neither of us knew what to say, so we didn't say anything while she looked at us so intently, it was like she was trying to will us to believe her. When we still didn't say anything, she pushed his arm away and jumped up, pushing one hand back through her hair.

"I . . ."

Matt reached for her hand, but she shied away to the steps. Rain fell behind her; her face was in shadow.

"My house, tonight, okay? About eight?"

She didn't say anything else. She hurried down the steps and started to run before she reached the sidewalk. A second later, the rain washed her away as if she'd never been there.

"Weird," Matt said, scratching his neck furiously, like he does when he doesn't know what else to say.

"It's just Ursula," I told him. "It's . . ." I shrugged, and watched the rain, felt the cold, and suddenly, as if a movie had started on an invisible screen, I saw Maynard Robson working in his garden, old and cranky and snarling at four little kids, who were standing on his lawn.

Angie, Matt, Rena, and me.
Ten years, at least, and he hadn't changed a bit.
I blinked, and the image was gone.
Then I looked at Matt, and knew that he had seen it too.
"Nah," we said at the same time.
"Everybody's old when you're a kid," he reminded me.
"Especially someone like him."
He agreed.
We said nothing more about it, instead talked about Ursula and what a bitch it was, and how there ought to be some kind of law, and stuff like that.
We didn't cry, not then, but I knew he felt like it. So did I.
We didn't say anything more about Mr. Robson.
But at eight o'clock that night, we stood in Rena's living room, and stared at a photocopy of a page of the *Station Herald*.
Rena had been working on her senior English project, an essay-with-pictures about the changes the Station had gone through since the Second World War.
There weren't that many.
Rena being Rena, she hardly ever forgot what she saw, which had made her wonder a little when she'd come across a photograph of Robson at a Boston flower show last year.
She did some digging.
What she found was on the table:
A picture of Mr. Robson down in the left-hand corner, standing proudly among his prize flowers.
He was old.
Very old.
The picture had been taken before any of us had been born.

We argued, and fought, and scared ourselves, and argued again, for almost three hours.
We talked about impossibilities and trick photography, mistaken identities and false memories; we called each other crazy for even thinking about something like this; we dumped hard on Rena for a really lousy joke the day a friend had died;

we argued, and we fought, and we only came up with one answer:

Mr. Robson wasn't dead, like Rena had thought.

He was very much alive.

But the picture in the paper had been taken over fifty years ago.

8

I was back in the corridor.

The giant, hammer and rock, still moved towards me.

It wasn't Theo.

It was Maynard Robson.

I was six or maybe seven, in a pirate costume, patch and tricorn and sword and everything, standing next to Angie at Mr. Robson's house, crying my eyes out because her name was on the Halloween tombstone, not mine.

I was ten or maybe eleven, in a Freddy Krueger costume, hat and awful shirt and dirty trousers and rubber knives for fingers, standing beside Matt at Mr. Robson's house, laughing because Ursula was furious her name was on the tombstone, and she threatened to sue him if he didn't take it off.

I was hanging from the maple tree, straw in my collar and sleeves and pants, swinging in the night wind, looking down at Theo Bronson, while he laughed, and dug my grave.

I woke up and whispered, "Oh, my God," and listened to the rain.

Scratching to get in.

Mom said it was all right, I didn't have to go to school on Friday. I didn't have to fake feeling rotten. Ursula had been part of my life since forever, and there was a hole there now I didn't think would fill for a real long time.

I wandered around the house until noon, listening to the steady drip and fall of the rain. Then I put on my coat and ran to the hospital.

Miracle time — I was allowed to see Angie.

She wasn't in a private room, but there was no-one in the other bed. She grinned when I walked in, and I had to grin back, just to hide the shock.

She looked awful.

She looked . . . old.

Dark circles around her eyes, her hair stringy, her cheeks sunken — all this in just a couple of days.

I sat on the edge of the mattress and took her hand, and she burst into tears, sobbing so hard the nurse came in to see what was wrong. I explained about Ursula, and the nurse nodded, sighed, and slipped out again, leaving us alone.

It was the same as with Matt and Rena — why Ursula, why now, how could it happen . . . all the questions that never had any real answers. She didn't even know about SJ, and I decided not to mention it.

And that's when I decided I wouldn't say anything about Robson either. I had an idea. It was stupid, and Angie would laugh me out of town, but I couldn't bring myself to tell her.

Instead, we talked about school, and I scolded her for letting herself get so rundown. She told me Theo had dropped in earlier.

"What?"

"Oh, Cody, come on. He's not that bad. Actually, he's kind of sweet."

I blinked. Theo Bronson, sweet?

Not in my lifetime.

Then the nurse stuck her head in and said I had to go.

Angie smiled. "Thanks, Cody."

"No sweat."

"You'll come back?"

"Now that they'll let me, sure."

We smiled.

And I kissed her.

I think that startled us both, especially when I kissed her again, and stroked her hair, and just did manage to get out of that awful room without crying.

I don't how I knew, but as sure as I knew I'd never see my dad again, I knew that if I didn't do something soon, Angie was going to die.

9

I called Matt and Rena from the lobby, telling them to meet me at the park. I didn't explain, and they didn't ask.

Then I walked all the way, even though I wanted to run. I needed time to think.

I needed to find the words.

We met at the park gate. There was a winding blacktop path that led towards the back; to the right was a line of bushes and trees on the other side of which was open ground, for ball-playing and soccer and music in the summer.

We kept going until the blacktop ended, pretty sure that with the rain no-one would see us back here.

The only bench was wrought iron and wood.

They sat, huddled under Rena's electric blue umbrella; I couldn't. I just let the rain soak me. After all, I don't think I could have got any wetter.

"What's up?" Matt asked.

I told them about visiting Angie and how bad she looked.

I told them about my dream, and told them what I thought.

I think I scared them.

See, I don't believe in ghosts or things like that. Maybe I used to, hoping someday I'd see Dad again. But I knew that was a lie, and I knew there was a reasonable explanation for everything, even ghosts and UFOs. Even that old tale about Hugh Morgan, who was supposed to haunt Mildenhall Woods . . . although there had been times when I'd heard strange noises out at the quarry, just like everyone else.

But I also knew that this was Oxrun Station.

No matter how much we want to convince ourselves otherwise, everyone who lives here for any length of time knows this place isn't normal.

So after I wasted a ton of time losing sleep, telling myself I was an idiot and a jerk and a total complete loon, I stopped kidding myself and did some thinking.

"He's not dead," I told them.

"No kidding," Matt muttered, shivering when a gust blew rain in his face.

"Hush," Rena snapped. This was important, and she had been the one to find that out.

"But if we take that picture as real—"

"It is!" she insisted hotly.

"—then Robson's up to something else."

"Yeah, sure," Matt grumbled. "He's a wizard or something, and he steals people's souls, right? God, Cody, get a life, okay? Man, I'm gonna catch pneumonia out here."

"Look, I don't know what he is," I said. I stopped pacing and stood in front of him, one hand slipped into my jeans pocket. "But what I think he does is stay alive by making other people die."

Matt's lips parted to laugh, then clamped together. He wasn't buying any of this, not a word.

I wasn't so sure I was, either.

"He's not dead," I reminded him. "He should be. He should have died years ago, but he hasn't." I pointed at him, making him jump. "All you have to do is look at the picture — he's still pretty much the same as he was when our parents were our age."

He squirmed, wanting to yell, wanting to go over all the arguments we'd been through last night. I knew how he felt, and I waited patiently, exchanging glances with Rena, who had gone from curious to scared to fascinated-but-scared.

Finally he waved one hand in disgust. "Nuts, right? You're nuts. I mean, come on, Cody, don't you think somebody would have noticed this old guy's still around after all these years?"

"People move away, new people come in," Rena said quickly, her voice shaking a little.

"And who notices old people anyway?" I added. "They're like us. We're just around." I kind of laughed, but it was bitter.

"Like trees, y'know? We're just around." I shrugged. "And then we're either grown up, or we're gone."

"Or dead," Rena whispered.

The rain stopped, and the only sound was water dripping from the leaves.

"All right," Matt said at last, reluctantly giving me the rope to hang myself. "So how does he do it?"

"If I knew that, we could . . . we could . . . "

I remembered my nightmare.

I grabbed Rena's hand and practically yanked her off the bench. "Can we get into the paper?"

"Now?"

I nodded. "Now. I mean, can we use the computer? To look back at old issues?"

"Hey," Matt said. "What the hell are you talking about?"

"An idea," I told him.

"Is it as crazy as the one you just told me?"

"Yep."

"Jesus." He pushed himself to his feet and headed for the gate. "Banning, you are going to get us grounded for life, you know that? I mean, as soon as we walk in the door, her old man's going to see us, and I don't think you want him to know you're going crazy."

Rena pushed him lightly. "My father's in Hartford. And Mr. Clayton's gone over to Boston. The only one there will be one of the temps, and they won't bother us because they know me." She looked at him smugly. "You are such a coward."

"I have a strong sense of survival," he countered sourly.

"Coward," she repeated, and was off, Matt and I trailing behind.

I don't know why, but I felt excited. If I was right, it would be easy to stop Robson from doing it — whatever, exactly, it was — again.

But if I was wrong . . .

My excitement died quickly.

I didn't want to think it, but I couldn't help it.

If I was wrong, the next one to die would be Angie Hanover, and nothing I could do would prevent it.

Or him from doing it again.

10

The *Herald* office is a small brick building on Williamston Pike. It's not very impressive, but as the owner, Marc Clayton, says, it gets the job done.

So did Rena.

She breezed right in, talking a mile a minute, making no sense at all, I swear, and the next thing we knew, we were in a closet-size office and she was doing mysterious things with a computer.

When she was ready, she looked over her shoulder at me.

The fear was in her eyes; I think she'd already figured it out.

"Halloween," I said. A quick shrug. "I don't know, fifty years ago, I guess." I rubbed a hand over my cheek. "We'll have to check the following week. For the pictures," I explained to Matt, who leaned against the window still, his arms folded over his chest, scowling.

She found it in less than a minute.

"Oh, boy," she whispered.

There he was, and there were the tombstones. We couldn't read the name on the one he'd painted that Halloween night, but that's not what bothered us.

It was him.

The same.

A little more hair, maybe, and he looked a little heavier, but otherwise, he was exactly the same. The caption said he was sixty-two.

Matt moved away from the window and looked over my shoulder. He inhaled sharply, but when I glanced at him, he ignored me. His lower lip was pulled between his teeth while he concentrated on something I couldn't see.

"Okay," I said, my throat dry, a slight buzzing in my head. "Now ten — no, twenty years ago." I frowned. "And every year after that, I guess, if you can."

That took a long time, because after she located what we wanted, she blew them up and printed them out.

There wasn't a picture for every year, but by the time she was done, it was enough.

You could have said the *Herald* just used the same picture over and over, but that wasn't true. Every so often it was clear enough to read the tombstones; the names were always different. Yet Matt still didn't say a word. He spread the copies over the desk and stared at them, shaking his head slowly.

"What?" Rena asked.

"I don't know," he answered. "I'm not sure."

"But what do you think?" I wanted to know. I needed him to believe me. Rena already did, but Matt was important.

He didn't say anything right away. He kept rubbing the back of his neck, kept chewing on his lip, kept shifting the pictures around as if he might be able to come up something that would prove me an idiot.

I wanted him to.

Honest to God, I really wanted him to.

Finally he said, "I think he killed Sara."

He asked Rena to check on the obituaries in the same issues that we found Robson's picture.

When she did, it suddenly got very cold in there.

Maybe once, maybe twice . . . but every time someone's name showed up on the old man's tombstone, they were dead in less ten years: SJ, Ursula, Sara, and other names we recognised.

We could have argued more, but none of us believed it was simple coincidence.

Maynard Robson was slowly killing the kids in Oxrun Station.

11

The wind was damp, not very strong, but as soon as we left the building, we looked up to watch the clouds darken and begin to move more quickly across the sky.

Branches rattled softly.

Or groaned.

Droplets fell on our heads, and shattered puddles in the street.

Nobody knew what to do next, because none of us knew what we really knew, or what we really, deep down believed.

We wandered for a while, not paying attention to where we were going. The light had begun to fail as the clouds thickened, and a few cars already had their headlamps glowing.

Before we knew it, we found ourselves at Robson's.

The tombstones were there, weathered, looking exactly like granite or mable.

The centre one still had no name.

That would come just before midnight, tomorrow.

A single light burned in one of his front windows, and I could see a folded newspaper lying by the door, waiting to be taken inside.

Suddenly the door opened, and we jumped.

Robson came out, saw us, and waved. "You kids ready for tomorrow?" he called.

We nodded dumbly.

He laughed, waved again, and went back inside.

He wasn't sick anymore.

It may have been . . . it must have been the light, but he actually looked a few years younger.

We stared at the tombstone.

"I'll knock it over," Matt volunteered grimly.

Rena shook her head. "That's no good. He'll just put it up again."

"Well, we gotta do something."

I touched their shoulders to move them on. "What we have to do first," I said, "is wait until dark. Meanwhile, we have to figure out if just getting rid of that thing is all there is to it."

"I doubt it," Matt said. "That's too easy."

I agreed, but had no ideas other than burning the old man at the stake. And when I said it aloud, I started to laugh. I mean, here we were, walking down the street, actually seriously talking about knocking off a guy who *maybe* stayed alive by *maybe* killing other people. The details weren't important; he did it, and we had to stop him. God, it sounded like a movie they show on TV just before dawn, when only the drunks are watching.

I couldn't stop laughing. Not loudly, but I couldn't stop it. It hurt my chest, hurt my stomach, but dammit, I couldn't stop.

When we reached my house, I invited them in, but they decided they'd better get home first, do some ego stroking so they could get out tonight, and stay out past their personal curfews.

It didn't work.

By the time my mother came home, I was huddled under a lap rug in the living room, feeling like my head had been stuffed with damp cotton. I was miserable. So was Matt, when I called.

"Nice, Banning," he said between sneezes. "Thanks a lot."

Rena was just fine.

That figures.

I talked to Angie for a few minutes, and hated how weak and small she sounded. She, however, spent most of the time giving me hell for walking around in the rain.

"How are you supposed to visit me when you've got a bad cold?" she demanded. "Cody, sometimes I wonder where you hide your brains."

"I'm sitting on them," I said, hoping she'd laugh.

She didn't.

That made me feel worse.

So bad, in fact, that I didn't argue when Mom tucked me up to bed, brought me chicken soup and crackers, and demanded I stay put until she told me differently.

The rain started again.

Patterns shifted across the ceiling and soon dropped me into a doze.

You hear noises inside, but you know it's only the house, talking to itself after everyone has gone to bed.

You hear noises outside, but you know it's only the rain hitting the roof, the leaves, the window.

You float into Dad's study, knowing you're dreaming, and you look out the window.

He's there again.

In the rain.

Blacker than the shadows.

Doing nothing but watching.

It doesn't take very long to realise that you're wrong.

He's not watching.

He's waiting.

12

Halloween in Oxrun Station:

The storm had stopped, but the clouds were still there. They hung so low, it was like the town had been put in a box whose lid was mottled grey.

They moved, but very slowly.

Colours were drab, even the brightest.

A constant light wind talked to itself in the bushes and trees.

Shopkeepers and clerks in costume; a pair of classic horror movies at the Regency; grade school kids on the prowl, roaming the streets in packs of ghosts and princesses and Power Rangers and hobos and Darth Maul and a Wonder Woman or two; leaves dried by the wind beginning to stir in the gutters.

A real skeleton hung on the iron gates to the park.

Cloud-filtered sunlight casting ghost-shadows on the ground.

Little kids in packs raced from house to house, urged on by the clear scent of coming rain, followed by their mothers who kept checking the sky.

I thought I saw Nicole Antrim, Chuck's little sister out with her best friend Merrilee and young David Trent, Eleanor's little brother. Tina Broadbent and her weird friend Cerise Fallon, who pretty much always looked like she was dressed for Halloween, were marching purposefully down the street.

The wind had come up around noon, not strong, but steady.

I stood in the dining room and looked out the side window. Down the street I could see the hanging man in Robson's tree, swinging slowly back and forth.

I didn't feel as bad as I had the night before, but I still got the shivers once in a while, and my legs were kind of wobbly. This was the first time I'd been up today, and the house seemed very big, very empty.

I kept telling myself there were things I had to do. Robson had to be stopped, Angie had to be saved. But I didn't know how. I didn't even really know if we were all just reacting in some bizarre way to Ursula's dying.

The wind punched the house.

I went upstairs and shook a shower, hoping it would clear my head. I dressed, found an old pullover in my bottom drawer and put that on too. I was going out, but I didn't know where, and didn't what I'd do when I got there.

I just knew I couldn't stay inside any longer.

Then Rena called.

"Hey," I said. "I was just going out."

"Angie," was all she said.

I sat on the floor and stared at the front door.

Everything stopped — the wind, my heart, time.

Angie wasn't dead; just after dawn, she had slipped into a coma, and none of the doctors knew why.

Robson, I thought, was going to take another one.

Rena was amazingly calm. She had been up most of the night, trying to figure out how the old man was doing it. What all her theories boiled down to was easy — she had failed.

"I don't want her to die, Cody," she said. "I don't want to die."

She hung up before I could say anything.

Almost immediately, the phone rang again.

This time it was Matt. He had already heard about Angie, and he was excited.

"Those pictures?" he said. "The ones I got from the newspaper?"

And still, nothing moved. I heard him as if he was talking from the far end of an alley, not quite echoing.

"Cody, you there?"

I nodded. "Yeah."

'Pay attention. I got a clue."

I sat a little straighter. "What?"

"In that first picture, Cody. I knew there was something weird, but I couldn't put my finger on it." He laughed, and I could tell he was close to hysteria. "It's his hand, Cody. It's his hand."

I shook my head. "What are you talking about?"

"Cody. In that first picture, he has all his fingers."

Nobody, my mother says constantly, gets something for nothing. Sooner or later, you're going to have to pay.

Mr. Robson paid with parts of himself.

13

I almost threw up, thinking about it, but Matt didn't stop. He told me that a later picture showed Robson with part of one finger missing; an even later one showed the whole finger gone.

There was no accident, no incident in the war.

He was paying for staying alive, one joint at a time. I jumped to my feet and almost shouted.

"Get over here," I said. "Call Rena, and you guys get over here as soon as you can after dark, understand?"

I didn't wait for an answer. I hung up, grabbed my coat, and hurried outside. I had to force myself to run up to the Kaler house, but I couldn't help thinking that the whole neighbourhood was watching. All the kids in their costumes, all the parents from behind their curtains and drapes.

But I went there once a week, and everyone knew it.

The only thing I had to be sure of was that Robson wasn't outside, tending to his graveyard.

He wasn't.

And as soon as I was in the house, I ran to the east side and looked through the window. The damn hedge was too high, though, so I ran upstairs, into one of the bedrooms, my footsteps loud on the bare floor, my breath even louder. I was sure the entire world could hear me.

Because there was nothing on the window there, I had to stand to one side, just in case. I don't know if it was good luck or bad luck, but when I pecked around the frame, I could see right into what I figured was his bedroom, not more than thirty feet away.

I could see part of a brass footboard, the edge of something dark on the mattress, and a dresser with a mirror on it framed in dark wood. Both windows were dirty, so I couldn't see all that clearly, and I wasn't even positive I would ever see anything.

But I had to know.

So I waited.

Thinking about Angie, willing her to come out of it, took up some of the time; thinking about Theo took up more; and thinking about what the old man would do to me if he caught me made me almost change my mind a couple of times.

I stayed, though.

I stayed while the clouds thickened, and a drizzle began to fall, I stayed while the shadow of the Kaler house crept across the side yard and up the edge, turning it black. Crept up Robson's house and covered the window.

This was dumb.

I ordered myself to go a couple of times, if only because Mom might call home. If I didn't answer, she'd practically fly home, find me gone, and there was no way she'd ever believe what I was doing.

Then a light went on.

I held my breath.

He was a blur through the grime, but I saw him stand in front of the mirror and examine himself. His gloves were off, and he turned his hands over slowly, as if he had never seen them before. The right one was wrapped in a bandage of some kind; even at this distance, I could tell it was bloody.

Then he leaned closed and started pulling at the skin on his face, looking at himself from as many different angles as he could.

Checking to see how old he looked, I thought; or maybe how much younger he would look after tonight.

I didn't care anymore about being spotted. What I wondered, while I felt my stomach get ready to empty, was how many years he got for every joint. One? Two? Five? Just enough so that people wouldn't notice. He was a tough old man, they probably said; he'll probably live forever.

I giggled.

Live forever.

He reached into a bottom drawer and took something out.

Live forever.

Suddenly he whipped around, and I jerked out of sight, pressing so hard against the wall, I thought I'd go right through it. I don't know if he saw me or not, but he sensed something, and I had to get out of there before he started snooping around.

I was finished anyway.

I had the last answer.

Now I knew why Angie was in her coma.

14

I didn't deserve the luck I had after that, getting home without Mom waiting for me, ready to lock me in a closet or something. But the others were there, waiting on the porch. When they saw me running, they came down to meet me, a zillion questions in the air that I couldn't answer until I rushed them inside.

Unfortunately, not a minute later, Mom came in too.

I never danced so fast in my life, telling her that the guys were over for some supper and maybe a rented video, since we were all too sick to go out that night. Matt was good with his coughing and red-rimmed eyes; Rena was pathetic. She didn't look or sound like she had a mild case of the sniffles, much less a stupid cold. But for some reason, it worked.

Mom was happy I wouldn't be alone. So happy, she made us all sit in the living room, while she made dinner in the kitchen.

A big dinner.

One that would take forever to eat.

That's the trouble with mothers — you can be as sick as a dog, and they always tell you to eat, you'll feel better, even if you throw it all up five minutes after you're done.

So we ate, and Mom watched and talked, shaking her head like mothers do. Then, just as I was ready to scream, she volunteered to go to the video store to get us a movie. That's when I put my foot down. Sort of. I reminded her she had to get back to work, that we weren't exactly dying here, that we could be there and back in less than twenty minutes, and there was no reason why she should stick around, right?

"Come on, Mom, don't you trust me?"

After a suspicious look at all of us, she gave in, kissed me, ordered me to cover up on the couch, and left with a cheery wave.

I felt like a rat.

Rena put her hands on her hips and glared at me.

"Well, what did you want me to say?" I snapped. "Hey, Mom, bug off, okay? because we have to stop this magic guy from killing us all before the sun comes up? Jeez."

"You didn't have to lie."

Matt punched her arm; she punched him back, and he yelped.

I will never, in my whole life, understand women.

I did understand, though, what was going on.

"He's leaving," I told them when they demanded to know why I was in such a panic. I explained what I done that afternoon, told Rena what Matt had said, and then: "There was a suitcase on the bed. He's going to leave town."

"But why?"

Rena's eye's brightened. "Because maybe somebody's been asking questions about him. You know, how do you live so long, what's your secret? He can't stay, so he's going to another town." The eyes widened. "Oh my God, he's going to start all over someplace else!"

I shook my head. "No, I don't think so. He took something out of his dresser just before he turned around." I swallowed heavily. "It was a cleaver."

Rena frowned, and Matt looked confused.

I held up my right hand. "He's a lefty, guys. He can get along." I wriggled my fingers. "That's why the missing joints are on this hand." I wriggled them again, and made them into a fist. "If he gets another couple of years with a joint . . . what would he get . . . how much younger would he get if he took the whole thing off?"

Matt got it. "Angie," he said softly.

Rena didn't say anything for a second. It was all too horrible and unbelievable. Then: "So whose name?"

"Nobody's," I said. "He's done here. Angie and Ursula give him what he needs, he pays with—" I couldn't say it, and shrugged instead.

The wind raced around the house, rattling a window, rattling the gutters.

I wondered if I was as pale as my friends. I felt it. We had got ourselves into something we didn't really understand, but we had to stop it anyway. For Angie, and everyone else who had gone before, and would come after.

The plan, when we finally worked it out, sitting at the kitchen table, was simple: we'd wait until we were sure all the trick-or-treaters were off the street — the weather was on our side, for a change — and then we'd go over there and knock over the tombstone. I was positive we'd find things buried under there, which was why he was so quick to reset that one and not the others. Part of a finger. Part of a toe. Then we'd make sure he didn't put anything else in the ground.

All we had to do was hold out until after midnight.

It was the flowers, you see.

Those pictures of him in his garden, holding those flowers up, sniffing them, and smiling.

A kid died, the flowers grew, and he took the life. The breath of life. Every spring, when everything was born again.

Why it happened didn't matter.

They agreed, and we waited around for what seemed like years.

Listening to the cars, the kids, the wind, the house.

We talked about Ursula, and Sara; we talked about how we couldn't wait to go to college somewhere else, anywhere else but Oxrun Station; we talked about how crazy we were, and how they'd lock us up if we were caught and tried to explain; we did not talk about what would happen if Robson caught us instead.

Finally Matt said, "It's eleven. Let's get going."

15

I felt like a gunfighter in those old westerns.

The three of us walking up the street side by side, the wind trying to push us back, while leaves crabbed around the street, once in a while jumping into our faces.

I was scared.

And I was mad.

And I didn't even hear anyone come up behind me just as we reached the hanging man, and the graveyard.

Suddenly my arms were pinned to my side, Rena and Matt yelled, and I was spun around.

Zack held me, and Theo leaned into my face. "I told you not to see her again, Banning," he said, smiling with only part of his face.

Rena tried to stop him, but he shoved her away, so hard she fell on her rump on the sidewalk. She cried out, more in surprise than pain, but when she tried to get up, he kicked her shin, hard.

"I'm gonna kill you," he said, no more disturbed than if a gnat had tried to bite him.

I couldn't break Zack's grip, and I couldn't get enough leverage to kick back.

I could only watch that fist fly out of the dark.

When it connected, the night grew amazingly bright, and I sagged. The pain didn't come for a second or two, right after he punched me again, high on the cheek.

Rena screamed.

Then Zack screamed, and I was free, and just aware enough to duck a third punch by dropping to my knees. I looked over my shoulder and saw Skelton rolling around on the sidewalk, holding his crotch, his legs drawn up, and Matt standing over him.

Then I faded out for a second, faded back in just as Theo, laughing almost as loud as the wind, reared back to kick me in the chin.

Before I could move, he fell when Rena wrapped herself around his leg, shrieking, trying to crawl up him to get at his eyes. I was too dazed to do anything but watch like an idiot while that monster tried to shake her off. By that time, Matt, kneeling beside him, clamped one hand to his throat and actually laughed once before clobbering him square on the jaw.

Theo didn't move.

Zack's screams became low moans, and the sound of retching.

I shook my head — big mistake, considering the fireworks that went off inside there — and staggered to my feet. All I could think of was the noise we had made, and I had to get to that tombstone before Robson did. So I did my best to turn around, while the whole world spun, and make my way to the yard.

Zack cursed at me and tried to grab my ankle, but it was easy to just kick his hand away and keep on.

Once I got there, though, I couldn't stand up. Dizziness made my vision blur and upset my balance. I fell forward grabbing that oak tombstone to keep from falling all the way.

I was cold, and the wind kept beating at me, but I grinned because I was there. In no shape to do much of anything, but I was there.

The rain started then. Not a drizzle, not a shower, but a downpour that instantly soaked me through to the bone. I could barely see as I put my shoulder to the wood and began to push.

The ground became instant mud.

"Help me!" I called to the others. "Hey, help me!"

The tombstone didn't budge.

My feet kept slipping, and I couldn't get a grip on the slick, slippery wood.

"Help me, dammit!"

The rain turned to sleet.

I pushed, grunting, practically crying in frustration, wondering why my friends weren't here.

I pushed, and I slipped, and a hand grabbed my hair and yanked me to my feet.

"Boy," said Mr. Robson, "you're going to die."

We faced each other in the storm, the nameless tombstone between us.

"I know what you're doing," I said, trying to catch my breath. "I know, and you're not going to do it anymore."

He was startled, then he laughed, tilting his head back until the sleet fell into his open mouth, his open eyes.

His left hand slapped me; his right hand was gone, nothing left but some bulky, red and white cloth wrapped tightly around the stump.

I lunged for him, and he grabbed my coat and pulled me so close the edge of the tombstone's top cut into my chest.

"Do you know what it's like to be old, Cody?" He grinned, his eyes wide. Crazy wide. "Do you know what it's like to want something so bad that it's all you can think of every second of every day?" He shook me, and a fire started in my chest; he had cracked one of my ribs. "Do you know?"

No smile now; his lips were pulled back, like an animal baring its fangs.

"Sometimes it burns, you want it so bad." He was whispering, but I could hear him. "Sometimes it drives you crazy, and sometimes it shows you the way."

"You're crazy!" I shouted.

His hair, thicker and darker, was plastered around his head.

His grip was so strong, I couldn't do anything but try to breathe, but the cracked rib wouldn't let me, and I felt myself blacking out.

"You have something I want, boy," he said. He began to pull me closer, and I realised that pretty soon another rib would break, and another, and one of them would eventually stab into a lung, or my heart. "You have it, I wasn't going to take it, but now you've made me mad."

I kept trying to break free, ignoring the pain as I pushed and twisted and clawed at his hand.

Then I heard a yell, and after that it was like a fever dream:

Theo leaping past me, and Robson swatting him away with his stumped arm;

Theo pinwheeling across the yard, landing a good fifty feet away;

Matt charging him from the back, and Robson swatting him too, right into the ground beneath the swaying, hanging man;

Rena stopping short of jumping him when he glared at her with those eyes, eyes that didn't blink when the wind lashed them with sleet.

His grip loosened on me, and I didn't even think about it. I kicked forward with a yell, felt another rib crack, and butted him under the chin.

I fell into the mud.

He stumbled back, slipped, and fell against the tombstone behind him.

I saw it. I saw his eyes widen for just a second, just as his neck struck the edge of the wood.

I saw him die.

16

The storm is still out there.

The sleet has turned to snow.

I'm not sure of everything that happened after Robson fell, because I finally blacked out. I do know that the police were there pretty quick; a neighbour had called them. I know that me and Theo and Rena were taken to the hospital for X-rays and stuff, and that Rena had a cast put on her lower leg, I have this wide bandage thing wrapped around my chest, and Theo has a neck brace.

I know I caught hell from Mom for being out so late, but I didn't mind because she cried the whole time.

I know Matt had the sense to come up with a story about Theo and Zack trying to knock over the tombstones, about Robson going crazy with anger, and we came along to help the guys out.

I also don't think anyone really believes it, but would you believe that Theo didn't contradict it after Matt visited him for a while? Neither did Zack.

I know this, too:

Angie is still in a coma, and I think it's because Robson didn't live until midnight; I thought then that she was going to stay that way forever.

Not now, though.

Now I understand.

Now I really know what the old man meant.

Wanting something so bad, you'd do anything to get it.

Wanting something so bad, it *burns*.

I thought, like Matt and Rena, that the something of ours was going to college to get out of this town.

I was wrong.

I want Angie.

And, oh God, it *burns*.

So not long after I got home, while Mom was working late, I went over to Robson's house. The tombstones are gone; so is the hanging man. The house is dark; it looks like nobody's lived there for years.

I dug up Robson's hand.

I've hidden it.

And when spring finally gets here, I'm going to have the most beautiful flowers my mom ever saw.

They're going to grow out there in back.

In my own private garden.

And when they do, I'm going to pick them, and I'm going to take them to Angie.

When she breathes them, she'll come back; and when she sees me, she'll smile.

And if she doesn't come back . . . well, I know something else.

I'm right-handed.

And it *burns*.

EPILOGUE

Epilogue

FLAKES SCRATCH AGAINST THE WINDOW PANE, and the wind talks to itself in the eaves.

I haven't moved.

I don't want to, because I can still see them out there, looking up, looking at me.

And I think I know why.

But it's not like we were a group or anything. We weren't even part of the same classes or clubs in school. We just kind of knew who the other guy was, the way kids do who see each other most days during the school year and once in a while during the summer.

But the point is, we did know each other.

The point is, we weren't strangers.

Things that happen to strangers don't matter, not really, not if you're honest with yourself. They're just names in a newspaper, or faces on TV. If they get hurt, or killed, you may think it's too bad, but it doesn't really touch you.

It doesn't really matter.

But we knew each other.

We did.

And all of those things that happened, to Sam and Eleanor and Tina and Chuck and Cody, all those things I could see in the falling snow, well, none of them happened to me.

Yet.

Now I think they're angry.

I think they don't like it that I got away, that I'm still here, nice and safe in my house.

I think they want me to go out there and join them.

I'm not, though.

No way.

But still . . . it's so quiet out there, and the snow looks so soft, and it doesn't really seem very cold at all. And it's not like they'd really hurt me, you know? I mean, we weren't *friends*, exactly, but we sure weren't enemies.

So maybe it wouldn't be that bad.

Maybe it would be okay anyway.

Because they're smiling now, and they're waving and laughing, and I think I can hear them calling my name.

It's as if they've forgotten all about Halloween . . .

Out there in the snow.

Out there in Oxrun Station.